The Idaho Stories
and
Far West Illustrations
of
Mary Hallock Foote

Edited by
Barbara Cragg
Dennis M. Walsh
Mary Ellen Walsh

Idaho State  University Press

Published 1988 by the
Idaho State University Press

Campus Box 8265
Idaho State University
Pocatello, Idaho 83209
William N. Harwood, Director
Phone (208) 236-3215

ISBN 0-937834-31-9

Contents

"It is our fate to be always in these queer places—and I forsee the time when I shall long for them and be homesick for the waste of moonlight, the silence, the night wind and the river! There is nothing that will ever quite take its place. Dreamers we are, dreamers we always will be, and what is folly and vain imaginings to some people is the stuff our daily lives are made of—and there are thousands like us! If there had not been, there would be no great West. . . ."

Mary Hallock Foote

Introduction

Mary Hallock Foote stepped from a car of the Oregon Short Line at Kuna Station in the summer of 1884 to begin an undefined stay in the territory of Idaho while her husband worked there to develop an irrigation project on the Boise River. When she left Boise in 1895, the territory had become a state, and Mary Hallock Foote had become the first writer and illustrator to publish a substantial body of work set in Idaho. As her novels, stories, essays, and illustrations appeared in *Century Magazine, The Atlantic Monthly,* and *St. Nicholas Magazine* (for children), Foote introduced a large national audience to the new West that she had found: the basalt canyons of the Boise River, the Thousand Springs area along the Snake River, ferry crossings and stage houses, the Arco desert, the Coeur d'Alene mining region, irrigation ditches, immigrant farmers and ranchers, the Bannock Indians. Although the genteel romance and pastoral art of the time influenced her fiction and illustrations, Foote produced a rounded and accurate portrait of Idaho as she saw it — a region where a booming agricultural and mining economy, a rapidly increasing population, and the coming of statehood signaled the end of the frontier.

Mary Hallock Foote had established her reputation as both an illustrator and a writer before she arrived in Idaho. Following early education at the Cooper Institute of Design for Women in New York City, she began her career as a professional illustrator and, by her early twenties, gained acclaim for illustrating works of writers such as Henry Wadsworth Longfellow, Nathaniel Hawthorne, and Alfred Lord Tennyson. Her career as a writer and her Western experience began after her marriage in 1876 to Arthur DeWint Foote, a mining engineer. In the following years, she wrote and illustrated essays and stories as well as three novels, all of which she based on her observations of mining towns and other places where her husband worked — New Almaden, California; Leadville, Colorado; Morelia,

Mexico. While her husband worked in camps such as Deadwood, South Dakota, which the Footes believed unsuitable for women and children, Foote returned to her family home in upper New York State.

When Foote arrived in Idaho, her attitude toward the West was ambivalent. Although she had written with skill and accuracy about the colorful mining communities in which she lived, she retained strong ties to literary and artistic circles centered in New York City. She considered herself and her husband "professional exiles" in the West. Consequently, she was pulled between her appreciation of the West's "natural beauty and expansive way of life" and her "yearning for the intellectual and social stimulation of the eastern seaboard" (Paul, 3). Her ambivalence is clear in *The Chosen Valley* and *Coeur d'Alene,* novels she wrote during her first years in Idaho, as well as in a number of the stories collected here. Her attitude toward Idaho and life in the West had changed, however, by the time she wrote "The Harshaw Bride." How definitely it had changed is apparent in her use of Idaho settings in two of her best novels — *The Desert and the Sown* and *Edith Bonham,* written after she moved from Boise to Grass Valley, California, her latest Western home. After leaving Idaho, Foote published seven novels, the last in 1919.

Mary Hallock Foote's memoirs, which she wrote in the 1920s, remained unpublished until 1972. Edited by Rodman Paul, *A Victorian Gentlewoman in the Far West: The Reminiscences of Mary Hallock Foote* revealed in Foote's life the stuff of which novels are made; her childhood as the daughter of Quaker farmers at Milton-on-the-Hudson; her education in New York City, where she formed a life-long friendship with Helen DeKay; her career as a professional illustrator; her marriage to a mining engineer and her subsequent life in California, Colorado, Mexico and Idaho; her career as a writer of western literature. Indeed, Wallace Stegner had already recognized the potential in the life of this extraordinary nineteenth century woman by making it the basis of a novel published in 1971. As he wrote *Angle of Repose,* Stegner paid an unusual tribute to Foote's excellence as a writer by frequently incorporating her own words into it — plagiarizing passages from her published essays about New Almaden and Mexico, from her unpublished letters, and from her then unpublished memoirs (Walsh). However, Stegner departs radically from the facts in Foote's life as he develops his heroine's life in Idaho.

The publication of *Angle of Repose* and *A Victorian Gentlewoman in the Far West* revived interest in Foote's work. Her fiction, admired in her day by writers such as Owen Wister and William Dean Howells, as well as by miners and engineers who praised its authenticity, went out of style as American reading tastes changed at the turn of the century and different critical standards emerged.[1] In order to assess it properly one hundred years later, one must see it in the context of a literary period which was primarily dominated by the influence of British and American Romantic and Victorian perceptions.

The pervasive influence of nineteenth century British authors on Mary Hallock Foote's thought is strongly evident in her literary allusions in *A Victorian Gentlewoman in the Far West*, written at the end of her career. She alludes frequently to William Wordsworth and Tennyson, but also to Sir Walter Scott, to Charles Dickens and William Thackeray, to George Eliot and to Rudyard Kipling, to John Keats, Samuel Taylor Coleridge, and Edward Fitzgerald, among others. Less frequently she alludes to American poets and novelists, among them John Greenleaf Whittier, Longfellow, Hawthorne, and Walt Whitman. In short, while living in and writing about the frontier West, Mary Hallock Foote continued to view herself primarily as an Easterner who made her strongest literary identification with nineteenth century British literature, particularly that of Wordsworth and Tennyson.

Because the Romantic view was important to educated Americans in the late nineteenth century, Foote's work appealed to her contemporaries. To understand the romanticism in Foote's work is to understand the influence of Wordsworth and Tennyson in poetry and of Scott and Dickens in fiction on educated Britons and Americans of Foote's generation. John R. Milton, in *The Novel of the American West*, remarks that "John Muir, among others, saw the hand of God in the mountains," and finds "a Wordsworthian attitude . . . in a segment of Western fiction" (61). He also notes: "Early nineteenth century travelers in the West were somewhat under the spell of the English Romantics . . . . It is not strange, then, to find a Wordsworthian vocabulary throughout the journals of Lewis and Clark" (71). One recognizes the influence of Wordsworth in Foote's acute visual description and her sense of the close relationship between the common people and the land. Likewise, her evocation of the pastoral reflects Wordsworth's belief in the natural goodness of human beings and their need to live in harmony with their natural surroundings. Furthermore, Foote's fiction sometimes contains the idealized characters, sentimental plots, and anti-urban bias of Wordsworth's poetry. Tennyson's influence on Foote is revealed most strongly in her fiction portraying conflict between Romantic idealism and Victorian demand for progress and change. In Scott, Foote found the sentimental Lochinvar as well as his remarkable rendering of dialects, his profound sense of social classes, and his skillfully observed detail.

Another appeal of Foote's Western writing is its authenticity. As the wife of a mining engineer who changed jobs often, Foote saw much of the West—but from a particular point of view. Because she was an educated, cultured woman, she did not associate with miners and cowboys. Thus, although she heard of their adventures from her husband and his professional associates, her stories reveal distance from the personal lives and rough talk of working-class men. Her knowledge of mining operations and irrigation projects, on the other hand, and of the relation between men and work and between people and land is noteworthy. Twentieth century scholars have agreed with Foote's contemporaries about the accuracy of her depictions of the West. After examining the historical backgrounds, themes, and characters of eighty-one mining novels set in the Rocky Mountain region, Harry H. Jones considers Foote the most authentic writer of mining fiction in the nineteenth century (101-24). In "The West in Magazine Fiction, 1870-1900," Lawana Shaul concludes from her examination of over two hundred short stories and serials that Foote's mining stories stand apart from those of her contemporaries; they "contain realistic details which enable a reader to imagine scenes in a mining camp" (42). Shaul finds, as many other readers have, that Foote's descriptions are often "photographically real" (52). Certainly this observation applies to Foote's descriptions of Idaho landscapes.

A third element of Foote's fiction presents the same problem for twentieth century readers as that of James Fenimore Cooper. She often centers the plot on a genteel love affair—a device used frequently in nineteenth century fiction. It was not her inclination, however, to demonstrate that such stories always have a happy ending—the Idaho love stories are not always genteel or always happy. That others do conform to the genteel tradition is partly the responsibility of the editors who published her work. William Dean Howells, who accepted her first story, "In Exile," for publication in *The Atlantic Monthly*, requested that she change the unhappy—and logical—ending. She did so, but protested in her reminiscences that her original ending was the authentic one (Paul, 155). Undoubtedly, the most important editorial influence on her writing was that of Richard Gilder. As editor of *Scribner's Monthly* and its successor, *Century Magazine,* he published and, consequently, shaped much of her fiction, although she did not readily agree to all his editorial suggestions (Shaul, 51).[2] According to Arthur John in *The Best Years of the Century,* Gilder's advice often stemmed from his view of himself as a "guardian of the 19th Century moral code," a shaper of "the fabric of gentility" which was woven of "lingering Puritanism and chronic national optimism, awareness of evil, and belief in perfectability" (153).

Foote's cast of characters differs greatly from those found in the fiction of the most influential nineteenth century Western writers—Cooper and Bret Harte. In Foote's fiction, Eastern engineers, like her husband, who went West to open mines, build railroads, develop irrigation systems, and make geological surveys appear prominently as characters. Drawing upon her personal experience, Foote cast many of her female characters as women who accompanied these men—Eastern women reared in genteel society who had to learn an entirely different way of life. In the Idaho stories, Foote sometimes develops local characters from the idealized perspective of the Romantic tradition, but she does not rely on totally stereotyped responses and actions as both Cooper and Harte often do—the tragedy of the heroine in "Maverick," for example, develops directly from the emotional and physical isolation of her life at a stage station on the Arco desert. Although Harte had firsthand experience in the West, he deliberately chose to disguise, exploit, and manipulate his materials. He aimed at a Dickens-oriented audience in the East and was indeed acclaimed there as a Western American Charles Dickens. Foote's "A Cup of Trembling" is the Idaho story which seems most influenced by Harte's Dickensian manner. Still, in Foote's West, there are no idealized or vilified Indians, no prostitutes with hearts of gold, no reformed gamblers. At one point, Foote illustrated some of Harte's work which was published in the *Century.*

Foote began writing of her Western experience at a time when the West was a popular subject in American magazines aimed at an educated reading public. Shaul found 226 Western stories and serials published in the last three decades of the nineteenth century in *The Atlantic Monthly, Century Magazine, Frank Leslie's Popular Magazine, Harper's Monthly* and *Weekly, Scribner's Magazine* and *Monthly* (30-1). Foote published stories and serialized novels in three of these publications. In 1885, the *Century*, where most of Foote's Idaho fiction was first published, had a circulation of 200,000 insuring that her work was widely read. There it appeared side-by-side with the work of Henry James, Howells, Kipling, and other notable writers.

*   *   *

The evaluations of Foote's fiction by twentieth century scholars are varied. Mary Lou Benn's early work emphasizes the impact of Foote's life on her art and sets the biographical tone of subsequent scholarship.[3]. Benn's discovery of the unpublished reminiscences led her to focus on Foote's Idaho novels because she could easily associate them with Foote's firsthand experiences. She dismisses the stories written in Idaho as trivial because Foote was writing under financial duress (as she nearly always was) and because Foote herself wrote deprecatingly in the reminiscences of her "pot-boiling" during that period (Paul, 350). Benn concludes, however, that Foote's Idaho novels show greater maturity because of their "variations in theme and tone as well as differences in locale" and because they show greater artistic involvement with Western scenes and greater personal sympathy toward the Western point of view (1974).

To a large extent, Lee Ann Johnson follows Benn's example by evaluating much of Foote's work biographically. In *Mary Hallock Foote* (1980), the most thorough extant literary biography, Johnson accepts, as Benn does, Foote's dismissive evaluation of some of the Idaho stories (77-78). When she examines Foote's Western fiction generally, Johnson tends to present Foote as a kind of third rate Bret Harte, without adequately taking into account the admiration that such writers as Wister and Stegner have had for Foote's work.

James H. Maguire's earlier and shorter introduction to Foote's life and work proceeds from a point of view that is different and more valuable than Benn's and Johnson's. In his Boise State Western Writers Series pamphlet on Foote, Maguire views her work from a broad cultural perspective and tends to evaluate her novels and stories on their own merits. In examining the Idaho stories, Maguire places Foote against a background of such writers as George Eliot and Edward Fitzgerald as well as Bret Harte and Frank Norris (passim). Thus, he recognizes the Romantic and Victorian context out of which Foote's work grows.

Rodman Paul's Introduction to *A Victorian Gentlewoman in the*

Far West is the most meticulous historical scholarship about Foote and her art. When Paul notes that "the Idaho phase of Mary Hallock Foote's life was the most elusive and yet in some respects the most crucial topic covered by research for this book" (viii), he undoubtedly points out the reason that biographically oriented scholars have had difficulty in assessing her Idaho fiction.

* * *

Foote expressed her sense of the Idaho landscape in the following passage from a letter she wrote to Helena DeKay Gilder several years after her arrival):

> There is something terribly sobering about these solitudes, these waste places of the Earth. They belittle everything one is, or tries to do. The vast wonderful sunsets, the solemn moonlights, and the noise the river makes on dark nights. (6-8 June 1887)

Here Foote not only praises the beauties of Idaho but also suggests certain of the themes which she develops in her fiction: the disquieting absence in the land of the taming human hand, the precarious hold humans have on desolate areas, the inadequacy of human effort in these places. Undoubtedly Foote's actual experience in Idaho suggested these themes.

One of the major strengths of the Idaho stories is Foote's ability to ground their themes and action in Idaho settings. In most, she begins with careful descriptions, which introduce her readers to some of the "solitudes" and "waste places" of Idaho. Such places evoked responses that show her intellectual reliance on a Romantic and Victorian literary heritage.

In "The Rapture of Hetty," one of the slighter stories, Foote transplants Sir Walter Scott's Lochinvar to Idaho's Payette River drainage. The opening description suggests the romantic isolation appropriate to such a tale: a "horse-ranch . . . situated in a high, watered valley . . . sixteen miles from the nearest town . . . ." This story has the virtues of economy and a certain suggestiveness about character and social relations that resembles Keats' "Eve of St. Agnes" or ancient ballads. Moreover, Foote's depiction of places and events (a country store and a local dance) are excellent. Finally, all elements of the story, including the literary allusions to a romantic escape on the Scottish or English moors, contribute to the sense of a powerful natural world where ill-equipped but scrappy humans search for freedom and meaning in their lives. The allusions tie that search to tradition. ·

"The Watchman" demonstrates both Foote's knowledge of irrigation projects such as her husband directed and the southwestern Idaho landscape. Foote's description of the "queer country along the new ditch," patrolled for "five crucial miles between the head-gates and Glenn's Ferry" by the watchman of the title, captures a Tennysonian conflict between the "progressive" view of the irrigation companies and that of the original settlers. While the obvious chief weaknesses of the story are uncertain narration and characters who are not fully realized, its strengths lie in its portrayal of immense stretches of arid country, the impotence of individuals against the large companies which came to control scarce, valuable water resources, the representation of people and their work; and, finally, the inclusion of the details of the irrigation ditch which are uniquely authentic in fiction of the time.

Foote achieves a finely tuned balance between setting and theme in "Pilgrim Station." The story opens with the following paragraph:

From the great plateau of the Snake River, at a point that is far from any main station, the stage-road sinks into a hollow which the winds might have scooped, so constantly do they pounce and delve and circle around the spot. Down in this pothole, where sand has drifted into the infrequent wheel tracks, there is a dead stillness which the perpetual land gale is roaring and troubling above.

Four travelers arrive here in search of Pilgrim Station, an abandoned spot on the former stage route which traced the old Oregon immigrant trail. The opening description sharply underlines the temporary nature of human habitation in the inhospitable desert. The empty land mirrors the emptiness of one traveler's assumptions about his murdered son's intended bride and about his son's friend. In contrast to the uncertain location of Pilgrim Station, Foote sets the closing scene at a precisely marked spot, the crossroads between Shoshone Falls and Bliss, and it is here that the relationships of all the characters are finally clarified.

"On a Side-Track" incorporates details of the train route from Omaha to Pocatello in mid-winter: "the dreary cattle-ranges of Wyoming," the halt for dinner at Cheyenne, the midnight shift on the Portland car at Green River from a "convoy" of the Union Pacific to a "train making up for the Oregon Short line," and the climb during the night to the Wind River divide during a heavy snow. Finally, unable to proceed because of the snow, the train halts on a side-track, "in the Bear Lake valley, just over the border of Idaho, about fifteen miles from the Squaw Creek divide." The desolation through which the train has traveled, the violence of the Idaho weather which halts it, and the isolated site of the side-track mirror the hero's desolation of spirit. All mock the Quaker optimism of the heroine and her father. Here Foote presents the hardships posed by the land, rather than its romantic and picturesque value, and places interesting characters in authentic circumstances appropriate to the action. As Shaul notes, this is one of the very rare railroad stories found in nineteenth century Western literature (45).

Most of Foote's Idaho stories are somber, encompassing treachery, murder or betrayal of one kind or another. One of the most elaborately plotted is "The Trumpeter" in which Foote incorporates the activities of the military post in Boise and a view of the Bannock Indian tribe from Fort Hall. In a tale whose characters could have ancestors in Cooper's novels, an enlisted Army man jilts a blonde heroine for her half-breed foster sister. Henniker, the trumpeter, subsequently betrays "the squaw's daughter," who inevitably, as the dark woman, must die. Finally Henniker commits suicide in the Snake River, and the blonde heroine marries a more conventional military man. Despite the Cooperesque racism, Foote's own elitism directed toward the union movements of the time, and some plot contrivance, "The Trumpeter" is successful in its descriptions of a minstrel show, military horsemanship, the frontier military posts and a Coxeyite gathering and trial. Foote's focus on human relationships in this isolated place and the establishment of respectability and order on the frontier is especially significant.

Foote uses regional environmental forces to accomplish the deaths of several women characters who find their lives unbearable. "A Cloud on the Mountain," her first published story with an Idaho setting, ends in such a way. A young girl, Ruth Mary Tully, loves the river and the mountain where it flows—the only home she has ever known. Her mother, on the other hand, feels the regret which most of Foote's transplanted Eastern women characters expressed for tamed and civilized places left behind. Ruth Mary's beloved river, however, is dangerous as well as idyllic; she drowns in the unpredictable waters of its spring flood. In death, Mary Ruth becomes a Wordsworthian innocent, a kind of Western Lucy Gray, joining with nature: "that fair young girl from the hills, . . . the simple features, the meek eyes, wide open on the searching light, . . . the pure young face."

In contrast, Esmee, in "The Cup of Trembling," finds the landscape completely foreign. Foote uses once again the unpredictability of a mountainous landscape to effect the end her character desires.

Esmee's alienation from the societal and moral codes of her Eastern upbringing is reflected in the isolated, wintry Coeur d'Alene mining district to which she and her lover flee in their illicit love. The solution to her moral dilemma is accomplished by "the soft wild gale, the chinook of the Northwest . . . the breath of May, but the voice of March" which creates an avalanche in which Esmee chooses to die. Foote also uses the Victorian convention of the preternaturally wise little dog. The story contains excellent dialect, clever narration, and a rich investigation of what characters of romantic sensibilities experience after a Lochinvar-like elopement. Lee Ann Johnson considers "The Cup of Trembling" to be the "most finished" of the Idaho stories (95), but she finds the collection in which it appears with "On a Side-Track," "Maverick," and "The Trumpeter," marred by "strained coincidences and melodramatic resolutions"; to Johnson these four stories seem thematically close to Harte's stories and to Frank Norris' naturalistic romances (96-97).

The third story in which a woman chooses death from the natural environment is "Maverick," which, ironically, alludes to the legend of Beauty and the Beast. Rose Gilroy, like Ruth Mary Tully, is a native and knows the dangerous nature of her home. Set in the Arco desert of southeastern Idaho, the story opens with a precise and authentic description of the desolate location of the principal character's home:

> Traveling Buttes is a lone stage-station on the road from Blackfoot to Boise . . . . The stage house is perhaps half a mile from the foot of the largest butte, one of three that loom on the horizon . . . . The country is destitute of water. To say that it is "thirsty" is to mock with vain imagery that dead and mummied land on the borders of the Black Lava.

The closest town is Arco, "a poor little seed of civilization dropped by the wayside." A long description of the Black Lava helps us to understand Rose's anguish when she realizes that she is trapped and that while she lives she will be unable to escape from the destitution of the Traveling Buttes station and the men who dominate her life: a half-crazy father, lawless brothers, and the mutilated Maverick. Rather than remain in that life, she enters the "stony-hearted wilderness" of the lava flow, choosing death.

In "The Fate of a Voice" the treacherous Western landscape brings not death but a lifetime of banishment to Madeline Hendric, who has a fine operatic voice. The story opens with a lengthy description of a river canyon, and closes with a discussion of its dangerous basalt walls. These basalt walls betray Madeline, crumbling and causing the man whom she does not wish to marry to fall into the canyon. Fear that he has been killed strikes her voiceless for a time and guilt weakens her into agreeing to marry him, dooming her to life in the wilderness. The story may be read as autobiographical in that it represents an artist figure giving up life and probable fame in the East to live in the Western wilderness with the man she marries. The somewhat ambiguous ending may represent Foote's realization that she owed much of the fame she was accruing to her Western experience.

In most of the stories, Foote accurately describes the Idaho landscape in which her characters move. In addition she incorporates what she perceives as "sobering" dangers of the "solitudes" and "waste places" in them. On the other hand, the last published of the Idaho stories, "The Harshaw Bride" marks a decided change in Foote's landscape depiction and in the attitudes of her characters toward the land. The story is one of Foote's most successful. A major source of its accomplishment is the narrative technique which takes the form of a serial letter from Mrs. Tom Daly to her sister. This method reflects Foote's own lenthy correspondence to Helena Gilder, and it allows Foote an informality and naturalness of expression that portrays the narrator, Mrs. Daly, vividly. Mrs. Daly displays grudging acceptance of her adopted Idaho home. She is amused at the prospect of the English bride-to-be coming to "the wilds of Idaho," as described in a trip from Boise to Thousand Springs. After riding through a dust storm and an alkali waste, they reach their Edenic camp at Thousand Springs, a natural wonder which Foote depicts in detail. Her closing sentences indicate the remarkably different attitude toward the landscape which this story conveys:

> Back of the bluffs, where it might be supposed to come from, there is nothing for a hundred miles but drought and desert plains. I don't care for any of their theories concerning its source. It is better as it is — the miracle of the smitten rock.

Mrs. Daly insists on accepting the springs as a miracle, not as a place of terror. Furthermore, the description does not, as elsewhere, set the stage for tragedy. When the jilted bride-to-be learns of her former fiance's perfidy but also receives a humiliating replacement offer of marriage, she and Mrs. Daly respond — atypically in Foote's fiction — with a hearty roar of laughter. A situation which in other stories might have called for the heroine to seek death is recognized here for what it is, not tragedy, merely absurdity — with the setting paralleling recognition of the incongruous in human affairs. The integrated references to Charles Lamb and to Tennyson aid the final, pastoral sense of balance and harmony in the story. And, in the British pastoral mode, "The Harshaw Bride" ends in marriage.

*   *   *

"If Mrs. Foote were not so identified with her work as a novelist," wrote W. A. Rogers in 1922, "she would be better known as one of the most accomplished illustrators in America . . . . There is a charm about her black-and-white drawings which cannot be described, but it may be accounted for by the fact that, more that any other American illustrator, she lived the pictures from day to day which she drew so sympathetically" (188). Rogers speaks of Foote's many illustrations prepared to accompany both her own stories and novels as well as the work of other writers.

Unfortunately, Foote is less well known as a visual artist than are some of her contemporaries who were also illustrators — Frederic Remington, for example — partly because she did not paint in watercolors or oils, except experimentally. She became, however, adept in the use of black and white values which an artist necessarily contrasts for the effects achieved by a print. Early in her career, she began drawing directly upon the wood blocks which engravers then prepared for the final woodcut print. For her excellence in using this technique, she was singled out from among her contemporaries, such as Thomas and Peter Moran, by W. J. Linton, who considered her "the best of our designers on wood" (464). The large collection of art she produced was published, and remains in magazines and books, but the fine woodcut prints of her drawings were never reproduced separately as gallery or museum pieces.

From the beginning, Foote drew people and places she could observe closely. Her models were her friends, her family, and members of the domestic staff in her parent's home. She continued this practice in Idaho. Thus, both the illustrations for her stories and the Far West series illustrations are generally precise and accurate in detail. In the illustrations for her stories, Foote paid close attention to setting, writing to Richard Gilder that she hoped "to enlarge upon the locality and environment and not try to repeat the personal situations of the story already described in words" (1 June 1981). As time passed in Idaho, Foote came to understand the possibilities envisioned by her husband and other engineers, and she faithfully recorded their day-by-day efforts in drawings such as "The Irrigating Ditch" and "The Winter's Camp".

Foote proposed the Far West series late in 1887 when she wrote to Richard Gilder outlining her intention to draw a series of full-page illustrations for the *Century*. Although Lee Ann Johnson credits Gilder with the plan, Foote's letter indicates that the idea, the request for a monthly sequence, and a plea for a collaborator to write "snatches of verse to go with the pictures" came from her (3 Nov. [1887]). Indeed, Edith Thomas did write verses to appear with "Looking for Camp," and "The Irrigating Ditch." Gilder, however, persuaded her to write her own commentary for the series of eleven full-page woodcuts which appeared in the *Century* in 1888 and 1889. Foote hoped the illustrations and essays might be published as a little book following their appearance in the magazine, a dream which remained unrealized until the publication of this edition.

Her pictures evoke the sentiment of home place in a land that is open, large, and treeless, except in the gulches and where irrigation ditches water it. When she sent the first four blocks to the *Century's* art editor, William L. Fraser, she insisted in an accompanying letter that she be allowed to treat the subjects horizontally because she could not see the West "perpendicularly." She wanted to draw pictures which "depend on the landscape and sky" as much as on the figures for effect (10 June [1888]). In this she succeeded admirably, for many of the series represent Foote's finest art work. As Robert M. Taft observed:

> These illustrations were beautifully engraved woodcuts, for this period marks the golden age of American woodcut illustration; a period which produced magazine illustrations which have never been excelled, and The Century was the leader in its field . . . . Mrs. Foote is the only woman who can claim company among the men in the field of the western picture. (174)

Because the essays accompanying the Far West illustrations seemed to call for a more personal point of view than did the pictures themselves, they capture something of the ambivalence about matters Western which troubled Foote and that must have confounded most pilgrims to the West. "There is certainly a simplicity of view here which one cannot help to a certain extent sharing," she wrote to Helena DeKay Gilder. "Life is younger, fresher, less subtle, *far less intellectual,* but also less timid and self-conscious" (10 Oct. 1888).

When Foote wrote these essays, Idaho was part of the last Western frontier where romance met reality head-on. As late as 1884, adventurers rushed to the Coeur d'Alene silver region, while the 1880 completion of the Utah and Northern Railway across southern Idaho to Montana encouraged settlement along its route. In the years from 1881 to 1883, the Union Pacific Railroad built the

Oregon Short Line which passed through Kuna just south of Boise. All around her Foote saw change as Boise grew — open range giving way to fenced claims and irrigated valleys, law and order of a sort taming the exuberance of wilderness, and culture-hungry Westerners creating their own branch of society. In the Far West series, Foote caught this middle ground between wilderness and civilization.

The influence of the Romantic perspective on landscape is particularly apparent in the essays for the Far West series. Foote tries to present a West which can be tied to a traditional past, a West which remains romantically compelling by virtue of its rough edges, and a West that is, at the same time, acquiring the morals and manners of the East. As Rodman Paul points out:

> Already a part of the genteel tradition when she went west, her continued reliance on the Gilders, who were the embodiment of eastern culture, kept her subject to what would today be called the viewpoint of the Eastern Establishment at a time when she was becoming know as a leading writer and illustrator of scenes that were regarded as being "authentically western." (9)

Foote's best work in the Far West series replicates those "restful" and "poetic" qualities of life in the Boise Canyon that appealed to her solitary and retiring nature. These drawings are essentially pastoral in conception, in accordance with the pastoral in her fiction. Unquestionably, Foote produced her best art and writing in this mode, where, as Regina Armstrong remarked in 1900, she "links the poetic and the actual in a manner which makes them seem inseparable" (131). The pastoral is appropriate to depicting certain scenes in the developing West, reflecting, as it did, Thomas Jefferson's vision for the West: ideally the pastoralist would occupy a place between the city and the wilderness, escaping the problems of both. In "The Orchard Windbreak," for example, the commonly held nineteenth century notion of the West as a garden in the wilderness finds expression; in this orchard, even the wild beast accepts human control. The setting of poplar windbreak and fruit trees is beautifully executed; the figures hold a rigid idealized pose. In the accompanying essay, Foote writes confidently of the irrigation systems which could make permanence possible in semi-arid and arid lands and speaks lovingly of trees transplanted from the East which symbolize a settler's acceptance of place. She is less hopeful for the fawn; it has no place in the garden.

"The Irrigating Ditch" also pictures that middle ground between wilderness and civilization. Foote's accompanying essay optimistically records the sequence taken by settlement in the arid lands she knew firsthand, her final paragraphs expressing the hope that future generations would give the "ancestral irrigators" their due. The evocative sketch, one of Foote's most frequently reproduced pictures, suggests a family within an irrigated garden. Edith Thomas's accompany in a poem, "The Water-Seeker," concludes:

> As day by day his toil the stream extends
> Sometimes the grasses harsh a footfall bends
> His wife and child, the genii of the stream,
> Before him rise as in a lovely dream!

American values of the time are here summed up: family, work, and progress in a rural setting free from the taint of city life.

With the Foote's own Boise Canyon house as setting, "Afternoon at a Ranch" and "A Pretty Girl in the West," further illustrate the pastoral ideal of Western settlement. Foote pictures the rural West as a safe place, healthy for children, and sufficiently tamed that a beautiful girl may serenade her young man from a hammock hung in the piazza. Foote's continuing allegiance to the East and her mixed emotions about the West, which contribute to a certain snobbery on her part, invest the accompanying essays with ambiguity. Reluctant acceptance of the possibility that she and her daughters might become Western women may have contributed to her moralizing about "A Pretty Girl in the West," for she saw that her children looked upon the West as their home, just as she had loved her childhood home in the East. "So while we are striving in exile in order that we may one day take our children home, they are striking deep roots into alien soil and may not consent to call any other home," she concluded.

"Cinching Up," the sixth illustration, reminds us that the West, for all its insistence otherwise, is merely the East brought West; all the country was at one time a frontier. What varies significantly is the land and responses to it. Foote creates a beautiful setting where figures engage in bringing the East to the West hold attractive positions among sage-dotted basalt cliffs. By alluding to Greek mythology and early fiction, her essay establishes a bridge between the men and women of the West and European knights and ladies.

Other illustrations in the series capture picturesque figures in wilderness landscapes which remain to be tamed. "Looking for Camp" shows a hunter or prospector whose day ends when he seeks shelter in an essentialy empty land. "The Coming of Winter" also addresses the West as frontier. Foote casts the man in the role of hunter and protector, the woman as the nurturing and somewhat apprehensive mother. The drawing captures the impermanence of the first frontier settlements which Foote's essay explains in realistic terms.

Foote preferred to call the third illustration "On the Range," but wrote to Fraser that someone in their engineer's camp in the Boise Canyon had titled it "The Sheriff's Posse," and so it remained (10 June [1888]). In the accompanying essay, Foote approached the subject of Western justice with a good deal of reluctance, although there is much veracity in her examples of the cattle-sheep wars. Given Foote's account, one could only conclude that she believed the West was still wild and likely to remain so.

In keeping with her perception of the West as "a land poor in tradition but rich in suggestion of a vague, large and melancholy sort," Foote sketched a pioneer looking westward as the fifth illustration in the series. The picture captures that quality which caused Charles Lummis to declare in 1898 that "her work has the undefinable but unmistakable largeness of soul which belongs to our horizons" (208). Once again Foote tempers the image of a male-dominated frontier West with the elements of home — a child and a well-protected camp. By naming the picture "The Choice of Reuben and Gad," she connects its figures with the biblical story of the exodus from Egypt and the "ten lost tribes of Israel." In the accompanying essay, Foote suggests that because the West lacks tradition, its people are, in her eyes, exiles. She uses the analogy to conclude that for many Westerners the promised land will always lie just beyond where they happen to be.[5]

Two illustrations record the work of people often neglected by Western art and literature, but whose work was essential to settlement — teamsters and engineers. "The Last Trip In" pictures a "freighter of the plains." Mule teams haul a covered wagon uphill through a landscape white with blowing snow. Civilization's marker, in the form of a telegraph pole, intrudes upon this stark scene which pays tribute to a little-honored pioneer of the West, and Foote reminds us that settlements and developmental schemes relied heavily on the freighter. She concludes the essay with the analogy of the West as a colony of the East, just as the East had been a colony of the "mother country."

The final picture, "The Winter Camp — A Day's Ride from the Mail," pictures those Foote knew best, the young engineers who saw themselves as a professional elite, exiled because of their occupation. This scene may have struck armchair adventurers as romantic for it shows the men living close to nature in a wilderness camp. But the accompanying essay reflects the Footes' unhappy experience in their Boise Canyon camp and adds a sobering note to the general optimism of the series. She describes the engineers' frustration when economic conditions slowed their work on expansive projects, thus revealing some sobering realities faced by those who took up the challenge to go West.

Foote's work contrasts markedly with that of her contemporaries who wrote about and illustrated the American West for *Century Magazine*. These contemporaries were, almost without exception, men: Frederic Remington and Teddy Roosevelt perpetuated the myth of the West as howling wilderness where men could still be men; John Wesley Powell and John Muir glorified the "grand" landscapes; sometimes artists who had never seen the West etched sublime and romantic panoramas. But Foote interpreted what was commonplace in her life. "My work," she wrote to Richard Gilder, "is a helplessly faithful rendering . . . of the experiences (my own and others) that have come under my observation" ([188?]). The Far West series, in particular, brings Foote's personal vision of the early Western experience into sharp focus. While the illustrations and essays encompass customary Western themes of open country and isolation, they also address the keynotes of settlement — adaptation to a new environment and the building of home places. In doing so, they contrast sharply with other illustrations of the time which depict the Far West as wilderness or playground for masculine adventure. The Far West series deserves praise for the balance it brings to early images of the American West. [6]

Barbara Cragg
Missoula, Montana

Dennis M. Walsh
Pocatello, Idaho

Mary Ellen Walsh
Pocatello, Idaho

NOTES

[1] Richard W. Etulain's review of scholarship and criticism, "Mary Hallock Foote (1847-1938)," describes the conflict among literary critics of the late nineteenth and early twentieth centuries about Foote's fiction, noting finally that "most observers—even those writing negative assessments—agreed that her descriptions were especially appealiing and pointed out that her style was clear and rarely cluttered with clumsy syntax" (*American Literary Realism* 5 [Spring 1972]: 144-150).

[2] After the publication of "In Exile," Foote wrote to H.E. Scudder in response to a request for another story: "I am under a long standing engagement to the *Century* to give them the first reading of my few stories" (MHF Collection. The Houghton, Cambridge). She did subsequently publish "The Trumpeter" and "Pilgrim Station" in the *Atlantic*.

[3] Benn's master's thesis was the first significant scholarly examination of Foote's fiction ("Mary Hallock Foote: Pioneer Woman Novelist." U of Wyoming, 1955).

[4] Foote expressed a different attitude toward her writing in a letter to H. E. Scudder. Responding after the *Atlantic* had published "The Trumpeter," Foote wrote: "I thank you for wanting another story, but they do not come as often as I wish they would. You wouldn't care for a written-on-purpose story, nor should I dare to risk the little reputation that I have by writing that kind" (12 Dec. 1894. MHF Collection. The Houghton, Cambridge). In an undated letter to Richard Gilder, responding to the editorial critisicm of "On a Side-Track," Foote shows once again her belief in her own work: "I wish to acknowledge the valuable grammatical help of your Proof Reader. I am very weak, as you know in my training: but I do prefer my own adjectives, and as a rule my own construction. I don't know why. I couldn't defend it; it must be because one gets used to the sound of one's own words. Or, perhaps we don't hear ourselves as others hear us" (MHF Collection. The Huntington, San Marino).

[5] Perhaps biblical references permeate this and other essays because Foote was reading to her children from *The Young People's Edition of the Scriptures* at the time that she was working on the series. She defended her references, citing Bartlett's *Young People's Edition,* in a letter to the "Editors of the Century": In the Choice of Reuben and Gad, I think you may depend on my biblical allusions, &c. I have taken pains to be correct. I am now able to give you the exact words from which I took the 'poorest thousand in Manasseh' " (10 Dec. [1888]. MHF Collection. The Huntington, San Marino). The biblical references suited the editorial stance of the *Century* which held Christianity central to western civilization, and they suited Foote's image of her family as among "the souls of the people. . .much discouraged because of the way," because of the failure of Arthur Foote's irrigation plan.

[6] The material concerning Foote's Far West Series is drawn from Barbara Cragg's master's thesis ("The Landscape Perceptions and Imagery of Mary Hallock Foote". U of Montana, 1980).

WORKS CITED

Armstrong, Regina. "Representative American Women Illustrators." *Critic* Aug. 1900: 131-41.

Benn, Mary Lou. "Mary Hallock Foote in Idaho." *University of Wyoming Publications* 20 (15 July 1956): 157-78.

Foote, Mary Hallock. Letter to Richard W. Gilder. 3 Nov. [1887]. MHF Collection. Stanford U Library, Stanford.

—. Letter to Richard W. Gilder. [188?] MHF Collection. Stanford U Library, Stanford.

—. Letter to Richard W. Gilder. 1 June 1891. MHF Collection. The Huntington, San Marino.

—. Letter to Helena DeKay Gilder. 6-8 June 1887. MHF Collection. Stanford U Library, Stanford.

—. Letter to Helena DeKay Gilder. 10 Oct. 1888. MHF Collection. Stanford U Library, Stanford.

—. Letter to William L. Fraser. 10 June [1888]. MHF Collection. Stanford U Library, Stanford.

John, Arthur. *The Best Years of the Century*. Urbana: U of Illinois P, 1981.

Johnson, Lee Ann. *Mary Hallock Foote*. TUSAS 369. Boston: Twayne, 1980.

Jones, Harry H. "The Mining Theme in Western Fiction." *University of Wyoming Publications* 20 (15 July 1956): 101-29.

Linton, W.J. "The History of Wood-Engraving in America: Part IV." In *American Art and American Art Collections*. Ed. Walter Montgomery. 2 vols. Boston, 1889. 1:464-70.
Lummis, Charles F. "The New League of Literature and the West." *Land of Sunshine* April 1898: 208.

Maguire, James H. *Mary Hallock Foote*. BSWW2. Boise: Boise State College, 1972.

Milton, John R. *The Novel of the American West*. Lincoln: U of Nebraska P, 1980.

Paul, Rodman W., ed. *A Victorian Gentlewoman in the Far West: The Reminiscences of Mary Hallock Foote*. San Marino: The Huntington, 1972.

Rogers, W.A. *A World Worthwhile: A Record of "Auld Acquaintance"*. New York: Harper, 1922.

Shaul, Lawana J. "The West in Magazine Fiction, 1870-1900." *University of Wyoming Publications* 20 (15 July 1956): 29-56.

Taft, Robert M. *Artists and Illustrators of the Old West*. New York: Scribner's, 1953.

Walsh, Mary Ellen Williams. "*Angle of Repose* and the Writings of Mary Hallock Foote: A Source Study." *Critical Essays on Wallace Stegner*. Ed. Anthony Arthur. Boston: Hall, 1982. 184-209.

The Idaho Stories

A Cloud on the Mountain

Ruth Mary stood on the high river bank, looking along the beach below to see if her small brother Tommy was lurking anywhere under the willows with his fishing pole. He had been sent half an hour before to the earth cellar for potatoes, and Ruth Mary's father, Mr. Tully, was waiting for his dinner.

She did not see Tommy; but while she lingered, looking at the river hurrying down the shoot between the hills, and curling up over the pebbles of the bar, she saw a team of bay horses and a red-wheeled wagon come rattling down the stony slope of the opposite shore. In the wagon she counted four men. Three of the men wore white, helmet-shaped hats that made brilliant spots of light against the bank. The horses were driven half their length into the stream and allowed to drink as well as they could for the swiftness of the current, while the men seemed to consult together, the two on the front seat turning back to speak with the two behind, and pointing across the river.

Ruth Mary watched them with much interest; for travelers, such as these seemed to be, seldom came as far up Bear River valley as the Tullys' cattle range. The visitors who came to them were mostly cow-boys looking up stray cattle, or miners on their way to the "Banner district," or packers with mule trains going over the mountains, to return in three weeks or three months as their journey prospered. Fishermen and hunters came up into the hills in the season of trout and deer; but they came, as a rule, on horseback, and at a distance were hardly to be distinguished from the cow-boys and the miners.

The men in the wagon were evidently strangers to that locality. They had seen Ruth Mary watching them from the hill, and now one of them rose up in the wagon, shouting across to her and pointing to the river.

She could not hear his words for the noise of the ripple and the wind which blew freshly downstream, but she understood that he was inquiring about the ford. She motioned up the river, and called to him, though she knew her words could not reach him, to keep on the edge of the ripple. Her gestures, however, aided by the driver's knowledge of fords, were sufficient; and turning his horses' heads upstream, they took water at the place she had tried to indicate. The wagon sank to the wheelhubs; the horses kept their feet well though the current was strong; the sun shone brightly on the white hats and laughing faces of the men, on the guns in their hands, on the red paint of the wagon and the warm backs of the horses breasting the stream. When they were halfway across, one of the men tossed a small, reluctant black dog over the wheel into the river, and all the company with the exception of the driver, who was giving his attention to his horses, broke into hilarious shouts of encouragement to the swimmer in his struggle with the current. It was carrying him, down and would probably land him, without effort of his own, on a strip of white sand beach under the willows above the bend; but now the unhappy little object, merely a black nose and two blinking anxious eyes above the water, had drifted into an eddy from which he cast forlorn glances toward his faithless friends in the wagon. The dog was in no real peril, but Ruth Mary did not know it, and her heart swelled with indignant pity. Only shyness kept her from wading to his rescue. But now one of the laughing young men, thinking, perhaps, the joke had gone far enough, and reckless of a wetting, leaped out into the water, and plunging along in his high boots, soon had the terrier by the scruff of his neck, and waded ashore with his sleek, quivering little body nestled in the bosom of his flannel hunting shirt.

A deep cut in the bank, through which the wagon was dragged, was screened by willows. When the fording party arrived at the top, Ruth Mary was nowhere to be seen. "Where's that girl got to all of a sudden?" one of the men demanded. They had intended to ask her several questions; but she was gone, and the road before them plainly led to the low-roofed cabin, and loosely built barn, with straw and daylight showing through its cracks, the newly planted poplar trees above the thatched earth cellar, and all the signs of a tentative home in this solitude of the hills.

They drove on slowly, the young man who had waded ashore, whom his comrades addressed as Kirkwood or Kirke, walking behind the wagon with the dog in his arms, responding to his whimpering claims for attention with teasing caresses. The dog seemed to be the butt as well as the pet of the party. As they approached the house, he scrambled out of Kirkwood's arms and lingered to take a roll in the sandy path, coming up a moment afterward to be received with blighting sarcasms as to his appearance. After his ignominious wetting, he was quite unable to bear up under them, and slunk to the rear with deprecatory blinks and waggings of his tail whenever one of the men looked back.

Ruth Mary had run home quickly to tell her father, who was sitting in the sun by the woodpile, of the arrival of strangers from across the river. Mr. Tully rose up deliberately and went to meet his guests, keeping between his teeth the sliver of pine he had been chewing while waiting for his dinner. It helped to bear him out in that appearance of indifference he thought it well to assume, as if such arrivals were an everyday occurrence.

"Hasn't Tommy got back yet, mother?" Ruth Mary asked as she entered the house. Mrs. Tully was a stout, low-browed woman, with grayish yellow hair of that dry and lifeless texture which shows declining health or want of care. Her blue eyes looked faded in the setting of her tanned complexion. She sat in a low chair, her knees wide apart, defined by her limp calico draperies, rocking a child of two years, a fat little girl, with flushed cheeks, and flaxen hair braided into tight knots on her forehead, who was asleep in the large cushioned rocking chair in the middle of the room. The room looked bare, for the shed room outside was evidently the more-used part of the house. The cookstove was there in the inclosed corner, and beside it a table and shelf with a tin hand-basin hanging beneath, while the crannies of the logs on each side of the doorway were utilized as shelves for all the household articles in frequent requisition that were not hanging from nails driven into the logs or from the projecting roofpoles against the light.

Tommy had not returned, and Mrs. Tully suggested as a reason for his delay that he had stopped somewhere to catch grasshoppers for bait.

"I should think he had enough of 'em in that bottle of his," Ruth Mary said, "to last him till the 'hoppers come again. Some strange men forded the river just now: Father's gone to speak to them. I guess he'll ask 'em to stop to dinner."

Mrs. Tully got up heavily and went to the door. "Here, Angy—" she addressed a girl of eight or ten years who sat on the flat bowlder which was the cabin door-step. "You go get them 'taters—that's a good girl," she added coaxingly, as Angy did not stir. "If your foot hurts you, you can walk on your heel."

Angy, who was complaining of a stonebruise, got up and limped

3

away, upsetting from her lap as she rose two kittens of tender years, who tumbled over each other before getting their legs under them, and staggered off, steering themselves jerkily with their tails.

"Oh, Angy!" Ruth Mary remonstrated; but she could not stay to comfort the kittens. She ran up the short, crooked stairs leading to the garret bedroom which she shared with Angy, hastily put on her shoes and stockings and braced her pretty figure, under the blue calico sack she wore, with her first pair of stays, an important purchase made on her last visit to the town in the valley, and to be worn now, if ever. It was hot at noon in the bedroom under the roof, and by the time Ruth Mary had fortified herself to meet the eyes of strangers, she was uncomfortably flushed and short of breath, besides, from the pressure of the new stays. She went slowly down the uneven stairs, wishing she could walk as softly in her shoes as she could barefoot.

Her father was talking to the strangers in the shed room. They looked tall and formidable, under the low roof against the flat glare of the sun on the hard swept ground in front of the shed. She waited inside until her mother reminded her of the dinner, half-cooked on the stove; then she went out shyly, the light falling on her downcast face and full white eyelids, on her yellow hair, sunfaded and meekly parted over a forehead low like her mother's, but smooth as one of the white stones of the river beach. Her fair skin was burned to a clear light red tint like a child's, and her blonde eyebrows and lashes looked silvery against it, but her chin was very white underneath, and there was a white space behind each of her little ears where her hair was knotted tightly away from her neck.

"This is my daughter," Mr. Tully said, briefly, and then he gave some hospitable orders about dinner which the strangers interrupted, saying they had a lunch with them and would not trouble his family until supper-time.

They gathered up their hunting gear and, lifting their hats to Ruth Mary, followed Mr. Tully, who had offered to show them the best fishing on that part of the river.

Mr. Tully explained to his wife and daughter, as the latter placed the dinner on the table, that three of the strangers were the engineers from the railroad camp at Moor's Bridge, and the fourth was a packer and teamster from the same camp; that they were all going up the river to look at timber, and wanted a little sport by the way. They had expected to keep on the other side of the river, but seeing the ranch on the opposite shore, with wheel-tracks going down to the water,

4

they had concluded to try the ford and the fishing and ask for a night's accommodation.

"They don't want we should put ourselves out any. They're used to roughin' it, they say. If you can git together somethin' to feed 'em on, mother, they say they'd as soon sleep on the straw in the barn as anywheres else."

"There's plenty to eat, such as it is, but Ruth Mary'll have it all to do. I can't be on my feet." Mrs. Tully spoke in a depressed way, but to her no less than to her husband was this little break welcome in the monotony of their life in the hills; even though it brought with it a more vivid consciousness of the family circumstances and a review of them in the light of former standards of comfort and gentility. For Mrs. Tully had been a woman of some social ambition in the small Eastern village where she was born. To all that to her guests made the unique charm of the place, she had grown callous, if she had ever felt it at all, while dwelling with an incurable regret upon the neatly painted houses and fenced door-yards, the gatherings of women in their best clothes in primly furnished parlors on summer afternoons, the churchgoing, the passing in the street, and, more than all, the house-keeping conveniences she had been used to, accumulated through many years' occupancy of the same house.

"Seems as though I hadn't any ambition left," she often complained to her daughter. "There's nothin' here to do with, and nobody to do for. The most of the folks we ever see wouldn't know sour-dough bread from saltrisin', and as for dressin' up, I might keep the same clothes on from Fourth July till Christmas—your father'd never know."

But Ruth Mary was haunted by no fleshpots of the past. As she dressed the chickens and mixed the biscuit for supper, she paused often in her work and looked towards the high pastures with the pale brown lights and purple shadows on them, rolling away and rising towards the great timbered ridges, and these lifting, here and there along their profiles a treeless peak or bare divide into the regions above vegetation. She had no misgivings about her home. Fences would not have improved her father's vast lawn, to her mind, or white paint the low-browed front of his dwelling; nor did she feel the want of a stair-carpet and a parlor-organ. She was sure that they, the strangers, had never seen anything more lovely than her beloved river, dancing down between the hills, tripping over rapids, wrinkling over sand-bars of its own spreading, and letting out its speed down the long reaches where the channel was deep.

About four o'clock she found leisure to stroll along the shore with Tommy, whose competitive energies as a fisherman had been stimulated by the advent of strange craftsmen with scientific-looking tackle. Tommy must forthwith show what native skill could do, with a willow pole and grasshoppers for bait. But Ruth Mary's sense of propriety would by no means tolerate Tommy's intruding his company upon the strangers, and to frustrate any rash, gregarious impulses on his part, she judged it best to keep him in sight.

Tommy knew of a deep pool under the willows which he could whip unseen in the shady hours of the afternoon. Thither he led Ruth Mary, leaving her seated upon the bank above him, lest she should be tempted to talk, and so interfere with his sport. The moments went by in silence, broken only by the river; Ruth Mary happy on the high bank in the sun, Tommy happy by the shady pool below, and now and then slapping a lively trout upon the stones. Across the river two Chinamen were washing gravel in a rude miner's cradle, paddling about on the river's brink and anon staggering down from the gravel bank above, with large square kerosene cans filled with pay dirt balanced on either end of a pole across their meager shoulders. Bare-headed, in their loose garments, with their pottering movements and wrinkled faces, shining with heat, they looked like two weird, unrevered old women working out some dismal penance. High up in the sky the great black buzzards sailed and sailed on slanting wing; the wood doves coo-oo-ed from the willow thickets that gathered the sunlight close to the water's edge. A few horses and cattle moved like specks upon the sides of the hills, cropping the bunch-grass, but the greater herds had been driven up into the high pastures where the snow falls early; and all these lower hills were bare of life, unless one might fancy that the far-off processions of pines against the sky marching up the northern sides of the divides, had a solemn personality, going up, like priests to a sacrifice, or that the restless river, flowing through the midst of all and bearing the light of the white noonday sky deep into the bosom of the darkest hills, had a soul as well as a voice. In its sparkle and everchanging motion, it was like a child among its elders at play. The hills seemed to watch it, and the great cloud-heads as they looked down between the parting summits, and the three tall pines, standing about a young bird's flight from each other by the shore, and mingling their fitful crooning with the river's babble.

It is pleasant to think of Ruth Mary, sitting high above the river in the peaceful afternoon, surrounded by the inanimate life that to her brought the fullness of companionship, and left no room for vain cravings; the shadow creeping upward over her hands folded in her lap, the light resting on her girlish face and meek, smooth hair. For this was during that unquestioning time of content which may not always last, even in a life as safe and as easily predicted as hers. But even now this silent communion was interrupted by the appearance of one of Tommy's rivals. It was the young man whose comrades called him Kirke, who came along the shore, stooping under the willow boughs and scattering all their shadows, lightly traced on the stones below. He held his fishing-rod couched like a lance in one hand, and a string of gleaming fish in the other.

Tommy, with his practiced eye, rapidly counted them and saw with chagrin that he was outnumbered, but another look satisfied him that the stranger's catch was nearly all white-fish instead of trout. He carassed his own dappled beauties complacently.

Kirkwood stopped and looked at them; he was evidently impressed by Tommy's superior luck.

"These are big fellows," he said; "did you catch them?"

"You don't suppose *she* did," said Tommy, with a jerk of his head towards Ruth Mary.

Kirkwood looked up and smiled, seeing the young girl on her sunny perch. The smile lingered pleasantly in his eyes as he seated himself on the stones,—deliberately, as if he meant to stay.

Tommy watched him while he made himself comfortable, taking from his pocket a short meerschaum pipe and a bag of tobacco, leisurely filling the pipe and lighting it with a wax match held in the hollow of his hands—apparently from habit, for there was no wind. He did not seem to mind in the least that his legs were wet and that his trout were nearly all white-fish. He was evidently a person of happy resources, and a joy-compelling temperament, that could find virtue in white-fish if it couldn't get trout. He began to talk to Tommy, not without an amused consciousness of Tommy's silent partner on the bank above, nor without an occasional glance up at the maidenly head serenely exalted in the sunlight. Nor did Ruth Mary fail to respond, with her down-bent looks, as simply and unawares as the clouds turning their bright side to the sun.

Tommy, on his part, was stoutly withholding in words the admiration his eyes could not help showing of the strange fisherman's tools. He cautiously felt the weight of the ringed and polished rod, and snapped it a little over the water; he was permitted to examine the book of flies and to handle the reel, things in themselves fascinating, but to Tommy's mind merely a hinderance and a snare to the understanding in the real business of catching fish. Still, he admitted, where a man could take a whole day, all to himself like that, without fear of being called off at any moment by the women on some frivolous household errand, he might afford to potter with such things. Tommy kept the conservative attitude of native experience and skill towards foreign contrivance.

"If Joe Enselman was here," he said, "I bet he could ketch more fish in half'n hour with a pole like this o'mine and a han'ful o' hoppers, than any of you can in a whole week o' fishing with them fancy things."

"Oh, Tommy!" Ruth Mary expostulated, looking distressed.

"Who is this famous fisherman?" Kirkwood asked, smiling at Tommy's boast.

"Oh, he's a feller I know. He's a packer, and he owns ha'f o' father's stock. He's goin' to marry our Sis soon's he gits back from Sheep Mountain, and then he'll be my brother." Tommy had been a little reckless in his desire for the distinction of a personal claim on the hero of his boyish heart. He was even conscious of this himself, as he glanced up at his sister.

Kirkwood's eyes involuntarily followed Tommy's. He withdrew them at once, but not before he saw the troubled blush that reddened the girl's averted face. It struck him, though he was not deeply versed in blushes, that it was not quite the expression of a happy, maidenly consciousness, when the name of a lover is unexpectedly spoken.

It was the first time in her life that Ruth Mary had ever blushed at Joe Enselman's name. She could not understand why it should pain her to have this young stranger hear of him in his relation to herself.

Before her blush had faded, Kirkwood had dismissed the subject of Ruth Mary's engagement with the careless reflection that Enselman was probably not the right man, but that the primitive laws which decide such haphazard unions, doubtless provided the necessary hardihood of temperament wherewith to meet their exigencies. She was a nice little girl, but possibly she was not so sensitive as she looked.

His pipe had gone out, and after relighting it, he showed Tommy the gayly pictured paper match-box which opened with a spring, and disclosed the matches lying in a little drawer within. Tommy's wistful eyes, as he returned the box, prompted Kirkwood to make prudent search in his pockets for a second box of matches before presenting Tommy with the one his eyes coveted. Finding himself secure against want in the immediate future, he gave himself up to the mild amusement of watching Tommy with his new acquisition.

Tommy could not resist lighting one of the little tapers, which burned in the sunlight with a still, clear flame like a Christmas candle. Then a second one was sacrificed. By this time the attraction was strong enough to bring Ruth Mary down from her high seat in the sun. She looked hardly less a child than Tommy, as with her face close to his, she watched the pale flame flower wasting on its waxen stem. Then she must needs light one herself and hold it, with a little fixed smile on her face, till the flame crept down and warmed her fingertips.

"There," she said, putting it out with a breath, "don't let us burn anymore. It's too bad to waste 'em in the daylight."

"We will burn one more," said Kirkwood, "not for amusement, but for information." And while he whittled a piece of drift-wood into the shape of a boat, he told Ruth Mary how the Hindoo maidens set their lighted lamps afloat at night on the Ganges, and watch them perilously voyaging, to learn, by the fate of the little flame, the safety of their absent lovers.

He told it simply and gravely, as he might have described some fact in natural history, for he rightly guessed that this little seed of sentiment fell on virgin soil. According to Tommy, Ruth Mary was betrothed and soon to be a wife, but Kirkwood was curiously sure that she knew not love, nor even fancy. Nor had he any rash idea of trying to enlarge her experience. He spoke of the lamps on the Ganges because they came into his mind while Ruth Mary was bending over the wasting match flame; any hesitation he might have had about introducing so delicate a topic was conquered by an idle fancy that he would like to observe its effect upon her almost pathetic innocence.

While he talked, interrupting himself as his whittling absorbed him, but always conscious of her eyes upon his face, the boat took shape in his hands. Tommy had failed to catch the connection between Hindoo girls and boatmaking, but was satisfied with watching Kirkwood's skillful fingers, without paying much heed to his words. He had a wonderful knife, too, with tools concealed in its handle, with one of which he bored a hole for the mast. In the top of the mast he fixed one of the wax tapers upright and steady for the voyage.

Ruth Mary's cheeks grew red, as she suddenly perceived the intention of Kirkwood's whittling.

"Now," he said, steadying the boat on the shallow ripple, "before we light our beacon you must think of someone you care for who is away. Perhaps Tommy's friend, on Sheep Mountain?" he ventured softly, glancing at Ruth Mary.

The color in her cheeks deepened, and again Kirkwood fancied it was not a happy confusion that covered her downcast face.

"No?" he questioned, as Ruth Mary did not speak; "that is too serious, perhaps. Well, then, make a little wish, and if the light is still alive when the boat passes that rock—the flat one with two stones on top—the wish will come true. But you must have faith, you know."

Ruth Mary looked at Kirkwood, the picture of faith in her sweet seriousness. His heart smote him a little, but he met her wide-eyed gaze with a gravity equal to her own.

"I would rather not wish for myself," she said, "but I will wish something for you, if you want me to."

"That is very kind of you. Am I to know what it will be?"

"Oh, yes. You must tell me what to wish."

"That is easily done," said Kirkwood gayly. "Wish that I may come back some other day, and sit here with you and Tommy by the river."

It was impossible not to see that Ruth Mary was blushing again. But she answered him with a gentle courtesy that rebuked the foolish blush: "That will be wishing for us all."

"Shall we light up then, and set her afloat?"

"I've made a wish," shouted Tommy; "I've wished Joe Enselman would bring me an injun pony—a good one that won't buck!"

"You must keep your wish for the next trip. This ship is freighted deep enough already. Off she goes then, and good luck to the wish," said Kirkwood, as the current took the boat with the light at its peak burning clearly, and swept it away. The pretty plaything dipped and danced a moment, while the light wavered, but still lived. Then a breath of wind shook the willows, and the light was gone.

"Now it's my turn," Tommy exclaimed, wasting no sentiment on another's failure. He rushed down the bank and into the shallow water to catch the wishing-boat before it drifted away.

"All the same, I'm coming back again," said Kirkwood, looking at Ruth Mary.

Tommy's wish fared no better than his sister's, but he bore up briskly, declaring it was "all foolishness anyway," and accused Kirkwood of having "just made it up for fun."

Kirkwood only laughed, and, ignoring Tommy, said to Ruth Mary, "The game was hardly worth the candle, was it?"

10

"Was it a game?" she asked. "I though you meant it for true."

"Oh, no," he said; "when we try it in earnest we must find a smoother river and a stronger light. Besides, you know, I'm coming back."

Ruth Mary kept her eyes upon his face, still questioning his seriousness, but its quick changes of expression baffled while fascinating her. She could not have told whether she thought him handsome or not, but she had a desire to look at him all the time.

Suddenly her household duties recurred to her, and refusing the help of Kirkwood's hand, she sprang up the bank and hurried back to the house. Kirkwood could see her head above the wild-rose thickets as she went along the high path by the shore. He was more than ever sure that Enselman was not the right man.

At supper Ruth Mary waited on the strangers in silence, while Angy kept the cats and dogs "corralled," as her father said, in the shed, that their impetuous appetites might not disturb the feast.

Mr. Tully stood in the doorway and talked with his guests while they ate, and Mrs. Tully, with the little two-year-old in her lap, rocked in the large rocking-chair and sighed apologetically between her promptings of Ruth Mary's attendance on the table.

Tommy hung about in a state of complete infatuation with the person and conversation of his former rival. He was even beginning to waver in his allegiance to his absent hero, especially as the wish about the Indian pony had not come true.

During the family meal the young men sat outside in the shed room and smoked, and lazily talked together. Their words reached the silent group at the table. Kirkwood's companions were deriding him as a recreant sportsman. He puffed his short-stemmed pipe and looked at them tranquilly. He was not dissatisfied with his share of the day's pleasure.

When Mr. Tully had finished his supper he took the young men down to the beach to look at his boat. Kirkwood had pointed it out to his comrades, where it lay moored under the bank, and ventured the opinion of a boating man that it had not been built in the mountains. But there he had generalized too rashly.

"I built her myself," said Mr. Tully; "ripsawed the lumber up here. My young ones are as *handy* with her!" he boasted cheerfully, warmed by the admiration his work called forth. "You'd never believe, to see'em knocking about in her, they hadn't the first one of 'em ever smelt salt water. Ruth Mary, now the oldest of 'em, is as much to home in that boat as she is on a hoss—and that's sayin'

11

enough. She looks quiet, but she's got as firm a seat and as light a hand as any cowboy that ever put leg over a cayuse."

Mr. Tully on being questioned admitted willingly that he was an Eastern man—a Down-East lumberman and boatbuilder. He couldn't say just why he'd come West. Got restless, and his wife's health was always poor back there. He had mined it some and had considerable luck—cleaned up several thousands the summer of '63 at Junction Bar. Put it in a saw-mill and got burned out. Then he took up this cattle range and went into stock in partnership with a young fellow from Montana, named Enselman. They expected to make a good thing of it, but it *was* a long ways from anywheres; and for months of the year they couldn't do any teaming. Had no way out except by the horseback trail. The women found it lonesome. In winter no team could get up that grade in the cañon they call the "freeze-out," even if they could cross for ice in the river; and from April to August the river was up so you couldn't ford.

All this in the intervals of business, for Mr. Tully in his circuitous way was agreeing to build a boat for the engineers after the model of his own. He would have to go down to the camp at Moor's Bridge to build it, he said, for suitable lumber could not be procured so far up the river, except at great expense. It would take him better'n a month anyhow, and he didn't know what his women folks would say to having him so long away. He would see about it.

The four men sauntered up the path from the shore, Tommy bringing up the rear with the little black-and-tan terrier. In default of a word from his master, Tommy tried to make friends with the dog, but the latter, wide awake and suspicious after dozing under the wagon all the afternoon, would none of him. Possibly he divined that Tommy's attentions were not wholly disinterested.

The family assembled for the evening in the shed room. The women were silent, for the talk was confined to masculine topics, such as the quality of the placer claims up the river, the timber, the hunting, the progress and prospects of the new railroad. Tommy, keeping himself forcibly awake, was seeing two Kirkwoods where there was but one. The terrier had taken shelter between Kirkwood's knees, after trying conclusions with the mother of the kittens—a cat of large experience and a reserved disposition, with only one ear, but otherwise in full possession of her faculties.

Betimes the young men arose and said good night. Mr. Tully was loath to have the evening, with its rare opportunity for conversation, come to a close, but he was too modest a host to press his company upon his guests. He went with them to their bed on the clean straw in the barn, and if good wishes could soften pillows the travelers would have slept sumptuously. They did not know, in fact, how they slept, but woke strong and joyous over the beauty of the morning on the hills, and the prospect of continuing their journey.

They parted from the family at the ranch with a light-hearted promise to stop again on their way down the river. When they would return they were gayly uncertain;—it might be ten days, it might be two weeks. It was a promise that nestled with delusive sweetness in Ruth Mary's thoughts as she went silently about her work. She was helpful in all ways, very gentle with the children, but she lingered more hours dreaming by the river, and often at twilight she climbed the hill back of the cabin and sat there alone, her cheek in the hollow of her hand, until the great planes of distance were lost, and all the hills drew together in one dark profile against the sky.

Mrs. Tully had been intending to spare Ruth Mary for a journey to town on some errands of a feminine nature which could not be intrusted to Mr. Tully's larger but less discriminating judgment. Ruth Mary had never before been known to trifle with an opportunity of this kind. Her rides to town had been the one excitement of her life; looked forward to with eagerness and discussed with tireless interest for many days after. But now she hung back with an unaccountable apathy, and made excuses for postponing the ride from day to day, until the business became too pressing to be longer neglected. She set off one morning at daybreak, following the horseback trail round the steep and sliding bluffs high above the river, or across beds of broken lava rock, arrested avalanches from the slowly crumbling cliffs which crowned the bluff; or picking her way at a soft-footed pace through the thickets of the river bottoms. In such a low and sheltered spot, scarcely four feet above the river she found the engineers' camp, a group of white tents shining among the willows. She keenly noted its location and surroundings. The broken timbers of the old bridge projected from the bank a short distance above the camp; a piece of weather-stained canvas stretched over them formed a kind of awning shading the rocks below, where the Chinese cook of the camp sat impassively fishing. The camp had a deserted look, for the men were all at work tunnelling the hill half a mile lower down. Her errands kept her so late that she was obliged to stay over night at the house of a friend of her father's, who owned a fruit ranch near the town. They were prosperous, talkative people, who loudly pitied the isolation of the family in the upper valley.

Ruth Mary reached home about noon the next day, tired and several shades more deeply sun-burned, to find that she had passed the engineers without knowing it on their way down the river by the wagon road on the other side. They had stopped over night at the ranch, and made an early start that morning. Ruth Mary was obliged to listen to enthusiastic reminiscences from each member of the family of the visit she had missed.

This was the last social event of the year. The willow copses turned yellow and threadbare; the scarlet hips of the rosebush looked as if tiny finger-tips had left their prints upon them. The wreaths of wild clematis turned ashen gray, and were scattered by the winds. The wood-dove's cooing no longer sounded at twilight in the leafless thickets. They had gone down the river and the wild duck with them.

But the voice of the river, rising with the autumn rains, was loud on the bar; the sky was hung with clouds that hid the hilltops or trailed their ragged pennants below their summits. The mists lay cold on the river; they rose with the sun, dissolving in soft haze that dulled the sunshine, and at night descending, shrouded the dark, hoarse water without stilling its lament. Then the first snow fell, and ghostly companies of deer came out upon the hills, or filed silently down the draws of the cañons at morning and evening. The cattle had come down from the mountain pastures, and at night congregated about the buildings with deep breathings and sighings; the river murmured in its fretted channel; now and then the yelp of a hungry coyote sounded from the hills.

The young men had said, among their light and pleasant sayings, that they would like to come up again to the hills when the snow fell, and get a shot at the deer; but they did not come, though often Ruth Mary stood on the bank and looked across the swollen ford, and listened for the echo of wheels among the hills.

About the first of November Mr. Tully went down to the camp at Moor's Bridge to build the engineers' boat. The women were now alone at the ranch, but Joe Enselman's return was daily expected. Mr. Tully, always cheerful, had been confident that he would be home by the 5th.

The 5th of November and the 10th passed, but Enselman had not returned. On the 12th, in the midst of a heavy fall of snow, his pack animals were driven in by another man, a stranger to the women at the ranch, who said that Enselman had changed his mind suddenly about coming home that fall, and decided to go to Montana and "prove up" on his ranch there.

Mr. Tully's work was finished before the 1st of December. On his return to the ranch he brought with him a great brown paper bundle which the children opened by the cabin fire on the joyous evening of his arrival. There were back numbers of the illustrated magazines and papers, stray copies of which now and then had drifted into the hands of the voracious young readers in the cabin. There were a few novels, selected by Kirkwood from the camp library, with especial reference to Ruth Mary. For Tommy there was a duplicate of the wonderful pocket-knife he had envied Kirkwood. Angy was remembered with a little music box which played "Willie, we have missed you," with a plaintive iteration that brought the sensitive tears to Ruth Mary's eyes; and for Ruth Mary herself there was a lace pin of hammered gold.

"He said it must be your wedding present from him, as you'd be married likely before he saw you again," Mr. Tully said, with innocent pride in the gift with which his daughter had been honored.

"Who said that?" Ruth Mary asked.

"Why, Mr. Kirkwood said it. He's the boss one of the whole lot to my thinkin'. He's got that *way* with him some folks has! We had some real good talks evenings, down on the rocks under the old bridge—I told him about you and Enselman—"

"Father, I wish you hadn't done that." The protest in Ruth Mary's voice was stronger than her words.

She had become slightly pale when Kirkwood's name was mentioned, but now, as she held out the box with the trinket in it, a deep blush covered her face.

"I cannot take it, father. Not with that message. He can wait till I'm married before he sends me his wedding present."

To her father's amazement, she burst into tears and went out into the shed room, leaving Kirkwood's ill-timed gift in his hands.

"What in all conscience's sake's got into her?" he demanded of his wife. "To take offense at a little thing like that! She didn't use to be so techy."

Mrs. Tully nodded her head at him sagely and glanced at the children, a hint that she understood Ruth Mary's state of mind, but could not explain before them.

At bedtime, the father and mother being alone together, Mrs. Tully revealed the cause of her daughter's sensitiveness, according to her theory of it. "She's put out because Joe Enselman chose to wait till spring before marryin' and went off to Montany instead of comin' home as he said he would."

"Sho, sho!" said Mr. Tully. "That don't seem like Ruth Mary! She ain't in any such a hurry as all that comes to. I've had it on my mind lately, that she took it a little *too* easy."

"*You'll* see," said the mother. "*She* ain't in any hurry, but she likes *him* to be. She feels's if he thought more of money-makin' than he does of her. She's like all girls. She won't use her reason and see it's all for her in the end he's doin' it."

"Why didn't you tell her 'twas my plan his goin' to Montany this fall. He wouldn't listen to it nohow, then. He'd rather lose his ranch than wait any longer for Sis, so he said—but I guess he's seen the sense of what I told him. Ruth Mary ain't a-goin' to run away, I says, even if ye don't prove up on her this fall. You ought to a-told her, mother, 'twas my proposition."

"I told her that and more too. I told her it showed he'd make a good provider. She looked at me solemn as a graven image all the time I was talkin' and not a word out of her. But that's Ruth Mary. I never said the child was sullen, but she is just like your sister Ruth—the more she feels, the less she talks."

"Well," said Mr. Tully, "that's all right, if that's it. That'll all straighten out with time. It was natural perhaps she should fire up at the talk about marryin' if she felt the bridegroom was hangin' back. Why, Joe,—he'd eat the dirt she treads on, if he couldn't make her like him no other way! He's most too foolish about her, to my thinkin'. That's what took me so by surprise when word came back he'd gone to Montany after all—I didn't expect anything so sensible of him."

"'Twas a reg'lar man's piece o' work anyhow," said Mrs. Tully disconsolately. "And you'll be sorry for it, I'm afraid. I never knew any good come of puttin' off a marriage where everything was suitable, just for a few hundred acres of wild land, more or less."

"No use your worryin'," said Mr. Tully. "Young folks always has their little troubles before they settle down—besides, what sort of a marriage would it be if you or I could make it or break it?" But he bore himself with a deprecating tenderness towards his daughter, in whose affairs he had meddled, perhaps disastrously, as his better-half feared.

The winters of Idaho are not long even in the higher valleys. Close on the cold footsteps of the retreating snows trooped the first wild flowers. The sun seemed to laugh in the cloudless sky. The children were let loose on the hills; their voices echoed the river's roar. Its waters, rising with the melting snows, no longer babbled childishly on their way; they shouted, and brawled, and tumbled over the bar, rolling huge pine trunks along as if they were sticks of kindling wood.

One cool May evening, Ruth Mary, climbing the path from the beach, saw there was a strange horse and two pack animals in the corral. She did not stop to look at them, but quickly guessing who their owner must be, she went on to the house, her knees weak and trembling, her heart beating heavily. Her father met her at the door and detained her outside. She was prepared for his announcement. She knew that Joe Enselman had returned, and that the time was come for her to prove her new resolve born of the winter's silent struggle.

"I thought I'd better have a few words with you, Ruthie, before you see him—to prepare your mind. Set down here." Mr. Tully took his daughter's hands in his own and held them while he talked.

"You thought it was queer Joe staid away so long, didn't you?" Ruth Mary opened her lips to speak, but no words came. "Well, I did," said the father. "Though it was my plan first off. I might a-know'd it was something more'n business that kep' him. Joe's had an accident. It happened to him just about the time he meant to a-started for home. It broke him all up,—made him feel like he didn't want to see any of us just then. He was goin' along a trail through the woods one dark night; he never knew what stunned him; must have been a twig or something struck him in the eye; he was giddy and crazy-like for a spell—his horse took him home. Well, he aint got but one eye left, Joe aint. There, Sis, I knew you'd feel bad. But he's well. It's hurt his looks some, but what's looks! We aint any of us got any to brag on. Joe had some hopes at first he'd git to seein' again out of the eye that was hurt, and so he sent home his animals and put out for Salt Lake to show it to a doctor there; but it wasn't any use. The eye's gone; and it does seem as if for the time bein' some of Joe's grit had gone with it. He went up to Montany and tended to his business, but it was all like a dumb show and no heart in it. It's cut him pretty deep, through his bein' alone so long perhaps, and thinkin' about how you'd feel. And then he's pestered in his mind about marryin'. He feels he's got no claim to you now. Says it aint fair to ask a young girl that's likely to have plenty good chances to tie up to what's left of *him*. I wanted you should know about this before you go inside. It might hurt him some to see a change in your face when you look at him first. As to his givin' you your word back, that you'll settle between yourselves, but however you fix it I guess you'll make it as easy as you can for Joe. I don't know as I ever see a big strappin' fellow so put down."

Mr. Tully had waited between his short and troubled sentences for some response from Ruth Mary, but she was still silent. Her hands felt cold in his. As he released them she leaned suddenly forward and hid her face against his shoulder. She shivered and her breast heaved, but she was not weeping.

"There, there!" said Mr. Tully, stroking her head clumsily with his large hand. "I've made a botch of it. I'd ought to let your mother told ye."

She pressed closer to him, and wrapped her arms around him without speaking.

"I expect I better go in now," he said gently, putting her away from him. "Will you come along o' me, or do you want to git a little quieter first?"

"You go in," Ruth Mary whispered. "I'll come soon."

It was not long before she followed her father into the house. No one was surprised to see her white and tremulous. She seemed to know where Enselman sat without raising her eyes; neither did he venture to look at her as she came to him and stooping forward laid her little cold hands on his.

"I'm glad you've come back," she said. Then sinking down suddenly on the floor at his feet, she threw her apron over her head and sobbed aloud.

The father and mother wept too. Joe sat still, with a great and bitter longing in his smitten countenance, but not daring to comfort her.

"Pick her up, Joe," said Mr. Tully. "Take hold of her, man, and show her you've got a whole heart if you aint got but one eye."

It was understood, as Ruth Mary meant it should be, without more words, that Enselman's misfortune would make no difference in their old relation. The difference it had made in that new resolve born of the winter's struggle, she told to no one—for to no one had she confided her resolve.

Joe stayed two weeks at the ranch, and was comforted into a semblance of his former hardy cheerfulness. But Ruth Mary knew that he was not happy. One evening he asked her to go with him down the high shore path. He told her that he was going to town the next day on business that might keep him absent about a fortnight, and entreated her to think well of her promise to him, for on his return he should expect its fulfillment. For God's sake, he begged her to let no pity for his misfortune blind her to the true nature of her feeling for him. He held her close to his heart and kissed her many times. Did she love him so—and so—he asked. Ruth Mary, trembling, said she did not know. How could she help knowing? he demanded passionately. Had her thoughts been with him all winter as his had been with her? Had she looked up the river towards the hills where he was staying so long and wished for him, as he had gazed southward into the valleys many and many a day, longing for the sweet blue eyes of his little girl so far away?

Alas, Ruth Mary! She gazed almost wildly into his stricken face, distorted by the anguish of his great love and his great dread. She wished that she were dead. There seemed no other way out of her trouble.

The next morning, before she was dressed, Enselman rode away and her father went with him.

She was alone now, in the midst of the hills she loved—alone as she would never be again! She foresaw that she would not have the strength to give that last blow to her faithful old friend,—the crushing blow that perfect truth demanded. Her tenderness was greater than her truth.

The river was now swollen to its greatest volume. Its voice that had been the babble of a child, and the tumult of a boy, was now deep and heavy like the chest notes of a strong man. Instead of the sparkling ripple on the bar there was a continuous roar of yellow turbid water that could be heard a mile away. There had been no fording for six weeks, nor would be again until late summer. The useless boat lay in the shallow wash that filled the deep cut among the willows. The white sand beach was gone; heavy waves swirled past the banks and sent their eddies up into the channels of the hills to meet the streams of melted snow. Thunder-clouds chased each other about the mountains, or met in sudden downfalls of rain.

One sultry noon when the sun had come out hot on the hills, after a wet morning, Ruth Mary, at work in the shed room, heard a sound that drove the color from her cheek. She ran out and looked up the river, listening to a distant but ever increasing roar which could be heard above the incessant laboring of the waters over the bar. Above the summit of Sheep Mountain, as it seemed, a huge turban-shaped cloud had rolled itself up and from its central folds was discharging gray sheets of water that veered and slanted with the wind, but were always distinct in their density against the rain-charged atmosphere. How far away the floods were descending she did not know, but that they were coming, in a huge wall of water, overtaking and swallowing up the river's current, she was as sure as that she had been bred in the mountains.

Bare-headed, bare-armed as she was, without a backward look, she ran down the hill to the place where the boat was moored. Tommy was there sitting in the boat and making the shallow water splash, as he rocked from side to side.

"Get out, Tommy, and let me have her, quick!" Ruth Mary called to him.

Tommy looked at her stolidly and kept on rocking. "What you want with her?" he asked.

"Come out, for mercy's sake! Don't you *hear* it? There's a cloud-burst on the mountain."

Tommy listened. He did hear it, but he did not stir. "It'll be a bully thing to see when it comes. What you doin'? You act like you was crazy," he exclaimed as Ruth Mary waded through the water and got into the boat.

"Tommy, you will kill me if you stop to talk! Don't you know the camp at Moor's Bridge? Go home and tell mother I've gone to give 'em warning."

Tommy was instantly sobered. "I'm going with you," he said. "You can't handle her alone in that current."

Ruth Mary, wild with the delay, every second of which might be the price of precious lives, seized Tommy in her arms, hugged him close and kissed him, and by main strength rolled him out into the water. He grasped the gunwale with both hands. "You're going to be drowned," he shrieked, as if she were already far away. She pushed off his hands and shot out into the current.

"Don't cry, Tommy, I'll get there somehow," she called back to him. She could not see anything for the first few minutes of her journey but his little wet, dismal figure toiling, sobbing, up the hill. It hurt her to have had to be rough with him. But all the while she sat upright, with her eyes on the current, plying her paddle right and left as rocks and driftwood and eddies were passed. She heard it coming, that distant roar from the hills, and prayed with beating heart that the wild current might carry her faster—faster—past the draggled willow copses—past the beds of black lava rock, and the bluffs with their patches of green moss livid in the sunshine—hurling along, past glimpses of the well-known trail she had followed dreamily on those peaceful rides she might never take again. The thought did not trouble her, only the fear that she might be overtaken before she reached the camp. For the waters were coming—or was it the wind that brought that dread sound so near! She dared not look round lest she should see through the gates of the cañon the black lifted head of the great wave, devouring the river behind her. How it would come swooping down between those high narrow walls of rock her heart stood still to think of! If the hills would but open and let it loose over the empty pastures—if the river would but hurry, hurry, hurry! She whispered the word to herself with frantic repetition, and the oncoming roar behind her echoed her whisper of fear with its awful response.

She trembled with joy as the canon walls lowered and fell apart, and she saw the blessed plains, the low green flats and the willows, and the white tents of the camp safe in the sunshine. Now if she be given but one moment's grace to swing into the bank! The roar behind her made her faint as she listened. For the first time she turned and looked back, and the cry of her despair went up and was lost, as boat and message and messenger were lost,—gone utterly, gorged, at one leap by the senseless flood.

At half past five o'clock that afternoon the men of the camp filed out of the tunnel along the new roadbed, with the low sunlight in their faces. It was "Saturday night," and the whole force was in good humor. As they tramped gayly along, tools and instruments glinting in the sun, word went down the line that something unusual had been going on by the river. There seemed to have been a wild uprising of its waters since they saw it last. Then a shout from those ahead proclaimed the disaster at the bridge. The Chinese cook, crouched among the rocks high up under the bluff, where he had fled for safety when he heard the waters coming, rushed down to them, with wild wavings and gabblings, to tell them of a catastrophe that was best described by its results. A few provisions were left them stored in a magazine under a rock on the hillside. They cooked their supper with the splinters of the ruined blacksmith's hut. After supper, in the clear, pink evening light they wandered about on the slippery rocks, seeking whatever fragments of their camp equipage the flood might have left them. Everything had been swept away, and tons of mud and gravel covered the little green meadow where their tents had stood. Kirkwood, straying on ahead of his comrades, came to the rocks below the bridge timbers, from which the awning had been torn away. The wet rocks glistened in the light, but there was a whiter gleam which caught his eye. He stooped and crawled under the timbers anchored in the bank, until he came to the spot of whiteness. Was this that fair young girl from the hills, dragged here by the waters in their cruel orgy, and then hidden by them as if in shame of their work? Kirkwood recognized the simple features, the meek eyes, wide open in the searching light. The mud that filled her garments had spared the pure young face. Kirkwood gazed into it reverently, but the passionate sacrifice, the useless warning, were sealed from him. She could not tell him why she was there.

The three young men watched in turn that night by the little motionless heap, covered by Kirkwood's coat. Kirkwood was very sad about Ruth Mary, yet he slept when his turn came.

In the morning they nailed together some boards into a long box. There was not a boat left on the river; fording was impossible. They could only take her home by the trail. So once more Ruth Mary traveled that winding path, high in the sunlight, or low in the shade of the shore. A log of driftwood left by the great wave, slung on one side of a mule's pack saddle, balanced the rude coffin on the other. No one meeting the three engineers and their pack-mule filing down the trail would have known they were a funeral procession. But they were heavy-hearted as they rode along, and Kirkwood would fain it had not been his part to ride ahead and prepare the family at the ranch for their child's coming.

The mother, with Tommy and Angy hiding their faces against her, stood on the hill and watched for it, and broke into cries as the mule with its burden came in sight.

Kirkwood walked with them down the hill to meet it. His comrades dismounted, and the three young men, with heads uncovered, carried the coffin over the hill and set it down in the shed room. Then Tommy, in a burst of childish grief, made them know that this piteous sacrifice had been for them.

The tunnel made its way through the hill; the sinuous road-bed wound up the valley; new camps were built along its course. But when the young men sat together of an evening, and looked at the hills in the strange pink light, a spell of quietness rested upon them which no one tried to explain.

The railroad has been built these two years. Every summer brings tourists up into the Bear River valley. They look with delight upon the mountain stream bounding down between the hills with the brightness of the morning on its breast.

"There should be an idyl or a legend to celebrate it," a pretty, dark-eyed girl, with a Boston accent, said to Kirkwood, one moonlight evening late in summer, when the river was low, as they drifted softly down between its dim shores. "Poor little Bear River, did nothing human ever happen near you to give you a place in poetry?"

The river did not answer as it rippled over the bar. Nor did Kirkwood speak for it; but the wood-dove's melancholy tremolo came from the misty willows by the shore; and in some suddenly illumined place in his memory he saw Ruth Mary sitting on the high bank in the peaceful afternoon, the sunshine resting on her smooth fair hair, the shadow lending its softness to her shy, down-bent face.

The pity of it, when he thinks of it sometimes, seems to him more than he can bear. Yet if Ruth Mary had still been there, at the ranch on the hills, she would have been to him only "that nice little girl of Tully's who married the one-eyed packer."

The Fate of A Voice

There are many loose pages of the earth's history scattered through the unpeopled regions of the Far West, known but to few persons, and these unskilled in the reading of Nature's dumb records. One of these unread pages, written over with prehistoric inscriptions, is the cañon of the Wallula River.

An ancient lava stream once submerged the valley. Its hardening crust, bursting asunder in places, left great crooked rents, through which the subsequent drainage from the mountain slopes found a way down to the desert plains. In one of these furrows, left by the fiery plowshare, a river, now called the Wallula, made its bed. Hurling itself from side to side, scouring out its straitened boundaries with tons of sand torn from the mountains, it slowly widened and deepened, and wore its ancient channel into the cañon as it may now be seen.

No one knows how long the river has been making the bed in which it lies so restlessly. Riding towards it across the sunburnt mountain pastures, its course may be traced by the black crests of the lava bluffs which line its channel, showing in the partings of the hills. From a distance the bluffs do not look formidable; they seem but a step down from the high sunlit slopes, an insignificant break in the skyward sweep of their long, buoyant lines. But ride on to the brink and look down. The bunch-grass grows to the very edge, its slight spears quivering in light against the cañon's depths of shadow. The roar of the river comes up to your ears in a continuous volume of sound, loud and low, as the wind changes. Here and there, where the speed of the river has been checked, it has left a bit of white sand beach, the only positive white in the landscape. The faded grasses of the hills look pale against the sky; it is a country of cloudless skies and long rainless summers—only the dark cañon walls dominate the intensity of its deep, unchanging blue. The broad light rests, still as in a picture, on the fixed black lines of the bluffs, on the slopes of wild pasture whose curves flatten and crowd together as they meet the horizon. A few black dots of cattle, grazing in the distance, may appear and then stray out of sight over a ridge, or a broad-winged bird may slowly mount and wheel and sink between the cañon walls. Meanwhile, your horse is picking his way, step by step, along the bluffs, cropping the tufts of dry bunch-grass, his hoofs clinking now and then on a bit of sunken rock, which, from the sound, might go down to the foundations of the hills; there are cracks, too, which look as if they went as deep. The basalt walls are reared in tiers of columns with hexagonal cleavage. A column or a group of columns becomes dislocated from the mass, rests so, slightly apart; a girl's weight might throw it over. At length the accumulation of slight, incessant propelling causes overcomes its delicate poise; it topples down; the jointed columns fall apart, and their fragments go to increase the heap of débris which has found its angle of repose at the foot of the cliff. A raw spot of color shows on the weather-worn face of the cliff, and beneath a shelf is left, or a niche, which the tough sage and the scented wild syringa creep down to and fearlessly occupy in company with straggling tufts of bunch-grass.

One summer a party of railroad engineers made their camp in the river canon, along the side of a gulch lined with willows and wild roses, up the first hill above it, and down on the white sand beach below. There were the quarters of the division engineer, who had ladies with him in camp that summer; the tents of the younger members of the corps, the cook-tent, and the dining-shed were on the hill, and the camp of the "force" was lower down the gulch. Work on that division of the new railroad was temporarily suspended; the engineer in charge, having finished his part of the line to its junction with the valley division, was awaiting orders from his chief.

It was September, and the last week of the ladies' sojourn in camp. They were but two, the division engineer's wife and the wife's younger sister, a girl with a voice. No one who knew her ever thought of Madeline Hendric without thinking of her voice, a fact she herself would have been the last to resent. At that time she was ordering her life solely with reference to the demands of that imperious organ. An obstinate huskiness that had changed it since the damp, late Eastern spring, and veiled its brilliancy, was the motive which had sent her, with her sister, to the dry, pure air of the foot-hills. In the autumn she would go abroad for two or three years' final study.

It was Sunday afternoon in camp. Since work on the line had ceased there was little to distinguish it from any other afternoon, except that the little Duncan girls wore white dresses and broad ribbons at lunch instead of their play frocks, and were allowed to come to the six o'clock dinner in the cook-tent. Mrs. Duncan had remarked to her husband that Madeline and young Aldis seemed to be making the most of their farewells. They had spent the entire afternoon together on the river beach, not in sight of the camp, but in a little cove secluded by willows, where the brook came down. Mrs. Duncan could see them now returning with lagging steps along the shore, not looking at each other and not speaking, apparently. The rest of the camp was on its way to dinner.

"I told you how it would be, if you brought her out here, you know," Mr. Duncan said, waiting for his wife to pass him, with her skirts gathered in one hand, along the foot-bridge that crossed the brook to the cook-tent.

"Oh, Madeline is all right," she replied.

But Aldis was missing at table, and Madeline came down late, though without having changed her dress, and during dinner avoided her sister's eye.

"You're not going out with him again, Madeline!" Mrs. Duncan found a chance to say to the girl after dinner, as she was hurrying up the trail with a light shawl on her arm. "*All* the afternoon, and now again! What can you be thinking of?"

Mrs. Duncan could see Aldis walking about in front of the tents on the hill, evidently on the watch for Madeline.

"I must," she said hurriedly. "It is a promise."

"Oh, if it has come to *that*—"

"It hasn't come to anything. You need not be troubled. To-night will be the last of it."

"Madeline, you must not go. Let me excuse you to Aldis. I can't let you go till I've had a chance to talk with you."

"That is what I have promised *him*—one more chance. You cannot help us, Sallie. Go back, dear, and don't worry about me."

These words were hastily whispered on the trail, Aldis walking about and gloomily awaiting the result of this flying conference between the sisters. Mrs. Duncan went back to the house only half-satisfied that she had done her duty. It was not the first time she had found it difficult to do her duty by Madeline, when it happened to conflict with the inclinations of that imperative youngest daughter of the house of Hendric. Besides, it was not for Madeline she was troubled.

The path leading to the bluffs was one of the many cattle-trails that wind upward with an even grade from base to summit of every grass-covered hill on the mountain ranges. Madeline and Aldis shortened the way by leaving the trail and climbing the side of the bluff where it jutted out above the river. It was a steep and breathless struggle upward, and Madeline did not refuse the accustomed help of her companion's hand, offered in silence with a look which she ignored. Mechanically they sought the place where it had been their custom to sit on other evenings of the summer they had spent together,—one of those ledges a few feet from the summit of the bluff where part of a row of columns had fallen. Cautiously they stepped down to it along a crevice slippery with dried grasses, he keeping always between her and the brink.

The sun had already set to the camp, but from their present height they could see it once more, drifting down the flaming west. Suddenly, as a fire ship burns to the water's edge and sinks, the darkening line of the distant plains closed above that intolerable splendor. All the cool subdued tones of the cañon sprang into life; the river took a steely gleam. Up through the gate of the cañon rolled the tide of hazy glory from the valley, touched the topmost crags, and mounted thence to fade in the evening sky. The two on the bluffs still sat in silence, their faces pale in the deepening glow, but Madeline had crept forward on the ledge, nearer to Aldis, to look down. It was the first confiding natural movement she had made towards him since the shock of this new phase of their friendship had startled her. Aldis was grateful for it, while resolved to take all possible advantage of it. At his first words she drew back, and he knew, before her answer came, that she had instantly resumed the defensive.

"Everything has been said, except things it would be unkind to say. Why need we go over it all again?"

"That is what we came up here for, isn't it? To go over it all once more, and get down to the very dregs of your argument."

"It isn't an argument. It's a decision, and it is made. There is nothing more I can say, except to indulge in the meanness of recrimination."

"Go on and recriminate, by all means! That is what I want,—to make you say everything you have on your mind. Then I want you to listen to me. What is it you are keeping back?"

"Well, then, was it quite honest of you to seem to accept the

27

conditions of our—being together this summer, as we have been, and all the while to be nursing this—hope,—for me to have to kill? Do you think I like to?"

"The conditions?" he repeated. "What conditions do you mean? I knew you intended yourself for a public singer."

The girl blushed hotly. "Why do you say 'intended myself'? I did not choose my fate. It has chosen me. You must have known that marrying"—the word came with a kind of awkward violence from her lips—"anybody was the last thing I should be likely to think of. A voice is a vocation in itself."

"I did not propose marriage to you as a vocation. As for that hope you accuse me of secretly harboring, I have never held you responsible for it. I took all the risks deliberately when I gave myself up to being happy with you and trying to make you happy with me. You have been happy sometimes, haven't you?"

"Yes," she confessed; "too happy, if this is the way it is to end."

"But it isn't? Perhaps I ought to thank you for being sorry for me, but that isn't what I want. I want to make you sorry for yourself and for the awful mistake you are making."

"Oh, the whole summer has been a mistake! And this place and everything have been fatal! But if you had only been honest with me, it would all have been different. I should have been on my guard."

"Thank Heaven you were not! Do you suppose the man lives who would put a girl on her guard, as you say, and endure her company on such terms?"

"You know what I mean. I am not free; I am not—eligible. I thought you understood that and admitted it. We were friends on that basis."

"I never admitted anything of the kind, or accepted any basis but the natural one. When you make your own conditions for a man and assume that he accepts them, you should ask yourself what sort of an animal he is. Most of us believe we have an inalienable right to try to win the woman we have chosen, if she is not bespoken or married to another man."

"I am bespoken then. Thank you for the word. My life is pledged to a purpose as serious as marriage itself. You need not smile. Love is not the only inspiration a woman's life can know. I shall reach far more people through my art than I could by just living for my own preferences."

"You still have preferences, then?"

"Why should I deny it? I don't call it being strong to be merely

28

indifferent. I can care for things and yet give them up. I don't expect to have a very good time these next three years. I dare say I shall have foolish dreams like other girls, and look back and count the time spent. But what I truly believe I was meant to do, that I will do, no matter what it costs. There is no other way to live. Listen!"—she stopped him with a gesture as he was about to speak. She raised her head. Her gray eyes, which had more light than color in them, were shining with something that looked like tears, as she gave voice to one long, heart-satisfying peal of harmony, prolonging it, filling the silence with its rich cadences, and waking from the rocks across the cañon a faint eerie repetition, an echo like the utterance of a voice imprisoned in the cliff. "There," she said, "are the two me's, the real me and what you would make of me—the ghost of a voice—an echo of other voices from the world I belonged to once, calling in the wild places where you would have me buried alive."

He smiled drearily at this girlish hyperbole. "I think there is room here even for a voice like yours. It need not perish for want of breath."

"No, but for want of listeners. I could not sing in an empty world."

"You would have one listener. I could listen for ten thousand."

"Oh, but I don't want you. I want the ten thousand. There are plenty of women with sweet voices meant for only one listener. You ought to find one of those voices and listen to it the rest of your life." There was a tremulous, insistent gayety in her manner which met with no response. "As for me," she continued, "I want to sing to multitudes. I want to lean my voice on the waves of great orchestra. I want to feel myself going crazy in the choruses, and then sing all alone in a hush. Oh, don't you know that intoxicating silence? It takes hundreds to make it. And can't you hear the first low notes, and feel the shudder of joy? I can. I can hear my own voice like a separate living thing. I love it better than I love myself! It isn't myself. I feel sometimes that it is a spirit that has trusted itself to my keeping. I will not betray it, even for you."

This little concession to the weakness of human preference escaped her in the ardor of her resolve. It was not lost upon Aldis.

"Do you think I wish to silence you?" he protested. "I love your voice, but not as a separate thing. If it is a spirit, it is your spirit. But I could dispense with it easily!"

"Of course you could. You don't care for me as I am. You have never admitted that I have a gift which is a destiny in itself. If you did, you would respect it; you could not think of me, mutilated, as I should be, if you took away my one means of expression."

"Oh, nobody who has anything to express is so limited as that. Besides, I wouldn't take it away. I would enlarge it, not force it into one channel. I would have the woman possess the voice, not the voice possess the woman. I should be the last to deny that you have a destiny; but I have one too. My destiny is to love you and to make you my wife. There is nothing in that that need conflict with yours."

"I should think there was everything!"

"You have never let me get so far as a single detail, but if you will listen."

"I thought I had listened pretty well for one who assumes it is her mission to be heard," Madeline said again, with a piteous attempt at lightness, which her hot cheeks and anxious eyes belied.

"Granting that it is your mission, this part of the world is not so empty as it looks. The people who would make your audiences here are farther apart than in the cities, but they have the enthusiasm that makes nothing of distance. They would make pilgrimages to hear you—whole families in plains-wagons with the children packed in bed-quilts. And the cowboys! They would gather as they do to a grand round-up. It would be a unique career for a singer," he continued, ignoring an interruption from Madeline, asking who would involve this widespread enthusiasm, and would he have her advertised in the "Wallula News Miner."

"There would be no money in it for us" (Madeline winced at the pronoun); "I would not have your lovely gift peddled about the country. There would be no floral tributes or press notices you would care for, or interviews with reporters or descriptions of your dresses in the papers. You might never have the pleasure of seeing your picture in the back of the monthlies, advertising superior toilet articles; but to a generous woman who believes in the regenerating influence of her art, I should think there would be a singular pleasure in giving it away to those who are cut off from all such joys. I know there are singers who boast of their five-thousand-dollar-a-night voices; I would rather boast that mine was the one free voice that could not be bought."

"There are no such vagrant, prodigal voices. A beautiful, trained voice is one of the highest products of civilization; it takes the most civilized listeners to appreciate it. It needs the stimulus of refined appreciation. It needs the inspiration of other voices and the spur of intelligent criticism. I know you have been making fun of my ambitions, but I choose to take you seriously. My standard would come down to the level of my audiences—the cowboys and the children in bed-quilts."

"Oh, no, it wouldn't. Your genius is its own standard, is it not? You would be like the early poets and the troubadours. They sang in rather an empty world, did they not, and not always to critical audiences? The knights and barons couldn't have been much above our cowboys."

"Oh, how absurd you are! No, not absurd, but unkind; you are making desperate fun of me and of my voice too, because I make so much of it—but you force me to. It is my whole argument."

"I'm desperate enough for anything, but I'm hardly in a position to make fun of any rival. Madeline, sometimes I hate your voice, and yet I love it too. I understand its power better than you think. It has just the dramatic quality which should make you the singer of a new people. Oh, how blind you are to a career so much finer, so much broader, so much sweeter, and more womanly! Your mission is here, in the camps of the Philistines. You are to bring a message to the heathen; to sing to the wandering, godless peoples,—to the Esaus and the Ishmaels of the Far West."

"That is all very fine, but you know perfectly well that your Esaus and your Ishmaels would prefer a good clog-dancer to all the 'messages' in the world."

"Oh, you don't know them,—and if they did, it would be the first part of your mission to teach them a higher sort of pleasure."

"And I am to go to Munich and study for the sake of coming out here to regenerate the cowboys?"

"That isn't the part of your destiny *I* insist upon," Aldis said, letting the weariness of discouragement show in his tones. "But you say you must have an audience. And I must have you—"

"But does it occur to you," Madeline interrupted quickly, "what a tremendous waste of effort and elaboration there would be between the means and the effect?"

"*I* don't ask for the effort and the elaboration. That is the part *you* insist upon. All I want is you, just as you are, voice or no voice. You need not go to Munich on my account."

"You expect me to give up everything."

"You would have to give up a good deal; I don't deny it. But is there any virtue in woman that becomes her better?"

"Perhaps not, from a man's point of view. But it is no use listening to you. You haven't the faintest conception of what my future is to me, as I see it, and all this you have been talking is either a burlesque on my ambition, or else it is the insanity of selfishness—masculine selfishness. I don't mean anything personal. You want to absorb into your own life a thing that was meant to have a life of its own, for all the world to share and enjoy. Yes, why not? I won't pretend to depreciate my gift! I am only the tenement in which a precious thing is lodged. You would drive out the divine tenant, or imprison it, for the sake of possessing the poor house it lives in."

"Good Heavens!" Aldis exclaimed, with a sort of awe of what seemed to him an almost blasphemous absurdity. "What nonsense you young geniuses can talk! I wish the precious tenant would evacuate and leave you to your sober senses, and to me."

"And this is what a man calls love!"

Aldis laughed fiercely. "Has there been any new kind of love invented lately? This is the kind that came into the world before art did."

"Art is love, without its selfishness," said Madeline, with innocent conclusiveness.

"Where the deuce do you girls learn this sort of talk?" Aldis demanded of the girl beside him.

She answered him with unexpected gentleness. She leaned towards him, and looked entreatingly in his face. "This is our last evening together. Don't let us spoil it with this wretched squabbling."

"She calls it squabbling—a man's fight for his life!" He turned and gave her back her look, with more fire than entreaty in his eyes.

"There is the moon," she said hurriedly. "It is time to go home."

The fringe of grasses above their heads was touched with silver light, and the shadow of the bluff lay broad and distinct across the valley.

"We must go home," Madeline urged. Aldis did not move.

"Madeline, would you marry me if I had a lot of money?"

"Oh, hush!"

"No, but would you? Answer me."

"Yes, I would." She was tired of choosing her words. "For then you would not have to earn a living in these wild places."

"You would take me then as a sort of appendage? You don't want a man with work of his own to do?"

"Not if it interferes with mine."

"That is your answer?"

"Can I make it any plainer?"

"You have not said you do not love me."

"I don't need to say it. It is proved by what I do—I might have been nicer to you, perhaps, but you are so unreasonable."

"Never mind if I am. Be nice to me now!"

"I meant to be. But it is too late. We must go home." She felt that she was losing command of herself through sheer exhaustion; it could only mislead him and prolong the struggle if she should now betray any signs of weakness. "Come," she said, "you will have to get up first."

He did not move.

"Oh, sit still a little longer," he pleaded. "I will not bother you any more. Let us have one half hour of our old times together—only a little better, because it is the last."

"No, not another minute." She rose quickly to her feet, tripped in her skirt, and tottered forward. Aldis had risen too. As she reeled and threw out her hands, he sprang between her and the brink, thrusting her back with the whole force of his sudden spring. The rock upon which he had leaped, regardless of his footing, gave its final quake and dropped into the abyss. It was the uppermost segment of a loosened column. The whole mass went down, narrowing the ledge so that Madeline, by turning her head, could look into the depths below. She did not move or cry; she lay still, but for the deep gasping breaths that would not cease, though all the life had seemed to go out from her when he went down. The relief of unconsciousness did not come to her. She was aware of the soft, dry night wind growing cool, of the river's soughing, of the long grasses fluttering wildly against the moon above her head. The perfume of wild syringa blossoms, hidden in some crevice of the rock, came to her with the breeze. There were crackling, rustling noises from the depth of shadow into which she dared not look; then silence, except the wind and the river's roar, borne strongly upwards, as it freshened—And all the words they had said to each other in their long, passionate argument kept repeating themselves, forcing themselves upon her stunned, passive consciousness, she lying there, not caring if she never stirred again, and he on the rocks below—and between them the sudden, awful silence. She might have crept to the brink and called, but she could not call to the dead.

Gradually it came to her that she must get herself back somehow to the camp with her miserable story. It would be easier, it seemed, to turn once over and drop off the cliff, and let someone else tell the story for them both. But the fascination of this impulse could not prevail over the awakening shuddering fact of her physical being. She despised herself for the caution with which she crept along the ledge and up the grass-grown crevice. If he had been cautious she would be where he was lying now. It was her own rash girl's fancy for getting on the brink of things and looking over that had brought them first to that fatal place. But these thoughts were but pin-pricks following the shock of that benumbing horror she was carrying with her back to the camp.

As she looked down upon its lights she felt like one already long estranged from the life she had been the gay center of but two hours before. She knew how her sister's little girls were asleep, the night wind softly stirring the leaves outside their bedroom window; how still the house was; how empty and white in the moonlight the tents on the hill; how the camp was assembled on the beach, waiting for her return with Aldis and for the evening singing. Sing! She could have shrieked, sobbed, and cried aloud at the thought of this homecoming—she alone with the burden of her sorrow, and by and by Aldis, borne in his comrades' arms and laid on his bed in that empty tent on the hill.

But there was a hard constriction, a dumb, convulsive ache in her throat. She felt as if no sound could ever be uttered by her again.

If Aldis had been lying dead at the foot of the bluffs, as Madeline believed, this story would never have been told in print, except in a cold-blooded newspaper paragraph which would have omitted to mention one curious fact connected with the accident, that a young girl who was the companion of the unfortunate young man, when it occurred, suffered a shock of the nerves from the sight of his fall that deprived her entirely of her voice, so that she could not speak except in whispers.

It was not Aldis who was the victim of this tragedy of the bluffs, but Aldis's successful rival, the voice. It was hushed at the very moment of its triumph. A blow from the brain upon those nerve-chords which were its life! Love shook the house in which music dwelt, jarred it to its center, and the imperious but frail tenant had fled.

At the moment when Madeline's tortured fancy was bringing home a mangled heap and laying him in the last of that row of tents on the hill, Aldis was getting himself home, by the lower trail, as fast as his bruises would let him.

He had fallen into a scrubby growth of wild syringa that flung its wax-white blossoms out from a cranny in the cliff less than half-way down. As he crashed into it, its tough and springy mass checked his fall enough to enable him to get a firm grasp with his hands. He hung dangling at arm's length against the cliff, groping for a temporary lodgment for his feet. In the darkness he dimly perceived something like a ledge, not too far below him, towards which the face of the bluff sloped slightly outwards.

Flattening himself against the rock he let go his hold and slid, clutching and grinding downward till his feet struck the ledge. From this vantage, after getting his breath and taking a deliberate view of his situation, it was not a difficult feat to reach the slope of broken rock below. He sat there while the trembling in his strained muscles subsided, scarcely conscious as yet of his torn and scratched and bruised condition. He was about to raise his voice in a shout to assure Madeline of his safety when the thought turned him sick, that, unnerved as she must be with the sight of his fall, she might mistake the call for a cry for help, and venture too near that treacherous edge to look down. He kept still, while the horror grew upon him of what might happen to Madeline alone on the ledge or trying to climb the slippery crevice in the shadow of the bluff. He knew that a mass of rock had fallen when he fell; was there space enough left on the ledge by which she could safely reach the crevice? He could not resist giving one low call, speaking her name as distinctly and quietly as he could, and bidding her not move but listen. There was no answer; the roar of the rapids, borne on the wind that nightly drew down the canyon, drowned his voice. Madeline did not hear him. He waited until the silence convinced him that she was no longer there; then he took his way toilsomely back to the camp.

A light showed in the window of the office, which in the evening was usually dark. He found the family assembled there in the light of a single kerosene lamp, the flame of which was streaming up the chimney unobserved, while all eyes were bent upon Madeline, seated in one of the revolving office chairs, with her back to the desk. She leaned shivering and whispering towards her sister, who knelt on the floor before her, holding her hands and staring, with a fearful interest, into the girl's colorless face.

The men who stood nearest the door turned and started as Aldis entered.

"Why, good God, Aldis!" Mr. Duncan exclaimed. "Why, man, we thought you were dead—you don't mean to say it's you—all of you?"

"I'm all here," said Aldis.

"He's all here, Madeline," Mrs. Duncan shouted hysterically to the girl, as if she were deaf as well as dumb.

The fateful voice was undoubtedly gone. Madeline could no longer plead ineligibility when the common destiny of woman was offered her. But if Aldis had thought to profit immediately by her release from the claims of art he was disappointed.

What was the new obstacle? Only some more of Madeline's high-flown nonsense, as her sister called it. She was always making a heroic situation out of everything that happened to her, and expecting her friends to bear her out in it.

She had been put to bed the night of the adventure on the cliff shaking with a nervous chill. Next day's packing had been suspended, and the eastward journey postponed. But in a day or two she was sufficiently recovered to be walking again with Aldis on the shore, and the old argument was resumed on a new basis. Madeline, pale and wistful, with Aldis's head very close to her's, that the river's intruding roar might not drown her whispers, protesting—sometimes with sobs, sometimes with sudden, tremulous laughter that shook her with dumb convulsions hardly more mirthful than the sobs—that she could not and she would not burden his life with the wreck she now passionately proclaimed herself to be.

But would she not give him what he wanted, had wanted, should continue to want and to try for so long as they both should live?

No, he didn't—he couldn't possibly want a ridiculous muttering shadow of a woman beside him all the days of his life. It was only his magnanimity. She wondered he could believe her capable of the meanness of taking advantage of it.

Aldis did not despair, but it was certainly difficult, with happiness almost within his reach, with the girl herself sometimes sobbing in his arms, to be obliged to treat this obstacle as seriously as Madeline insisted it should be treated. He appealed to Mrs. Duncan, who scolded and laughed at her sister alternately, and quoted with elaborate particulars a surprising number of similar cases of voices lost and found again by means of care and skillful treatment. But hers was *not* a similar case, Madeline vehemently declared. It was *not* from a cold, like Mrs. So and So's; it had not come on gradually, beginning with a hoarseness, like someone's else. It was; the girl believed in her heart that she had been made a singular and impressive example of the folly and wickedness of pride in an exceptional gift, and triumph in its corresponding destiny. The spirit she had boasted of harboring had deserted her. She deserved her punishment, but she would not permit another's life to be shadowed by it, especially one so generous—who, so far from resenting her refusal of the whole loaf, was content, or pretended to be, with the broken and rejected fragments. But all this Madeline was careful to keep from the cheerful irreverence of her sister's comments. She faltered something like it to Aldis in one of their long talks by the river; his low tones answering briefly, and at long intervals, her piercing whispers that sometimes almost shrieked her trouble in his ear. He could feel that she was still thrilling with the double shock she had suffered; he was infinitely tender with her, and patient with her extravagant expositions of the situation between them. He longed to heap savage ridicule upon them, but he forbore. He listened and waited and let her talk until she was worn out, and then they were happiest together. For a few moments each day it seemed that she might drift back to him on the ebb of that overstrained tide of resistance and be at rest.

Madeline was always impatient of any discussion of the chances of her recovery, but one day, just before the time of their parting, Aldis surprised and captured an admission from her that there might be such a chance. Would she, then, on the strength of that possibility, consent to be engaged to him and treat him as her accepted lover, since nothing but her pride now kept them apart?

"Pride," Madeline repeated; "I don't know what I have left to be proud of."

"There is a kind of stiff-necked humility that is worse than pride," said Aldis, smiling at the easy way in which she shirked the logic of the conclusion he was forcing upon her. "You won't consent to the meanness, as you call it, of giving me what you are pleased to consider a damaged article, a thing with a flaw in it; as if a woman would be more lovable if she could be warranted proof against all wear and tear. But if the flaw can be healed, if there is a possibility that the voice may come back, why should we not be engaged on that hope?"

"And if it never does, will you promise to let me release you?"

"You can release me anytime—now, if you like."

"But will you promise to take your release when I give it to you?"

"We will see about that. Perhaps by the time your voice doesn't come back I shall have been able to make you believe that it isn't the voice I care for."

"And if it should come back," cried Madeline with sudden enthusiasm, "I shall have my triumph! I am done forever with all that nonsense about Art and Destiny. If my voice ever should come back, I shall not let it bully me. It shall not decide my fate. You will see. Oh, how I wish you *might* see! I have learned my lesson in the true, awful values of things. Thank Heaven it has cost no more! There is one less singer in the world, perhaps, but there is not one less life. Your life. If you had lost it that night, and I had kept my voice, do you think I should ever have had any joy in it again—even lifted it up, as I boasted to you I would some day, before crowds of listeners? Could I have gone before the footlights, bowing and smiling, with my arms full of flowers, and remembered your face and your last look as you went down?

"Then it is settled at last, voice or no voice?"

"Yes,—but I am so sorry for you! It will not come back; I know it never will, and I shall go on whispering and gibbering to the end of my days, and all your friends will pity you; it is such a painfully conspicuous thing!"

"I want to be pitied. I am just pining to be an object of general compassion. Only I want to choose what I shall be pitied for."

"Choose?" said Madeline stupidly. "What *do* you mean?"

"I *have* chosen. Now be as sorry for me as you like. And we'll ask for the sympathy of the camp to-night. It will be a blow to the boys—my throwing myself away like this!"

"How ridiculous you are!" sighed Madeline. It was a luxury, after all, to yield. And perhaps in the depths of her consciousness, bruised and quivering as it was, there lingered a faint image of herself, as a charming girl sees herself reflected in those flattering mirrors, the eyes of friends, kindred, and adorers. Voiceless, futureless, spoiled as was the budding prima donna, the girl remained: eighteen years old and fair to look upon, with perfect health, and all the mysterious, fitful but unquenchable joy of youth thrilling through her pulses. Perhaps she was not so sorry for Aldis after all, in the innocent joy of her own intentions towards him. The sobs, the frantic whispers died away, and were hushed in a blissful acquiescence. She was not less fascinating to her lover—half amazed at his own sudden triumph—in her blushing, starry-eyed silences, than she had been in all the eager redundance of her lost utterance. That was a wonderful last day for the young man to dream over in the long months before they should meet again!

The camp had moved out of the cañon and down upon the desert plains. It was an open winter; up to the first of January the contractors had been able to keep their men at work, following closely the locating party.

Aldis rode up and down the line, putting in fresh stakes for the contractors, keeping them true to the line, and watching incidentally that they did not pod their embankments with sage-brush. His summer camp-dress of broad-shouldered, breezy, flannel shirt, and slender-waisted trousers, was changed to a reefing-jacket, double-buttoned to the chin, long boots, and helmet-shaped cap, pulled low down to keep the wind out of his eyes. Strong wintry reds and brown replaced, on his thin cheek, the summer's pallor.

Madeline Hendric, dressing for dinner at the Sutherland in New York, where she and her sister were spending the winter, would stand before her toilet-glass fastening her laces, her eyes fixed alternately on her own reflection in the mirror and on a dim photograph that leaned against the frame. It was not a bad specimen of amateur photography; it represented a young man on horseback in a wide and windy country, with an expression of sadness and determination in the dark eyes that looked steadfastly out of the gray, toneless picture.

They were the most beautiful eyes in the world, Madeline thought to herself, and sinking on her knees before the low table, with her arms crossed on the lace, rose-lined cover, she would brood in a fond, luxurious melancholy over the picture—over the somber line of plain and distant mountain, and the chilly little cluster of tents huddled close together by the river's dark, swift flood, flowing between icy beaches, below barren shores where a few leafless willows shivered, and the wild-twisted clumps of sage defied the cold.

A moment later she would be rustling softly down the corridor at her sister's side, passing groups of ladies who looked after them with that comprehensive but impersonal scrutiny which is a woman's recognition of anything unusual in another's dress or appearance. Mrs. Duncan looked her sister over with a quick, intelligent side glance, for those silent eye comments were all turned upon Madeline. She could see nothing amiss with the girl; she was looking very lovely, a trifle absent; Madeline had a way lately of looking as if she were alone with her own thoughts, on occasions when other women's faces took on habitually a neutral and impassive expression. It made her conspicuous, as if hers were the only sensitive human countenance exposed in a roomful of masks.

"Why do you never wear your light dresses, Madeline?" said Mrs. Duncan, with the intention of rousing the girl from her untimely dream. "You are very effective in black, with your hair, but I should think you would like once in a while to vary the effect."

"Do you suppose I am studying effects for the benefit of these people? I am *saving* my light dresses."

"Saving them! What for?"

"Do you never save up a pretty dress that Will likes, when you are away from him?"

"No, indeed I don't. It would get out of style, and he would see there was something wrong with it, though he might not know what it was. Dresses *won't* keep! Besides—do you think you are never to have any new ones, now you are engaged to an engineer?"

"I shall not need many, if I go West, and a year or two behind won't matter to—*my* engineer!"

"Oh, you poor innocent! You don't know your engineer yet—and you don't know your West, either. And one is always having to pack up and come East at short notice, and I know of nothing more insupportable than finding one's self dumped off an overland train in New York, in the middle of winter, for instance, with a veteran outfit one hasn't had the strength of mind to 'give to the poor,' as Will says. You never know how your clothes look till you have packed them up on one side of the continent and unpacked them on the other. And let me tell you it pays to dress well in camp. Nothing is too good for them, poor things, so long as it's not inappropriate. Do you suppose a man ever forgets how a woman *ought* to look? Wear out your things, my dear, and take the good of them before they get *passé*, and let the future take care of itself."

Madeline was laughing, and the dreamy, soft abstraction had vanished. A stranger might look into her liquid, half-averted eyes, and see no more there than was meant for the passing glance.

Aldis had the promise of a month's leave of absence in March, but soon after the 1st of January the weather turned suddenly cold. The contractors took their men off the work, and the time of Aldis's leave was thus anticipated by two months.

He telegraphed to Mrs. Duncan that he would be in New York by the 15th, allowing for all contingencies.

Madeline's joy over the telegram was increased by one small item of relief, from the necessity of delaying a communication which she dreaded making by letter.

With rest and skillful treatment her voice had come back, as her sister had prophesied, in its full compass and purity. Her musical instructor had urged her to try it once upon an audience, in a not too conspicuous role, before she went abroad to study; for Madeline had not yet found courage to confess her apostasy.

The temptation to sing once as she had so often dreamed of singing, with the support of a magnificent orchestra, the longing to know just how much she was resigning in turning her back upon a musical career, were overmastering.

Moreover, her music was the sole dowry with which she could enrich her husband's life. She had a curious, persistent humility about herself, apart from the gift, which she had grown to consider the essential quality of her being. She desired intensely to know just how much it was in her power to endow her lover with over and above what his generosity, as she insisted upon calling it, demanded. For Madeline did nothing by halves; she could abandon herself to a passion of surrender as completely as she had done to the fire of resistance; and while she was about it, she wished to feel that it was no paltry thing she was giving up. But she was wise enough in her love to feel that possibly Aldis might not be able fully to enter into the joy of her magnificent renunciation. There might be a pang, an uneasiness to him, so far away from her, in the thought that his old enemy was again in the field. So Aldis only knew this much of her recovery, that she could speak once more in her natural voice. She would reserve her triumph, if so it should prove, until his homecoming, when she could lay it at his feet with a joyous humility and such assurances of her love as no letter could convey.

On the 13th of January she was to be the soloist at one of a series of popular concerts to be given that evening, where the character of the music and of the audience was exceedingly good, and the orchestral support all that a singer's heart could desire. On the 15th Aldis would come home.

It was all delightfully dramatic; and Madeline was not yet so in love with obscurity as to be quite indifferent to the scenic element in life.

In his telegram Aldis had allowed for a two days' delay on business at Denver. Arriving at that city, however, he found that, in the absence of one of the principal parties concerned, his business would have to be deferred. He was therefore due in New York on the 13th. He had not telegraphed again to his Eastern friends; it had seemed like making too much of a ceremony of his homecoming. He dropped off the train from the North at the Grand Central depot in the white early dusk of a snowy afternoon, when the quiet up-town streets were echoing to the sound of snowshovels, and the muffled tinkle of car-bells came at long intervals from the neighboring avenues. He hurried ahead of the long line of passengers, jumped on the rear platform of a crowded car that was just moving off, and in twenty minutes was at his hotel. He tried to master his great but tremulous joy, to dine deliberately, to do his best for his outer man, before presenting himself to Madeline, but his lonely fancy had dwelt so long and with such intensity on this meeting that now he was almost unnerved by the nearness of the reality.

The reality was after all only a neat maid, who said, as he offered his card at the door of Mrs. Duncan's apartment, that the ladies were both out. It was impossible to accept the statement simply and go away. Were the ladies out for the evening? he asked. Yes they had gone to a concert or the opera, or something at the Academy of Music. Mrs. Duncan always left word where she was going when she and Miss Madeline both went out, on account of the children. The maid looked at him with intelligent friendliness. She was perfectly aware of the significance of the name on the card she held. She waited while Aldis scribbled a few words on another card which she was to give to Mrs. Duncan when the ladies returned, in case he missed them at the concert. In the street he debated briefly whether to endure a few more hours of waiting, or hasten on to the mixed joy of a meeting in a crowd. Yet such meetings were not always infelicitous. Delicious moments of isolation might come to two in a great assembly, hushed, driven together in a storm of music. There seemed a peculiar fascinating fitness in the situation. Music, that had threatened to part them, should celebrate, like a hireling, their reunion. The violins were in full cry, mingled with the clear, terse notes of a piano, behind the green baize doors, as he passed into the lobby of the Academy. While he waited for the concerto to end, his eyes rested mechanically upon the portraits of prima donnas, whose names were new to him, in smiles and low corsages and wonderful coiffures of the latest fashion; and he said to himself that well it was for those fair dames but not for his lady—his little girl, she was safe among the listeners, unknown, unpublished. *For* her, not *of* her, the loud instruments were speaking, in that vast, hushed, resounding temple of music.

He would see her first, with her rapt face turned towards the stage. He would know her by her cheek, her little ear, and the soft light tangle of curls hiding her temples. She would not be exalted above him in the Olympian circle of the boxes; she would be in the balcony, not in full-dress, but with some marvel of a little bonnet framing the color and light and sweetness of her face. Her cloak would have slipped down from her smooth, silken arms and shoulders. In his restless, waiting dream he could see her with distracting vividness, while the music sank and swelled in endless cadences behind the barriers: her listening attitude, her lifted, half-averted face, her slender, passive hands in her lap, her soft, deep, joyous breathing stirring the fall of lace or ribbons at her throat.

He was prepared to find her very dainty and unapproachably elegant; there had been a hint of such formidable but delightful possibilities in the cut of her simple camp dresses and in the very way she wore them. He glanced disconsolately at his own modestly dressed person, with which he was so monotonously familiar, and wondered if Madeline would find him "Western."

The concerto was over at last. He passed down the aisle and along the rear wall of the balcony, keeping under the shadow of the first tier of boxes, while he took a survey of the house. It seemed bewilderingly brilliant to Aldis, seeing it, for the first time in three years, in a setting of frontier life; a much more complex emotion to one born to the life around him, and estranged from it, than to him who sees it for the first time as a spectacle in which he has never had a part. It was with rather a heart-sick gaze he searched the rows and rows of laughing women's faces, banked like flowers against the crimson and white and gold of the partitions.

Suddenly the murmur pervading the house sank into an expectant silence—the musicians' chairs were filling up; but only the gray-headed first violins were leaning to their instruments and fingering their music. The leader's music-stand had been moved to one side to make room for the soloist, a young débutante, so the whispers around him announced, who was now coming forward, winding her silken train past the musicians' stands, her hand in that of the leader. Now she sank before the hushed crowd, dedicating to it, as it were, herself, her beauty, her song, her whole blissful young presence there.

43

Aldis crushed the unfolded programme he held in his hand. He did not need to consult it for the name of the fair young candidate. The blood rushed into his face, and then left it deadly white. His heart was pounding with a raging excitement, but he did not move or take his eyes from Madeline's face. She stood, faintly smiling down upon the crowd, folding and unfolding the music in her hands, while the orchestra played the prelude. Then on the deepening silence came the first notes of her voice. Aldis had never imagined anything like the pang of delicious pain it gave him. Its personality pierced his very soul. Every word of the recitative, in the singer's pure enunciation, could be heard. The song was Heine's "*Lorelei*," with Liszt's music, and the orchestration was worthy of the music.

"I know not what it presages,"—the recitative began,—"This heart with sadness fraught." Aldis took a deep, hard breath. He knew the story that was coming. The rocks, the river, the evening sky, he knew them all. Had she forgotten? Did the great god Music deprive a woman of her memory, her tender womanly compunction, as well as her heart? Was this beautiful creature with eyes alight and soft throat swelling to the notes of her song merely a voice, after all, celebrating its own triumph and another's allurement and despair? Was the heart that beat under the laces that covered that white bosom merely a subtle machine for setting free those wonderful sounds that floated down to him and seemed to bid him farewell?

Now, in a wild crescendo, with a hurry of chords in the accompaniment, the end has come; the boat and man are lost. Then an interlude, and the pure, pitiless voice again lamenting now, not triumphing—"And this, with her magic singing, the Lorelei hath done—the Lorelei hath done." The song died away and ceased in mournful repetitions, and the audience gave itself up to a transport of applause. It had won—a new singer; and he had lost—only his wife. He stood there, unknown and unheeded, a pitiful minority of one, and accepted his defeat.

The frantic clappings continued. They were demanding an encore; the friendly old fellows in the orchestra were looking back across the stage to welcome the singer's return. They had assisted at the triumph of so many young aspirants and queens of the hour. This one was coming back, flushed and smiling, her face beautiful in its new joy, as she sank down again with her arms full of flowers, gratefully, submissively, before the audience at whose command she was there. The great house was enchanted with her and with its own unexpected enthusiasm. A joyous thrill and murmur, the very breath of that adulation which is dearest to the goddess of the foot-lights, floated up to the intoxicated girl, wrapt in the wonder of her own success. Aldis could bear no more. He made his way out, pursued by the furious clappings, by the silence, by the first thrilling notes of the encore. He walked the streets for hours, then he went to his room, and threw himself, face downward, on his bed. The lace curtains of his window let in a pallid glimmer from the electric lights in the square,—a ghastly fiction of a moon that never waxes nor wanes. The night spent itself, the tardy winter morning crept slowly over the city wrapt in chill sea fog.

Mrs. Duncan woke with a hoarse feverish cold, and wished she had given Aldis's card and message to Madeline the night before. She had kept them from her, sure that the excited girl would lose what was left of her night's sleep in consequence. Now she felt too ill to make the disclosure and face Madeline's alarm. She waited, with cowardly procrastination until the late breakfast was over, and her little girls had been hurried off to school. She and Madeline had drawn their chairs close to the soft coal fire to talk over the concert, Madeline with a heap of morning papers in her lap, through which she was looking for the musical notices, when Mrs. Duncan gave her Aldis's note. It needed no explanation or comment. It said that he hoped to find them at the Academy of Music, but if he failed to do so, this was to prepare them for an early call; he was coming as early as he could hope to see them,—nine o'clock, he suggested, with insistence that made itself felt even in the careless words of the note. It was now nearly ten o'clock; he had not come. The gray morning turned a sickly yellow, and the streets looked wet and dirty; the papers were tossed into a corner of the sofa where Mrs. Duncan had taken refuge from Madeline's restless wanderings about the room.

A mass of hot-house roses, trophies of the evening's triumph, were displayed on the closed piano, shedding their languid sweetness unheeded, except once when Madeline stopped near them, and exclaimed to her sister:

"Oh, do tell Alice to take those flowers away!" and the next moment seemed to forget they were still there.

The ladies breakfasted and lunched in their own rooms, dining only in the restaurant below. When lunch was announced, Mrs. Duncan rose from her heap of shawls and sofa-cushions and went to the window where Madeline stood gazing out into the yellow mist

45

that hid the square.

"Come, girlie, come out and keep me company. A watched pot never boils, you know."

"Do you *want* any lunch?" Madeline asked incredulously.

Mrs. Duncan did not want any, but she was willing to pretend she did for the sake of interrupting the girl's unhappy watch.

The two women sat down opposite each other in the little dark dining-room, the one window of which looked into a dingy well inclosed by the many-storied walls of the house. The gas was burning, but enough gray daylight mingled with it to give a sickly paleness to the faces it illumined.

There was a letter lying by Madeline's plate.

"When did this come?" she demanded of Alice, the maid.

"They sent it up, miss, with the lunch tray."

"Oh!" cried Madeline. "It may have been lying there in the office for hours!"

She read a few words of the letter, got up from the table, and left the room. Mrs. Duncan gave her a few moments to herself, and then followed her. She was in the parlor, turning over the heap of papers in a distracted search for something which she could not seem to find.

"Oh, Sallie," she exclaimed, looking up piteously at her sister, "won't you find when the Boston shore-line train goes out? I think it is two o'clock, and it's after one now."

"Why do you want to know about the Boston trains?"

"Read that letter—I'm going to try to see him before he starts—read the letter!" she repeated, in answer to her sister's amazed expostulatory stare. She ran out of the room while Mrs. Duncan was reading the letter, and in her own chamber tore off her wrapper and began dressing for the street. Mrs. Duncan heard bureau-drawers flying open and hurried footsteps as she read. This was Aldis's letter:

"Wednesday morning.

"DEAR MADELINE: I saw you at the Academy last night when the verdict was given that separates us.

"The destiny I would not believe in has become a reality to me at last. I must stand aside, and let it fulfill itself.

"Last night I accused you of bitter things, you can imagine what, seeing you so, without any forewarning; but I am tolerably sane this morning. I know that nothing of all that maddened me is true, except that I love you and must give you back to your fate that claims you. You were never mine except by default.

"I am going on to Boston this afternoon. I cannot trust myself to see you. I could not bear your compassion or your remorse, and if you were to offer me more than that, God knows what sacrifice I might not be base enough to accept, face to face with you again.

"Good-bye, my dearest, my only one. I think nothing can ever hurt me much after this. But do not grieve over what neither of us could have helped.

"The happiness of one man should not stand in the way of the free exercise of a divine gift like yours, and the memory of our summer in the canyon—of our last days there together, when my soul set itself to the music of those silences between us—that is still mine. Nothing can take that from me. Yours always,

"HUGH ALDIS."

"Madeline, you are not going after him!" Mrs. Duncan protested, looking up from the letter with tears in her eyes, as her sister entered the parlor, in cloak and bonnet.

Madeline heard the protest; she did not see the tears.

"Don't *talk* to me,—help me, Sallie! Can't you see what I have done? Find me that Boston train, won't you? I know there is one in the evening, but he said afternoon. Where *is* it?" she wailed, turning over with trembling hands sheet after sheet of bewildering columns which mocked her with advertisements of musical entertainments, and even with her own name, staring at her in print.

"The *train* goes at two o'clock, but you shall not go racing up there after him, you crazy girl! I'd go myself, only I'm too sick. I'm awfully sorry for him, but he'll come back—they always do—and give you a chance to explain."

"Explain! I'm going to see him for one instant if I can. I've got just twenty minutes, and nothing on earth shall stop me!"

"Alice," Mrs. Duncan called down the passage, as Madeline shut the outer door, "put on your things and go after Miss Madeline, quick—Third Avenue Elevated to the Grand Central; you'll catch her if you hurry before she gets up the steps."

Mistress and maid reached the Grand Central station together, a few minutes before the train moved out. The last of the line of passengers, ticket in hand, were filing past the door-keeper. It needed but a glance to see that Aldis was not among them. It would be safer, Madeline decided quickly, to get out upon the platform in broadside view from the windows of the train. If Aldis were already on the train, or better still, on the platform, and saw her, Madeline felt sure he would instantly know why she was there.

"I only want to see a friend who is going by the Boston train," she said to the door-keeper. "I'm not going myself." He hesitated, and said something about his orders. "If I must have a ticket, my maid will get me one, but I cannot wait; you must let me through!" She handed her purse to Alice; the man at the gate said he guessed it was no matter about a ticket; he looked curiously after her as she sped along the platform, such a pretty girl, her cheeks red, and her hair all out of crimp with the dampness, but with a sob in her voice, and eyes strained wide with trouble!

"Last train down on the right!" he called after her. "You'll have to hurry." Ominous clouds of steam were puffing out of a smokestack far ahead of her; men were swinging themselves aboard from the platform where they had been walking up and down.

"Boston Shore-line, miss?" a porter lounging by his empty truck called to Madeline as she came panting up to the rear car.

"Oh, yes!" she sobbed. "Is it gone?"

The train gave one heavy, clanking lurch forward. The porter laughed, caught her by the arms, and swung her lightly up to the platform of the last car. The brakeman seized her and shunted her in at the door. The train was in motion. She clung wildly to the door-handle a moment, looking back, and then sank into the nearest seat and burst into tears. Curious glances were cast at her from the neighboring seats, but Madeline was oblivious of everything but the grotesque misery of her situation. What would Alice think, and what would poor, frantic Sallie think, what even would the man at the gate think, who had taken her word instead of a ticket! The conductor came round after a while, and Madeline appealed to him. She had been put on the train by mistake. She had no money and no ticket, but there was, she thought, a friend of hers aboard—would the conductor kindly find out for her if a Mr. Aldis were in any of the forward cars, and tell him a lady, a friend of his, wished to see him?

The conductor had a broad, purple, smooth-shaven cheek, which overflowed his stiff shirt collar; he stroked the tuft of coarse beard on the end of his chin, as he assured the young lady that she need not distress herself. He would find the gentleman if he were on the train. Was he a young gentleman, for instance?

"Yes, he was young and tall, and had dark eyes—" and suddenly Madeline stopped and blushed furiously, meeting the conductor's small and merry eye fixed upon her in the abandonment of her trouble.

The door banged behind him; the car swayed and leaped on the track as the motion of the train increased. A long interval, then a loud crash of noise from the wheels as the door opened again at the forward end of the car. A gentleman was coming down the aisle, looking from side to side as if in search of someone.

Madeline squeezed herself back into the corner of her seat next the window. The blood dropped out of her hot cheeks and stifled her breathing. She turned away her face, and buried it in her muff as someone stopped at her seat, and said, leaning with one hand on the back of it, "Is this the lady who wished to see me?"

Aldis's face was as white as her own; his hand gripped the seat to hide its shaking; Madeline swept back her skirts, and he took the seat beside her. A long silence; Madeline's cheek and profile emerged from the muff and became visible in rosy silhouette against the blank white mist outside the window. Her color had come back.

"Did you get my letter?"

"Yes. That is what brought me here."

Another silence. Madeline slid the hand next to Aldis out of her muff. He took no notice of it at first, then suddenly his own closed over it, and crushed it hard.

"You must not go to Boston to-night," she whispered.

"Why not?"

"Because I am in such trouble!—I had to see you, after that letter. I ran after the train, and they caught hold of me and put me on before I knew what they were doing; and here I am without a ticket or a cent of money—and because you would not come and let me—tell you—" She had hidden her face again in her muff.

"Tell me—what?" His head was close to hers, his arm against her shoulder. He could feel her long, shuddering sobs.

"How *could* I come?" he said.

She did not answer. The roar and rattle of the train went sounding on. It was very interesting to the people in the car; but Madeline had forgotten them, and Aldis cared no more for the files of faces than if they had been the rock fronts of the bluffs that had kept a summer's watch over him and the girl beside him, and the noise of the train had been the far-off river's roar. He was in a dream which could not last too long.

Madeline lifted her head, and through the lulling din he heard her voice, saying:

"Oh, the river! I seemed to hear it last night when I was singing,—and the light on the rocks—do you remember? And I was so glad the rest was not true. And then your letter came—"

"Never mind; nothing is true—only this," he roused himself to say.

The crowded train went roaring and swaying on, as it had during all the days and nights of his journey home, mingling its monotone with the dream that was coming true at last.

Somewhere in that vague and rapidly lessening region known as the frontier, there disappeared, a few years ago, a woman's voice. A soprano with a wonderful mezzo quality, those who knew it called it, and the girl, besides her beauty, had quite a distinct promise of dramatic power. But, they added, she seemed to have no imagination, no conception, of the value of her gifts. She threw away a charming career, just at its outset, and went West with a husband—not anybody in particular. It was altogether a great pity. Perhaps she had not the artistic temperament, or was too indolent to give the time and labor required for the perfecting of her rare gift—at all events the voice was lost.

But in the camps of engineers, within sound of unknown waters, on mountain trails, or crossing the windy cattle-ranges, or in the little churches of the valley towns, or at a lonely grave, perhaps, where his comrades are burying some unwitting, unacknowledged hero, dead in the quiet doing of his duty, a voice is sometimes heard, in ballad or gay roulade, anthem or requiem,—a voice those who have heard it say they will never forget.

Like the hermit-thrush, it sings in the deep woods and the solitudes. Lost it may be to the history of famous voices, but the treasured, self-prized gifts are not those which always carry a blessing with them; and the soul of music, wherever it is purely uttered, will find its listeners, though it be a voice singing in the wilderness, in the dawn of the day of art and beauty which is coming to a new country and a new people.

The Rapture of Hetty

The dance was set for Christmas night at Walling's, a horse-ranch where there were women, situated in a high, watered valley, shut in by foothills, sixteen miles from the nearest town. The cabin with its roof of "shakes," the sheds and corrals, can be seen from any divide between Packer's ferry and the Payette.

The "boys" had been generally invited, with one exception to the usual company. The youngest of the sons of Basset, a pastoral and nomadic house, was socially under a cloud, on the charge of having been "too handy with the frying-pan brand."

The charge could not be substantiated, but the boy's name had been roughly handled in those wide, loosely defined circles of the range, where the force of private judgment makes up for the weakness of the law in dealing with crimes that are difficult of detection and uncertain of punishment. He that has obliterated his neighbor's brand, or misapplied his own, is held as in the age of tribal government and ownership was held the remover of his neighbor's landmarks. A word goes forth against him potent as the Levitical curse, and all the people say amen.

As society's first public and pointed rejection of him, the slight had rankled with the son of Basset; and grievously it wore on him that Hetty Rhodes was going with the man who had been his earliest and most persistent accuser—Hetty, prettiest of all the bunch-grass belles, who never reproached nor quarreled, but judged people with her smile and let them go. He had not complained, though he had her promise,—one of her promises,—nor asked a hearing in his own defense. The sons of Basset were many and poor; their stock had dwindled upon the range; her men-folk condemned him, and Hetty believed, or seemed to believe, as the others.

Had she forgotten the night when two men's horses stood at her father's fence—the Basset boy's and his that was afterward his accuser, and the other's horse was unhitched when the evening was

51

but half spent, and furiously ridden away, while the Basset boy's stood at the rails till close upon midnight? Had the coincidence escaped her that from this night, of one man's rage and another's bliss, the ugly charge had dated? Of these things a girl may not testify.

They met in town on the Saturday before the dance, Hetty buying her dancing-shoes at the back of the store, where the shoe-cases framed in a snug little alcove for the exhibition of a "fit," the boy, in his belled spurs and "chaps" of goat-hide, lounging disconsolate and sulky against one of the front counters. She wore a striped ulster—an enchanted garment his arm had pressed—and a pink crocheted Tam-o'-Shanter cocked bewitchingly over her dark eyes. Her hair was ruffled, her cheeks were red with the wind she had faced two hours on the spring-seat of her father's "dead ax" wagon. Critical feminine eyes might have found her a trifle blowzy; the sick-hearted Basset boy looked once—he dared not look again.

Hetty coquetted with her partner in the shoe-bargain, a curly-headed young Hebrew, who flattered her familiarly and talked as if he had known her from a child, but always with an eye to business. She stood, holding back her skirts and rocking her instep from right to left while she considered the effect of the new style—patent-leather foxings and tan-cloth tops, and heels that came under the middle of her foot, and narrow toes with tips of stamped leather; but what a price! More than a third of her chicken-money gone for that one fancy's satisfaction. But who can know the joy of a really distinguished choice in shoe-leather as one that in her childhood has trotted barefoot through the sage-brush and associated shoes only with cold weather or going to town? The Basset boy tried to fix his strained attention upon anything rather than upon that tone of high jocosity between Hetty and the shiny-haired clerk. He tried to summon his own self-respect and leave the place.

What was the tax, he inquired, on those neck-handkerchiefs, and he pointed with the loaded butt of his braided leather "quirt" to a row of dainty silk mufflers signaling custom from a cord stretched above the gentlemen's furnishing-counter.

The clerk explained that the goods in question were first class, all silk, brocaded, and of an extra size. Plainly he expected that a casual mention of the price would cool the inexperienced customer's curiosity, especially as the colors displayed in the handkerchiefs were not those commonly affected by the cowboy cult. The Basset boy threw down his last half-eagle and carelessly called for the one with a blue border. The delicate "baby blue" attracted him by its perishability, its suggestion of impossible refinements beyond the soilure and dust of his grimy circumstances. Yet he pocketed his purchase as though it were any common thing, not to show his pride in it before the patronizing salesman.

He waited foolishly for Hetty, not knowing if she would even speak to him. When she came at last loitering down the shop, with her eyes on the gay Christmas counters, her arms filled with bundles, he silently fell in behind her and followed her to her father's wagon, where he helped her unload her purchases.

"Been buying out the store?" he opened the conversation.

"Buying more than father'll want to pay for," she drawled, glancing at him sweetly. Those entoiling looks of Hetty's dark-lashed eyes had grown to a habit with her; even now the little Jewish salesman was smiling over his brief portion in them. Her own coolness made her careless, as children are, in playing with fire.

"Here's some Christmas the old man won't have to pay for." A soft paper parcel was crushed into her hand.

"Who is going to pay for it I'd like to know? If it's some of your doings, Jim Basset, I can't take it—so there!"

She thrust the package back upon him. He tore off the wrapper and let the wind carry his rejected token into the trampled mud and slush of the street.

Hetty screamed, and pounced to the rescue. "What a shame! It's a beauty of a handkerchief. It must have cost a lot of money. I sha'n't let you use it so."

She shook it, and wiped away the spots from its delicate sheen, and folded it into its folds again.

"*I* don't want the thing." He spurned it fiercely.

"Then give it to someone else." She endeavored coquettishly to force it into his hands or into the pockets of his coat. He could not withstand her thrilling little liberties in the face of all the street.

"I'll wear it Monday night," said he. "Maybe you think I won't be there?" he added hoarsely, for he had noted her look of surprise mingled with an infuriating touch of pity. "You kin bank on it I'll be there."

Hetty toyed with the thought that after all it might be better that she should not go to the dance. There might be trouble, for certainly Jim Basset had looked as if he meant it when he said he would be there;

and Hetty knew the temper of the company, the male portion of it, to well to doubt what their attitude would be toward an inhibited guest who disputed the popular verdict and claimed social privileges which, it had been agreed, he had forfeited. But it was never really in her mind to deny herself—at least the excitement. She and her escort were among the first couples to cross the snowy pastures stretching between her father's claim and the lights of the lonely horse-ranch.

It was a cloudy night, the air soft, chill, and springlike. Snow had fallen early and frozen upon the ground; the stockmen welcomed the "chinook wind" as the promise of a break in the hard weather. Shadows came out and played on the pale slopes as the riders rose and dropped past one long swell and another of dim country, falling away like a ghostly land seeking a ghostly sea. And often Hetty looked back, fearing yet half hoping that the interdicted one might be on his way, among the dusky, straggling shapes behind.

The company was not large, nor up to nine o'clock particularly merry. The women were engaged in cooking supper, or up in the roof-room brushing out their crimps by the light of an unshaded kerosene-lamp placed on the pine washstand which did duty as a dressing-table. The men's voices came jarringly through the loose boards of the floor from below.

About that hour came the unbidden guest, and like the others he had brought his "gun." He was stopped at the door and told that he could not come in among the girls to make trouble. He denied that he had come with any such intention. There were persons present—he mentioned no names—who were no more eligible, socially speaking, than himself, and he ranked himself low in saying so; where such as these could be admitted, he proposed to show that he could. He offered, in evidence of his good faith and peaceable intentions, to give up his gun; but on condition that he be allowed one dance with the partner of his choosing, regardless of her previous engagements.

This unprecedented proposal was referred to the girls, who were charmed with its audacity. But none of them spoke up for the outcast till Hetty said she could not think what they were all afraid of. A dozen to one, and that one without his weapon! Then the other girls chimed in, and added their timid suffrages. There may have been some twinges of disappointment, there could hardly have been surprise, when the black sheep directed his choice without a look elsewhere to Hetty. She stood up, smiling but rather pale, and he rushed her to the head of the room, the most conspicuous place before his rival, who with his partner took the place of second couple opposite.

"Keep right on!" the fiddler chanted, in sonorous cadence to the music, as the last figure of the set ended with "Promenade all!" He swung into the air of the first figure again, smiling, with his cheek upon his instrument and his eyes upon the floor. Hetty fancied that his smile meant more than merely the artist's pleasure in the joy he evokes.

"Keep your places!" he shouted again, after the "Promenade all!" a second time had raised the dust and made the lamps flare, and lighted with smiles of sympathy the rugged faces of the elders ranged against the walls. The side couples dropped off exhausted, but the tops held the floor, and neither of the men was smiling.

The whimsical fiddler invented new figures, which he "called off" in time to his music, to vary the monotony of a quadrille with two couples missing.

The opposite girl was laughing hysterically; she could no longer dance or stand. The rival gentleman looked about him for another partner. One girl jumped up, then hesitating, sat down again. The music passed smoothly into a gallop, and Hetty and her bad boy kept the floor, regardless of shouts and protests warning the trespasser that his time was up and the game in other hands.

Thrice they circled the room. They looked neither to right nor left; their eyes were upon each other. The men were all on their feet, the music playing madly. A group of half-scared girls were huddled, giggling and whispering, near the door of the dimly lighted shed-room. Into the midst of them Hetty's partner plunged with his breathless, smiling dancer in his arms, passed into the dim outer place to the door where his horse stood saddled, and they were gone.

They crossed the little valley known as Seven Pines, they crashed through the thin ice of the creek, they rode double sixteen miles before midnight—Hetty wrapped in her lover's "slicker," with the blue bordered handkerchief, her only wedding gift, tied over her blowing hair.

The Watchman

The far-Eastern company was counting its Western acres under water contracts. The acres were in first crops, waiting for the water. The water was dallying down its untried channel, searching the new dry earth banks, seeping, prying, insinuating sly, minute forces which multiplied and insisted tremendously the moment a rift had been made. And the orders were to "watch" and "puddle"; and the watchmen were as other men, and some of them doubtless remembered they were working for a company.

Travis, the black-eyed young lumberman from the upper Columbia, had been sent down with a special word from the manager commending him as a tried hand, equal to any post or service. The ditch superintendent was looking for such a man. He gave him those five crucial miles between the head-gates and Glenn's Ferry, the notorious beat that had sifted Finlayson's force without yet finding a man who could keep the banks. Some said it was the arc-light saloon at Glenn's Ferry; some said it was the pretty girl at Lark's.

Whatever it was, Travis raged at it in the silent hours of his one-man watch, and the report went up the line, now three times since he had taken hold, of breaks on his division. And the engineer would by no means "weaken" on a question of the work, nor did the loyal watchman ask that anyone should weaken, to spare him. He was all eyes and ears; he watched by daylight and listened by dark, and the sounds he heard in his dreams were sounds of water searching the banks, swirling and sinking in holes, or of mud subsiding with a wretched flop into the insidious current.

It was a queer country along the new ditch below the head-gates: as old and sunbleached and bony as the stony valleys of Arabia Petrea, all but that strip of green that led the eye to where the river wandered, and that warm brown strip of sown land extending field by field below the ditch.

Lark's ranch was the first one below the head-gates, lying between the river and the ditch, an old homesteader's claim, subirrigated by means of rude dams ponding the natural sloughs. The worn-out land, never drained, was foul and sour, lapsing into swamps, the black alkali oozing and spreading from pools in its boggy pastures.

A few pioneer fruit-trees still bloomed and bore, undiscouraged by neglect, and cast home-like shadows on the weedy grass around the cabin and sheds that slouched at all angles, with nails starting and shingles warping in the sun.

Similar weather-stains and odd kicks and bulges the old rancher's person exhibited when he came out to sun himself of a rimy morning, when cobwebs glittered on the short, late grass, and his joints reminded him that the rains were coming. And up and down the cow-trail below the ditch, morning and evening, went his dairy-herd to pasture; and after them loitered Nancy, on a strawberry pony with milk-white mane and tail.

The lights and shadows chased her in and out among the willows and fleecy cottonwoods and tall swamp-grasses; but Travis rode in the glare, on the high ditch-bank, and although they passed each other daily, he had never had a good look at the "pretty girl at Lark's." But one morning the white-faced heifer broke away and bolted up the ditch-bank, and, in a cloud of sun-smitten dust, Nancy followed, a figure of virginal wrath, with scarlet cheeks and wind-blown hair. Reining her pony on the narrow bank, she called across to Travis, in a voice as clear and fresh as her colors:

"Head her off, can't you? *What* are you about!" This last to the pony, who was behaving "mean."

"Ride to the bridge, and head her this way. I can drive her up the bank," Travis responded.

Nancy obeyed him, and waited at the bridge, while he endeavored to persuade the heifer of the error of her ways. The heifer was not easily persuaded, and Travis was wet to the waist before he had got her out; but he lost nothing of the bright figure guarding the bridge, a slender shape, all pink and blue and dark blue, with hair like the sun on brown water, and a perfect seat and ringing voice, calling thanks and bewildering encouragement to her ally in the stream. And this was old Solomon's daughter!

But "Oh, my, Nancy!" the boys would groan, with excess of appreciation beyond words, and for that Nancy heeded them not; and now Travis knew that the boys were right.

"Thank you ever so much!" her clear voice lilted, as the discomfited runaway dashed down the bank to the path she had forsaken. "I'm ever so sorry she dug all those bad tracks in the ditch. Will they do any harm?"

Travis assured her that nothing did harm if only it were known in time.

"What is the matter with it, anyhow—the ditch? Isn't it built right?"

"The ditch is the prettiest I ever saw," Travis responded, with all the warmth of his unrequited devotion to that faithless piece of engineering. "All new ditches need watching till the banks get settled."

"Well, I should say that *you* watched! Don't you ever stir off that bank?"

"I eat and sleep, sometimes."

"You must have a pretty dry camp up above. Wouldn't you like some milk once in a while?"

"Thanks; I never happen to fall in with the milkman on my beat."

"We have lots to spare, and buttermilk too, if you're not too proud to come for it. The others used to."

"I guess I don't quite catch on."

"The other watchmen—the boys who were here before you."

"Oh," said Travis, coldly.

"Well, any time you choose to come down I'll save some for you," said the girl, as if that matter were settled.

"I'm afraid it is rather off my beat," Travis hesitated; "but I'm just as much obliged."

Nancy straightened herself haughtily. "Oh, it is nothing to be obliged for, if you don't care to come."

"I did not say I didn't care," Travis protested; but she was gone. The dust flew, and presently her dark blue skirt and the pony's silver tail flashed past the willows in the low grounds.

"I shall never see her again," he mourned. "So much for those other fellows spoiling her idea of a watchman's duty. Of course she thought I could come if I wanted to. Did she ask them, I wonder?"

Nancy was piqued, but not resentful. The more he did not come, as evening after evening smiled upon the level land, the more she thought of Travis alone in his dusty camp, alone on his blinding beat; the more she dwelt upon the singularity and constancy of his refusal, the more she respected him for it.

So, one day, he did see her again. She was sitting on the bridge-planks, leaning forward, her arms in her lap, her hat tipped back, a star of white sunlight touching her forehead. She lifted her head when she heard him coming, and put her hand over her eyes, as if she were dizzy with watching the water.

"How's the ditch?" she called in a voice of sweetest cheer. She was on her feet now, and he saw how entrancing she was in a blue muslin frock and a broad white hat with a wreath of pink roses bestrewing the tilted brim. Had they got company at the ranch? was his jealous reflection?

"How's the ditch behaving itself these days?" she repeated.

"Much as usual, thank you," Travis beamed from his saddle.

"Breaking, as usual?"

"Yes; it broke night before last."

"Well, I don't believe it's much of a ditch, anyhow. I wouldn't fret about it if I was you. Don't you think I'm very good-natured, after your snubbing me so? Here I've brought you a basket of apples, seeing you wouldn't spare time from your old ditch to come for them yourself. That, in the napkin, is a little pat of fresh butter." She lifted the grape-leaves which covered the basket. "I thought it might taste good in camp."

"Good! Well, I rather guess it will taste good! See here, I can't ever thank you for this—for bringing it yourself." He had few words, but his looks were moderately expressive.

Nancy blushed with pleasure. "Well, I had to—when folks are so wrapped up in their business. There, with Susan's compliments! Susan's the heifer you rounded up for me in the ditch. I know she made you a lot of work, tracking holes in your banks you're so fussy about. Do you really think it is a good ditch?"

"I am positive it is."

"Then, if anything goes wrong down here, they will lay the blame on you."

"They are welcome to. That's what I am here for."

Nancy openly acknowledged her approval of a man that stood right up to his work, and would take no odds of anyone.

"The other boys were always complaining, and saying it was the ditch. But there, I know it is mean of me to talk about them."

"I guess it won't go any further," said Travis, dryly.

"Well, I hope not. They were good boys enough, but pretty trifling watchmen, I shouldn't wonder."

Travis had nothing to say to this, but he made a mental note or two.

"When shall you give me a chance to return your basket?"

"Why, anytime; there's no hurry about the basket. Have you any regular times?"

He looked away, dissembling his joy in the question, and answered as if he were making an official report.

"I leave camp at six, patrol the line to the ferry and back; lay off an hour, and down again at eleven. Back in camp at three, and two hours for dinner. On again at five, and back in camp at nine. I pass this bridge, for instance, at seven and nine of a morning, twelve and two afternoons, and six and eight in the evening."

"Six and eight," Nancy mused, with a slight increase of color. "Well, I can stop some evening, after cow-time, I suppose; but it isn't any matter about the basket."

Six evenings, going and coming, Travis delayed in passing the bridge, on the watch for Nancy; six times he filled the basket with such late field flowers as he could find; and she never came. On the seventh evening his heart announced her for as far as his eyes beheld. This time she was in white, without her hat, and she wore a blue ribbon in her gold-brown braids—a blue ribbon in her braids and a red, red rose in each cheek; and her colors and the colors of the sky floated like flowers on the placid water.

"Well, where is the basket, then?" she merrily demanded.

"I left it behind, for luck."

"For luck? What sort of luck?"

"Six times I brought it, and you were never here; so to-night I just kicked it into the tent and came off without it. It seems to have been about the right thing to do."

"What—my basket!"

"Your basket. And it was filled with wild flowers, the prettiest I could find. It's your own fault for not coming before."

"I never set any day that I know of. I have been up to town."

Travis was not pleased to hear it.

"Yes; and I saw your company's manager. What a young man he is! I had no idea managers were ever young. And stylish—my! I'm sure I hope he'll know me when he sees me again," she added, coloring, and dropping her eyes.

Travis grimly coincided in the opinion that he would. Nancy continued to strike the wrong note with cruel precision; she could not have done better had she calculated her words. And all the while

60

looking as innocent as the shining water under her feet; and that last time she had been so kind!

And the ditch was as provoking as Nancy, rewarding his devotion with breaks that defied all explanation. It was not possible that the patience of the management could hold out much longer; and when he should have been dismissed in disgrace from his post, Nancy would lightly class him as another of those "good boys enough, but pretty trifling watchmen."

II.

The first dry moon was just past the full. At nine o'clock the sky began to whiten above the long bare ridge of the side-hill cut. At half-past, the edge of the moon's disk clove the skyline, and the shadow of the ridge crept down among the willows and tule-beds of the bottom. At ten the shadow had shrunk; it lay black on the ditch-bank, but the whispering tree-tops below were turning in silver light that flickered along the cow-path and caught the still eye of a dark, shallow pool among the tules.

Nancy had chosen this night for a stroll to the bridge, where Travis might be expected to pass any time between eight o'clock and moonrise. Instead of Travis came a man whom she recognized as one of the watchmen from a lower division. He saluted her, after the custom of the country, claiming nothing on personal grounds but the privilege to look rather hard at the girlish figure silhouetted against the water. It was yet early enough for sky-gleams to linger on still pools, or to color the wimpling reaches of the ditch.

Nancy was disappointed: she had not come out to see a strange rider passing on Travis's gray horse. Her little plans were disconcerted. She had waited what she considered a dignified interval before seeming to take cognizance of her watchman's hours; now it appeared that the part of dignity might be overdone. Had Travis been superseded on his beat? She was conscious of missing him already. Her walk home alone through the confidential willows struck a chill of loneliness which the aspect of the house did not dispel. All was as dark and empty as she had left it. Was her father still at work at those tedious dams? This had been his given reason for frequent absences of late, after his usual working hours; though why he should choose the dark nights for mending his dams Nancy had not asked herself. To-night she wanted him or somebody to drive away this queer new ache that made the moonlight too large and still for one little girl to wander in alone.

She hunted for him. He was in none of the expected places; the dark fields were as empty as the house. She turned back to the ditch; from its high bank she could see farther into the shadowy places of the bottom.

Travis, meanwhile, had been leisurely pursuing his evening beat. He had overtaken one of his fellow-watchmen, on foot, walking to town, had lent him his horse for the last two miles to camp, and invited him to help himself to what he could find for supper, without waiting for his host.

"It is a still night," said Travis; "I will mog along slowly up the ditch, and put in a little extra listening: it's at night the water talks."

Long after the rider had passed on, the tread of his horse's hoofs was heard diminishing on the hard-tramped bank; a loosened stone rattled down and splashed into the water; the wind rustled in the tule-beds; then all surface sounds ceased, and the only talker was the ditch, chuckling and dawdling like an idle child, on its errand, which it could not be persuaded to take seriously, to the desert lands.

Travis came to a ticklish spot near the bridge, and stopped to listen. Here the ditch cut through beds of clean sand, where the water might sink and work back into the old ground, the sand holding it like a sponge, till all the bottom became a bog, and the banks sank in one wide-spread general wash-out. The first symptom of such deep-seated trouble would be the water's motion in the ditch—whirling round and round as if boring a hole in the bottom.

Travis laid his ear to the current, for he could check the water's movement by the sound, as a musician knows when his instrument is in tune. All seemed right at the bridge, but far up the ditch he was aware of a new demonstration. He listened awhile, and then walked on, with long, light steps, and gained upon the sound, which persisted, defining itself as a muffled churning at marked intervals, with now and then a wait between. The prodding was of some tool at work underwater at the ditch-bank.

He crossed to the upper side, and moved forward cautiously along the ridge, crouching, that his figure might not be seen against the sky.

Nancy had gone up the cow-trail, past the low grounds, and was just climbing the bank when a dark shape, of man or beast, crashed down the opposite slope and shot like a slide of rock into the water.

A half-choked cry followed the plunge, then ugly sounds of a scuffle under the ditch-bank—men breathing hard, sighing and snorting, and somebody gasped as if he were being held down till his breath was gone.

"Get in there, you old muskrat! You shall stop your own breaks if it takes your cursed carcass to do it! Now, then, have you got your breath?"

Nancy stayed only to hear that it was her father's voice, convulsed with terror and the chill of his repeated duckings, begging to be spared the anguish of drowning by night in three feet of ditch water.

"Mr. Travis," she screamed, "you let my father be, whatever you are doing to him! Father, you come right home and get on dry clothes!"

Travis was as much amazed as if Diana with the moon on her forehead had appeared on the ditch-bank to take old Solomon Lark under her maiden protection; but no less he stuck to his prize of war.

"Your father hasn't time to change his clothes just yet, Miss Nancy; he's got some work to do first."

"Who are you, to be setting my father to work? Let go of him this minute! You are drowning him; you are choking him to death!" sobbed the frantic girl. The shadow fortunately withheld the details of her father's condition, but she had seen enough. Had Travis been drinking? Was the man bereft of his senses?

He was quite himself, apparently—hideously cool, yet roused, and his voice cut like steel.

"You had better go home, Miss Nancy, and light a fire, and warm a blanket for your father's bed. He'll be pretty cold before he gets through with this night's work."

After his cruel speech he took no more notice of Nancy, but leaped upon the ditch-bank, and began hurling earth in great shovelfuls, patting the old man on the head with his cold tool whenever he tried to clamber up after him.

"You better not try *that*," he roared in a terrible voice that wounded Nancy like a blow. "Get in there, now! Puddle, puddle, or I'll have you buried to the ears in five minutes!"

It was shocking, hideous, like a horrible dream. The earth rattled down all about Solomon, and frequently upon him, the water was thick with mud, and the wretched old man tramped and puddled for dear life, helping to mend the hole he had secretly dug where no eye could discover till the water had fingered it, and enlarged the mischief to a break.

It was the work of vermin, and as such Travis had treated his prisoner. Nancy felt the insult as keenly as she abhorred the cruelty. She fled, hysterical with wrath and despair at her own helplessness. But while she made ready the means of consolation at home, her thinking powers came back, and between what she suspected and what she remembered, she was not wholly in the dark as to the truth between her father and Travis.

There was no one to warm Travis's blankets when he fell back upon camp about daybreak, reeking with cold perspiration, soaked with ditch-water, and sore in every muscle from his frenzy of shoveling. He had had no supper the night before; his guest had eaten all the cooked food, burned all his light wood kindlings, and forgotten to cover the bread-pail, and his bread was full of sand. He didn't think much of those tenderfeet who called themselves ditch-men, on that lower division where there was no work at all to speak of.

He began—worse comfort—to consider his police work from a daughter's point of view: alas for himself and Nancy! His idyl of the ditch was shattered like the tender sky-reflections that bloomed on its still waters and vanished when the waters were troubled. His own thoughts were as that roily pool, where he had ducked the old man in the darkness. He overslept himself, after thinking he should not sleep at all, and started down his beat not until noon of the next day. Half way to the bridge he met on the ditch-bank Nancy Lark. She gave him a note, which he dismounted to take, she vouchsafing no greeting, not even a look, and standing apart, while he read it, with the air of a martyr to duty.

Mr. Travis [the letter ran], I am a death-struck man in consequence of your outrageous treatment of me last evening. I've took a dum chill, and it has hit me in the vitals through standing in water up to my waist with the blood soaking out of me. If you think your fool ditch is worth more than a Human's life though your company's enemy, that's for you to settle as you can when the time comes you'll have to. I don't ask any favors. But if you got anny desency left in you through working for that fish-livered company of bondholders coming out here to stomp us farmers into the dirt, you will call this bizness quits. I ain't in no shape to fight ditches no more. You have put me where I be, and the less said on both sides, the better, it looks to me. If that's so you can say so by word or writing. I should prefer writing as I ain't got that confidence I might have.

Yours truly,
SOLOMON LARK.

"Miss Nancy," said Travis, gently, "is your father very sick this morning?"

"I don't know," Nancy replied.

"Have you sent for a doctor?"

"He won't let me."

"Have you read this letter?"

She flashed an indignant look at him.

"I wish you would, then."

"It is not my letter. I don't know what's in it, and I don't care to know."

"Do you know what your father was doing in the ditch last night?"

"Helping you to mend it, at the risk of his life, because you made him," Nancy answered quickly.

"Helping to mend a hole he made himself, so there would be a nice little break in the morning."

The subject rested there, till Travis, forced to take the defensive, asked:

"Do you believe me?"

"Believe what?"

"What I have just told you about your father?"

"Oh," she said, "it makes no difference to me. I knew my father pretty well before I ever saw you. If you think he was doing that, why, I suppose you will have to think so. But even if he was, I don't call that any reason you should half drown him, and make him work himself to death beside."

"But the water was warm! And I did the work. What was it to tread dirt for an hour or so on a summer's night? Wasn't he in the ditch when I found him?"

"I don't know, I'm sure," said Nancy. "I know that you kept him there."

"Well, I hope he'll keep out of the ditch after this. Working at ditches at night isn't good for his health. But you needn't be alarmed about him this time. I think he'll recover. But remember this: last night I was the company's watchman. I had an ugly piece of work to do, and I did it; but fair play or foul, whatever may happen between

65

your father and me, remember, it is only my work, and you are not in it."

"Well, I guess I'm in it if my father is," said Nancy; "and that is something for you to remember."

"Oh, hang the work and the ditch and all the ditches!" thought Travis; yet it was the ditch that had put color and soul and meaning into his life—that had given him sight of Nancy. And it was not his work nor his convictions about it that stood between them now; it was her woman's contempt for justice and reason where her feelings were concerned. The case was simple, as Nancy saw it; too simple, for it left him out in the cold. He would have had it complicated by a little more feeling in his direction.

"Well, have I got your answer?" she asked. "Father said I was to bring an answer, but not to let you come."

"He need not be afraid," said Travis, bitterly. "If he will leave my ditch-banks alone, I shall not meddle with him. Tell him, if there are no more breaks there will be nothing to report: this break is mended—the break in the ditch, I mean."

"Then you will not tell?" Nancy stole a look at him that was half a plea.

"You would even promise to like me a little, wouldn't you, if you couldn't get the old man off any other way?" he mocked her sorrowfully. "Well, I had rather you hated me than have you stoop to coax me, as I've seen girls do—"

He might be satisfied, she passionately answered; she hated him enough. She hated his work, and the hateful way he did it.

"You are an unmerciful man!" she accused him, with a sob in her voice. "You don't know the trouble my father has had, how many years he has worked, with nothing but his hands; and now your company comes and claims the water, and turns the river, that belongs to everybody, into their big ditch. I'd like to know how they came to own this river! And when they have got it all in their ditch, all the little ditches and the ponds will go dry. We were here years before any of you ever thought of coming, or knew there was a country here at all. It's claim-jumping; and not a cent will they pay, and laugh at us besides, and call us mossbacks! I don't blame my father one bit, if he did break the ditch, and if you are here to watch, then watch!—watch me! Perhaps you think I've had a hand in your breaks!"

Travis turned pale. He had made the mistake of trying to reason with Nancy, and now he felt he must go on, in justice to his case, though she was far away from all his arguments, rapt in the grief, the wrath, the conviction, of her plea.

"You talk as women talk who only hear one side," he replied. "But you people down here don't know the company's intentions; they don't ask, and when they do they won't believe what they are told. That talk against companies is an old politician's drive. This country is too big for single men to handle; companies save years of waiting. This one will bring the railroads and the markets, and boom up the price of land. The ditch your father hates so will make him a rich man in five years, if he does nothing but sit still and let it come.

"As for water, why do you cry before you are hurt? Nobody can steal a river! That is more politicians' talk, to make out they are the settlers' friends. We are the settlers' friends, because we are the friends of the country's boom. It can't boom without us. Why should I believe in this company? I'm a poor man, a settler like your father. I've got land of my own: but I can see we farmers can't do everything for ourselves; it's cheaper to pay a company to help us. They are just peddlers of water and we buy it. Who owns the other, then? Don't we own them just as much as they own us?

"Come, if you can't feel it's so, leave hating us at least till we have done all these things you accuse us of. Wait till we take all the water and ruin your land. Most of these farmers along the river have got too much water. They are ruining their own land. So I tell your father, but he thinks he knows it all."

"He is some older than you are, anyhow."

"He is too old to be working nights in ditches. Tell him so from me, will you?"

"Oh, I'll tell him! I don't think you will be troubled much with us around your ditch, after this. I went to the bridge last night because I thought you were nice and a friend. I had a respect for you more than for any of the others. I might have come to think better of the ditch—but I've had all the ditch I want, and all the watchmen. Never till I die shall I forget how my father looked," she passionately returned to the charge. "An old man like him! Why didn't you put me in and make me tread dirt for you? The water was *warm;* and I'm enough better able than he was!"

"I'll get right down here and let you tread on me, and be proud to have you, if it will cure the sight of what you saw me do last night. I was mad, don't you understand? I have to answer for all this foolishness of your father's, remember. It had to be stopped."

"Was there no way to stop it but half-drowning him and insulting him besides?"

"Yes, there is another way; inform the company, and have him shut up in the Pen. *I* thought I let the old man off pretty easy. But if you prefer the other way, why, next time there's a break, we can try it."

"I'm sure we ought to thank you for your kindness," said Nancy. "And if we are companied out of house and home and father made a criminal, we shall thank you still more. Good morning."

Their eyes met, and hers fell; she turned away, and he remounted, and rode on up the ditch, angry as a man only can be with one he might have loved, down to those dregs of bitterness that lurk at the bottom of the soundest heart.

III.

He was but an idle watchman all that day, so sure he was that the ditch was right and Solomon the author of all his troubles; and Solomon was "fixed" at last. Weariness overcame him, and at the end of his beat he slept under the lee of the ditch bank instead of returning to his camp.

Next morning he was riding along at his usual pace when it struck him how incredibly the ditch had fallen. The line of silt which marked the water's normal depth now stood exposed and dry full two feet above its running, and the pulse of the current had weakened as though it were ebbing fast.

He put his horse to a run, and lightened ship as he went, casting off his sack of oats, then his coat, and such tools as he could spare; he might have been traced to the scene of disaster by his impedimenta strewing the ditch bank.

The water had had hours the start of him; its work was sickening to behold. A part of the bank had gone clean out, and the ditch was returning to the river by way of Solomon Lark's alfalfa fields; the homestead itself was in danger.

He cut sage-brush, and tore up tules by the roots, and piled them as a wing-dam against the outer bank, and heaped dirt like mad upon the mats; and as he worked, alone, where forty men were needed, came Nancy, with glowing face, flying down the ditch bank, calling the word of exquisite relief:

"I've shut off the water. Was that right?"

Right! He had been wishing himself two men, nay, three; one at the bank, and one at the gates, and one carrying word to Finlayson.

"Can I do anything else?"

"Yes; make Finlayson's camp quick as you can." Travis panted over a shovelful of dirt he was heaving.

"Yes, what shall I tell him?"

"Tell him to send up everything he has got; every man, and team, and scraper."

Nancy was gone, but in a few moments she was back again, wringing her hands and as white as a cherry blossom.

"The water is all down round the house, and father is alone in bed crying like a child."

"There's nothing to cry about now. You turned off the water; see, it has almost stopped."

"Can I leave him with you?"

"Great Scott! I'll take care of him! But go, there's a blessed girl. You will save the ditch."

Nancy went, covering the desert miles as a bird flies; she exulted in this chance for reparation. But long after Finlayson's forces had arrived and gone to work, she came lagging wearily homeward, all of a color, herself and the pony, with the yellow road. She had refused a fresh horse at the ditch-camp, and, sparing the whip, reached home not until after dark.

Her father's excitement in his hours of loneliness had waxed to a pitch of childish frenzy. He wept, he cursed, he counted his losses, and when his daughter said, to comfort him, "Why, father, surely they must pay for this!" he threw himself about in his bed, and gave way to lamentations in which the secret of his wildness came out. He had done the thing himself; and he dared not risk suspicion, and the investigation that would follow a heavy claim for damages.

Nancy could not believe him. "Father, do be quiet; you didn't do any such thing," she insisted. "How could you, when I know you haven't stirred out of this bed since night before last? Hush, now; you are dreaming; you are out of your head."

"I guess I know what I done. I ain't crazy, and I ain't a fool. I made this hole first, before he caught me at the upper one. I made this one to keep him busy on his way up, so's the upper one could get a good start. The upper one wouldn't a-hurt us. It's jest like my cussed luck! I knew it was a-comin', but I didn't think I'd get it like this. It's all his fault, the great lazy loafer, sleepin' at the bottom of his beat 'stead o'comin' up as he'd ought to have done last evening. He wasted the whole night—and calls himself a watchman!"

"Well, I'm glad of it," Nancy cried excitedly. "I'm just *glad* we are washed out, and I hope this will end it!" and she burst into tears, and ran out of the room.

She sat weeping and storming by herself in the dark little shed-room where her chickens were gathered from the flood.

"Nancy!" she heard her father calling, "Nancy, child! Where's that gal taken herself off to? Are you a-settin' up your back on account of that ditch? If you are, you ain't no child of mine. I'm dum sorry I let on a word to her about it. How do I know but she's off with it now, to that watchman feller—I'll be put in the papers—an old man informed on by his darter, and he on his last sick-bed! Nancy, I say, where be you a-hidin' yourself?"

Nancy returned to her forlorn charge, and after a while the old man fell asleep. She put out the lamp, for she could see to move about the room by the light of the sage-brush bonfires that flared along the ditch, lighting the men and teams, all Finlayson's force, at work upon the broken banks.

The sight was wild and alluring; she went out to watch the strange army of shadows shifting and intermingling against a wall of flame.

There was a distressful space to cross, of sand and slippery mud and drowned vegetation, including the remains of her garden; the look of everything was changed. Only the ditch-bank against the reddened sky supplied the usual landmark. Its crest was black with shovelers, and up and down, in lurid light, climbed the scraper-teams; climbed, and dumped, and dropped over the bank, to climb again, like figures in a stage procession. There was a bedlam roar and crackle of pitchy fires, rattle of harness, clank of scraper-pans, shouts of men to the cattle, oaths and words of command; and this would go forward unceasingly till the banks held water. And what was the use of contending?

Nancy felt bitterly the insignificance of such small scattered folk as her father, pitiful even in their spite. Their vengeance was like the malice of field-mice or rabbits, which the farmers fenced out of their fields into the desert where they belonged. What could such as they do either to help or hinder this invincible march of capital into the country where they with untold hardships had located the first claims? And some of them were ready enough for a little temporary relief to part with their birthright to these clever sons of Jacob.

"Out we go, to find some other wilderness for them to take away from us! We are only mossbacks," said the daughter of Esau.

As she spoke half aloud to herself, a man rushed past her down the bank, flattened himself on his hands, laid his face to the water, and drank, and paused to pant, and drank again, while she could have counted a score. Then he lifted his head, sighed, and stretched himself back with a groan of complete exhaustion.

The firelight touched his face, and showed her Travis: haggard, hollow-eyed, soaked with ditch water, and matted with mud, looking as if he had been dragged bodily through the ditch-bank, like thread through a piece of cloth.

Nancy did not try to avoid him.

"Oh, is it you?" he marveled, softly smiling up at her. "What a splendid ride you made! Did nobody thank you? Finlayson said he couldn't find you when he was leaving camp."

Nancy answered not a word: she was trembling so that she feared to betray herself by speaking.

"I was coming to say good-by when I had washed my face," he continued. "I got my time tonight."

"Your time?"

"My time-check. They are going to put another man in my place. So you needn't hate me any longer on account of the ditch; you can transfer all that to the next fellow."

"Isn't that just like them! They never can do anything fair!"

"Like who? Do you suppose I'm going to kick about it? The only wonder is they kept me on so long."

Every word of Travis's was a knife in Nancy's conscience, to say nothing of her pride. She hugged her arms in her shawl, and rocked herself to and fro. Travis crawled up the bank a little way further, and stretched himself humbly beside her. The dark shadows under his aching eyes started a pang of pity in the girl's heart, sore beset as she was with troubles of her own.

"I'm glad it's duskish," he remarked, "so you can't see the sweet state I'm in. I'm all over top soil. You might rent me to a Chinaman for twenty-five dollars an acre; and I don't need any irrigating either."

An irresponsible laugh from Nancy was followed by a sob. Then she gathered herself to speak.

"See here, do you want to stay on this ditch?"

"Of course I do. I wanted to stay till I had straightened out my own record, and shown what the ditch can do. But no management under heaven could stand such work as this."

"Then stay, if you want to. You have only to say the word. You said you'd inform if there was a next time, and there is. Father did it. He made this break, too. He made them both the same night, and didn't dare to tell of this one. Now, go and clear yourself, and get back your beat."

"Are you sure of this you are telling me?"

"Well, I guess so. It isn't the sort of thing I'd be likely to make up. And I say you can tell if you want to. I make you a present of the information. If father isn't willing to take the consequences, I am; and they half belong to me. I won't have anybody sheltering us, or losing by us. We have got no quarrel with you."

"That is brave of you. I wish it was something more than brave," sighed Travis. "But I want it all myself. I can't spare this information to the company. You didn't do it for them, did you?"

"When I go telling on my father to save a ditch, I guess it will be after now," said Nancy. "If that rich company, with all its men and watchmen and teams and money, can't protect itself from one poor old man—"

"Never mind the company," said Travis. "What's mine is mine. This word you gave to me, it doesn't belong to my employers. You have saved me to myself; now I shall not go kicking myself for sleeping that night on my beat. It's not so bad—oh, not half so bad—for me!"

"Then go tell them, and get the credit for it. Don't you mean to?"

She could not see him smile. "When I tell, you will hear of it."

"But you talked about your record."

"I shall have to go to work and make a new record. Ah, if you would be as kind as you are brave! Was it all just for pride you told me this? Don't you care, not the least bit, about my part—that I am down and out of everything?"

"It's your own fault, then. I have told you how you can clear yourself and stay."

"And lose my chance with you! I was thinking of coming back

someday, to tell you—what you must know already. Nancy, you do know!"

"You forget," shivered Nancy; "I am the daughter of the man you called—"

"Is that fair—to bring that up now?"

"You mustn't deceive yourself. There are some things that can't be forgotten."

"How did *I* know what I was saying? A man isn't always responsible."

"I heard you," said Nancy. "There are things we say when we are raging mad at a person, and there are things we say when we think them the dirt under our feet. You kept him down with your dirt-shovel, and you called him—what I can't ever forget."

"And is this the only hitch between us?"

"I should think it was enough. Who despises my father despises me."

"But I do not despise him," Travis did not scruple to assert. "The quarrel was not mine; and I'm not a ditchman any longer. I will apologize to your father."

"Oh, I know it costs you nothing to apologize. You don't mind father—an old man like him! You'd take him in, and give him his meals, and pat him on the head as you would the house-dog that bites because he's old and cross. Well, I'll let you know I don't want you to forgive him, and apologize, and all that stuff. I want you to get even with him."

"Be satisfied," said Travis. "The only count I have against your father is through his daughter. There is no way for me to get even with you. And when you have spoiled a man's life just for one angry word—"

"Not angry," she interrupted. "I could have forgiven you that."

"For one word, then. And you call it square when you have given me a piece of information to use for myself against you! I will go back, now, and go to work. They can't say I haven't earned my wages on this beat."

He looked down at her, longing to gather her with all her thorny sweetness to his breast; but her attitude forbade him.

"Can't we shake hands?" he said. They shook hands in silence, and he went back and finished the night in the ranks of the shovelers, to work well, to love well, and to get his discharge at last. Yet Travis was not sorry that he had taken those five miles below Glenn's Ferry.

He had found something to work for.

The company's officials marveled as the weeks went by that nothing was heard of Solomon Lark. He had ever been the sturdiest beggar for damages on the ditch. If he lacked an occasion he could invent one; he was known to be a fanatic on the subject of the small farmers' wrongs; yet now, with a veritable claim to sue for, the old protestant was dumb. Had Solomon turned the other cheek? There were jokes about it in the office; they looked to have some fun with Solomon yet.

In the early autumn the joking ceased. There was a final reason for the old man's silence: Solomon was dead. His ranch was rented to a Chinese vegetable-gardener, who bought water from the ditch.

The company, through its officials, was disposed to recognize this unspoken claim that had perished on the lips of the dead. They made an estimate, and offered Nancy Lark a fair sum in consideration of her father's losses by the ditch.

It was unusual for a company to volunteer a settlement of this kind, it was still more unusual for the indemnity to be refused. Nancy declined by letter, first; the manager asked her to call at the office. She did not come. He took pains to hunt her up at the house of her friends in town. He might have delegated the call, but he made it in person, and was struck by an added dignity, a finer beauty, in the saddened face of the girl he remembered as a bit of a rustic coquette.

He went over the business with her. She was perfectly intelligent in the matter; there had been no misunderstanding. Why, then, should she not take what belonged to her? Companies were not in the habit of paying claims that were claims of sentiment.

"I have made no claim," said Nancy.

"But you have one. You inherited one. We do not propose to rob—"

She put out her hand with a gesture of appeal.

"My father had no claim. He never made one, nor meant to make one. I am the best judge of what belongs to me. I don't want this money, and I will never take one cent of it. But there is a claim you can settle, if you are hunting up claims. It won't cost you anything," she faltered, as if some unguarded impulse had hurried her into a subject she hardly knew how to go on with. She moved her chair back a little from the light.

"There was one of your watchmen on the Glenn's Ferry beat who lost his place on account of those breaks coming one after

74

another—"

"Yes," said the manager; "there were several that did. Which man do you refer to?"

The name, she thought, was Travis. Then, blushing, she spoke out courageously.

"It was Mr. Travis. He was discharged just after the big break. You thought it was his carelessness, but it was not. I am the only one that can say so, and I know it. You lost the best watchman you ever had on the ditch when you took his name off your pay-roll. He worked for more than just his money's worth, and it hurt him to lose that place."

"Are you aware that he made the worst record of any man on the line?"

"I don't care what his record was; he kept a good watch. It's no concern of mine to say so," she said. Trembling, and red and white, the tears shining in her honest eyes, she persisted: "He had his reasons for never explaining, and they were nothing to be ashamed of. I think you might believe me!"

"I do," said the manager, willing to spare her. "I will attend to the case of Mr. Travis when I see him. I do not think he has left the country. In fact, he was inquiring about you only the other day, in the office, and he seemed very much concerned to hear of your—of the loss you have suffered. Shall I say that you spoke a good word for him?"

"You need not do that," she answered with spirit. "He knows whether he kept watch. But you may say that I ask as a favor that he will answer all your questions; and you need not be afraid to question him."

Travis was given back his beat, but no more explicit exoneration would he accept. The reason of his reinstatement was not made public, and naturally there was gossip about it among other discharged watchmen who had not been invited to try again.

Two of these cynic philosophers, popularly known as sore-heads, foregathered one morning at Glenn's Ferry, and began to discuss the management and the ditch.

"Travis don't seem to have so much trouble with the water this year as he had last," the first ex-watchman remarked. "Used to get away with him on an average once a week, so I hear."

"He's married his girl," the other exclaimed sarcastically. "He's got more time to look after the ditch."

There is no sand, now, in Travis's bread. The prettiest girl on the ditch makes it for him, and walks beside him when the lights are fair and the shadows long on the ditch-bank. And it is a pleasure to record that both Nancy and the ditch are behaving as dutifully as girls and water can be expected to do when taken from their self-found paths and committed to the sober bounds of responsibility.

Flowers bloom upon its banks, heaven is reflected in its waters, fair and broad are the fertile pastures that lie beyond; but the best-trained ditch can never be a river, nor the gentlest wife a girl again.

Maverick

Traveling Buttes is a lone stage-station on the road, largely speaking, from Blackfoot to Boise. I do not know whether the stages take that road now, but ten years ago they did, and the man who kept the stage-house was a person of primitive habits and corresponding appearance named Gilroy.

The stage-house is perhaps half a mile from the foot of the largest butte, one of three which loom on the horizon, and appear to "travel" from you, as you approach them from the plains. A day's ride with the Buttes as a landmark is like a stern chase in that you seem never to gain upon them.

From the stage-house the plain slopes up to the foot of the Big Butte, which rises suddenly in the form of an enormous tepee, as if Gitche Manito, the mighty, had here descended and pitched his tent for a council of the nations.

The country is destitute of water. To say that it is "thirsty" is to mock with vain imagery that dead and mummied land on the borders of the Black Lava. The people at the stage-house had located a precious spring, four miles up, in a cleft near the top of the Big Butte; they piped the water down to the house, and they sold it to travelers on that Jericho road at so much per horse. The man was thrown in, but the man usually drank whisky.

Our guide commented unfavorably on this species of husbandry, which is common enough in the arid West, and as legitimate as selling oats or hay; but he chose to resent it in the case of Gilroy, and to look upon it as an instance of individual and exceptional meanness.

"Any man that will jump God's water in a place like this, and sell it the same as drinks—he'd sell water to his own father in hell!"

This was our guide's opinion of Gilroy. He was equally frank, and much more explicit, in regard to Gilroy's sons. "But," he concluded, with a philosopher's acceptance of existing facts, "it ain't likely that any of that outfit will ever git into trouble s' long as Maverick is sheriff of Lemhi County."

We were about to ask why, when we drove up to the stage-house, and Maverick himself stepped out, and took our horses.

"What the—infernal has happened to the man?" my companion, Ferris, exclaimed; and our guide answered indifferently, as if he were speaking of the weather:

"Some Injuns caught him alone in an out-o'-the-way ranch, when he was a lad, and took a notion to play with him. This is what was left of him when they got through. I never see but one worse-looking man," he added, speaking low, as Maverick passed us with the team: "him a bear wiped over the head with its paw. 'T was quicker over with, I expect, but he lived, and *he* looked worse than Maverick."

"Then I hope to the Lord I may never see him!" Ferris ejaculated; and I noticed that he left his dinner untasted, though he had boasted of a hunter's appetite.

We were two college friends on a hunting-trip, but we had not got into the country of game. In two days more we expected to make Hagar's Hole, and I may mention that "hole," in this region, signifies any small, deep valley, well hidden amidst high mountains, where moisture is perennial, and grass abounds. In these pockets of plenty, herds of elk gather and feed as tame as park pets; and other hunted creatures, as wild but less innocent, often find sanctuary here, and cache their stolen stock and other spoil of the road and the range.

We did not forget to put our question concerning Maverick, that unhappy man, in his character of legalized protector of the Gilroy gang. What did our free-spoken guide mean by that insinuation?

We were told that Gilroy, in his rough-handed way, had been as a father to the lad, after the savages wreaked their pleasure on him; and his people being dead or scattered, Maverick had made himself useful in various humble capacities at the stage-house, and had finally become a sort of factotum there and a member of the family. And though perfectly square himself, and much respected on account of his personal courage and singular misfortunes, he could never see the old man's crookedness, nor the more than crookedness of his sons. He was like a son of the house, himself; but most persons agreed that it was not as a brother he felt toward Rose Gilroy. And a tough lookout it was for the girl; for Maverick was one that no man would lightly cross, and in her case he was acting as "general dog around the place," as our guide called it. The young fellows were shy of the house, notwithstanding the attraction it held. It was likely to be Maverick or nobody for Rose.

We did not see Rose Gilroy, but we heard her step in the stage-house kitchen and her voice, as clear as a lark's, giving orders to the tall, stooping, fair young Swede, who waited on us at table, and did other work of a menial character in that singular establishment.

"How is it the watch-dog allows such a pretty sprig as that around the place?" Ferris questioned, eying our knight of the trencher, who blushed to feel himself remarked.

"He won't stay," our guide pronounced; "they don't none of 'em stay when they're good-lookin'. The old man he's failin' considerable these days,—gettin' kind o'silly,—and the boys are away the heft of the time. Maverick pretty much runs the place. I don't justly blame the critter. He's watched that little Rose grow up from a baby. How's he goin' to quit bein' fond of her now she's a woman? I dare say he'd a heap sooner she'd stayed a little girl. And these yere boys around here they're a triflin' set, not half so able to take care of her as Maverick. He's got the sense and he's got the sand; but there's that awful head on him! I don't blame him much, lookin' the way he does, and feelin' the same as any other man."

We left Traveling Buttes and its cruel little love-story, but we had not gone a mile when a horseman overtook us with a message for Ferris from his new foreman at the ranch, a summons which called him back for a day at the least. Ferris was exceedingly annoyed: a day at the ranch meant four days on the road; but the business was imperative. We held a brief council, and decided that, with Ferris returning, our guide should push on with the animals and camp outfit into a country of grass, and look up a good camping spot (which might not be the first place he struck) this side of Hagar's Hole. It remained for me to choose between going with the stuff, or staying for a longer look at the phenomenal Black Lava fields at Arco; Arco being another name for desolation on the very edge of the weird stone sea. This was my ostensible reason for choosing to remain at Arco; but I will not say the reflection did not cross me that Arco is only sixteen miles from Traveling Buttes—not an insurmountable distance between geology and a pretty girl, when one is five and twenty, and has not seen a pretty face for a month of Sundays.

Arco, at that time, consisted of the stage-house, a store, and one or two cabins—a poor little seed of civilization dropped by the wayside, between the Black Lava and the hills where Lost River comes down and "sinks" on the edge of the lava. The station is somewhat back from the road, with its face—a very grimy, unwashed countenance—to the lava. Quaking asps and mountain birches follow the water, pausing a little way up the gulch behind the house, but the eager grass tracks it all the way till it vanishes; and the dry bed of the stream goes on and spreads in a mass of coarse sand and gravel, beaten flat, flailed by the feet of countless driven sheep that have gathered here. For this road is on the great overland sheep-trail from Oregon eastward—the march of the million mouths, and what the mouths do not devour the feet tramp down.

The staple topic of conversation at Arco was one very common in the far West, when a tenderfoot is of the company. The poorest place can boast of some distinction, and Arco, though hardly on the highroad of fashion and commerce, had frequently been named in print in connection with crime of a highly sensational and picturesque character. Scarcely another fifty miles of stage-road could boast of so many and such successful road jobs; and although these affairs were of almost biennial occurrence, and might be looked for to come off always within that noted danger-limit, yet it was a fact that the law had never yet laid finger on a man of the gang, nor gained the smallest clue to their hide-out. It was a difficult country around Arco, one that lent itself to secrecy. The road-agents came, and took, and vanished as if the hills were their copartners as well as the receivers of their goods. As for the lava, which was its front dooryard, so to speak, for a hundred miles, the man did not live who could say he had crossed it. What it held, or was capable of hiding, in life or in death, no man knew.

The day after Ferris left me I rode out upon that arrested tide—those silent breakers which for ages have threatened, but never reached, the shore. I tried to fancy it as it must once have been, a sluggish, vitreous flood, filling the great valley, and stiffening as it slowly pushed toward the bases of the hills. It climbed and spread, as dough rises and crawls over the edge of the pan. The Black Lava is always called a sea—that image is inevitable; yet its movement had never in the least the character of water. "This is where hell pops," an old plainsman feelingly described it, and the suggestion is perfect. The colors of the rock are those produced by fire; its texture is that of slag from a furnace. One sees how the lava hardened into a crust, which cracked and sank in places, mingling its tumbled edges with the creeping flood not cooled beneath. After all movement had

80

ceased, and the mass was still, time began upon its tortured configurations, crumbled and wore and broke, and sifted a little earth here and there, and sealed the burnt rock with fairy print of lichens, serpent-green and orange and rust-red. The spring rains left shallow pools which the summer dried. A few dim trails wander a little way and give out, like the water.

For a hundred miles to the Snake River, this Plutonian gulf obliterates the land—holds it against occupation or travel. The shoes of a marching army would be cut from their feet before they had gone a dozen miles across it; horses would have no feet left; and water would have to be packed as on an ocean, or a desert, cruise.

I rode over places where the rock rang beneath my horse's hoofs like the iron cover of a manhole. I followed the hollow ridges that mounted often forty feet above my head, but always with that gruesome effect of thickening movement—that sluggish, atomic crawl; and I thought how one man, pursuing another into this frozen hell, might lose himself but never find the object of his quest. If he took the wrong furrow, he could not cross from one blind gut into another, nor hope to meet the fugitive at any future turning.

I don't know why the fancy of a flight and pursuit should so have haunted me in connection with the Black Lava; I suppose it must have been the desperate and lawless character of our conversation at the stage-house.

I fell completely under the spell of that skeleton flood. I watched the sun sink, as it sinks at sea, beyond its utmost ragged ridges; I sat on the borders of it, and stared across it in the gray moonlight; I rode out upon it when the Buttes, in their delusive nearness, were as blue as the gates of amethyst, and the morning was as fair as one great pearl: but no peace or radiance of heaven or earth could change its aspect more than that of a mound of skulls. When I began to dream about it, I thought I must be getting morbid. This is worse than Gilroy's, I said; and I promised myself I would ride up there next day and see if by chance one might get a peep at the Rose that all were praising, but none dared put forth a hand to pluck. Was it indeed so hard a case for the Rose? There are women who can love a man for the perils he has passed. Alas, Maverick! Could anyone get used to a face like that?

Here, surely, was the story of Beauty and her poor Beast humbly awaiting, in the mask of a brutish deformity, the recognition of Love pure enough to divine the soul beneath, and unselfish enough to deliver it. Was there such love as that at Gilroy's? However, I did not make that ride.

It was the fourth night of clear, desert moonlight since Ferris had left me: I was sleepless, and so I heard the first faint throb of a horse's feet approaching from the east, coming on at a great pace, and making the turn to the stage-house. I looked out, and on the trodden space in front I saw Maverick dismounting from a badly blown horse.

"Halloo! What's up?" I called from the open window of my bedroom on the ground floor.

"Did two men pass here on horseback since dark?"

"Yes," I said. "About twelve o'clock a tall man and a little short fellow."

"Did they stop to water?"

"No, they did not and they seemed in such a tearing hurry that I watched them down the road—"

"I am after those men, and I want a fresh horse," he cut in. "Call up somebody quick!"

"Shall you take one of the boys along?" I inquired, with half an eye to myself, after I had obeyed his command.

He shook his head. "Only one horse here that's good for anything: I want that myself."

"There is my horse," I suggested. "But I'd rather be the one who rides her. She belongs to a friend."

"Take her, and come on, then, but understand—this ain't a Sunday-school picnic."

"I'm with you, if you'll have me."

"I'd sooner have your horse," he remarked, shifting the quid of tobacco in his cheek.

"You can't have her without me, unless you steal her," I said.

"Git your gun, then, and shove some grub into your pockets. I can't wait for nobody."

He swung himself into the saddle.

"What road do you take?"

"There ain't but one," he shouted, and pointed straight ahead.

I overtook him easily within the hour; he was saving his horse, for this was his last chance to change until Champagne Station, fifty miles away.

He gave me rather a cynical smile of recognition as I ranged alongside, as if to say, "You'll probably get enough of this before we are through." The horses settled down to their work, and they "humped theirselves," as Maverick put it, in the cool hours before sunrise.

At daybreak his awful face struck me all afresh, as inscrutable in its strange distortion as some stone god in the desert from whose graven hideousness a thousand years of mornings have silently drawn the veil.

"What do you want those fellows for?" I asked, as we rode. I had taken for granted that we were hunting suspects of the road-agent persuasion.

"I want 'em on general principles," he answered shortly.

"Do you think you know them?"

"I think they'll know me. All depends on how they act when we get within range. If they don't pay no attention to us, we'll send a shot across their bows. But more likely they'll speak first."

He was very gloomy, and would keep silence for an hour at a time. Once he turned on me as with a sudden misgiving.

"See here, don't you git excited; and whatever happens, don't you meddle with the little one. If the big fellow cuts up rough, he'll take his chances, but you leave the little one to me. I want him—I want him for State's evidence," he finished hoarsely.

"The little one must be the Benjamin of the family," I thought—"one of the bad young Gilroys, whose time has come at last; and Sheriff Maverick finds his duty hard."

I could not say whether I really wished the men to be overtaken, but the spirit of the chase had undoubtedly entered into my blood. I felt as most men do, who are not saints or cowards, when such work as this is to be done. But I knew I had no business to be along. It was one thing for Maverick, but the part of an amateur in a man-hunt is not one to boast of.

The sun was now high, and the fresh tracks ahead of us were plain in the dust. Once they left the road and strayed off into the lava, incomprehensibly to me; but Maverick understood, and pressed forward. "We'll strike them again further on. D— fool!" he muttered, and I observed that he alluded but to one, "huntin' waterholes in the lava in the tail-end of August!"

They could not have found water, for at Belgian Flat they had stopped and dug for it in the gravel, where a little stream in freshet time comes down the gulch from the snow-fields higher up, and sinks, as at Arco, on the lip of the lava. They had dug, and found it, and saved us the trouble, as Maverick remarked.

Considerable water had gathered since the flight had paused here and lost precious time. We drank our fill, refreshed our horses, and shifted the saddle-girths; and I managed to stow away my lunch during the next mile or so, after offering to share it with Maverick, who refused it as if the notion of food made him sick. He had considerable whisky aboard, but he was, I judged, one of those men on whom drink has little effect; else some counter-flame of excitement was fighting it in his blood.

I looked for the development of the personal complication whenever we should come up with the chase, for the man's eye burned, and had his branded countenance been capable of any expression that was not cruelly travestied, he would have looked the impersonation of wild justice.

It was now high noon, and our horses were beginning to feel the steady work; yet we had not ridden as they brought the good news from Ghent: that is the pace of a great lyric; but it's not the pace at which justice, or even vengeance, travels in the far West. Even the furies take it coolly when they pursue a man over these roads, and on these poor brutes of horses, in fifty-mile stages, with drought thrown in.

Maverick had had no mercy on the pony that brought him sixteen miles; but this piece of horse-flesh he now bestrode must last him through at least to Champagne Station, should we not overhaul our men before. He knew well when to press and when to spare the pace, a species of purely practical consideration which seemed habitual with him; he rode like an automaton, his baleful face borne straight before him—the Gorgon's head.

Beyond Belgian Flat—how far beyond I do not remember, for I was beginning to feel the work, too, and the country looked all alike to me as we made it, mile by mile—the road follows close along by the lava, but the hills recede, and a little trail cuts across, meeting the road again at Deadman's Flat. Here we could not trust to the track, which from the nature of the ground was indistinct. So we divided our forces, Maverick taking the trail,—which I was quite willing he should do, for it had a look of most sinister invitation,—while I continued by the longer road. Our little discussion, or some atmospheric change,—some breath of coolness from the hills,—had brought me up out of my stupor of weariness. I began to feel both alert and nervous; my heart was beating fast. The still sunshine lay all around us, but where Maverick's white horse was climbing, the shadows were turning eastward, and the deep gulches, with their patches of aspen, were purple instead of brown. The aspens were left shaking where he broke through them and passed out of sight.

I kept on at a good pace, and about three o'clock I, being then as much as half a mile away, saw the spot which I knew must be Deadman's Flat; and there were our men, the tall one and his boyish mate, standing quietly by their horses in broad sunlight, as if there were no one within a hundred miles. Their horses had drunk, and were cropping the thin grass, which had set its tooth in the gravel where, as at the other places, a living stream had perished. I spurred forward, with my heart thumping, but before they saw me I saw Maverick coming down the little gulch; and from the way he came I knew that he had seen them.

The scene was awful in its treacherous peacefulness. Their shadows slept on the broad bed of sunlight, and the gulch was as cool and still as a lady's chamber. The great dead desert received the silence like a secret.

Tenderfoot as I was, I knew quite well what must happen now; yet I was not prepared—could not realize it—even when the tall one put his hand quickly behind him and stepped ahead of his horse. There was the flash of his pistol, and the loud crack echoing in the hill; a second shot, and then Maverick replied deliberately, and the tall one was down, with his face in the grass.

I heard a scream that sounded strangely like a woman's; but there were only the three, the little one, acting wildly, and Maverick bending over him who lay with his face in the grass. I saw him turn the body over, and the little fellow seemed to protest, and to try to push him away. I thought it strange he made no more of a fight, but I was not near enough to hear what those two said to each other.

Still, the tragedy did not come home to me. It was all like a scene, and I was without feeling in it except for that nervous trembling which I could not control.

Maverick stood up at length, and came slowly toward me, wiping his face. He kept his hat in his hand, and, looking down at it, said huskily:

"I gave that man his life when I found him las' spring runnin' loose like a wild thing in the mountings, and now I've took it; 'n' God above knows I had no grudge ag'in' him, if he had stayed in his place. But he would have it so."

"Maverick, I saw it all, and I can swear it was self-defense."

His face drew into the tortured grimace which was his smile. "This here will never come before a jury," he said. "It's a family matter. Did ye see how he acted? Steppin' up to me like he was a first-class shot, or else a fool. He ain't nary one; he's a poor silly tool, the whip-hand of a girl that's boltin' from her friends like they was her mortal enemies. Go and take a look at him; then maybe you'll understand."

He paused, and uttered the name of Jesus Christ, but not as such men often use it, with an inconsequence dreadful to hear; he was not idly swearing, but calling that name to witness solemnly in a case that would never come before a jury.

I began to understand.

"Is it—is the girl—"

"Yes, it's our poor little Rose—that's the little one, in the gray hat. She'll give herself away if I don't. She don't care for nothin' nor nobody. She was runnin' away with that fellow—that dishwashin' Swede what I found in the mountings eatin' roots like a ground-hog, with the ends of his feet froze off. Now you know all I know—and more 'n she knows, for she thinks she was fond of him. She wa'n't, never—for I watched 'em, and I know. She was crazy to git away, and she took him for the chance."

His excitement passed, and we sat apart and watched the pair at a distance. She—the little one—sat as passively by her dead as Maverick pondering his cruel deed; but with both it was a hopeless quiet.

"Come," he said at length, "I've got to bury him. You look after her, and keep her with you till I git through. I'm givin' you the hardest part," he added wistfully, as if he fully realized how he had cut himself off from all such duties, henceforth, to the girl he was consigning to a stranger's care.

I told him I thought that the funeral had more need of me than the mourner, and I shrank from intruding myself.

"I dassent leave her by herself—see? I don't know what notion she may take next, and she won't let me come within a rope's len'th of her."

I will not go over again that miserable hour in the willows, where I made her stay with me out of sight of what Maverick was doing. Ours were the tender mercies of the wicked, I fear; but she must have felt that pity at least was near her, if not help. I will not say that her youth and distressful loveliness did not help my perception of a sweet life wasted, gone utterly astray, which might have brought God's blessing into some man's home—perhaps Maverick's, had he not been so hardly dealt with. She was not of that great disposition of heart which can love best that which has sorest need of love; but she was all woman, and helpless and distraught with her tangle of grief and despair, the nature of which I could only half comprehend.

We sat there by the sunken stream, on the hot gravel where the sun had lain, the willows sifting their inconstant shadows over us; and I thought how other things as precious as "God's water" go astray on the Jericho road, or are captured and sold for a price, while dry hearts ache with the thirst that asks a "draught divine."

The man's felt hat which she wore pulled down over her face was pinned to the coil of braids; this had slipped from the crown of her head. The hat was no longer even a protection; she cast it off, and the blond braids, which had not been smoothed for a day and a night, fell like ropes down her back. The sun had burned her cheeks and neck to a clear crimson; her blue eyes were as wild with weeping as a child's. She was a rose, but a rose that had been trampled in the dust; and her prayer was to be left there, rather than that we should take her home.

I suppose I must have had some influence over her, for she allowed me to help her to arrange her forlorn disguise, and put her on her horse, which was more than could have been expected from the way she received me. And so, about four o'clock, we started back.

There was a scene when we headed the horses to the west; she protesting with wild sobs that she would not, could not, go home, that she would rather die, that we should never get her back alive, and so on. Maverick stood aside bitterly, and left her to me, and I was aware of a grotesque touch of jealousy—which, after all, was perhaps natural—in his dour face whenever he looked back at us. He kept some distance ahead, and waited for us when we fell too far in the rear.

This would happen when from time to time her situation seemed to overpower her, and she would stop in the road, and wring her hands, and try to throw herself out of the saddle, and pray me to let her go.

"Go where?" I would ask. "Where do you wish to go? Have you any plan, or suggestion, that I could help you to carry out?" But I said it only to show her how hopeless her resistance was. This she would own piteously, and say: "Nobody can help me. There ain't nowhere for me to go. But I can't go back. You won't let him make me, will you?"

"Why cannot you go back to your father and your brothers?"

This would usually silence her, and, setting her teeth upon her trouble, she would ride on, while I reproached myself, I knew not why.

After one of these struggles, when she had given in to the force of circumstances, still unconsenting and rebellious, Maverick fell back, and ranged his horse on her other side.

"I know partly what's troubling you, and I'd rid you of that part quick enough," he said, with a kind of dogged patience in his hard voice; "but you can't get on there without me. You know that, don't you? You don't blame me for staying?"

"I don't blame you for anything but what you've done to-day. You've broke my heart, and ruined me, and took away my last chance, and I don't care what becomes of me, so I don't have to go back."

"You don't have to any more than you have to live. Dyin' is a good deal easier, but we can't always die when we want to. Suppose I found a little lost child on the road, and it cried to go home, and I didn't know where 'home' was, would I leave it there just because it cried and hung back? I'd take you to a better home if I knew of one; but I don't. And there's the old man. I suppose we could get some doctor to certify that he's out of his mind, and get him sent up to Blackfoot; but I guess we'd have to buy the doctor first."

"Oh, hush, do, and leave me alone," she said.

Maverick dug his spurs into his horse, and plunged ahead.

"There," she cried, "now you know part of it; but it's the least part—the least, the least! Poor father, he's awful queer. He don't more than half the time know who I am," she whispered. "But it ain't him I'm running away from. It's myself—my own life."

"What is it—can't you tell me?"

She shook her head, but she kept on telling, as if she were talking to herself.

"Father he's like I told you, and the boys—oh, that's worse! I can't get a decent woman to come there and live, and the women at Arco won't speak to me because I'm livin' there alone. They say—they think I ought to get married—to Maverick or somebody. I'll die first! I *will* die, if there's any way to."

This may not sound like tragedy as I tell it, but I think it was tragedy to her. I tried to persuade her that it must be her imagination about the women at Arco; or, if some of them did talk—as indeed I myself had heard, to my shame and disgust,—I told her I had never known that place where there was not one woman, at least, who could understand and help another in her trouble."

"I don't know of any," she said simply.

There was no more to do but ride on, feeling like her executioner; but

Ride hooly, ride hooly, now, gentlemen,
Ride hooly now wi' me,

came into my mind; and no man ever kept beside a "wearier burd," on a sadder journey.

At dusk we came to Belgian Flat, and here Maverick, dismounting, mixed a little whisky in his flask with water which he dipped from the pool. She must have recalled who dug the well, and with whom she had drunk in the morning. He held it to her lips. She rejected it with a strong shudder of disgust.

"Drink it!" he commanded. "You'll kill yourself, carryin' on like this." He pressed it on her, but she turned away her face like a sick and rebellious child.

"Maybe she'd drink it for you," said Maverick, with bitter patience, handing me the cup.

"Will you?" I asked her gently. She shook her head, but at the same time she let me take her hand, and put it down from her face, and I held the cup to her lips. She drank it, every drop. It made her deathly sick, and I took her off her horse, and made a pillow of my coat, so that she could lie down. In ten minutes she was asleep. Maverick covered her with his coat after she was no longer conscious.

We built a fire on the edge of the lava, for we were both chilled and both miserable, each for his own part in that day's work.

The flat is a little cup-shaped valley formed by high hills, like dark walls, shutting it in. The lava creeps up to it in front.

We hovered over the fire, and Maverick fed it, savagely, in silence. He did not recognize my presence by a word—not so much as if I had been a strange dog. I relieved him of it after a while, and went out a little way on the lava. At first all was blackness after the strong glare of the fire; but gradually the desolation took shape, and I stumbled about in it, with my shadow mocking me in derisive beckonings, or contracting close to my heels, as the red flames towered or fell. I stayed out there till I was chilled to the bone, and then went back defiantly. Maverick sat as if he had not moved, his elbows on his knees, his face in his hands. I wondered if he were thinking of that other sleeper under the birches of Deadman's Gulch, victim of an unhappy girl's revolt. Had she loved him. Had she deceived him as well as herself? It seemed to me they were all like children who had lost their way home.

By midnight the moon had risen high enough to look at us coldly over the tops of the great hills. Their shadows crept forth upon the lava. The fire had died down. Maverick rose, and scattered the winking brands with his boot-heel.

"We must pull out," he said. "I'll saddle up, if you will—" The hoarseness in his voice choked him, and he nodded toward the sleeper.

I dreaded to waken the poor Rose. She was very meek and quiet after the brief respite sleep had given her. She sat quite still, and watched me while I shook the sand from my coat, put it on, and buttoned it to the chin, and drew my hat down more firmly. There was a kind of magnetism in her gaze; I felt it creep over me like the touch of a soft hand.

When the horse was ready, Maverick brought it, and left it standing near, and went back to his own, without looking toward us.

"Come, you poor, tired little girl," I said, holding out my hand. She could not find her way at first in the uncertain light, and she seemed half asleep still, so I kept her hand in mine, and guided her to her horse. "Now, once more up," I encouraged her; and suddenly she was clinging to me, and whispering passionately:

"Can't you take me somewhere? Where are those women that you know?" she cried, shaking from head to foot.

"Dear little soul, all the women I know are two thousand miles away," I answered.

"But can't you take me *somewhere*? There must be some place. I know you would be good to me; and you could go away afterward, and I wouldn't trouble you any more."

"My child, there is not a place under the heavens where I could take you. You must go on like a brave girl, and trust to your friends. Keep up your heart, and the way will open. God will not forget you," I said, and may he forgive me for talking cant to that poor soul in her bitter extremity.

She stood perfectly still one moment while I held her by the hands. I think she could have heard my heart beat; but there was nothing I could do. Even now I wake in the night, and wonder if there was anyway but one.

"Yes; the way will open," she said very low. She cast off my hands, and in a second she was in the saddle, and off up the road, riding for her life. And we two men knew no better than to follow her.

I knew better, or I think, now, that I did. I told Maverick we had pushed her far enough. I begged him to hold up and at least not to let her see us on her track. But he never spoke a word, but kept straight on, as if possessed. I don't thing he knew what he was doing. At least there was only one thing he was capable of doing—following that girl till he dropped.

Two miles beyond the Flat there is another turn, where the shoulder of a hill comes down and crowds the road, which passes out of sight. She saw us hard upon her as she reached this bend. Maverick was ahead. Her horse was doing all he could, but it was plain he could not do much more. She looked back, and flung out her hand in the man's sleeve that half covered it. She gave a little whimpering cry, the most dreadful sound I ever heard from any hunted thing.

We made the turn after her, and there lay the road white in the moonlight, and as bare as my hand. She had escaped us.

We pulled up the horses, and listened. Not a sound came from the hills or the dark gulches, where the wind was stirring the quaking asps; the lonesome hush-sh made the silence deeper. But we heard a horse's step go clink, clinking—a loose, uncertain step wandering away in the lava.

"Look! look there! My God!" groaned Maverick.

There was her horse limping along one of the hollow ridges, but the saddle was empty.

"She has taken to the lava!"

I had no need to be told what that meant, but if I had needed, I learned what it meant before the night was through. I think that if I were a poet, I could add another "dolorous circle" to the wailing-place for lost souls.

But she had found a way. Somewhere in that stony-hearted wilderness she is at rest. We shall see her again when the sea—the stupid, cruel sea that crawls upon the land—gives up its dead.

The Trumpeter

When the trumpets at Bisuka barracks sound retreat, the girls in the Meadows cottage, on the edge of the Reservation, begin to hurry with the supper things, and Mrs. Meadows, who has been young herself, says to her eldest daughter, "You go now, Callie; the girls and I can finish." Which means that Callie's colors go up as the colors on the hill come down; for soon the tidy infantrymen and the troopers with their yellow stripes will be seen, in the first blush of the afterglow, tramping along the paths that thread the sagebrush common between the barracks and the town; and Callie's young man will be among them, and he will turn off at the bridge that crosses the acéquia, and make for the cottage gate by a path which he ought to know pretty well by this time.

Callie's young man is Henniker, one of the trumpeters of K troop,—th cavalry; *the* trumpeter, Callie would say, for though there are two of the infantry and two of the cavalry who stand forth at sunset, in front of the adjutant's office, and blow as one man the brazen call that throbs against the hill, it is only Henniker that Callie hears. That trumpet blare, most masculine of all musical utterances, goes straight from his big blue-clad chest to the heart of his girl, across the clear lit evening; but not to hers alone. There is only one Henniker, but there is more than one girl in the cottage on the common.

At this hour, nightly, a small dark head, not so high above the sage as Callie's auburn one, pursues its dreaming way, in the wake of two cows and a half-grown heifer, towards the hills where the town herd pastures. Punctually at the first call it starts out behind the cows from the home corral; by the second it has passed, very slowly, the foot-bridge, and is nearly to the corner post of the Reservation; but when "sound off" is heard, the slow-moving head stops still. The cheek turns. A listening eye is raised; it is black, heavily lashed; the tip of a silken eyebrow shows against the narrow temple. The cheek is round

92

and young, of a smooth clear brown, richly under-tinted with rose,—a native wild flower of the Northwest. As the trumpets cease, and the gun fires, and the brief echo dies in the hill, the liquid eyes grow sad.

"Sweet, sweet! too sweet to be so short and so strong!" The dumb childish heart swells in the constriction of a new and keener sense of joy, an unspeakable new longing.

What that note of the deep-colored summer twilight means to her she hardly understands. It awakens no thought of expectation for herself, no definite desire. She knows that the trumpeter's sunset call is his good-bye to duty on the eve of joy; it is the paean of his love for Callie. Wonderful to be like Callie; who after all is just like any other girl,—like herself, just as she was a year ago, before she had ever spoken to Henniker.

Henniker was not only a trumpeter, one of four who made music for the small two-company garrison; he was an artist with a personality. The others blew according to tactics, and sometimes made mistakes; Henniker never made mistakes except that he sometimes blew too well. Nobody with an ear listening nightly for taps could mistake when it was Henniker's turn, as orderly trumpeter, to sound the calls. He had the temperament of the joyous art; and with it the vanity, the passion, the forgetfulness, the unconscious cruelty, the love of beauty, and the love of being loved that made him the flirt constitutional as well as the flirt military,—which not all soldiers are, but which all soldiers are accused of being. He flirted not only with his fine gait and figure, and bold roving glances from under his cap-peak with the gold sabres crossed above it; he flirted in a particular and personal as well as promiscuous manner, and was ever new to the dangers he incurred, not to mention those to which his willing victims exposed themselves. For up to this time in all his life Henniker had never yet pursued a girl. There had been no need, and as yet no inducement, for him to take the offensive. The girls all felt his irresponsible gift of pleasing, and forgot to be afraid. Not one of the class of girls he met but envied Callie Meadows, and showed it by pretending to wonder what he could see in her.

It was himself Henniker saw, so no wonder he was satisfied, until he should see himself in a more flattering mirror still. The very first night he met her, Callie had informed him, with the courage of her bright eyes, that she thought him magnificent fun; and he had laughed in his heart, and said, "Go ahead, my dear!" And ahead they went headlong, and were engaged within a week.

Mother Meadows did not like it much, but it was the youthful way, in pastoral frontier circles like their own; and Callie would do as she pleased,—that was Callie's way. Father Meadows said it was the women's business; if Callie and her mother were satisfied, so was he.

But he made inquiries at the post, and learned that Henniker's record was good in a military sense. He stood well with his officers, had no loose, unsoldierly habits, and never was drunk on duty. He did not save his pay; but how much "pay" had Meadows ever saved when he was a single man? And within two years, if he wanted it, the trumpeter was entitled to his discharge. So he prospered in this as in former love affairs that had stopped short of the conclusive step of marriage.

Meta, the little cow-girl, the youngest and fairest, though many shades the darkest of the Meadows household, was not of the Meadows blood. On her father's side, her ancestry, doubtless, was uncertain; some said carelessly, "Canada French." Her mother was pure squaw of the Bannock breed. But Mother Meadows, whose warm Scotch-Irish heart nourished a vein of romance together with a feudal love of family, upheld that Meta was no chance slip of the murky half-bloods, neither clean wild nor clean tame. Her father, she claimed to know, had been a man of education and of honor on the white side of his life, a well-born Scottish gentleman, exiled to the wilderness of the Northwest in the service of the Hudson's Bay Company. And Meta's mother had broken no law of her rudimentary conscience. She had not swerved in her own wild allegiance, nor suffered desertion by her white chief. He had been killed in some obscure frontier fight, and his goods, including the woman and child, were the stake for which he had perished. But Father Josette, who knew all things and all people of those parts, and had baptized the infant by the sainted name of Margaret, had traced his lost plant of grace and conveyed it out of the forest shades into the sunshine of a Christian white woman's home. Father Josette—so Mrs. Meadows maintained—had known that the babe would prove worthy of transplantation.

She made room for the little black-headed stranger, with soft eyes like a mouse (by the blessing of God she had never lost a child, and the nest was full), in the midst of her own fat, fair-haired brood, and cherished her in her place, and gave her a daughter's privilege.

In a wild, woodlandish way, Meta was a bit of an heiress in her own right. She had inherited through her mother a share in the yearly increase of a band of Bannock ponies down on the Salmon meadows; and every season, after the grand round-up, the settlement was made,—always with distinct fairness, though it took some time, and good deal of eating, drinking, and diplomacy, before the business could be accomplished.

"What is a matter of a field worth forty shekels betwixt thee and me?" was the etiquette of the transaction, but the outcome was practically the same as in the days of patriarchal transfers of real estate.

Father Meadows would say that it cost him twice over what the maiden's claim was worth to have her cousins the Bannocks, with their wives and children and horses, camped on his borders every summer; for Meta's dark-skinned brethren never sent her the worth of her share in money, but came themselves with her ponies in the flesh, and spare ponies of their own, for sale in the town; and on Father Meadows was the burden of keeping them all good natured, of satisfying their primitive ideas of hospitality, and of pasturing Meta's ponies until they could finally be sold for her benefit. No account was kept, in this simple, generous household, of what was done for Meta, but strict account was kept of all that was Meta's own.

The Bannock brethren were very proud of their fair kinswoman who dwelt in the tents of Jacob. They called her, amongst themselves, by the name they give to the mariposa lily, the closed bud of which is pure white as the whitest garden lily; but as each Psyche-wing petal opens it is mooned at the base with a dark purplish stain which marks the flower with startling beauty, yet, to some eyes, seems to mar it as well. With every new bud the immaculate promise is renewed, but the leopard cannot change his spots nor the wild hill lily her natal stain.

This year the sale of pony flesh amounted to nearly a hundred dollars, which Father Meadows put away for Meta's future benefit,—all but one gold piece, which the mother showed her, telling her that it represented a new dress.

"You need a new white one for your best, and I shall have it made long. You're filling out so, I don't believe you'll grow much taller."

Meta smiled sedately. In spite of the yearly object lesson her dark kinsfolk presented, she never classed herself among the hybrids. She accepted homage and tribute from the tribe, but in her consciousness, at this time, she was all white. This was due partly to Mother Meadows's large-hearted and romantic theories of training, and partly to an accident of heredity. The woman who looks the squaw is the squaw, when it comes to the flowering time of her life. To Meta had succeeded the temperament of her mother expressed in the features of her father; whether Canadian trapper or Scotch grandee, he had owned an admirable profile.

A great social and musical event took place that summer in the town, and Meta's first long dress was finished in time to play its part, as such trifles will in the simple fates of girlhood. It was by far the prettiest dress she had ever put over her head; the work of a professional, to begin with. Then its length persuaded one that she was taller than nature had made her. Its short waist suited her youthful bust and flat back and narrow shoulders. The sleeves were puffed and stood out like wings, and were gathered on a ribbon which tied in a bow just above the bend of her elbow. Her arms were round and soft as satin, and pinkish-pale inside, like the palms of her small hands. All her skin, though dark, was as clear as wine in a colored glass. The neck was cut down in a circle below her throat, which she shyly clasped with her hands, not being accustomed to feel it bare. And as naturally as a bird would open its beak for a worm, she exclaimed to Mother Meadows, "Oh, how I wish I had some beads!" And before night she had strung herself a necklace of the gold-colored pompons with silver-gray stems that spangle the dry hills in June,—"butter-balls" the Western children call them,—and, in spite of the laughter and gibes of the other girls, she wore her sylvan ornament on the great gala night, and its amazing becomingness was its best defense.

So Meta's first long dress went, in company with three other unenvious white dresses and Father Meadows's best coat, to hear the "Coonville Minstrels," a company of amateur performers representing the best musical talent in the town, who would appear for one night only, for the benefit of the free circulating library fund.

Henniker was not in attendance on his girl as usual.

"What a pity," the sisters said, "that he should have to be on guard to-night!" But Meta remembered, though she did not say so, that Henniker had been on guard only two nights before, so it could not be his turn again, and that could not explain his absence.

But Callie was as gay as ever, and did not seem put out even at her father's bantering insinuations about some other possible girl who might be scoring in her place.

The sisters were enraptured over every number on the programme. The performers had endeavored to conceal their identity under burnt cork and names that were fictitious and humorous, but everybody was comparing guesses as to which was which, and who was who. The house was packed, and "society"was there. The feminine half of it did not wear its best frock to the show and its head uncovered, but what of that! A girl knows when she is looking her prettiest, and the young Meadowses were in no way concerned for the propriety of their own appearance. Father Meadows, looking along the row of smiling faces belonging to him, was as well satisfied as any man in the house. His eyes rested longer than usual on little Meta tonight. He saw for the first time that the child was a beauty; not going to be,—she was one then and there. Her hair, which she was accustomed to wear in two tightly braided pigtails down her back, had been released and brushed out all its stately maiden length, "crisped like a war-steed's encolure." It fell below her waist, and made her face and throat look pale against its blackness. A spot of white electric light touched her chest where it rose and fell beneath the chain of golden blossom balls,—orange gold, the cavalry color. She looked like no other girl in the house, though nearly every girl in town was there.

Part I. of the programme was finished; a brief wait,—the curtain rose, and behold the colored gentlemen from Coonville had vanished. Only the interlocutor remained, scratching his white wool wig over a letter which he begged to read in apology for his predicament. His minstrelsy had decamped, and spoilt his show. They wrote to inform him of the obvious fact, and advised him, facetiously, to throw himself upon the indulgence of the house, but "by no means to refund the money."

Poor little Meta believed that she was listening to the deplorable truth, and wondered how Father Meadows and the girls could laugh.

"Oh, won't there be any second part, after all?" she despaired; at which Father Meadows laughed still more, and pinched her cheek, and some persons in the row of chairs in front half turned and smiled.

"Goosey," whispered Callie, "don't you see he's only gassing? This is part of the fun."

"Oh, is it?" sighed Meta, and she waited for the secret of the fun to develop.

"Look at your program," Callie instructed her. "See, this is the Impressario's Predicament—The Wandering Minstrel comes next. He will be splendid, I can tell you."

"Mr. Piper Hide-and-Seek," murmured Meta, studying her programme. "What a funny name!"

"Oh, you child!" Callie laughed aloud, but as suddenly hushed, for the sensation of the evening, to the Meadows party, had begun.

A very handsome man, in the gala dress of a stage peasant, of the Bavarian Highlands possibly, came forward with a short, military step, and bowed impressively. There was a burst of applause from the bluecoats in the gallery, and much whistling and stamping from the boys.

"Who is it?" the lady in front whispered to her neighbor.

"One of the soldiers from the post," was the answer.

"Really!"

But the lady's accent of surprise conveyed nothing beside the speechless admiration of the Meadows family. Callie, who had been in the exciting secret all along, whispered violently with the other girls, but Meta had become quite cold and shivery. She could not have uttered a word.

Henniker made a little speech in an assumed accent which astonished his friends almost more than his theatrical dress and bearing. He said he was a stranger, piping his way through a foreign land, but he could "spik ze Engleesh a leetle." Would the ladies and gentlemen permit him, in the embarrassing absence of better performers, to present them with a specimen of his poor skill upon a very simple instrument? Behold!

He flung back his short cloak, and filled his chest, standing lightly on his feet, with his elbows raised.

No rattling trumpet blast from the artist's lips to-night, but, still and small, sustained and clear, the pure reed note trilled forth. Willow whistles piping in springtime in the stillness of deep meadow lands before the grass is long, or in flickering wood paths before the full leaves darken the boughs,—such was the pastoral simplicity of the instrument with which Henniker beguiled his audience. Such was the quality of sound, but the ingenuity, caprice, delicacy, and precision of its management were quite his own. They procured him a wild encore.

Henniker had been nervous at the first time of playing; it would have embarrassed him less to come before a strange house; for there were the captain and the captain's lady, and the lieutenants with their best girls; and forty men he knew were nudging and winking at one another; and there were the bonny Meadowses, with their eyes upon him and their faces all aglow. But who was she, the little big-eyed dark one in their midst? He took her in more coolly as he came before the house the second time; and this time he knew her, but not as he ever had known her before.

Is it one of nature's revenges that in the beauty of their women lurks the venom of the dark races which the white man has put beneath his feet? The bruised serpent has its sting; and we know how from Moab and Midian down the daughters of the heathen have been the unhappy instruments of proud Israel's fall, and how the shaft of his punishment reaches him through the body of the woman who cleaves to his breast.

That one look of Henniker's at Meta, in her strange yet familiar beauty, sitting captive to his spell, went through his flattered senses like the intoxication of strong drink. He did not take his eyes off her again. His face was pale with the complex excitement of a full house that was all one girl, and all hushed through joy of him. She sat so close to Callie, his reckless glances might have been meant for either of them; Callie thought at first they were for her, but she did not think so long.

Something followed on the programme at which everybody laughed, but it meant nothing at all to Meta. She thought the supreme moment had come and gone, when a big Zouave in his barbaric reds and blues marched out and took his stand, back from the footlights, between the wings, and began that amazing performance with a rifle which is known as the "Zouave drill."

The dress was less of a disguise than the minstrel's had been, and it was a sterner, manlier transformation. It brought out the fighting look in Henniker. The footlights were lowered, a smoke arose behind the wings, strange lurid colors were cast upon the figure of the soldier magician.

"The stage is burning!" gasped Meta, clutching Callie's arm.

"It's nothing but red fire. You mustn't give yourself away so, Meta; folks will take us for a lot of Sagebrushers."

Meta settled back in her place with a fluttering sigh, and poured her soul into this new wonder.

But Henniker was not doing himself justice to-night, his comrades thought. No one present was so critical of him or so proud of him as they. A hundred times he had put himself through this drill before a barrack audience, and it had seemed as if he could not make a break. But to-night his nerve was not good. Once he actually dropped his piece, and a groan escaped the row of uniforms in the gallery. This made him angry; he pulled himself up and did some good work for a moment, and then—"Great Scott! he's lost it again! No, he hasn't. Brace up, man!" The rifle swerves, but Henniker's knee flies up to catch it; the sound of the blow on the bone makes the women shiver; but he has his piece, and sends it savagely whirling, and that miss was his last. His head was like the centre of a spinning-top or the hub of a flying-wheel. He felt ugly from the pain of his knee, but he made a dogged finish, and only those who had seen him at his best would have said that his drill was a failure.

Henniker knew, if no one else did, what had lost him his grip in the rifle act. His eyes, which should have been glued to his work, had been straying for another and yet one more look at Meta. Where she sat so still was the storm centre of emotion in the house, and when his eyes approached her they caught the nerve shock which shook his whole system and spoiled his fine work. He cared nothing for the success of his piping when he thought of the failure of his drill. The failure had come last, and, with other things, it left its sting.

On the way home to barracks, the boys were all talking, in their free way, about Meta Meadows,—the little broncho, they called her, in allusion to her great mane of hair,—which made Henniker very hot.

He would not own that his knee pained him, he would not have it referred to, and was ready, next day, to join the riders in squad drill, a new feature of which was the hurdles and ditch-jumping and the mounted exercises, in which, as usual, Henniker had distinguished himself.

The Reservation is bounded on the southeast side, next the town, by an irrigation ditch, which is crossed by as many little bridges as there are streets that open out upon the common. (All this part of the town is laid out in "additions," and is sparsely built up.) Close to this division line, at right angles with it, are the dry ditches and hurdle embankments over which the stern young corporals put their squads, under the eye of the captain.

Out in the centre of the plain other squads are engaged in the athletics of horsemanship, a series of problems in action which embraces every sort of emergency a mounted man may encounter in the rush and throng of battle, and the means of instantly meeting it, and of saving his own life or that of a comrade. So much more is made in these days of the individual powers of the man and horse that it is wonderful to see what an exact yet intelligently obedient combination they have become; no less effective in a charge as so many pounds of live momentum to be hurled on the bayonet points, but much more self-reliant on scout service, or when scattered singly, in defeat, over a wide, strange field of danger.

On the regular afternoons for squad and troop drill, the ditch bank on the town side would be lined with spectators: ladies in light cotton dresses and beflowered hats, small barelegged boys and muddy dogs, the small boys' sisters dragging bonnetless babies by the hand, and sometimes a tired mother who has come in a hurry to see where her little truants have strayed to, or a cowboy lounging sideways on his peaked saddle, condescending to look on at the riding of Uncle Sam's boys. The crowd assorts itself as the people do who line the barriers at a bullfight: those who have parasols, to the shadow; those who have barely a hat, to the sun.

Here, on the field of the gray-green plain, under the glaring tent roof of the desert sky, the national free circus goes on, to the screaming delight of the small boys, the fear and exultation of the ladies, and the alternate pride and disgust of the officers who have it in charge.

A squad of the boldest riders are jumping, six in line. One can see by the way they come that every man will go over: first the small ditch, hardly a check in the pace; then a rush at the hurdle embankment, the horses' heads very grand and Greek as they rear in a broken line to take it. Their faces are as strong and wild as the faces of the men. Their flanks are slippery with sweat. They clear the hurdles, and stretch out for the wide ditch.

"Keep in line! Don't crowd!" the corporal shouts. They are doing well, he thinks. Over they all go; and the ladies breathe again, and say to each other how much finer this sport is because it is work, and has a purpose in it.

Now the guidon comes, riding alone, and the whole troop is proud of him. The signal flag flashes erect from the trooper's stirrup; the horse is new to it, and fears it as if it were something pursuing him; but in the face of horse and man is the same fixed expression, the sober recklessness that goes straight to the finish. If these do not go over, it will not be for want of the spur in the blood.

Next comes a pale young cavalryman just out of the hospital. He has had a fall at the hurdle the week before and strained his back. His captain sees that he is nervous and not yet fit for the work, yet cannot spare him openly. He invents an order, and sends him off to another part of the field where the other squads are manoeuvring.

If it is not in the man to go over, it will not be in his horse, though a poor horse may put a good rider to shame; but the measure of every man and every horse is taken by those who have watched them day by day.

The ladies are much concerned for the man who fails,—"so sorry" they are for him, as his horse blunders over the hurdle, and slackens when he ought to go free; and of course he jibs at the wide ditch, and the rider saws on his mouth.

"Give him his head! Where are your spurs, man?" the corporal shouts, and adds something under his breath which cannot be said in the presence of his captain. In they go, floundering, on their knees and noses, horse and man, and the ladies cannot see, for the dust, which of them is on top; but they come to the surface panting, and the man, whose uniform is of the color of the ditch, climbs on again, and the corporal's disgust is heard in his voice as he calls, "Ne-aaxt!"

It need not be said that no corporal ever asked Henniker where were *his* spurs. To-day the fret in his temper fretted his horse, a young, nervous animal who did not need to know where his rider's heels were quite so often as Henniker's informed him.

"Is that a non-commissioned officer who is off, and his horse scouring away over the plain? What a dire mortification," the ladies say, "and what a consolation to the bunglers!"

No, it is the trumpeter. He was taking the hurdle in a rush of the whole squad; his check-strap broke, and his horse went wild, and slammed himself into another man's horse, and ground his rider's knee against his comrade's carbine. It is Henniker who is down in the dust, cursing the carbine, and cursing his knee, and cursing the mischief generally.

The ladies strolled home through the heat, and said how glorious it was and how awfully real, and how one man got badly hurt; and they described in detail the sight of Henniker limping bare-headed in the sun, holding on to a comrade's shoulder; how his face was a "ghastly brown white," and his eyes were bloodshot, and his black head dun with dust.

"It was the trumpeter who blew so beautifully the other night—who hurt his knee in the rifle drill," they said. "It was his knee that was hurt to-day. I wonder if it was the same knee?"

It was the same knee, and this time Henniker went to the hospital and stayed there; and being no malingerer, his confinement was bitterly irksome and a hurt to his physical pride.

The post surgeon's house is the last one on the line. Then comes the hospital, but lower down the hill. The officer's walk reaches it by a pair of steps that end in a slope of grass. There are moisture and shade where the hospital stands, and a clump of box-elder trees is a boon to the convalescents there. The road between barracks and canteen passes the angle of the whitewashed fence; a wild syringa bush grows on the hospital side, and thrusts its blossoms over the wall. There is a broken board in the fence, which the syringa partly hides.

After three o'clock in the afternoon this is the coolest corner of the hospital grounds; and here, on the grass, Henniker was lying, one day of the second week of his confinement.

He had been half asleep when a soft, light thump on the grass aroused him. A stray kitten had crawled through the hole in the fence, and, feeling her way down with her forepaws, had leaped to the ground beside him.

"Hey, pussy!" Henniker welcomed her pleasantly, and then was silent. A hand had followed the kitten through the hole in the fence—a smooth brown hand no bigger than a child's, but perfect in shape as a woman's. The small fingers moved and curled enticingly.

"Pussy, pussy? Come, pussy!" a soft voice cooed. "Puss, puss, puss? Come pussy!" The fingers groped about in empty air. "Where are you, pussy?"

Henniker had quietly possessed himself of the kitten, which, moved by these siren tones, began to squirm a little and meekly to "miew." He reached forth his hand and took the small questing one prisoner; then he let the kitten go. There was a brief speechless struggle, quite a useless one.

"Let me go! Who is it? Oh *dear!*"

Another pull. Plainly, from the tone, this last was femine profanity.

Silence again, the hand struggling persistently, but in vain. The soft bare arm, working against the fence, became an angry red.

"Softly, now. It's only me. Didn't you know I was in hospital, Meta?"

"Is it you, Henniker?"

"Indeed it is. You wouldn't begrudge me a small shake of your hand, after all these days?"

"But you are not in hospital now?"

"That's what I am. I'm not in bed, but I'm going on three legs when I'm going at all. I'm a house-bound man." A heavy sigh from Henniker.

"Haven't you shaken hands enough now, Henniker?" beseechingly from the other side. "I only wanted kitty; please put her through the fence."

"What's your hurry?"

"Have you got her there? Callie left her with me. I mustn't lose her. Please?"

"Has Callie gone away?"

"Why, yes, didn't you know? She has gone to stay with Tim's wife." (Tim Meadows was the eldest, the married son of the family.) "She has a little baby, and they can't get any help, and father wouldn't let mother go down because it's bad for her to be over a cook stove, you know."

"Yes, I know the old lady feels the heat."

"We are quite busy at the house. I came of an errand to the quartermaster-sergeant's, and kitty followed me, and the children chased her. I must go home now," urged Meta. "Really, I did not think you would be so foolish, Henniker. I can't see what fun there is in this!"

"Yes, but Meta, I've made a discovery—here in your hand."

"In my hand? What is it? Let me see." A violent determined pull, and a sound like a smothered explosion of laughter from Henniker.

"Softly, softly, now. You'll hurt yourself, my dear."

"Is my hand dirty? It was the kitten, then; her paws were all over sand."

"Oh, no. Great sign! It's worse than that. It'll not come off."

"I *will* see what it is!"

"But you can't see unless I was to tell you. I'm a hand reader, did you know it? I can tell your fortune by the lines on your palm. I'm reading them off here just like a book."

"Good gracious! What do you see?"

"Why, it's a most extraordinary thing! Your head line is that mixed up with your heart line, 'pon me word I can't tell which is which. Which is it, Meta? Do you choose your friends with your head entirely, or is it the other way with you, dear?"

"Oh, is that all? I thought you could tell fortunes really. I don't care what I *am;* I want to know what I'm going to *do*. Don't you see anything that's going to happen to me?"

"Lots of things. I see something that's going to happen to you right now. I wonder did it ever happen to you before?"

"What is it? When is it coming?"

"It has come. I will put it right here in your hand. But I shall want it back again, remember; and don't be giving it away, now, to anybody else."

A mysterious pause. Meta felt a breath upon her wrist, and a kiss from a mustached lip was pressed into the hollow of her hand.

"Keep that till I ask you for it," said Henniker quite sternly, and closed her hand tight with his own. The hand became an expressive little fist.

"I think you are just as mean and silly as you can be! I'll never believe a word you say again."

"Pussy," remarked Henniker, in a mournful aside, "go ask your mistress will she please forgive me. Tell her I'm not exactly sorry, but I couldn't help it. Faith, I couldn't."

"I'm not her mistress," said Meta.

It was a keen reminder, but Henniker did not seem to feel it much.

"Go tell Meta," he corrected. "Ask her please to forgive me, and I'll take it back—the kiss, I mean."

"I'm going now," said Meta. "Keep the kitten, if you want her. She isn't mine, anyway."

But now the kitten was softly crowded through the fence by Henniker, and Meta, relenting, gathered her into her arms and carried her home.

It was certainly not his absence from Callie's side that put Henniker in such a bad humor with his confinement. He grew morbid, and fell into treacherous dreaming, and wondered jealously about the other boys, and what they were doing with themselves these summer evenings, while he was loafing on crutches under the hospital trees. He was frankly pining for his freedom before Callie should return. He wanted a few evenings which he need not account for to anybody but himself; and he got his freedom, unhappily, in time to do the mischief of his dream, to put vain, selfish longings into the simple heart of Meta, and to spoil his own conscience toward his promised wife.

Henniker knew the ways of the Meadows cottage as well as if he had been one of the family. He knew that Meta, having less skill about the house than the older girls, took the part of chore-boy, and fetched and drove away the cows.

It were simple enough to cross her evening track through the pale sagebrush, which betrayed every bit of contrasting color, the colors of Meta's hair-ribbon and her evening frock; it were simple enough, had she been willing to meet him. But Meta had lost confidence in the hero of the household. She had seen Henniker in a new light; and whatever her heart line said, her head line told her that she had best keep a good breadth of sagebrush between herself and that particular pair of broad blue shoulders that moved so fast above it. So as Henniker advanced the girl retreated, obscurely, with shy doublings and turnings, carefully managed not to confess that she was running away; for that might vex Henniker, and she was too loyal to the family bond to wish to show her sister's lover an open discourtesy. She did not dream of the possibility of his becoming her own lover, but she thought him capable of going great lengths in his very peculiar method of teasing.

As soon as he understood her tactics Henniker changed his own. Without another glance in her direction he made off for the hills, but not too far from the trail the cows were taking; and choosing a secluded spot, behind a thickset clump of sage, he took out his rustic pipe and waited, and when he saw her he began to play.

Meta's heart jumped at the first note. She stole along, drinking in the sounds, no one molesting or making her afraid. Ahead of her, as she climbed, the first range of hills cast a glowing reflection in her face; but the hills beyond were darker, cooler, and the blue-black pines stood out against the sky like trees of a far cloud-country cut off by some aerial gulf from the most venturesome of living feet.

Henniker saw the girl coming, her face alight in the primrose glow, and he threw away all moments but the present. His breath stopped; then he took a deep inspiration, laid his lips to the pipe, and played, softly, subtly, as one who thinks himself alone.

She had discovered him, but she could not drag herself very far away from those sounds. She sat down upon the ground, at last, and gave herself up to listening. A springy sagebush supported her as she let herself sink back; one arm was behind her head, to protect it from the prickly shoots.

"Meta," said Henniker, "are you listening? I'm talking to you now."

It was all the same; his voice was like another phrase of music. He went on playing, and Meta did not stir.

Another pause. "Are you there still, Meta? I was lonesome to-night, but you ran away from me. Was that friendly? You like my music; then why don't you like me? Well, here's for you again, ungrateful!" He went on playing.

The cows were wandering wide of the trail, towards the upper valley. Meta began to feel herself constrained, and not in the direction of her duty. She rose, cast her long braids over her shoulder, and moved resolutely away.

Henniker was absorbed in what he was saying to her with his pipe. When he had made a most seductive finish he paused, and spoke. He rose and looked about him. Meta was a long way off, down the valley, walking fast. He bounded after her, and caught her rudely around the waist.

"See here, little girl, I won't be made game of like this! I was playing to you, and you ran off and left me tooting like a fool. Was that right?"

"I had to go; it is getting late. The music was too sweet. It made me feel as if I could cry." She lifted her long-lashed eyes swimming in liquid brightness. Henniker caught her hand in his.

"I was playing to you, Meta, as I play to no one else. Does a person steal away and leave another person discoursin' to the empty air? I didn't think you would want to make a fool of me."

Meta drew away her hand and pressed it in silence on her heart. No woman of Anglo-Saxon blood, without a vast amount of training, could have said so much and said it so naturally with a gesture so hackneyed.

Henniker looked at her from under his eyebrows, biting his mustache. He took a few steps away from her, and then came back.

"Meta," he said, in a different voice, "what was that thing you wore around your neck, the other night, at the minstrels—that filigree gold thing, eh?"

The girl looked up, astonished; then her eyes fell, and she colored angrily. No Indian or dog could hate to be laughed at more than Meta; and she had been so teased about her innocent make-believe necklace! Had the girls been spreading the joke? She had suddenly outgrown the childish good faith that had made it possible for her to deck herself out in it, and she wished never to hear the thing mentioned again. She hung her head and would not speak.

Henniker's suspicions were characteristic. Of course a girl like that must have a lover. Her face confessed that he had touched upon a tender spot.

"It was a pretty thing," he said coldly. "I wonder if I could get one like it for Callie?"

"I don't think Callie would wear one even if you gave it to her," Meta answered with spirit.

"I say, won't you tell me which of the boys it is, Meta? Won't I wear the life out of him, just!" he added to himself.

"Is what?"

"Your best fellah; the one who gave you that."

"There isn't any. It was nothing. I won't tell you what it was! I made it myself, there! It was only 'butter-balls.' "

"Oh, good Lord!" laughed Henniker.

Meta thought he was laughing at her. It was too much! The

107

sweetness of his music was all jangled in her nerves. Tears would come, and then more tears because of the first.

Had Meta been the child of her father, she might have been sitting, that night, in one of the vine-shaded porches of the houses on the line, with several young lieutenants at her feet, and in her wildest follies with them she would have been protected by all the traditions and safeguards of her class. As she was the child of her mother, instead, she was out on the hills with Henniker. And how should the squaw's daughter know the difference between protection and pursuit?

When Henniker put his arm around her and kissed the tears from her eyes, she would not have changed places with the proudest lady of the line—captain's wife, lieutenant's sweetheart, or colonel's daughter of them all. Her chief, who blew the trumpet, was as great a man in Meta's eyes as the officer who buckled on his sabre in obedience to the call.

As for Henniker, no girl's head against his breast had ever looked so womanly dear as Meta's; no shut eyelids that he had ever kissed had covered such wild, sweet eyes. He did not think of her at all in words, any more than of the twilight afterglow in which they parted, with its peculiar intensity, its pang of color. He simply felt her; and it was nearest to the poetic passion of any emotion that he had ever known.

That night Meta deceived her foster-mother, and lying awake beside Callie's empty cot, in the room which the two girls shared together, she treacherously prayed that it might be long before her sister's return. The wild white lily had opened, and behold the stain!

It had been a hard summer for Tim Meadows's family,—the second summer on a sagebrush ranch, their small capital all in the ground, the first hay crop ungathered, and the men to board as well as to pay. The boarding was Mrs. Tim's part; yet many a young wife would have thought that she had enough to do with her own family to cook and wash for, and her first baby to take care of.

"You'll get along all right," the older mothers encouraged her. "A summer baby is no trouble at all."

No trouble, when the trouble is twenty years behind us, among the joys of the past. But Tim's wife was wondering if she could hold out till cool weather came, when the rush of the farm work would be over, and her "summer baby" would be in short clothes and able to sit alone. The heat in their four-roomed cabin, in the midst of the treeless land, was an ordeal alone. To sleep in the house was impossible; the rooms and the windows were too small to admit enough air. They moved their beds outside, and slept like tramps under the stars; and the broad light awoke them at earliest dawn, and the baby would never sleep till after ten at night, when the dry Plains wind began to fan the face of the weary land. Even Callie, whose part in the work was subsidiary, lost flesh, and the roses in her cheeks turned sallow, in the month she stayed on the ranch; but she would have been ashamed to complain, though she was heartsick for a word from Henniker. He had written to her only once.

It was Mrs. Meadows who thought it high time that Callie should come home. She had found a good woman to take her daughter's place, and arranged the matter of pay herself. Tim had said they could get no help, but his mother knew what that meant; such help as they could afford to pay for was worse than none.

It seemed a poor return to Callie for her sisterly service in the valley to come home and find her lover a changed man. Mrs. Meadows said he was like all the soldiers she had ever known, — light come, light go. But this did not comfort Callie much, nor more to be reminded what a good thing it was she had found him out in time.

Henniker was not scoundrel enough to make love to two girls at once, two semi-sisters, who slept in the same room and watched each other's movements in the same looking-glass. It was no use pretending that he and Callie could "heat their broth over again;" so the coolness came speedily to a breach, and Henniker no longer openly, in fair daylight, took the path to the cottage gate. But there were other paths.

He had found a way to talk to Meta with his trumpet. He sent her messages at guard-mounting, as the guard was forming, when, as senior trumpeter, he was allowed a choice in the airs he played; and when he was orderly trumpeter, and could not come himself to say it, he sent her his good-night in the plaintive notes of taps.

This was the climax of Henniker's flirtations: all that went before had been as nothing, all that came after was much worse than nothing. It was the one sincere as it was the one poetic passion of his life; and had it not cost him his self-respect through his baseness to Callie, and the treachery and dissimulation he was teaching to an innocent child, it might have made him a faithful man. As it was, his soldier's honor slept; it was the undisciplined part of him that spoke to the elemental nature of the girl; and it was fit that a trumpet's reckless summons, or its brief inarticulate call, like the note of a wild bird to its mate, should be the language of his love.

Retreat had sounded, one evening in October, but it made no stir any more in the cottage where the girls had been so gay. Callie, putting tea on the table, remembered, as she heard the gun fire, how in the spring Henniker had said that when "sound off" was at six he would drop in to supper some night, and show her how to make *chili con carne,* a dish that every soldier knows who has served on the Mexican border. Her face grew hard, for these foolish, unsleeping reminders were as constant as the bugle calls.

The women waited for the head of the house; but as he did not come, they sat down and ate quickly, saving the best dish hot for him.

They had finished, and the room was growing dusk, when he came in breezily, and called at once, as a man will, for a light. Meta rose to fetch it. The door stood open between the fore-room and the kitchen, where she was groping for a lamp. Mr. Meadow's spoke in a voice too big for the room. He had just been conversing across the common with the quartermaster-sergeant, as the two men's footsteps diverged by separate paths to their homes.

"I hear there's going to be a change at the post!" he shouted. "The —th is going to leave this department, and C troop of the Second is coming from Custer. Sergeant says they are looking for orders any day now.

Mrs. Meadows, before she thought, glanced at Callie. The girl winced, for she hated to be looked at like that. She held up her head and began to sing audaciously, drumming with her fingers on the table:—

> " ' When my mother comes to know
> That I love the soldiers so,
> She will lock me up all day,
> Till the soldiers march away.' "

"What sort of a song is that?" asked her father sharply.

Callie looked him in the eyes. "Don't you know that tune?" said she. "Henniker plays that at guard-mount; and sometimes he plays this:—

> " ' Oh, whistle, and I'll come to you, my lad,
> Though father and mither and a' should go
> mad.' "

"Let him play what he likes," said the father angrily. "His saucy jig tunes are nothing to us. I'm thankful no girl of mine is following after the army. It's a hard life for a woman, I can tell you, in the ranks."

Callie pushed her chair back, and looked out of the window as if she had not heard.

"Where's Meta with that lamp? Go and see what's keeping her."

"Sit still," said Mrs. Meadows. She went herself into the kitchen, but no one heard her speak a word, yet the kitchen was not empty.

There was a calico-covered lounge that stood across the end of the room; Meta sat there, quite still, her back against the wall. Mrs. Meadows took one look at her; then she lighted the lamp and carried it into the dining-room, and went back and shut herself in with Meta.

" ' When my mother comes to know,' "

hummed Callie. Her face was pale. She hardly knew that she was singing.

"Stop that song!" her father shouted. "Go and see what's the matter with your sister."

"Sister?" repeated Callie. "Meta is no sister of mine."

"She's your tent-mate, then. Ye grew nest ripe under the same mother's wing."

"Meta can use her own wings now, you will find. She grew nest-ripe very young."

Father Meadows knew that there was trouble inside of that closed door, as there was trouble inside the white lips and shut heart of his frank and joyous Callie, but it was "the women's business." He went out to attend to his own.

Irrigation on the scale of a small cottage garden is tedious work. It has intervals of silence and leaning on a hoe while one little channel fills or trickles into the next one; and the water must be stopped out here, and floated longer there, like the bath over the surface of an etcher's plate. Water was scarce and the rates were high, that summer, and there was a good deal of "dry-point" work with a hoe in Father Meadows's garden.

He had come to one of the discouraging places where the ground was higher than the water could be made to reach without a deal of propping and damming with shovelfuls of earth. This spot was close to the window of the kitchen chamber, which was "mother's room." She was in there talking to Meta. Her voice was deep with the maternal note of remonstrance; Meta's was high and sharp with excitement and resistance. Her faintness had passed, but Mother Meadows had been inquiring into causes.

"I am married to him, mother! He is my husband as much as he can be."

"It was never Father Magrath married you, or I should be knowing of it before now."

"No, we went before a judge, or a justice, in the town."

"In town! Well, that is something; but be sure there is a wrong or a folly somewhere when a man takes a young girl out of her home and out of her church to be married. If Henniker had taken you 'soberly, in the fear of God' "—

"He *was* sober!" cried Meta. "I never saw him any other way."

"Mercy on us! I was not thinking of the man's habits. He's too good to have done the way he has. That's what I have against him. I don't know what I shall say to Father Josette. The disgrace of this in on me, too, for not looking after my house better. 'Never let her be humbled through her not being all white,' the father said when he brought you to me, and God knows I never forgot that you little heart was white. I trusted you as I would one of my own, and was easier on you for fear of a mother's natural bias toward her own flesh and blood; and now to think that you would lie to me, and take a man in secret that had deceived your sister before you—as if nothing mattered so that you got what you wanted! And down in the town, without the priest's blessing or a kiss from any of us belonging to you! It's one way to get married, but it's not the right way."

"Did no white girl ever do as I have?" asked Meta, with a touch of sullenness.

"Plenty of them, but they didn't make their mothers happy."

Meta stirred restively on the bed. "Will Father Magrath have to talk to me, and Father Josette, and *all* the fathers?" she inquired. "He said he never would have married Callie anyway,—not even if he couldn't have had me."

"And the more shame to him to say such a thing to one sister of another! Callie is much the best off of you two." Mrs. Meadows rose and moved heavily away from the bed. "Well," she said, "most marriages are just one couple more. It's very little of a sacrament there is about the common run of such things, but I hoped for something better when it came to my girls' turn. However, sorrow is the sacrament God sends us, to give us a chance to learn a little something before we die. I expect you'll learn your lesson."

She came back to the bed, and Meta moaned as she sat down again, to signify that she had been talked to enough. But the mother had something practical to say, though she could not say it without emotional emphasis, for her outraged feelings were like a flood that has come down, but has not yet subsided.

"If there's any way for you to go with Henniker when the troop goes, it's with him you ought to be; but if he has married without his captain's consent, he'll get no help at barracks. Do you know how that is, Meta?"

Meta shook her hear; presently she forced herself to speak the truth. She did know that Henniker had told no one at the post of his marriage. She had never asked him why, nor had thought that it mattered.

"Oh my! I was afraid of that," said Mrs. Meadows. "The major knows it was Callie he was engaged to. Father went up to see him about Henniker, and the major as good as gave his word for him that he was a man we could have in the family. A commanding officer doesn't like such goings-on with respectable neighbors."

Mrs. Meadows possibly overestimated the post commandant's interest in these matters, but she had gratefully remembered his civility to her husband when he went to make fatherly inquiries. The major was a father himself, and had seemed to appreciate their anxiety about Callie's choice. It was just as well that Meta should know that none of the constituted authorities were on the side of her lover's defection.

Meta said nothing to all this. It did not touch her only as it bore on the one question, Was Henniker going to leave her behind him?

"How long is it since you have seen him, that he hasn't told you this news himself?" asked the mother.

"Last night; but perhaps he did not know."

Henniker had known, as Mrs. Meadows supposed, but having to shift for himself in the matter of transportation for the wife he had never acknowledged, and seeing no way of providing for her without considerable inconvenience to himself, he had put off the pain of breaking to her the parting that must come. In their later consultations Meta had mentioned her "pony money," as she called it, and Henniker had privately welcomed the existence of such a fund. It lightened the pressure of his own responsibility in the future, in case—but he did not formulate his doubts. There are more uncertainties than anything else, except hard work, in the life of an enlisted man.

Father Meadows purposely would not speak of Meta's resources. He felt that Henniker had not earned his confidence in this or any other respect where his girls were concerned. Till Meta should come of age—she was barely sixteen—or until it could be known what sort of a husband she had got in Henniker, her bit of money was safest in her guardian's hands.

So the orders came, and the transfer of troops was made; and now it was the trumpeter of C troop that sounded the calls, and Henniker's bold messages at guard-mounting and his tender good-night at taps called no more across the plain. The summer lilies were all dead on the hills, and the common was white with snow. But something in Meta's heart said, —

> " ' Weep no more! Oh, weep no more!
> Young buds sleep in the root's white core.' "

And she dried her eyes. The mother was very gentle with her, and Callie, hard-eyed, saying nothing, watched her, and did her little cruel kindnesses that cut to the quick of her soreness and her pride.

When the Bannock brethren came, late in September, the next year, she walked the sagebrush paths to their encampment with her young son in her arms. They looked at the boy and said that it was good; and when they asked after the father, and Meta told them that he had gone with his troop to Fort Custer, and that she waited for word to join him, they said it was not good, and they turned away their eyes in silence from her shame. The men did, but the women looked at her in a silence that said different things. Her heart went out to them, and their dumb soft glances brought healing to her wounds. What sorrow, what humiliation, was hers that they from all time had not known? The men took little notice of her after that: she had lost caste both as maid and wife; she was nothing now but a means of existence to her son. But between her and her dark sisters the natural bond grew strong. Old lessons that had lain dormant in her blood revived with the force of her keener intelligence, and supplanted later teachings that were of no use now except to make her suffer more.

It was impossible that Mother Meadows should not resent the wrong and insult to her own child; she felt it increasingly as she came to realize the girl's unhappiness. It grew upon her, and she could not feel the same towards Meta, who kept herself more and more proudly and silently aloof. She was one alone in the house, where no one spoke of the past to reproach her, where nothing but kindness was ever shown. The kindness was like the hand of pardon held out to her. Why did they think she wanted their forgiveness? She was not sorry for what she had done. She wanted nothing, only Henniker. So she crept away with her child and sat among the Bannock women, and was at peace with them whom she had never injured; who beheld her unhappiness, but did not call it her shame.

When she walked the paths across the common, her eyes were always on the skyward range of hills that appeared to her farther away than ever, beyond a wider gulf, now that their tops were white and the clouds came low enough to hide them. Often yellow gleams shot out beneath the clouds and turned the valleys green. It seemed to her that Henniker was there; he was in the cold, bright north, and the trumpets called her, but she could not go, for the way was very long. Such words as these she would sometimes whisper to her dark sisters by the camp-fire, and once they said to her, "Get strong and go; we will show you the way."

Henniker was taking life as it comes to an enlisted man in barracks. He thought of Meta many times, and of his boy, very tenderly and shamefully; and if he could have whistled them to him, or if a wind of luck could have blown them thither, he would have embraced them with joy, and shared with them all that he had. There was the difficulty. He had so little besides the very well fitting clothes on his back. His pay seemed to melt away, month by month, and where it went to the mischief only knew. Canteen got a good deal of it. Henniker was one of the popular men in barracks, with his physical expertness, his piping and singing and story-telling, and his high good humor at all times with himself and everybody else. He did not drink much except in the way of comradeship, but he did a good deal of that. He was a model trumpeter, and a very ornamental fellow when he rode behind his captain on full-dress inspection, more bedight than the captain himself with gold cords and tags and bullion; but he was not a domestic man, and the only person in the world who might perhaps have made him one was a very helpless, ignorant little person, and—she was not there.

It was a bad season for selling ponies. The Indians had arrived late with a larger band than usual, which partly represented an unwise investment they had made on the strength of their good fortune the year before. Certain big ditch enterprises had been starting then, creating a brisk demand for horses at prices unusual, especially in the latter end of summer. This year the big ditch had closed down, and was selling its own horses, or turning them out upon the range, and unbroken Indian ponies could hardly be given away.

The disappointment of the Bannocks was very great, and their comprehension of causes very slow. It took sometime for them to satisfy themselves that Father Meadows was telling them a straight tale. It took more time still for consultations as to what should now be done with their unsalable stock. The middle of October was near, and the grumbling chiefs finally decided to accept their loss and go hunting. The squaws and children were ordered home to the Reservation by rail, as wards of the nation travel, to get permission of the agent for the hunt, and the men, with their ponies, were to ride overland and meet the women at Eagle Rock.

Thus Meta learned how an Indian woman may pass unchallenged from one part of the country to another, clothed in the freedom of her poverty. In this way the nation acknowledges a part of its ancient indebtedness to her people. No word had come from Henniker, though he had said that he should get his discharge in October. Meta's resolve was taken. The Bannock women encouraged her, and she saw how simple it would be to copy their dress and slip away with them as far as their roads lay together; and thence, having gained practice in her part and become accustomed to its disguises, to go on alone to Custer, where her chief, her beautiful trumpeter, was sounding his last calls. She was wise in this resolution to see her husband, at whatever cost, before the time of his freedom should come; but she was late in carrying it out.

Long before, she had turned over fruitlessly in her mind every means of getting money for this journey besides the obvious way of asking Father Meadows for her own. She had guessed that her friends were suspicious of Henniker's good faith, and believed that if they should come to know of her intention of running away to follow him they would prevent her for her own good, —which was quite the case.

That was the point Father Meadows made with his wife, when she argued that Meta, being a married woman now, ought to learn the purchasing power of money and its limitations by experimenting with a little of her own.

"We shall do wrong if we keep her a child now," she said.

"But if she has money, she'll lay it by till she get enough to slip off to her soldier with. There's that much Injun about her; she'll follow to heel like a dog."

Father Meadows could not have spoken in this way of Meta a year ago. She had lost caste with him, also.

"Don't, father," the mother said, with a hurt look. "She'll not follow far with ten dollars in her pocket; but that much I want to try her with. She's like a child about shopping. She'll take anything at all, if it looks right and the man persuades her. And those Jew clerks will charge whatever they think they can get."

Mrs. Meadows had her way, and the trial sum was given to Meta one day, and the next day she and the child were missing.

At dusk, that evening, a group of Bannock squaws, more or less encumbered with packs and children, climbed upon one of the flat cars of a freight train bound for Pocatello. The engine steamed out of the station, and down the valley, and away upon the autumn plains. The next morning the Bannocks broke camp, and vanished before the hoar frost had melted from the sage. Their leave-taking had been sullen, and their answers to questions about Meta, with which Father Meadows had routed them out in the night, had been so unsatisfactory that he took the first train to the Fort Hall Agency. There he waited for the party of squaws from Bisuka; but when they came, Meta was not with them. They knew nothing of her, they said; even the agent was deceived by their counterfeit ignorance. They could tell nothing, and were allowed to join their men at Eagle Rock, to go hunting into the wild country around Jackson's Hole.

Father Meadows went back and relieved his wife's worst fear,—that the girl had fulfilled the wrong half of her destiny, and gone back to hide her grief in the bosom of her tribe.

"Then you'll find her at Custer," said she. "You must write to the quartermaster-sergeant. And be sure you tell him she's married to him. He may be carrying on with someone else by this time."

Traveling as a ward of the nation travels; suffering as a white girl would suffer, from exposure and squalor, weariness and dirt, but bearing her misery like a squaw, Meta came at last to Custer station. In five days, always on the outside of comforts that other travelers pay for, she had passed from the lingering mildness of autumn in southern Idaho into the early winter of the hard Montana north.

She was only fit for a sick-bed when she came into the empty station at Custer, and learned that she was still thirty miles away from the fort. In her make-believe broken English, she asked a humble question about transportation. The station-keeper was called away that moment by a summons from the wire. It was while she stood listening to the tapping of the message, and waiting to repeat her question, that she felt a frightening pain, sharp, like a knife sticking in her breast. She could take only short breaths, yet longed for deep ones to brace her lungs and strengthen her sick heart. She stepped outside and spoke to a man who was wheeling freight down the platform. She dared not throw off her fated disguise and say, "I am the wife of Trumpeter Henniker. How shall I get to the fort?" for she had stolen a ride of a thousand miles, and she knew not what the penalty of discovery might be. She had borrowed a squaw's wretched immunity, and she must pay the price for that which she had rashly coveted. She pulled her blanket about her face and muttered, "Which way—Fort Custer?"

The freight man answered by pointing to the road. Dark wind clouds rolled along the snow-white tops of the mountains. The plain was a howling sea of dust.

"No stage?" she gasped.

The man laughed and shook his head. "There's the road. Injuns walk." He went on with his baggage-truck, and did not look at her again. He had not spoken unkindly: the fact and his blunt way of putting it were equally a matter of course. Squaws who "beat" their way in on freight trains do not go out by stage.

Meta crept away in the lee of a pile of freight, and sat down to nurse her child. The infant, like herself, had taken harm from exposure to the cold; his head passages were stopped, and when he tried to nurse he had to fight with suffocation and hunger both, and threw himself back in the visible act of screaming, but his hoarse little pipe was muted to a squeak. This, which sounds grotesque in the telling, was acute anguish for the mother to see. She covered her face with her blanket, and sobbed and coughed, and the pain tore her like a knife. But she rose, and began her journey. She had little conception of what she was undertaking, but it would have made no difference; she must get there on her feet, since there was no other way.

She no longer carried her baby squaw-fashion. She was out of sight of the station, and she hugged it where the burden lay heaviest, on her heart. Her hands were not free, but she had cast away her bundle of food; she could eat no more; and the warmth of the child's nestling body gave her all the strength she had,—that and her certainty of Henniker's welcome. That he would be faithful to her presence she never doubted. He would see her coming, perhaps, and he would run to catch her and the child together in his arms. She could feel the thrill of his eyes upon her and the half groan of joy with which he would strain her to his breast. Then she would take one deep, deep breath of happiness,—ah, that pain!—and let the anguish of it kill her if it must.

The snows on the mountains had come down and encompassed the whole plain; the winter's siege had begun. The winds were iced to the teeth, and they smote like armed men. They encountered

Meta carrying some precious hidden thing to the garrison at Custer; they seized her and searched her rudely, and left her, trembling and disheveled, sobbing along with her silly treasure in her arms. The dust rose in columns, and traveled with mocking becks and bows before her, or burst like a bomb in her face, or circled about her like a band of wild horses lashed by the hooting winds.

Meantime, Henniker, in span-new civilian dress, was rattling across the plain on the box seat of the ambulance, beside the soldier driver. The ambulance was late to catch the east-bound train, and the paymaster was inside; so the four stout mules laid back their ears and traveled, and the heavy wheels bounded from stone to stone of the dust-buried road. Henniker smoked hard in silence, and drew great breaths of cold air into his splendid lungs. He was as warm and clean and sound and fit, from top to toe. He had been drinking bounteous farewells to a dozen good comrades, and though sufficiently himself for all ordinary purposes, he was not that self he would have wished to be had he known that one of the test moments of his life was before him. It was a mood with him of headlong, treacherous quiet, and the devil of all foolish desires was showing him the pleasures of the world. He was in dangerously good health; he had got his discharge, and was off duty and off guard, all at once. He was a free man, though married. He was going to his wife, of course. Poor little Meta! God bless the girl, how she loved him! Ah, those black-eyed girls, with narrow temples and sallow, deep-fringed eyelids, they knew how to love a man! He was going to her by way of Laramie, or perhaps the coast. He might run upon a good thing over there, and start a bit of a home before he sent for her or went to fetch her; it was all one. She rested lightly on his mind, and he thought of her with a tender, reminiscent sadness,—rather a curious feeling considering that he was to see her now so soon. Why was she always "poor little Meta" in his thoughts?

Poor little Meta was toiling on, for "Injuns walk." The dreadful pain of coughing was incessant. The dust blinded and choked her, and there was a roaring in her ears which she confused with the night and day burden of the trains. She was in a burning fever that was fever and chill in one, and her mind was not clear, except on the point of keeping on; for once down, she felt that she could never get up again. At times she fancied she was clinging to the rocking, roaring platforms she had ridden on so long. The dust swirled around her—when had she breathed anything but dust! The ground swam like water under her feet. She swayed, and seemed to be falling,—perhaps she did fall. But she was up and on her feet, the blanket cast from her head, when the ambulance drove straight towards her, and she saw him—

She had seen it coming, the ambulance, down the long, dizzy rise. The hills above were white as death; a crooked gash of color rent the sky; the toothed pines stood black against that gleam, and through the ringing in her ears, loud and sweet, she heard the trumpets call. The cloud of delirium lifted, and she saw the uniform she loved; and beside the soldier driver sat her white chief, looking down at her who came so late with joy, bringing her babe,—her sheaves, the harvest of that year's wild sowing. But he did not seem to see her. She had not the power to speak or cry. She took one step forward and held up the child.

Then she fell down on her face in the road, for the beloved one had seen her, and had not known her, and had passed her by. And God would not let her make one sound.

How in Heaven's name could it have happened! Could any man believe it of himself? Henniker put it to his reason, not to speak of conscience or affection, and never could explain, even to himself, that most unhappy moment of his life. If he had not a heart for any helpless thing in trouble, who had? He was the joke of the garrison for his softness about dogs and women and children. Yet he had met his wife and baby on the open road, and passed them by, and owned them not, and still he called himself a man.

What he had seen at first had been the abject figure of a little squaw facing the wind, her bowed head shrouded in her blanket, carrying something which her short arms could barely meet around,—a shapeless bundle. He did not think it a child, for a squaw will pack her baby always on her back. He had looked at her indifferently, but with condescending pity; for the day was rough, and the road was long, even for a squaw. Then, in all the disfigurement of her dirt and wretchedness and wild attire, it broke upon him that this creature was his wife, the rightful sharer of his life and freedom; and that animal-like thing she held up, that wrung its face and squeaked like a blind kitten, was his son.

Good God! He clutched the driver's arm, and the man swore and jerked his mules out of the road, for the woman had stopped right in the track where the wheels were going. The driver looked back, but could not see her; he knew that he had not touched her, only with the wind of his pace, so he pulled the mules into the road again, and the ambulance rolled on.

"Stop; let me get off. That woman is my wife." Henniker heard himself saying the words, but they were never spoken to the ear. "Stop; let me get down," the inner voice prompted; but he did not make a sound, and the curtains flapped and the wheels went bounding along. They were a long way past the spot, and the station was in sight, when Henniker was heard to say hoarsely, "Pick her up, can't you, as you go back?"

"Pick up which?" asked the driver.

"The—that woman we passed just now."

"I'll see how she's making it," the man answered coolly. "I ain't much stuck on squaws. Acted like she was drunk or crazy."

Henniker's face flushed, but he shuddered as if he were cold.

"Pick her us, for the child's sake, by God!" No man was ever more ashamed of himself than he as he took out a gold piece and handed it to the soldier. "Give her this, Billy—from yourself, you know. I ain't in it."

Billy looked at Henniker, and then at the gold piece. It was a double eagle; all that the husband had dared to offer as alms to his wife, but more than enough to arouse the suspicions that he feared.

"Ain't in it, eh?" thought the soldier. "You knew the woman, and she knew you. This is conscience money." But aloud he said, "A fool and his money are soon parted. How do you know but I'll blow it in at canteen?"

"I'll trust you," said Henniker.

The men did not speak to each other again.

"She's one of them Bannocks that camped by old Pop Meadows's place, down at Bisuka, I bet," said the soldier to himself.

Henniker went on fighting his fight as if it had not been lost forever in that instant's hesitation. A man cannot bethink himself: "By the way, it strikes me that was my wife and child we passed on the road!" What he had done could never be explained without grotesque lying which would deceive nobody.

It could not be undone; it must be lived down. Henniker was much better at living things down than he was at explaining or trying to mend them.

After all, it was the girl's own fault, putting up that wretched squaw act on him. To follow him publicly, and shame him before all the garrison, in that beastly Bannock rig! Had she turned Bannock altogether and gone back to the tribe? In that case let the tribe look after her; he could have no more to do with her, of course.

He stepped into the smoking-car, and lost himself as quickly as

121

possible in the interest of new faces around him, and the agreeable impressions of himself which he read in eyes that glanced and returned for another look at so much magnificent health and color and virility. His spot of turpitude did not show through. He was still good to look at; and to look the man that one would be goes a long way toward feeling that one is that man.

II.

It was at Laramie, between the mountains, and Henniker was celebrating the present and drowning the past in a large, untrammeled style, when he received a letter from the quartermaster-sergeant at Custer—a plain statement until the end, where Henniker read: —

"If you should happen at any time to wish for news of your son, Meadows and his wife have taken the child. They came on here to get him, and Meadows insisted on standing the expense of the funeral, which was the best we could give her for the credit of the troop. He put a handsome stone over her, with 'Meta, wife of Trumpeter Henniker, K Troop —th U.S. Cavalry,' on it; and there it stands to her memory, poor girl, and to your shame, a false, cruel, and cowardly man in your treatment of her. And so everyone of us holds you, officers and men the same—of your old troop that walked behind her to her grave. And where were you, Henniker, and what were you doing this day two weeks, when we were burying your poor wife? The twenty dollars you sent her by Billy, Meadows has, and says he will keep it till he sees you again. Which some of us think it will be a good while he will be packing that Judas piece around with him.—And so good-by, Henniker. I might have said less, or I might have said nothing at all, but that the boy is a fine child, my wife says, and must have a grand constitution to stand what he has stood; and I have a fondness for you myself when all is said and done.

"P.S. I would take a thought for that boy once in a while, if I was you. A man doesn't care for the brats when he is young, but age cures us of all wants but the want of a child."

But Henniker was not ready to go back to the Meadows cottage and be clothed in the robe of forgiveness, and receive his babe like a pledge of penitence on his hand.

The shock of the letter sobered him at first, and then the sting of it drove him to drinking harder than ever. He did not run upon that "good thing" at Laramie, nor in any of the cities westward that one after another beheld the progress of his deterioration. It does not take long in the telling, but it was several years before he finally struck upon the "Barbary Coast" in San Francisco, where so many mothers' sons who never were heard of have gone down. He went ashore, but he did not quite go to pieces. His constitution had matured under healthy conditions, and could stand a good deal of ill-usage; but we are "no stronger than our weakest part," and at the end of all he found himself in a hospital bed under treatment for his knee,—the same that had been mulcted for him twice before.

He listened grimly to the doctor's explanations,—how the past sins of his whole impenitent system were being vicariously reckoned for through this one afflicted member. It was rough on his old knee, Henniker remarked; but he had hopes of getting out all right again, and he made the usual sick-bed promises to himself. He did get out, eventually, without a penny in the world, and with a stiff knee to drag about for the rest of his life. And he was just thirty-four years old.

His splendid vitality, that had been wont to express itself in so many attractive ways, now found its chief vent in talk—inexpensive, inordinate, meddlesome discourse—wherever two or three were gathered together in the name of idleness and discontent. The members of these congregations were pessimists to a man. They disbelieved in everybody and everything except themselves, and secretly, at times, they were even a little shaken on that head; but all the louder they exclaimed upon the world that had refused them the chance to be the great and successful characters nature had intended them to be.

It need hardly be said that when Henniker raved about the inequalities of class, the helplessness of poverty, the tyranny of wealth, and the curse of labor; and devoted in eloquent phrases the remainder of a blighted existence to the cause of the "Poor Man," he was thinking of but one poor man, namely, himself. He classed himself with "Labor" only as he might feel his superiority to the laboring masses. There were few situations in which he could taste his superiority, in these days. The "ego" in his Cosmos was very hungry; his memories were bitter, his hopes unsatisfied; his vanity and artistic sense were crucified through poverty, lameness, and bad clothes. Now all that was left him was the conquests of the mind. For the smiles of women, give him the hoarse plaudits of men. The dandy of the garrison began to shine in saloon coteries and primaries of the most primary order. He was the star of sidewalk convocations and vacant lot meetings of the Unemployed. But he despised the mob that echoed his perorations and paid for his drinks, and was at heart the aristocrat that his old uniform had made him.

In the summer of 1894, a little black-eyed boy with chestnut curls used to swing on the gate of the Meadows cottage that opens upon the common, and chant some verses of domestic doggerel about Coxey's army, which was then begging and bullying its way eastward, and demanding transportation at the expense of the railroads and of the people at large.

He sang his song to the well-marked tune of Pharaoh's Army, and thus the verses ran: —

> "The Coxeyites they gathered,
> The Coxeyites they gathered,
> And stole a train of freight-cars in the morn,
> And stole a train of freight-cars in the morning,
> And stole a train of freight-cars in the morn.

> "The engine left them standing,
> The engine left them standing,
> On the railroad-track at Caldwell in the morn.
> Very sad it was for Caldwell in the morning
> To feed that hungry army in the morn.

> "Where are all the U.S. marshals,
> The deputy U.S. marshals,
> To jail that Coxey army in the morn,
> That 'industrious, law-abiding' Coxey's army
> That stole a train of freight-cars in the morn?"

Where indeed were all the U.S. marshals? The question was being asked with anxiety in the town, for a posse of them had gone down to arrest the defiant train-stealers, and it was rumored that the civil arm had been disarmed, and the deputies carried on as prisoners to Pocatello, where the Industrials, two hundred strong, were intrenched in the sympathies of the town, and knocking the federal authorities about at their law-abiding pleasure. Pocatello is a division town on the Union Pacific Railroad; it is full of the company's shops and men, the latter all in the American Railway Union or the Knights of Labor, and solid on class issues, right or wrong; and it was said that the master workman was expected at Pocatello to speak on the situation, and, if need arose, to call out the trades all over the land in support of the principle that tramp delegations shall not walk. Disquieting rumors were abroad, and there was relief in the news that the regulars had been called on to sustain the action of the federal court.

The troops at Bisuka barracks were under marching orders. While the town was alert to see them go they tramped away one evening, just as a shower was clearing that had emptied the streets of citizens; and before the ladies could say "There they go," and call each other to the windows, they were gone.

Then for a few days the remote little capital, with Coxeyites gathering and threatening its mails and railroad service, waited in apprehensive curiosity as to what was going to happen next. The party press on both sides seized the occasion to point a moral on their own account, and some said, "Behold the logic of McKinleyism," and others retorted, "Behold the shadow of the Wilson Bill stalking abroad over the land. Let us fall on our faces and pray!" But most people laughed instead, and patted the Coxeyites on the back, preferring their backs to their faces.

It seemed as if it might be time to stop laughing and gibing and inviting the procession to move on, when a thousand or more men, calling themselves American citizens, were parading their idleness through the land as authority for lawlessness and crime, and when our sober regulars had to be called out to quell a Falstaff's army. The regulars, be sure, did not enjoy it. If there is a sort of service our soldiers would like to be spared, doubtless it is disarming crazy Indians; but they prefer even that to standing up to be stoned and insulted and chunked with railroad iron by a mob which they are ordered not to fire upon, or to entering a peaceful country which has been sown with dynamite by patriotic labor unions, or prepared with cut-bridges by sympathetic strikers.

We are here to be hurt, so the strong ones tell us, and perhaps the best apology the strong can make to the weak for the vast superiority that training gives is to show how long they can hold their fire amidst a mob of brute ignorances, and how much better they can bear their hurts when the senseless missiles fly. We love the forbearance of our "unpitied strong;" it is what we expect of them; but we trust also in their firmness when the time for forbearance is past.

Little Ross Henniker—named for that mythical great Scotchman, his supposed grandfather—was deeply disappointed because he did not see the soldiers go. To have lived next door to them all his life, seven whole years, and watched them practicing and preparing to be fit and ready to go, and then not to see them when they did march away for actual service in the field, was hard indeed.

Ross was not only one of those brightest boys of his age known to parents and grandparents by the million, but he was really a very bright and handsome child. If Mother Meadows, now "granny," had ever had any doubts at all about the Scottish chief of the Hudson's Bay Company, the style and presence of that incomparable boy were proof enough. It was a marked case of "throwing-back." There was none of the Bannock here. Could he not be trusted like a man to do whatever things he liked to do; as riding to fetch the cows and driving them hillward again, on the weird little spotted pony, hardly bigger than a dog, with a huge head and a furry cheek and a hanging underlip, which the tributary Bannocks had brought him? It was while he was on cow-duty far away, but not out of sight of the post, that he saw the column move. "Great Scott!" how he did ride! He broke his stick over the pony's back, and kicked him with his bare heels, and slapped him with his hat, till the pony bucked him off into a sagebush, whence he picked himself up and flew as fast as his own legs would spin; but he was too late. Then, for the first time in six months at least, he howled. Aunt Callie comforted him with fresh strawberry jam for supper; but the lump of grief remained, until, as she was washing the dishes, she glanced at him, laughing out of the corner of her eye, and began to make up the song about Coxey's army. For some time Ross refused to smile, but when it came to the chorus about the soldiers who were going

"To turn back Coxey's army, hallelujah!
To turn back Coxey's army, halleloo!"

he began to sing "hallelujah" too. Then gun-fire broke in with a lonesome sound, as if the cavalry up on the hill missed its comrades of the white stripes who were gone to "turn back" that ridiculous army.

Mother Meadows wished "that man Coxey had never been born," so weary did she get of the Coxey song. Coxeyism had taken complete possession of the young lord of the house, now that his friends the soldiers had gone to take a hand in the business.

In a few days the soldiers came back escorting the Coxey prisoners. The "presence of the troops" had sufficed. The two hundred Coxeyites were to be tried at Bisuka for crimes committed within the State. They were penned meanwhile in a field by the river, below the railroad track, and at night they were shut into a rough barrack which had been hastily put up for the purpose. A skirt of the town little known, except to the Chinese vegetable gardeners and makers of hay on the river meadows and small boys fishing along the shore, now became the centre of popular regard; and "Have you been down to the Coxey camp?" was as common a question as "Are you going to the Natatorium Saturday night?" or "Will there be a mail from the West today?"

One evening, Mother Meadows, with little Ross Henniker by the hand, stood close to the dead-line of the Coxey field, watching the groups on the prisoners' side. The woman looked at them with perplexed pity, but the child swung himself away and cried, "Pooh! only a lot of dirty hobos!" and turned to look at the soldiers.

The tents of the guard of regulars stood in a row in front of a rank of tall poplar-trees, their tops swinging slow in the last sunlight. Behind the trees stretched the green river-flats in shadow. Frogs were croaking; voices of girls could be heard in a tennis-court with a high wall that ran back to the street of the railroad.

Roll-call was proceeding in front of the tents, the men firing their quick, harsh answers like scattering shots along the line. Under the trees at a little distance the beautiful sleek cavalry horses were grouped, unsaddled and calling for their supper. Ross Henniker gazed at them with a look of joy; then he turned a contemptuous eye upon the prisoners.

"Which of them two kinds of animals looks most like what a man ought to be?" he asked, pointing to the horses and then to the Coxeyites, who in the cool of the evening were indulging in unbeautiful horse-play, not without a suspicion of showing off before the eyes of visitors. The horses in their free impatience were as unconscious as lords.

"What are you saying, Ross?" asked Mrs. Meadows, rousing herself.

"I say, suppose I'd just come down from the moon, or some place where they don't know a man from a horse, and you said to me: 'Look at these things, and then look at them things over there, and say which is boss of t'other.' Why, I'd say *them* things, everytime." Ross pointed without prejudice to the horses.

"My goodness!" cried Mrs. Meadows, "if these Coxeys had been taken care of and coddled all their lives like them troop horses, they might not be so handsome, but they'd look a good deal better than what they do. And they'd have more sense," she added in a lower voice. "Very few poor men's sons get the training those horses have had. They've learned to mind, for one thing, and to be faithful to the hand that feeds them."

"Not all of them don't," said Ross, shaking his head wisely. "There's kickers and biters and shirks amongst them; but if they won't learn and can't learn, they get 'condemned.' "

"And what becomes of them then?"

"Why, you know," answered the boy, who began to suspect that there was a moral looming in the distance of this bold generalization.

"Yes," said Mother Meadows, "I know what becomes of some of them, because I've seen; and I don't think a condemned horse looks much better in the latter end of him than a condemned man."

"But you can't leave them in the troop, for they'd spoil all the rest," objected the boy.

"It's too much for me, dear," replied the old woman humbly. "These Coxeys are a kind of folks I don't understand."

"I should think you might understand, when the troops have to go out and run 'em in! I'm on the side of the soldiers, every time."

"Well, that's simple enough," said Mrs. Meadows. She was a very mild protagonist, for she could never confine herself to one side of a question. "I'm on the side of the soldiers, too. A soldier has to do what he's told, and pays with his life for it, right or wrong."

"And I think it's a shame to send the beautiful clean soldiers to shove a lot of dirty hobos back where they belong."

"My goodness! Hush! you'd better talk less till you get more sense to talk with," said Mrs. Meadows sternly. A man standing near, with his back to them, had turned around quickly, and she saw by his angry eye that he had overheard. She looked at him again, and knew the man. It was the boy's father. Ross had bounded away to talk to his friend Corporal Niles.

"Henniker!" exclaimed Mrs. Meadows in a low voice of shocked amazement. "It don't seem as if this could be you!"

"Let that be!" said Henniker roughly. "I didn't enlist by that name in this army. Who's that young son of a gun that's got so much lip on him?"

"God help you! Don't you know your own son?"

"What? No! Has he got to be that size already?" The man's weather-beaten face turned a darker red under the week-old beard that disfigured it. He sat down on the ground, for suddenly he felt weak, and also to hide his lameness from the woman who should have hated him, but who simply pitied him instead. Her face showed a sort of motherly shame for the change that she saw in him. It was very hard to bear. He had not realized fully the change in himself till its effect upon her confronted him. He tried to bluff it off carelessly.

"Bring the boy here. I have a word to say to him."

"You should have said it long ago, then." Mrs. Meadows was hurt and indignant at his manner. "What has been said is said, for good and all. It's too late to unsay it now."

"What do you mean by that, Mrs. Meadows? Am I the boy's father or am I not?"

"You are not the father he knows. Do you think I have been teaching him to be ashamed of the name he bears?"

"Old lady," cried Henniker the Coxeyite, "have you been stuffing that boy about his dad as you did the mother about hers?"

"I have told him the truth, partly. The rest, if it was not the truth, ought to have been," answered Mrs. Meadows stoutly. "I have put the story right, as an honest man would have lived it. Whatever you've been doing with yourself these years, it's your own affair, not the boy's nor mine. Keep it to yourself now. You were too good for them once,—the mother and the child; they can do without you now."

"That's all right," said Henniker, wincing; "but as a matter of curiosity let me hear how you have put it up."

"How I have what?"

"How you have dressed up the story to the boy. I'd like to see myself with a woman's eyes once more."

Mrs. Meadows looked him over and hesitated; then her face kindled. "I've told him that his father was a beautiful clean man," she said, using unconsciously the boy's words, "and rode a beautiful horse, and saluted his captain so!" She pointed to the corporal of the guard who was at that moment reporting. "I told him that when the troops went you had to leave your young wife behind you, and she could not be kept from following you with her child; and by a cruel mischance you passed each other on the road, and you never knew till you had got to her old home and heard she was dead and buried; and you were so broke up that you couldn't bear your life in the place where you used to be with her; and you were a sorrowful wandering man that he must pray for, and ask God to bring you home. You never came near us, Henniker, or thought of coming; but could I tell your own child that? Indeed, I would be afraid to tell him what did happen on that road from Custer station, for fear when he's a man

129

he'd go hunting you with a shotgun. Now where is the falsehood here? Is it in me, or in you, who have made it as much as your own life is worth to tell the truth about you to your son? *Was* it the truth, Henniker? Sure, man, you did love her! What did you want with her else? Was it the truth that they told us at Custer? There are times when I can't believe it myself. If there is a word you could say for yourself,—say it, for the child's sake! You wouldn't mind speaking to an old woman like me? There was a time when I would have been proud to call you my son."

"You are a good woman, Mrs. Meadows, but I cannot lie to you, even for the child's sake. And it's not that I don't know how to lie, for God knows I'm nothing but a lie this blessed minute! What do I care for such cattle as these?" He had risen, and waved his hand contemptuously toward his fellow-martyrs. "Well, I must be going. I see they're passin' around the flesh-pots. We're livin' like fighting-cocks here, on a restaurant contract. There'll be a big deal in it for the marshal, I suspect." Henniker winked, and his face fell into the lowest of its demoralized expressions.

"There's no such thing!" said Mrs. Meadows indignantly. "Some folks are willing to work for very little these hard times, and give good value for their money. You had better eat and be thankful, and leave other folks alone!"

Little Ross coming up heard but the last words, and saw his granny's agitation and the familiar attitude of the strange Coxeyite. His quick temper flashed out: "Get out with you! Go off where you belong, you dirty man!"

Mrs. Meadows caught the boy, and whirled him around and shook him. "Never, never let me hear you speak like that to any man again!"

"Why?" he demanded.

"I'll tell you why, someday, if I have to. Pray God I may never need to tell you!"

"Why?" repeated the boy, wondering at her excitement.

"Come away,—come away home!" she said, and Ross saw that her eyes were red with unshed tears. He hung behind her and looked back.

"He's lame," said he, half to himself. "I wouldn't have spoken that way if I'd known he had a game leg."

"Who's lame?" asked Mrs. Meadows.

"The Coxeyite. See. He limps bad."

"Didn't I tell you! We never know, when we call names, what sore spots we may be hitting. You may have sore spots of your own someday."

"I hope I sha'n't be lame," mused the boy. "And I hope I sha'n't be a Coxey."

The Coxeyites had been in a camp a fortnight when their trial began. Twice a day the prisoners were marched up the streets of Bisuka to the court-house, and back again to camp, till the citizens became accustomed to the strange, unrepublican procession. The prisoners were herded along the middle of the street; on either side of them walked the marshals, and outside of the line of civil officers the guard of infantry or cavalry, the officers riding and the men on foot.

This was the last march of the Coxeyites. Many citizens looking on were of the opinion that if these men desired to make themselves an "object-lesson" to the nation, this was their best chance of being useful in that capacity.

For two weeks, day by day, in the prisoner's field, Henniker had been confronted with the contrast of his old service with his present demoralization. He had been a conspicuous figure among the Industrials until they came in contact with the troops, and then suddenly he subsided, and was heard and seen as little as possible. Not for all that a populist congress could vote, out of the pockets of the people into the pockets of the tramp petitioners, would he have posed as one of them before the eyes of an officer, or a man, of his old regiment, who might remember him as Trumpeter Henniker of K troop. But the daily march to the court-house was the death-sickness of his pride. Once he had walked these same streets with his head as high as any man's; and it had been, "How are you, Henniker?" and "Step in, Henniker;" or Callie had been laughing and falling out of step on his arm, or Meta—poor little Meta—waiting for him when the darkness fell!

Now the women ran to the windows and crowded the porches, and stared at him and his ill-conditioned comrades as if they had been animals belonging to a different species.

But Henniker was mistaken here. The eyes of the pretty girls were for the "pretty soldiers." It was all in the day's work for the soldiers, who tramped indifferently along; but the officers looked bored, as if they were neither proud of the duty nor of the display of it which the times demanded.

On the last day's march from the court-house to the camp, there was a clamor of voices that drowned the shuffling and tramping of the feet. The prisoners were all talking at once, discussing the sentences which the court had just announced: the leaders and those taken in acts of violence to be imprisoned at hard labor for specified times; the rank and file to be put back on their stolen progress as far westward, whence they came, as the borders of the State would allow; there to be staked out, as it were, on the banks of the Snake River, and guarded for sixty days by the marshals, supported by the inevitable "presence of the troops."

But the sentence that Henniker heard was that private one which his own child had spoken: "Get out with you! Go back where you belong, you dirty man!" He had wished at the time that he could make the proud youngster feel the sting of his own lash: but that thought had passed entirely, and been merged in the simple hurt of a father's longing for his son. "If he were mine," he bitterly confessed, "if that little cock-a-whoop rascal would own me and love me for his dad, I swear to God I could begin my life again! But now, what next?"

There had been a stoppage ahead, the feet pressing on had slackened step, when there, with his back to the high iron gates of the capitol grounds, was the beautiful child again. A young woman stood beside him, a fine, wholesome girl like a full-blown cottage rose, with auburn hair, an ivory-white throat, and a back as flat as a trooper's. It was Callie, of course, with Meta's child. The cup of Henniker's humiliation was full.

The boy stood with his chin up, his hat on the back of his head, his plump hands spread on the hips of his white knickerbockers. He was dressed in his best, as he had come from a children's fête. Around his neck hung a prize which he had won in the games, a silver dog-whistle on a scarlet ribbon. He caught it to his lips and blew a long piercing trill, his dark eyes smiling, the wind blowing the short curls across his cheek.

"There he is, the lame one! I made him look round," said Ross.

Henniker had turned, for one long look—the last, he thought—at his son. All the singleness and passion of the mother, the fire and grace and daring of the father, were in the promise of his childish face and form. He flushed, not a self-conscious, but an honest, generous blush, and took his hat away off his head to the lame Coxeyite—"because I was mean to him; and they are down and done for now, the Coxeys."

"Whose kid is that?" asked the man who walked beside Henniker, seeing the gesture and the look that passed between the man and the boy. "He's as handsome as they make 'em," he added, smiling.

Henniker did not reply in the proud word "Mine." A sudden heat rushed to his eyes, his chest was tight to bursting. He pulled his hat down and tramped along. The shuffling feet of the prisoners passed on down the middle of the street; the double line of guards kept step on either side. The dust arose and blended the moving shapes, prisoners and guards together, and blotted them out in the distance.

Callie had not seen her old lover at all. "Great is the recuperative power of the human heart." She had been looking at Corporal Niles, who could not turn his well-drilled head to look at her. But a side-spark from his blue eye shot out in her direction, and made her blush and cease to smile. Corporal Niles carried his head a little higher and walked a little straighter after that; and Callie went slowly through the gates, and sat a long while on one of the benches in the park, with her elbow resting on the iron scroll and her cheek upon her hand.

She was thinking about the Coxeyites' sentence, and wondering if the cavalry would have to go down to the stockade prison on the Snake; for in that case Corporal Niles would have to go, and the wedding be postponed. Everybody knows it is bad luck to put off a wedding-day; and besides, the yellow roses she had promised her corporal to wear would all be out of bloom, and no other roses but those were the true cavalry yellow.

But the cavalry did not go down till after the wedding, which took place on the evening appointed at the Meadows cottage between "Sound off" and "Taps." The ring was duly blessed, and the father's and mother's kiss was not wanting. The primrose radiance of the summer twilight shone as strong as lamplight in the room, and Callie, in her white dress, with her auburn braids gleaming through the wedding veil and her lover's colors in the roses on her breast, was as sweet and womanly a picture as any mother could wish to behold.

When little Ross came up to kiss the bride, he somehow forgot, and flung his arms first around Corporal Niles's brown neck.

"Corporal, I'm twice related to the cavalry now," said he. "I had a father in it, and now I've got an uncle in it."

"That's right," the corporal agreed; "and if you have any sort of luck you'll be in it yourself someday."

"But not in the ranks," said Ross firmly. "I'm going to West Point, you know."

"Bless his heart!" cried Callie, catching the boy in her arms; "and how does he think he's going to get there?"

"I shall manage it somehow," said Ross, struggling. He was very fond of aunt Callie, but a boy doesn't like to be hugged so before his military acquaintances, and in Ross's opinion there had been a great deal too much kissing and hugging, not to speak of crying, already. He did not see why there should be all this fuss just because Aunt Callie was going up to the barracks to live, in the jolliest little whitewashed cabin, with a hop-vine hanging, like the veil on an old woman's bonnet, over the front gable. He only wished that the corporal had asked him to go too!

A slight misgiving about his last speech was making Ross uncomfortable. If there was a person whose feelings he would not have wished to hurt for anything in the world, it was Corporal Niles.

"Corporal," he amended affectionately, "if I should be a West Pointer, and should be over you, I shouldn't put on any airs, you know. We should be better friends than ever."

"I expect we should, captain. I'm looking forward to the day."

A mild species of corvée had been put in force down on the Snake River while the stockade prison was building. The prisoners as a body rebelled against it, and were not constrained to work; but a few were willing, and these were promptly stigmatized as "scabs," and ill-treated by the lordly idlers. Hence they were given a separate camp and treated as trusties.

When the work was done, the trusties were rewarded with their freedom, either to go independently, or to stay and eat government rations till the sixty days of their sentence had expired.

Henniker, in spite of his infirmity, had been one of the hardest volunteer workers. But now the work was done, and the question returned. What next?

Again he was a free man, as he sat one evening by the river. A dry embankment, warm as an oven to the touch, sloped up to the railroad track above his head; tufts of young sage and broken stone strewed the face of it; there was not a tree in sight. He heard the river boiling down over the rapids and thundering under the bridge. He heard the trumpets calling the men to quarters. "Lights out" had sounded some time before. He had been sitting motionless, his knees drawn up, his head resting on his crossed arms. The sound of the trumpets made him choke up like a homesick boy. He sat there till, faintly in the distance, "Taps" breathed its slow and sweet good-night.

"Last call," he said. "Time to turn in." He took off the rags in which his child had spurned him.

"The next time I'm inspected," he muttered, "I shall be a clean man." So, naked, he slipped into the black water under the bank. The river bore him up and gave him one more chance, but he refused it; with two strokes he was in the midst of the death-current, and it seized him and took him down.

On A Side-Track

It was the second week in February, but winter had taken a fresh hold; the stockmen grumbled, freight was dull, and travel light on the white Northwestern lines.

In the Portland car from Omaha there were but four passengers: father and daughter,—a gentle, unsophisticated pair,—and two strong-faced men, fellow-travelers also, keeping each other's company in a silent but close and conspicuous proximity. They shared the same section, the younger man sleeping above, going to bed before, and rising later than, his companion; and whenever he changed his seat or made an unexpected movement, the eyes of the elder man followed him, and they were never far from him at any time.

The elder was a plain farmer type of man, with a clean-shaven, straight upper lip, a grizzled beard covering the lower half of his face, and humorous wrinkles spreading from the corners of his keen gray eyes.

The younger showed in his striking person that union of good blood with hard conditions so often seen in the old-young graduates of the life schools of the West. His hands and face were dark with exposure to the sun, not of parks and club-grounds and seaside piazzas, but the dry, untempered light of the desert and the plains. His dark eye was distinctively masculine,—if there be such a thing as gender in features,—bold, ardent, and possessive; but now it was clouded with sadness which did not pass like a mood, though he looked capable of moods.

He was dressed in the demi-toilet which answers for dinners in the West, on occasions where a dress-coat is not required. In itself the costume was correct, even fastidious, in its details, but on board an overland train there was a foppish unsuitability in it that "gave the wearer away," as another man would have said—put him at a disadvantage, notwithstanding his admirable physique, and the sad, rather fine preoccupation of his manner. He looked like a very real person dressed for a trifling part, which he lays aside between the scenes while he thinks about his sick child, or his debts, or his friend with whom he has quarreled.

But these incongruities, especially the one of dress, might easily have escaped a pair of eyes so confiding and unworldly as those of the young girl in the opposite section; they had escaped her, but not the incongruity of youth with so much sadness. The girl and her father had boarded the car at Omaha, escorted by the porter of one of the forward sleepers on the same train. They had come from farther East. The old gentleman appeared to be an invalid; but they gave little trouble. The porter had much leisure on his hands, which he bestowed in making up arrears of sleep on the end seat forward. The conductor made up his accounts in the empty drawing-rooms, or looked at himself in mirrors, or stretched his legs on the velvet sofas. He was a young fellow, with a tendency to jokes and snatches of song and talk of a light character when not on duty. He talked sometimes with the porter in low tones, and then both looked at the pair of travelers in No. 8, and the younger man seemed moodily aware of their observation.

On the first morning out from Omaha the old gentleman kept his berth until nine or ten o'clock. At eight his daughter brought him a cup of chocolate and a sandwich, and sat between his curtains, chatting with him cozily. In speaking together they used the language of the Society of Friends.

The young man opposite listened attentively to the girl's voice; it was as sweet as the piping of birds at daybreak. Phebe her father called her.

Afterward Phebe sat in the empty section next her father's. The table before her was spread with a fringed doily, and a few pieces of old household silver and china which she had taken from her lunch-basket. She and her father were economical travelers, but in all their belongings there was the refinement of modest suitability and an exquisite cleanliness. Her own order for breakfast was confined to a cup of coffee, which the porter was preparing in the buffet-kitchen.

"Would you mind changing places with me?"

The young man in No. 8 spoke to his companion, who sat opposite reading a newspaper. They changed seats, and by this arrangement the younger could look at Phebe, who innocently gave him every advantage to study her sober and delicate profile against the white snow-light as she sat watching the dreary cattle-ranges of

Wyoming swim past the car window.

Her hair had been brushed, and her face washed in the bitter alkaline water of the plains, with the uncompromising severity of one whose standards of personal adornment are limited to the sternest ideals of neatness and purity. Yet her fair face bloomed, like a winter sunrise, with tints of rose and pearl and sapphire blue, and the pale gold of winter sunshine was in her satin-smooth hair.

The young man did not fail to include in his study of Phebe the modest breakfast equipment set out before her. He perfectly recalled the pattern of the white-and-gold china, the touch, the very taste, of the thin, bright old silver spoons; they were like his grandmother's tea-things in the family homestead in the country, where he had spent his summers as a boy. The look of them touched him nearly, but not happily, it would seem, from his expression.

The porter came with the cup of coffee, and offered a number of patronizing suggestions in the line of his service, which the young girl declined. She set forth a meek choice of food, blushing faintly in deprecation of the young man's eyes, of which she began to be aware. Evidently she was not yet hardened to the practice of eating in public.

He took the hint, and retired to his corner, opening a newspaper between himself and Phebe.

Presently he heard her call the porter in a small, ineffectual voice. The porter did not come. She waited a little, and called again, with no better result. He put down his newspaper.

"If you will press the button at your left," he suggested.

"The button!" she repeated, looking at him helplessly.

He sprang to assist her. As he did so his companion flung down his paper, and jumped in front of him. The eyes of the two met. A hot flush rose to the young man's eyebrows.

"I am calling the porter for her."

"Oh!" said the other, and he sat down again; but he kept an eye upon the angry youth, who leaned across Phebe's seat, and touched the electric button.

"Little girl hadn't got on to it, eh?" the grizzled man remarked pleasantly, when his companion had resumed his seat.

There was no answer.

"Nice folks; from the country, somewheres back East, I should guess," the imperturbable one continued. "Old man seems sort of sickly. Making a move on account of his health, likely. Great mistake—old folks turning out in winter huntin' a climate."

The young man remained silent, and the elder returned to his paper.

At Cheyenne, where the train halts for dinner, the young girl helped her father into his outer garments, buttoned herself hastily into her homespun jacket bordered with gray fur, pinned her little hat firmly to her crown of golden braids, hid her hands in her muff,—she did not wait to put on gloves,—and led the way to the dining-room.

The travelers in No. 8 disposed of their meal rapidly, in their usual close but silent conjunction, and returned at once to the car.

The old gentleman and his daughter walked the windy platform, and cast rather forlorn glances at the crowd bustling about in the bleak winter sunlight. When they took their seats again, the father's pale blue eyes were still paler, his face looked white and drawn with the cold; but Phebe was like a rose: with her wonderful, pure color the girl was beautiful. The young man of No. 8 looked at her with startled reluctance, as if her sweetness wounded him.

Then he seemed to have resolved to look at her no more. He leaned his head back in his corner, and closed his eyes; the train shook him slightly as he sat in moody preoccupation with his thoughts, and the miles of track flew by.

At Green RIver, at midnight, the Portland car was dropped by its convoy of the Union Pacific, and was coupled with a train making up for the Oregon Short Line. There was hooting and backing of engines, slamming of car doors, flashing of conductors' lanterns, voices calling across the tracks. One of these voices could be heard, in the wakeful silence within the car, as an engine from the west steamed past in the glare of its snow-wreathed headlight.

"No. 10 stuck this side of Squaw Creek. Bet you don't make it before Sunday!"

The outbound conductor's retort was lost in the clank of couplings as the train lurched forward on the slippery rails.

"Phebe, is thee awake?" the old gentleman softly called to his daughter, about the small hours.

"Yes, father. Want anything?"

"Are those ventilators shut? I feel a cold draft in the back of my berth."

The ventilators were all shut, but the train was now climbing the Wind River divide, the cold bitterly increasing, and the wind dead ahead. Cinders tinkled on the roaring stove-pipes, the blast swept the car roofs, pelting the window-panes with fine, dry snow, and searching every joint and crevice defended by the company's upholstery.

Phebe slipped behind the berth-curtains, and tucked a shawl in at her father's back. Her low voice could be heard, and the old man's self-pitying tones in answer to her tender questionings. He coughed at intervals till daybreak, when there was silence in section No. 7.

In No. 8, across the aisle, the young man lay awake in the strength of his thoughts, and made up passionate sentences which he fancied himself speaking to persons he might never be brought face to face with again. They were people mixed in with his life in various relations, past and present, whose opinions had weighed with him. When he heard Phebe talking to her father, he muttered, with a sort of anguish:

"Oh, you precious lamb!"

He and his companion made their toilet early, and breakfasted and smoked together, and their taciturn relation continued as before. Snow filled the air, and blotted out the distance, but there were few stationary dark objects outside by which to gage its fall. They were across the border now, between Wyoming and Idaho, in a featureless white region, a country of small Mormon ranches, far from any considerable town.

The old man slept behind his curtains. Phebe went through the morning routine by which women travelers make themselves at home and pass the time, but obviously her day did not begin until her father had reported himself. She had found a hole in one of her gloves, which she was mending, choosing critically the needle and the silk for the purpose from a very complete housewife in brown linen bound with a brown silk galloon. Again the young man was reminded of his boyhood, and of certain kind old ladies of precise habits who had contributed to his happiness, and occasionally had eked out the fond measure of paternal discipline.

The snow continued; about noon the train halted at a small water-station, waited awhile as if in consideration of difficulties ahead, and then backed quietly down upon a side-track. A shock of silence followed. Every least personal movement in the thinly peopled car, before lost in the drumming of the wheels, asserted itself against this new medium. The passengers looked up and at one another; the Pullman conductor stepped out to make inquiries.

The silence continued, and became embarrassing. Phebe dropped her scissors. This time the young man sat still, but the flush rose to his forehead as before. The old gentleman's breathing could be heard behind his curtains; the porter rattling plates in the cooking-closet; the soft rustling of the snow outside. Phebe stepped to her father's berth, and peeped between his curtain; he was still sleeping. Her voice was hushed to the note of a sick-room as she asked:

"Where are we now, do you know?"

The young man was looking at her, and to him she addressed the question.

With a glance at his companion, he crossed to her side of the car, and took the seat beside her.

"We are in the Bear Lake Valley, just over the border of Idaho, about fifteen miles from the Squaw Creek divide," he answered, sinking his voice.

"Did you hear what that person said in the night, when a train passed us, about our not getting through?"

"I wondered if you heard that." He smiled. "You did not rest well, I'm afraid."

"I was anxious about father. This weather is a great surprise to us. We were told the winters were short in southern Idaho—almost like Virginia; but look at this!"

"We have nearly eight thousand feet of altitude here, you must remember. In the valleys it is warmer. There the winter does break usually about this time. Are you going on much farther?"

"To a place called Volney."

"Volney is pretty high; but there is Boisé City, farther down. Strangers moving into a new country very seldom strike it right the first time."

"Oh, we shall stay at Volney, even if we do not like it; that is, if we can stay. I have a married sister living there. She thought the climate would be better for father."

After a pause she asked, "Do you know why we are stopping here so long?"

"Probably because we have had orders not to go any farther."

"Do you mean that we are blocked?"

"The train ahead of us is. We shall stay here until that gets through."

"You seem very cheerful about it," she said, observing his expression.

"Ah, I should think so!"

His short lip curled in the first smile she had seen upon his strong, brooding face. She could not help smiling in response, but she felt bound to protest against his irresponsible view of the situation.

"Have you so much time to spend upon the road? I thought the men of this country were always in a hurry."

"It makes a difference where a man is going, and on what errand, and what fortune he meets with on the way. *I* am not going to Volney."

She did not understand his emphasis, nor the bearing of his words. His eyes dropped to her hands lying in her lap, still holding the glove she had been mending.

"How nicely you do it! How can you take such little stitches without pricking yourself, when the train is going?"

"It is my business to take little stitches. I don't know how to do anything else."

"Do you mean it literally? Is it your business to sew?"

The notion seemed to surprise him.

"No, I mean in a general sense. Some of us can do only small things, a stitch at a time,—take little steps, and not know always where they are going."

"Is this a little step—to Volney?"

"Oh, no; it is a very long one, and rather a wild one, I'm afraid. I suppose everybody does a wild thing once in a lifetime?"

"How should *you* know that?"

"I only said so. I don't say that it is true."

"People who take little steps are sometimes picked up and carried off their feet by those who take long, wild ones."

"Why, what are we talking about?" she asked herself, in surprise."

"About going to Volney, was it not?" he suggested.

"What is there about Volney, please tell me, that you harp upon the name? I am a stranger, you know; I don't know the country allusions. Is there anything peculiar about Volney?"

"She is a deep little innocent," he said within himself; "but oh, so innocent!" And again he appeared to gather himself in pained resistance to some thought which jarred with the thought of Phebe. He rose and bowed and so took leave of her, and settled himself back into his corner, shading his eyes with his hand.

He ate no luncheon, Phebe noticed, and he sat so long in a dogged silence that she began to cast wistful glances across the aisle, wondering if he were ill, or if she had unwittingly been rude to him. Anyone could have shaken her confidence in her own behavior; moreover, she reminded herself, she did not know the etiquette of an overland train. She had heard that the Western people were very friendly; no doubt they expected a frank response in others. She resolved to be more careful the next time, if the moody young man should speak to her again.

Her father was awake now, dressed and sitting up. He was very chipper, but Phebe knew his color was not natural, nor his breathing right. He was much inclined to talk, in a rambling, childish, excited manner that increased her anxiety.

The young man in No. 8 had evidently taken his fancy; his formal, old-fashioned advances were modestly but promptly met.

"I suppose it is not usual, in these parts, for travelers to inquire each other's names?" said the old gentleman to his new acquaintance; "but we seem to have plenty of time on our hands; we might as well improve it socially. My name is David Underhill, and this is my daughter Phebe. Now what might thy name be, friend?"

"My name is Ludovic," said the youth, looking a half-apology at Phebe, who saw no reason for it.

"First or family name?"

"Ludovic is my family name."

"And a very good name it is," said the old gentleman. "Not a common name in these parts, I should say, but one very well and highly known to me," he added, with pleased emphasis. "Phebe, thee remembers a visit we had from Martin Ludovic when we were living at New Rochelle?"

"Thee knows I was not born when you lived at New Rochelle, father dear."

"True, true! It was thy mother I was thinking of. She had a great esteem for Martin Ludovic. He was one of the world's people, as we say—in the world, but not of the world. Yet he made a great success in life. He was her father's junior partner; rose from a clerk's stool in his counting-room—and a great success he made of it. But that was after Friend Lawrence's time. My wife was Phebe Lawrence."

Young Ludovic smiled brightly in reply to this information, and seemed about to speak, but the old gentleman forestalled him.

"Friend Lawrence had made what was considered a competence in those days—a very small one it would be called now; but he was satisfied. Thee may not be aware that it is a recommendation among the Friends, and it used to be a common practice, that when a merchant had made a sufficiency for himself and those depending on him, he should show his sense of the favor of Providence by stepping out and leaving his chance to the younger men. Friend Lawrence did so—not to his own benefit ultimately, though that was no one's fault that ever I heard; and Martin Ludovic was his successor, and a great and honorable business was the outcome of his efforts. Now does thee happen to recall if Martin is a name in thy branch?"

"My grandfather was Martin Ludovic of the old New York house of Lawrence and Ludovic," said the cadet of that name; but as he gave these credentials a profound melancholy subdued his just and natural pride.

"Is it possible!" Friend Underhill exulted, more pleased than if he had recovered a lost bank-note for many hundreds. There are no people who hold by the ties of blood and family more strongly than the Friends; and Friend Underhill, on this long journey, had felt himself sadly insolvent in those sureties which cannot be packed in a trunk or invested in irrigable lands. It was as if on the wild, cold seas he had crossed the path of a bark from home. He yearned to have speech with this graciously favored young man, whose grandfather had been his Phebe's grandfather's partner and dearest friend. The memory of that connection had been cherished with ungrudging pride through the succeeding generations in which the Ludovics had gone up in the world and the Lawrences had come down. Friend Underhill did not recall—nor would he have thought it of the least importance that a Lawrence had been the benefactor in the first place, and had set Martin Ludovic's feet upon the ladder of success. He took the young man's hand affectionately in his own, and studied the favor of his countenance.

"Thee has the family look," he said in a satisfied tone; "and they had no cause, as a rule, to be discontented with their looks."

Young Ludovic's eyes fell, and he blushed like a girl; the dark-red blood dyed his face with the color almost of shame. Phebe moved uneasily in her seat.

"Make room beside thee, Phebe," said her father; "or, no, friend Ludovic; sit thee here beside me. If the train should start, I could hear thee better. And thy name—let me see—thee must be a Charles Ludovic. In thy family there was always a Martin, and then an Aloys, and then a Charles; and it was said—though a foolish superstition, no doubt—that the king's name brought ill luck. The Ludovic whose turn it was to bear the name of the unhappy Stuart took with it the misfortunes of three generations."

"A very unjust superstition I should call it," pronounced Phebe.

"Surely, and a very idle one," her father acquiesced, smiling at her warmth. "I trust, friend Charles, it has been given thee happily to disprove it in thy own person."

"On the contrary," said Charles Ludovic, "if I am not the unluckiest of my name, I hope there may never be another."

He spoke with such conviction, such energy of sadness, only silence could follow the words. Then the old gentleman said most gently and ruefully:

"If it be indeed as thee says, I trust it will not seem an intrusion, in one who knew thy family's great worth, to ask the nature of thy trouble—if by chance it might be my privilege to assist thee. I feel of rather less than my usual small importance—cast loose, as it were, between the old and the new; but if my small remedies should happen to suit with thy complaint, it would not matter that they were trifling—like Phebe's drops and pellets she puts such faith in," he added, with a glance at his daughter's downcast face.

"Dear sir, you *have* helped me, by the gift of the outstretched hand. Between strangers, as we are, that implies a faith as generous as it is rare."

"Nay, we are not strangers; no one of thy name shall call himself stranger to one of ours. Shall he, Phebe? Still, I would not importune thee—"

"I thank you far more than you can know; but we need not talk of my troubles. It was a graceless speech of mine to obtrude them."

"As thee will. But I deny the lack of grace. The gracelessness was mine to bring up a foolish saying, more honored in the forgetting."

Here Phebe interposed with a spoonful of the medicine her father had referred to so disparagingly. "I would not talk anymore now, if I were thee, father. Thee sees how it makes thee cough."

At this, Ludovic rose to leave them; but Phebe detained him, shyly doing the honors of their quarters in the common caravan. He stayed, but a constrained silence had come upon him. The old gentleman closed his eyes, and sometimes smiled to himself as he sat so, beside the younger man, and Phebe had strange thoughts as she looked at them both. Her imagination was greatly stirred. She talked very easily and with perfect unconsciousness to Ludovic, and told him little things she could remember having heard about the one generation of his family that had formerly been connected with her own. She knew more about it, it appeared, than he did. And more and more he seemed to lose himself in her eyes, rather than to be listening to her voice. He sat with his back to his companion across the aisle; at length the latter rose, and touched him on the shoulder. He turned instantly, and Phebe, looking up, caught the hard, roused expression which altered him into the likeness of another man.

"I am going outside." No more was said, but Ludovic rose, bowed to Phebe, and followed his curt fellow-passenger.

"What can be the connection between them?" thought the girl. "They seem inseparable, yet not friends precisely. How could they be friends?" And in her prompt mental comparison the elder man inevitably suffered. She began to think of all the tragedies with which young lives are fatalistically bound up; but it was significant that none of her speculations included the possibility of anything in the nature of error in respect to this Charles Ludovic who called himself unhappy.

II.

"Stop a moment. I want to speak to you," said Ludovic. The two men were passing through the gentlemen's toilet-room; and Ludovic turned his back to the marble wash-stand, and waited, with his head up, and the tips of his long hands resting in his trousers' pockets. "I have a favor to ask of you, Mr. Burke."

"Well, sir, what's the size of it?"

"You must have heard some of our talk in there; you see how it is? They will never, of themselves, suspect the reason of your fondness for my company. Is it worthwhile, for the time we shall be together, to put them on to it? It's not very easy, you see; make it as easy as you can."

"Have I tried to make it hard, Mr. Ludovic?"

"Not at all. I don't mean that."

"Am I giving you away most of the time?"

"Of course not. You have been most awfully good. But you're—you're damnably in my way. I see you out of the corner of my eye always, when you aren't square in front of me. I can't make a move but you jump. Do you think I am such a fool as to make a break now? No, sir; I am going through with this; I'm in it most of the time. Now see here, I give you my word—and there are no liars of my name—that you will find me with you at Pocatello. Till then let me alone, will you? Keep your eyes off me. Keep out of range of my talk. I would like to say a word now and then without knowing there's a running comment in the mind of a man across the car, who thinks he knows me better than the people I am talking to—understand?"

"Maybe I do, maybe I don't," said Mr. Burke, deliberately. "I don't know as it's any of my business what you say to your friends, or what they think of you. All I'm responsible for is your person."

"Precisely. At Pocatello you will have my person."

"And have I got your word for the road between?"

"My word, and my thanks—if the thanks of a man in my situation are worth anything."

"I'm dum sorry for you, Mr. Ludovic, and I don't mind doing what little I can to make things easy—" Mr. Burke paused, seeing his companion smile. "Well, yes, I know it's hard—it's dooced almighty hard; and it looks like there was a big mistake somewheres, but it's no business of mine to say so. Have a cigar?"

Young Mr. Ludovic had accepted a number of Mr. Burke's palliative offers of cigars during their journey together; he accepted the courtesy, but he did not smoke the cigars. He usually gave them to the porter. He had an expensive taste in cigars, as in many other things. He paid for his high-priced preferences, or he went without. He was never willing to accept any substitute for the thing he really wanted; and it was very hard for him, when he had set his heart upon a thing, not to approach it in the attitude that an all-wise Providence had intended it for him.

About dusk the snow-plow engines from above came down for coal and water. They brought no positive word, only that the plows and shovelers were at work at both ends of the big cut, and they hoped the track would be free by daybreak. But the snow was still falling as night set in.

Ludovic and Phebe sat in the shadowed corner behind the curtains of No. 7. Phebe's father had gone to bed early; his cough was worse, and Phebe was treating him for that and for the fever which had developed as an attendant symptom. She was a devotee in her chosen school of medicine; she knew her remedies within the limits of her household experience, and used them with the courage and constancy that are of no school, but which better the wisdom of them all.

Ludovic observed that she never lost count of the time through all their talk, which was growing more and more absorbing; he was jealous of the interruption when she said, "Excuse me," and looked at her watch, or rose and carried her tumblers of medicine alternately to the patient, and woke him gently; for it was now a case for strenuous treatment, and she purposed to watch out the night, and give the medicines regularly every hour.

147

Mr. Burke was as good as his word; he kept several seats distant from the young people. He had a private understanding, though, with the car officials; not that he put no faith in the word of a Ludovic, but business is business.

When he went to his berth about eleven o'clock he noticed that his prisoner was still keeping the little Quaker girl company, and neither of them seemed to be sleepy. The table where they had taken supper together was still between them, with Phebe's watch and the medicine tumblers upon it. The panel of looking-glass reflected the young man's profile, touched with gleams of lamplight, as he leaned forward with his arms upon the table.

Phebe sat far back in her corner, pale and grave; but when her eyes were lifted to his face they were as bright as winter stars.

It was Ludovic's intention, before he parted with Phebe, to tell her his story—his own story; the newspaper account of him she would read, with all the world, after she had reached Volney. Meantime he wished to lose himself in a dream of how it might have been could he have met this little Phebe, not on a side-track, his chance already spoiled, but on the main line, with a long ticket, and the road clear before them to the Golden Gate.

Under other circumstances she might not have had the same overmastering fascination for him; he did not argue that question with himself. He talked to her all night long as a man talks to the woman he has chosen and is free to win, with but a single day in which to win her; and underneath his impassioned tones, shading and deepening them with tragic meaning, was the truth he was withholding. There was no one to stand between Phebe and this peril, and how should she know whither they were drifting?

He told her stories of his life of danger and excitement and contrasts, East and West; he told her of his work, his ambitions, his disappointments; he carried her from city to city, from camp to camp. He spoke to sparkling eyes, to fresh, thrilling sympathies, to a warm heart, a large comprehension, and a narrow experience. Every word went home; for with this girl he was strangely sure of himself, as indeed he might have been.

And still the low music of his voice went on; for he did not lack that charm, among many others—a voice for sustained and moving speech. Perhaps he did not know his own power; at all events, he was unsparing of an influence the most deliberate and enthralling to which the girl had ever been subjected.

He was a Ludovic of that family her own had ever held in highest consideration. He was that Charles Ludovic who had called himself unhappiest of his name. Phebe never forgot this fact, and in his pauses, and often in his words, she felt the tug of that strong undertow of unspoken feeling pulling him back into depths where even in thought she could not follow him.

And so they sat face to face, with the watch between them ticking away the fateful moments. For Ludovic life ended at Pocatello, but not for Phebe.

What had he done with that faith they had given him—the gentle, generous pair! He had resisted, he thought that he was resisting, his mad attraction to this girl—of all girls the most impossible to him now, yet the one, his soul averred, most obviously designed for him. His wild, sick fancy had clung to her from the moment her face had startled him as he took his last backward look upon the world he had forfeited.

His prayer was that he might win from Phebe, before he left her at Pocatello, some sure token of her remembrance that he might dwell upon and dream over in the years of his buried life.

It would not have been wonderful, as the hours of that strange night flew by, if Phebe had lost a moment now and then, had sometimes wandered from the purpose of her vigil. Her thoughts strayed, but they came back duly, and she was constant to her charge. Through all that unwholesome enchantment her hold upon herself was firm, through her faithfulness to the simple duties in which she had been bred.

Meanwhile the train lay still in the darkness, and Ludovic thanked God, shamelessly, for the snow. How the dream outwore the night and strengthened as morning broke gray and cold, and quiet with the stillness of the desert, we need not follow. More and more it possessed him, and began to seem the only truth that mattered.

He took to himself all the privileges of her protector; the rights, indeed—as if he could have rights such as belong to other men, now, in regard to any woman.

If the powers that are named of good or evil, according to the will of the wisher, had conspired to help him on, the dream could not have drawn closer to the dearest facts of life; but no spells were needed beyond those which the reckless conjurer himself possessed—his youth, his implied misfortunes, his unlikeness to any person she had known, his passion, "meek, but wild," which he neither spoke nor attempted to conceal.

And Phebe sat like a charmed thing while he wove the dream

about her. She could not think; she had nothing to do while her father slept; she had nowhere to go, away from this new friend of her father's choosing. She was exhausted with watching, and nervously unstrung. Her hands were ice; her color went and came; her heart was in a wild alarm. She blushed almost as she breathed, with his eyes always upon her; and blushing, could have wept, but for the pride that still was left her in this strange, unnerved excitement.

It was an ordeal which should have had no witnesses but the angels; yet it was seen of the porter and the conductor and Mr. Burke. The last was not a person finely cognizant of situations like this one; but he felt it and resented it in every fiber of his honest manhood.

"What's Ludovic doing?" he asked himself in heated soliloquy. "He's out of the running, and the old man's sick abed, and no better than an old woman when he's well. What's the fellow thinking of?"

Mr. Burke took occasion to ask him, when they were alone together—Ludovic putting the finishing touches to a shave; the time was not the happiest, but the words were honest and to the point.

"I didn't understand," said Mr. Burke, "that the little girl was in it. Now, do you call it quite on the square, Mr. Ludovic, between you and her? I don't like it, myself; I don't want to be a party to it. I've got girls of my own."

Ludovic held his chin up high; his hands shook as he worked at his collar-button.

"Have you got any boys?" he flung out in the tone of a retort.

"Yes, one about your age, I should guess."

"How would you like to see him in the fix I'm in?"

"I couldn't suppose it, Mr. Ludovic. My boy and you ain't one bit alike."

"Are your girls like her?"

"No, sir; they are not. I ain't worrying about them any, nor wouldn't if they was in her place. But there's points about this thing—"

"We'll leave the points. Suppose, I say, your boy was in my fix: would you grudge him any little kindness he might be able to cheat heaven, we'll say, out of between here and Pocatello?"

"Heaven can take care of itself; that little girl is not in heaven yet. And there's kindnesses and kindnesses, Mr. Ludovic. There's some that cost like the mischief. I expect you're willing to bid high on kindness from a nice girl, about now; but how about her? Has kindness gone up in her market? I guess not. That little creetur's goods can wait; she'd be on top in any market. I guess it ain't quite a square deal between her and you."

Ludovic sat down, and buried his hands in his pockets. His face was a dark red; his lips twitched.

"Are you going to stick to your bargain, or are you not?" he asked, fixing his eyes on a spot just above Mr. Burke's head.

"You've got the cheek to call it a bargain! But say it was a bargain. I didn't know, I say, that the little girl was in it. Your bank's broke, Mr. Ludovic. You ought to quit business. You got no right to keep your doors open, taking in money like hers, clean gold fresh from the mint."

"O Lord!" murmured Ludovic; and he may have added a prayer for patience with this common man who was so pitilessly in the right. A week ago, and the right had been easy to him. But now he was off the track; every turn of the wheels tore something to pieces.

"There are just two subjects I cannot discuss with you," he said, sinking his voice. "One is that young lady. Her father knows my people. She shall know me before I leave her. They say we shall go through to-night. You must think I am the devil if you think that, without the right even to dispense with your company, I can have much to answer for between here and Pocatello."

"You are as selfish as the devil, that's what I think; and the worst of it is, you look as white as other folks."

"Then leave me alone, or else put the irons on me. Do one thing or the other. I won't be dogged and watched and hammered with your infernal jaw! You can put a ball through me, you can handcuff me before her face; but my eyes are my own, and my tongue is my own, and I will use them as I please."

Mr. Burke said no more. He had said a good deal; he had covered the ground, he thought. And possibly he had some sympathy, even when he thought of his girls, with the young fellow who had looked too late in the face of joy and gone clean wild over his mischance.

It was his opinion that Ludovic would "get" not less than twenty-five years. There were likely to be Farmers' Alliance men on that jury; the prisoner's friends belonged to a clique of big monopolists; it would go harder with him than if he had been an honest miner, or a playful cow-boy on one of his monthly "tears."

When Ludovic returned to his section, Phebe had gone to sleep in the corner opposite, her muff tucked under one flushed cheek; the other cheek was pale. Shadows as delicate as the tinted reflections in the hollow of a snowdrift slept beneath her chin, and in the curves around her pathetic eyelids, and in the small incision that defined her pure red under lip. Again the angels, whom we used to believe in, were far from this their child.

Ludovic drew down all the blinds to keep out the glare, and sat in his own place, and watched her, and fed his aching dream. He did not care what he did, nor who saw him, nor what anybody thought.

In the afternoon he took her out for a walk. The snow had stopped; her father was up and dressed, and very much better, and Phebe was radiant. Her sky was clearing all at once. She charged the porter to call her in "just twenty minutes," for then she must give the medicine again. On their way out of the car Ludovic slipped a dollar into the porter's hand. Somehow that clever but corrupted functionary let the time slip by, to Phebe's innocent amazement. Could he have gone to sleep? Surely it must be more than twenty minutes since they had left the car.

"He's probably given the dose himself," said Ludovic. "A good porter is always three parts nurse."

"But he doesn't know which medicine to give."

"Oh, let them be," he said impatiently. "He's talking to your father, and making him laugh. He'll brace him up better than any medicine. They will call you fast enough if you are needed."

They walked the platform up and down in front of the section-house. They were watched, but Ludovic did not care for that now.

"Will you take my arm?"

She hesitated, in amused consideration of her own inexperience.

"Why, I never *did* take any one's arm that I remember. I don't think I could keep step with thee."

The intimate pronoun slipped out unawares.

"I will keep step with *thee*."

"I don't know that I quite like to hear you use that word."

"But you used it, just now, to me."

"It was an accident, then."

"Your father says 'thee' to me."

"He is of an older generation; my mother wore the Friends' dress. But those customs had a religious meaning for them to which I cannot pretend. With me it is a sort of instinct. I can't explain it, nor yet quite ignore it."

"Have I offended that particular instinct of yours which attaches to the word 'thee'?"

He seemed deeply chagrined. He was one who did not like to make mistakes, and he had no time to waste in apologizing and recovering lost ground.

"People do say it to us sometimes in fun, not knowing what the word means to us," said Phebe.

In the fresh winter air she was regaining her tone—escaping from him, Ludovic felt, into her own sweet, calm self-possession.

"Then you distinctly refuse me whatever—the least—that word implies? I am one of those who 'rush in'?"

"Oh, no; but you are much too serious. It is partly a habit of speech; we cannot lose the habit of speaking to each other as strangers in three days."

"You were never a stranger to me. I knew you from the first moment I saw you; yet each moment since you have been a fresh surprise."

"I cannot keep up with you," she said, slipping her hand out of his arm. In the grasp of his passionate dream he was striding along regardless, not of her, but of her steps.

"Oh, little steps," he groaned within himself—"oh, little doubting steps, why did we not meet before?"

Oh, blessed hampering steps, how much safer his would have gone beside them!

"What a charming pair!" cried a lady passenger from the forward sleeper. She too was walking, with her husband, and her eye had been instantly taken by the gentle girl with the delicate wild-rose color, halting on the arm of a splendid youth with daredevil eyes, who did not look as happy as he ought with that sweet creature on his arm.

"Isn't it good to know that the old stories are going on all the same?" said the sentimental traveler. "What do you say—will that story end in happiness?"

"I say that he isn't good enough for her," the husband replied.

"Then he'll be sure to win her," laughed the lady. "He has won her, I believe," she added more seriously, watching the pair where they stood together at the far end of the platform; "but something is wrong."

"Something usually is at that stage, if I remember. Come, let's get aboard."

The sun was setting clear in the pale saffron west. The train from the buried cut had been released, and now came sliding down the track, welcomed by boisterous salutations. Behind were the mighty snowplow engines, backing down, enwreathed and garlanded with snow.

"A-a-all aboard!" the conductor drawled in a colloquial tone to the small waiting group upon the platform.

Slowly they crept back upon the main track, and heavily the motion increased, till the old chant of the rails began again, and they were thundering westward down the line.

III.

Phebe was much occupied with her father, perhaps purposely so, until his bedtime. She made him her innocent refuge.

Ludovic kept subtly away, lest the friendly old gentleman should be led into conversation, which might delay the hour of his retiring. He went cheerfully to rest about the time the lamps were lighted, and Phebe sought once more her corner in the empty section, shaded by her father's curtains.

Ludovic asked, dropping his voice below the roar of the train, if he might take the seat beside her.

He took it, and turned his back upon the car. He looked at his watch. He had just three hours before Pocatello. The train was making great speed; they would get in, the conductor said, by eleven o'clock. But he need not tell her yet. Half an hour passed, and his thoughts in the silence were no longer to be borne.

She was aware of his intense excitement, his restlessness, the nervous action of his hands. She shrank from the burning misery in his questioning eyes. Once she heard him whisper under his breath; but the words she heard were, "*My love! my love!*" and she thought she could not have heard aright. Her trouble increased with her sense of some involuntary strangeness in her companion, some recklessness impending which she might not know how to meet. She rose in her place, and said tremulously that she must go.

"Go!" He sprang up. "Go where, in Heaven's name? Stay," he implored, "and be kind to me! We get off at Pocatello."

"We?" she asked with her eyes in his.

"That man and I. I am his prisoner."

She sank down again, and stared at him mutely.

"He is the sheriff of Bingham County, and I am his prisoner," he repeated. "Do the words mean nothing to you?" He paused for some sign that she understood him. She dropped her eyes; her face had become as white as a snowdrop.

"He is taking me to Pocatello for the preliminary examination—

154

oh, must I tell you this? If I thought you would never read it in the ghastly type—"

"Go on," she whispered.

"Examination," he choked, "for—for homicide. I don't know what the judge will call it; but the other man is dead, and I am left to answer for the passion of a moment with my life. And you will not speak to me?"

But now she did speak. Leaning forward so that she could look him in the eyes, she said:

"I thought when I saw that man always with you, watching you, that he might be taking you, with your consent, to one of those places where they treat persons for—for unsoundness of the mind. I knew you had some trouble that was beyond help. I could think of nothing worse than that. It haunted me till we began to speak together; then I knew it could not be; now I wish it had been."

"I do not," said Ludovic. "I thank God I am not mad. There is passion in my blood, and folly, perhaps, but not insanity. No, I am responsible."

She remained silent, and he continued defensively:

"But I am not the only one responsible. Can you listen? Can you hear the particulars? One always feels that one's own case is peculiar; one is never the common sinner, you know.

"I have a friend at Pocatello; he is my partner in business. Two years ago he married a New York girl, and brought her out there to live. If you knew Pocatello, you would know what a privilege it was to have their house to go to. They made me free of it, as people do in the West. There is nothing they could not have asked of me in return for such hospitality; it was an obligation not less sacred on my part than that of family.

"When my friend went away on long journeys, on our common business, it was my place in his absence to care for all that was his. There are many little things a woman needs a man to do for her in a place like Pocatello; it was my pride and privilege to be at all times at the service of this lady. She was needlessly grateful, but she liked me besides: she was one who showed her likes and dislikes frankly. She had grown up in a small, exclusive set of persons who knew one another's grandfathers, and were accustomed to say what they pleased inside; what outsiders thought did not matter. She had not learned to be careful; she despised the need of it. She thought Pocatello and the people there were a joke. But there is a serious side even to Pocatello: you cannot joke with rattlesnakes and vitriol

155

and slow mines. She made enemies by her gay little sallies, and she would never condescend to explain. When people said things which showed they had interpreted her words or actions in a stupid or vulgar way, she gave the thing up. It was not her business to adapt herself to such people; it was theirs to understand her. If they could not, then it did not matter what they thought. That was her theory of life in Pocatello.

"One night I was in a place—not for my pleasure—a place where a lady's name is never spoken by a gentleman. I heard her name spoken by a fool; he coupled it with mine, and laughed. I walked out of the place, and forgot what I was there for till I found myself down the street with my heart jumping. That time I did right, you would say.

"But I met him again. It was at the depot at Pocatello. I was seeing a man off—a stranger in the place, but a friend of my friends; we had dined at their house together. This other—I think he had been drinking—I suppose he must have included me in his stupid spite against the lady. He made his fool speech again. The man who was with me heard him, and looked astounded. I stepped up to him. I said—I don't know what. I ordered him to leave that name alone. He repeated it, and I struck him. He pulled a pistol on me. I grabbed him, and twisted it out of his hand. How it happened I cannot tell, but there in the smoke he lay at my feet. The train was moving out. My friend pulled me aboard. The papers said I ran away. I did not. I waited at Omaha for Mr. Burke.

"And there I met you, three days ago; and all I care for now is just to know that you will not think of me always by that word."

"What word?"

"Never mind; spare me the word. Look at me! Do I seem to you at all the same man?"

Phebe slowly lifted her eyes.

"Is there nothing left of me? Answer me the truth. I have a right to be answered."

"You are the same; but all the rest of it is strange. I do not see how such a thing could be."

"Can you not conceive of one wild act in a man not inevitably always a sinner?"

"Oh, yes; but not that act. I cannot understand the impulse to take a life."

"I did not think of his miserable life; I only meant to stop his talking. He tried to take mine. I wish he had. But no, no; I should have missed this glimpse of you. Just when it is too late I learn what life is worth."

"Do men truly do those things for the sake of women? Were you thinking of your friend's wife when you struck him?"

"I was thinking of the man—what a foul-mouthed fool he was—not fit to—." He stopped, seeing the look on Phebe's face.

"Oh, I'm impossible, I know, to one like you! It's rather hard I should have to be compared, in your mind, to a race of men like your father. Have you never known any other men?"

"I have read of all the men other people read of. I have some imagination."

"I suppose you read your Bible."

"Yes, the men in the Bible were not all of the Spirit; but they worshiped the Spirit—they were humble when they did wrong."

"Did women ever love them?"

Phebe was silent.

"Do not talk to me of the Spirit," Ludovic pleaded. "I am a long way from that. At least I am not a hypocrite—not yet. Wait till I am a 'trusty,' scheming for a pardon. Can you not give me one word of simple human comfort? There are just forty minutes more."

"What can I say?"

"Tell me this—and oh, be careful! Could you, if it were permitted a criminal like me to expiate his sin in the world among living men, in human relations with them—could we ever meet? Could you say 'thee' to me, not as to an afflicted person or a child? Am I to be only a text, another instance—"

"Many would not blame you. Neither do I blame you, not knowing that life or those people," said Phebe. "But there was One who turned away from the evil-speakers, and wrote upon the sand."

"But those evil-speakers spoke the truth."

"Can a lie be stopped by a pistol-shot? But we need not argue."

"No, I see how it is. I shall be to you only another of the wretched sons of Cain."

"I am thy sister," she said, and gave him her hand.

He held it in his strong, cold, trembling clasp.

"Darling, do you know where I am going? I shall never see you, never again—unless you are like the sainted women of your faith who walked the prisons, and preached to them in bonds."

"Thy bonds are mine: but I am no preacher."

The drowsy lights swayed and twinkled, the wheels rang on the frozen rails as the wild, white wastes flew by.

157

"Father shall never know it," Phebe murmured. "He shall never know, if I can help it, why you called yourself unhappy."

"Is it such an unspeakable horror to you?" He winced.

"He has not many years to live; it would only be one disappointment more." She was leaning back in her seat; her eyes were closed; she looked dead weary, but patient, as if this too were life, and not more than her share.

"Has you father any money, dear?"

She smiled: "Do we look like people with money?"

"If they would only let me have my hands!" he groaned. "To think of shutting up a great strong fellow like me—"

It was useless to go on. He sat, bitterly forecasting the fortunes of those two lambs who had strayed so far from the green pastures and still waters, when he heard Phebe say softly, as if to herself:

"We are almost there."

Mr. Burke began to fold his newspapers and get his bags in order. His hands rested upon the implements of his office—he carried them always in his pockets—while he stood balancing himself in the rocking car, and the porter dusted his hat and coat.

The train dashed past the first scattered lights of the town.

"Po-catello!" the brakeman roared in a voice of triumph, for they were "in" at last.

The porter came, and touched Ludovic on the shoulder.

"Gen'leman says he's ready, sir."

He rose, and bent over Phebe. If she had been like any other girl he must have kissed her, but he dared not. He had prayed for a sign, and he had won it—that look of dumb and lasting anguish in her childlike eyes.

Yet, strange passion of the man's nature, he was not sorry for what he had done.

Mr. Burke took his arm in silence, and steered him out of the car; both doors were guarded, for he had feared there might be trouble. He was surprised at Ludovic's behavior.

"What's the matter with him?" the car-conductor asked, looking after the pair as they walked up the platform together. "Is he sick?"

"Mashed," said the porter, gloomily; for Ludovic had forgotten the parting fee. "Regular girl mash, the worst I ever saw."

"He's late about it if he expects to have any fun," said the conductor; and he began to dance, with his hands in his great-coat pockets, for the night air was raw. He was at the end of his run, and was going home to his own girl, whom he had married the week

158

before.

Friends and family influence mustered strong for Ludovic at the trial six weeks later. His lawyer's speech was the finest effort, it was said, ever listened to by an Idaho jury. The ladies went to hear it, and to look at the handsome prisoner, who seemed to grow visibly old as the days of the trial went by.

But those who are acquainted with the average Western jury need not be told that it was not influence that did it, nor the lawyer's eloquence, nor the court's fine-spun legal definitions, nor even the women's tears. They looked at the boy, and thought of their own boys, or they looked inside, and thought of themselves; and they concluded that society might take its chances with that young man at large. They stayed out an hour, out of respect to their oath, and then brought in a verdict of "Not guilty;" and the audience had to be suppressed.

But after the jury's verdict there is society, and all the tongues that will talk long after the tears are dry. And then comes God in the silence—and Phebe.

The men all say she is too good for him, whose name has been in everybody's mouth. They say it, even though they do not know the cruel way in which he won her love. But the women say that Phebe, though undeniably a saint (and the "sweetest thing that ever lived"), is yet a woman, incapable of inflicting judgment upon the man she loves.

The case is in her hands now. She may punish, she may avenge, if she will; for Ludovic is the slave of his own remorseless conquest. But Phebe has never discovered that she was wronged. There is something in faith, after all; and there is a good deal in blood, Friend Underhill thinks. "Doubtless the grandson of Martin Ludovic must have had great provocation."

The Cup Of Trembling

A miner of the Coeur d'Alêne was returning alone, on foot, one winter evening, from the town in the gulch to his solitary claim far up on the timbered mountain-side.

His nearest way was by an unfrequented road that led to the Dreadnaught, a lofty and now abandoned mine that had struck the vein three thousand feet above the valley, but, the ore of which being low-grade, could never be made to pay the cost of transportation.

He had cached his snow-shoes, going down, at the Bruce boys' cabin, the only habitation on the Dreadnaught road, which from there was still open to town.

The snows that camp all summer on the highest peaks of the Coeur d'Alêne were steadily working downward, driving the game before them; but traffic had not ceased in the mountains. Supplies were still delivered by pack-train at outlying claims and distant cabins in the standing timber. The miner was therefore traveling light, encumbered with no heavier load than his personal requisition of tobacco and whisky and the latest newspapers, which he circulated in exchange for the wayside hospitalities of that thinly peopled but neighborly region.

His homeward halt at the cabin was well timed. The Bruce boys were just sitting down to supper; and the moon, which would light his lonelier way across the white slopes of the forest, would not be visible for an hour or more. The boys threw wood upon their low cooking-fire of coals, which flamed up gloriously, spreading its immemorial welcome over that poor, chance suggestion of a home. The supper was served upon a board, or literally two boards, nailed shelf-wise across the lighted end of the cabin, beneath a small window where, crossed by the squares of a dusty sash, the austere winter twilight looked in: a sky of stained-glass colors above the clear heights of snow; an atmosphere as cold and pure as the air of a fireless church; a hushed multitude of trees disguised in vestments of snow, a mute recessional after the benediction has been said.

Each man dragged his seat to the table, and placed himself sidewise, that his legs might find room beneath the narrow board. Each dark face was illumined on one side by the fitful fire-glow, on the other by the constant though fading ray from the window; and, as they talked, the boisterous fire applauded, and the twilight, like a pale listener, laid its cold finger on the pane.

They talked of the price of silver, of the mines shutting down, of the bad times East and West, and the signs of a corrupt generation; and this brought them to the latest ill rumor from town — a sensation that had transpired only a few hours before the miner's departure, and which friends of the persons discussed were trying to keep as quiet as possible.

The name of a young woman was mentioned, hitherto a rather disdainful favorite with society in the Coeur d'Alêne — the wife of one of the richest mine-owners in the State.

The "Old Man," as the miners called him, had been absent for three months in London, detained from week to week on the tedious but paramount business of selling his mine. The mine, with its fatalistic millions (which, it was surmised, had spoken for their owner in marriage more eloquently than the man could have spoken for himself), had been closed down pending negotiations for its sale, and left in charge of the engineer, who was also the superintendent. This young man, whose personal qualities were in somewhat formidable contrast to those of his employer, nevertheless, in business ways, enjoyed a high measure of his confidence, and had indeed deserved it. The present outlook was somewhat different. Persons who were fond of Waring were saying in town that "Jack must be off his head," as the most charitable way of accounting for his late eccentricity. The husband was reported to be on ship-board, expected in New York in a week or less; but the wife, without explanation, had suddenly left her home. Her disappearance was generally accounted a flight. On the same night of the young woman's evanishment, Superintendent Waring had relieved himself of his duties and responsibilities, and taken himself off, with the same irrevocable frankness, leaving upon his friends the burden of his excuses, his motives, his whereabouts, and his reputation.

Since news of the double desertion had got abroad, tongues had been busy, and a vigorous search was afoot for evidence of the generally assumed fact of an elopement, but with trifling results.

The fugitives, it was easily learned, had not gone out by the railroad; but Clarkson's best team, without bells, and a bob-sleigh with two seats in it had been driven into the stable-yard before daylight on the morning of the discovery, the horses rough and jaded, and white with frozen steam; and Clarkson himself had been the driver on this hard night trip. As he was not in the habit of serving his patrons in this capacity, and as he would give none but frivolous, evasive answers to the many questions that were asked him, he was supposed to be accessory to Waring in his crime against the morals of the camp.

While the visitor enlarged upon the evidence furnished by Clarkson's night ride, the condition of his horses, and his own frank lying, the Bruce boys glanced at each other significantly, and each man spat into the fire in silence.

The traveler's halt was over. He slipped his feet into the straps of his snow-shoes, and took his pole in hand; for now the moon had risen to light his path, and faint boreal shadows began to appear on the glistening slopes. He shuffled away, and his shape was soon lost in the white depths of the forest.

The brothers sat and smoked by their sinking fire, before covering its embers for the night; and again the small window, whitening in the growing moonlight, was like the blanched face of a troubled listener.

"That must 'a' been them last night, you recollect. I looked out about two o'clock, and it *was* a bob-sleigh, crawlin' up the grade, and the horses hadn't no bells on. The driver was a thick-set man like Clarkson, in a buffaler coat. There was two on the back seat, a man and woman plain enough, all muffled up, with their heads down. It was so still in the woods I could 'a' heard if they'd been talkin' no louder than I be now; but not a word was spoke all the way up the hill. I says to myself, 'Them folks must be pretty well acquainted, 'less they're all asleep, goin' along through the woods the prettiest kind of a night, walkin' their horses, and not a word in the whole blasted outfit.' "

"I'm glad you didn't open your head about it," said the elder brother. "We don't know for certain it was them, and it's none of our funeral, anyhow. Where, think, could they have been going to, supposin' you was right? Would Jack be likely to harbor up there at the mine?"

"Where else could they get to, with a team, by this road? Where else could they be safer? Jack's inside of his own lines up there, and come another big snow the road'll be closed till spring; and who'd

162

bother about them, anyway, exceptin' it might be the Old Man? And a man that leaves his wife around loose the way he done ain't likely to be huntin' her on snow-shoes up to another man's mine."

"I don't believe Jack's got the coin to be meanderin' very far just about now," said the practical elder brother. "He's staked out with a pretty short rope, unless he's realized on some of his claims. I heard he was tryin' to dig up a trade with a man who's got a mine over in the Slocan country. That would be convenient over the line among the Canucks. I wouldn't wonder if he's hidin' out for a spell till he gathers his senses, and gets a little more room to turn in. He can't fly far with a woman like her, unless his pockets are pretty well lined. Them easy-comers easy-goers ain't the kind that likes to rough it. I'll bet she don't bile his shirts or cook his dinners, not much."

"It's a wild old nest up there," said the younger and more imaginative as well as more sympathetic of the brothers—"a wild road to nowhere, only the dropping-off place."

"What gets me is that talk of Jack's last fall, when you was in the Kootenai, about his intentions to 'bach' it up there this winter, if he could coax his brother out from Manitoba to bach with him. I wouldn't like to think it of Jack, that he'd lie that way, just to turn folks off the scent. But he did, sure, pack a lot of his books and stuff up to the mine; grub, too, a lot of it and done some work on the cabin. Think he was fixin' up for a hideout, in case he should need one? Or wa'n't it anything but a bluff?"

"Naw," the other drawled impatiently. "Jack's no such a deep schemer as all that comes to. More'n likely he seen he was workin' the wrong lead, and concluded 't was about time for him to be driftin' in another direction. 'T ain't likely he give in to such foolishness without one fight with himself. And about when he had made up his mind to fire himself out, and quit the whole business, the Old Man puts out for London, stuck on sellin' his mine, and can't leave unless Jack stays with it. And Jack says to himself, 'Well, blast it all, I done what I could! What is to be will be.' That's about the way I put it up."

"I wouldn't be surprised," the other assented; "but what's become of the brother, if there ever was a brother in it at all?"

"Why, Lord! A man can change his mind. But I guess he didn't tell his brother about this young madam he was lookin' after along with the rest of the Old Man's goods. I hain't got nothin' against Jack Waring; he's always been square with me, and he's an awful good minin' man. I'd trust him with my pile, if it was millions, but I wouldn't trust him, nor any other man, with my wife."

"Sho! She was poor stuff; she was light, I tell ye. Think of some of the women we've known! Did they need watchin'? No, sir; it ain't the man, it's the woman, when it's between a young man and a married woman. It's her foolishness that gits away with them both. Girls is different. I'd skin a man alive that set the town talkin' about my sister like *she's* bein' talked about, now."

The brothers stepped outside, and stood awhile in silence, regarding the night, and breathing the pure, frosty air of the forest. A commiserating thankfulness swelled in their breasts with each deep, clean inspiration. They were poor men, but they were free men—free, compared with Jack. There was no need to bar their door, or watch suspiciously, or skulk away and hide their direction, choosing the defense of winter and the deathlike silence of the snows to the observation of their kind.

They stared with awe up the white, blank road that led to the deserted mine, and they marveled in homely thinking: "Will it pay?" It was "the wrong lead this time, sure."

The brothers watched the road from day to day, and took note that not a fresh track had been seen upon it; not a team, or a traveler on snow-shoes, had gone up or down since the night when the bob-sleigh with its silent passengers had creaked up it in the moonlight. Since that night of the full moon of January not another footprint had broken the smoothness of that hidden track. The snow-tides of midwinter flowed over it. They filled the gulch, and, softly mounting, snow on snow, rose to the eaves of the little cabin by the buried road. The Bruce boys dug out their window; the hooded roof protected their door. They walked about on top of the frozen tide, and entered their house, as if it were a cellar, by steps cut in a seven-foot wall of snow.

One gray day in February a black dog, with a long nose and bloodshot eyes, leaped down into the trench, and pawed upon the cabin door. Opening to the sound, the Bruce boys gave him a boisterous welcome, calling their visitor by name. The dog was Tip, Jack Waring's clever shepherd spaniel, a character as well known in the mountains as his master. Indeed, he was too well known, and too social in his habits, for a safe member of a household cultivating strict seclusion; therefore, when Tip's master went away with his neighbor's wife, Tip had been left behind. His reappearance on this road was regarded by the Bruce boys as highly suggestive.

Tip was a dog that never forgave an injury or forgot a kindness. Many a good bone he had set down to the Bruce boys' credit in the days when his master's mine was supposed to be booming, and his own busy feet were better acquainted with the Dreadnaught road. He would not come in, but stood at the door, wagging his tail inquiringly. The boys were about to haul him into the cabin by the hair of his neck, or shut him out in the cold, when a shout was heard from the direction of the road above. Looking out, they saw a strange young man, on snow-shoes, who hailed them a second time, and stood still, awaiting their response. Tip seemed to be satisfied now; he briskly led the way, the boys following up the frozen steps cut in their moat-wall of snow, and stood close by, assisting, with all the eloquence his honest, ugly phiz was capable of, at the conference that ensued. He showed himself particularly anxious that his old friends should take his word for the stranger whom he had introduced and appeared to have adopted.

Pointing up the mountain, the young man asked, "Is that the way to the Dreadnaught mine?"

"There ain't nobody workin' up there now," Jim Bruce replied indirectly, after a pause in which he had been studying the stranger's appearance. His countenance was exceedingly fresh and pleasing, his age about twenty years. He was buttoned to the chin in a reefing-jacket of iron-gray Irish frieze. His smooth, girlish face was all over one pure, deep blush from exertion in the cold. He wore Canadian snow-shoes strapped upon his feet, instead of the long Norweigian skees on which the men of the Coeur d'Alene make their winter journeys in the mountains; and this difference alone would have marked him for a stranger from over the line. After he had spoken, he wiped away the icy moisture of his breath that frosted his upper lip, stuck a short pipe between his teeth, drew off one mitten, and fumbled in his clothing for a match. The Bruce boys supplied him with a light, and as the fresh, pungent smoke ascended, he raised his head and smiled his thanks.

"Is this the road to the Waring mine—the Dreadnaught?" he asked again, deliberately, after a pull or two at his pipe.

And again came the evasive answer: "Mine's shut down. Ain't nobody workin' up there now."

The youngster laughed aloud. "Most uncommunicative population I ever struck," he remarked, in a sort of humorous despair. "That's the way they answered me in town. I say, is this a hoodoo? If my brother isn't up there, where in the devil is he? All I ask is a straight answer to a straight question."

The Bruce boys grinned their embarrassment. "You'll have to ask us somethin' easier," they said.

"This is the road to the mine, ain't it?"

"Oh, that's the road all right enough," the boys admitted; "but you can see yourself how much it's been traveled lately."

The stranger declined to be put off with such casual evidence as this. "The wind would wipe out any snow-shoe track; and a snow-shoer would as soon take across the woods as keep the road, if he knew the way."

"Wal," said Jim Bruce, conclusively, "most of the boys, when they are humpin' themselves to town, stops in here for a spell, to limber up their shins by our fire; but Jack Waring hain't fetched his bones this way for two months an better. Looks mighty queer that we hain't seen track nor trace of him if he's been livin' up there since winter set in. Are you the brother he was talkin' of sending for to come out and back it with him?"

The boys were aware of their own uneasy looks as the frank eyes of the stranger met theirs at the question.

"I'm the only brother he's got. He wrote to me last August that he'd taken a fit of the sulks, and wanted me to come and help him work it off up here at his mine. I was coming, only a good job took me in tow; and after a month or so the work went back on me, and I wrote to Jack two weeks ago to look out for me; and here I am. And the people in town where he's been doing business these six years, acted as if they distantly remembered him. 'Oh, yes,' they say, 'Jack Waring; but he's gone away, don't you know? Snowed under somewhere; don't know where.' I asked them if he'd left no address. Apparently not. Asked if he'd seemed to be clothed in his proper senses when last seen. They thought so. I went to the post-office, expecting to find his mail piled up there. Every scrap had been cleaned up since Friday last; but not the letter I wrote him, so he can't be looking for me. The P.M. squirmed, like everybody else, when I mentioned my brother; but he owned that a man's mail can't leave the box without hands, and that the hands belonged usually to some of the boys at the Mule Deer mine. Now, the Mule Deer is next neighbor to the Dreadnaught, across the divide. It's a friendly power, I know; and that confirms me that my brother has done just what he said he was going to do. By the tone of his letter I judged that he was feeling a bit seedy. He seemed to have soured on the town for some reason, which might mean that the town has soured on him. I don't ask what it is, and I don't care to know, but something has queered the whole crowd. I asked Clarkson to let me have a man to show me the way to the Dreadnaught. He calmly lied to me a blue streak, and he knew that I knew he was lying. And then Tip, here, looked me in the eye, with his head on one side, and I saw that he was on to the whole business."

"Smartest dog that ever lived!" Jim Bruce ejaculated. "I wouldn't wonder if he knew you was Jack's brother."

"I won't swear that he could name the connection; but he knows that I'm looking for his master, and he's looking for him too; but he's afraid to trail after him without a good excuse. See? I don't know what Tip's been up to, that he should be left with a man like Clarkson; but whatever he's done, he's a good dog now. Ain't you, Tip?"

"*He* done!" Jim Bruce interrupted sternly. "Tip never done nothing to be punished for. Got more sense of what's right than most humans, and lives up to it straight along. I'd quar'l with any man that looked cross at that dog. You old brute, you rascal! What you doin' up here? Ain't you 'shamed, totin' folks 'way up here on a wild-goose chase? What you doin' it fer, eh? Pertendin' you're so smart! You know Jack ain't up here. Jack, ain't up here, I say. Go along with ye, tryin' to fool a stranger!"

Tip was not only unconvinced by these unblushing assertions on the part of a friend whose word he had never doubted: he was terribly abashed and troubled by their manifest disingenuousness. From a dog's point of view it was a poor thing for the Bruce boys to do, to try to pass upon him like this. He blinked apologetically, and licked his chaps, and wagged the end of his tail, which had sunk a trifle from distress and embarrassment at his position.

The three men stood and watched the workings of his mind, expressed in his humble, doggish countenance; and a final admission of the truth that he had been trying to conceal escaped Jim Bruce in a burst of admiration for his favorite's unswerving sagacity.

"Smartest dog that ever lived!" he repeated, triumphant over his own defeat; and the brothers wasted no more lies upon the stranger.

There was something uncanny, thought the young man, in this mystery about his brother that grew upon him, and waxed formidable, and pursued him even into the depths of the snow-buried wilderness. The breath of gossip should have died on so clean an air, unless there had been more than gossip in it.

The Bruce boys ceased to argue with him on the question of his brother's occupancy of the mine. They urged other considerations by

167

way of delaying him. They spoke of the weather; of the look of snow in the sky, the feeling of snow in the air, the yellow stillness of the forest, the creeping cold. They tried to keep him over-night, on the offer of their company up the mountain in the morning, if the weather should prove fit. But he was confident, though graver in manner than at first, that he was going to a supper and a bed at his brother's camp, to say nothing of a brother's welcome.

"I'm positive he's up there. I froze on to it from the first," he persisted. "And why should I sleep at the foot of the hill when my brother sleeps at the top?"

The Bruce boys were forced to let him go on, with the promise, merely allowing for the chance of disappointment, that if he found nobody above he would not attempt to return after nightfall by the Dreadnaught road, which hugs the peak at a height above the valley where there is always a stiff gale blowing, and the combing drifts in midwinter are forty feet high.

"Trust Tip," they said; "He'll show you the trail across the mountain to the Mule Deer"—a longer but far safer way to shelter for the night.

"Tip is fly; he'll see me through," said Jack's brother. "I'd trust him with my life. I'll be back this way possibly in the mornng; but if you don't see me, come up and pay us a visit. We'll teach the Dreadnaught to be more neighborly. Here's hoping," he cried, and the three drank in turn out of the young fellow's flask, the Bruce boys almost solemnly as they thought of the forthcoming meeting between the brothers, the sequel to that innocent hope. Unhappy brother, unhappy Jack!

He turned his face to the snows again, and toiled on up the mountain, with Tip's little figure trotting on ahead.

"Think of Jack's leavin' a dog like that, and takin' up with a woman!" said Jim Bruce, as he squared his shoulders to the fire, yawning and shuddering with the chill he had brought with him from outside. "And such a woman!" he added. "I'd want the straight thing, or else I'd manage to get along without. Anything decent would have taken the dog too."

" 'T was mortal cute, though, of the youngster to freeze on to Tip, and pay no attention to the talk. He knows a dog, that's sure. And Tip knowed him. But I wished we could 'a' blocked that little rascal's game. 'T was too bad to let him go on."

"I never see anybody so stuck on goin' to a place," said the elder Bruce. "I calc'late we'll see him back in the morning; but I'll bet he don't jaw much about brother Jack."

The manager's house at the Dreadnaught had been built in the time of the mine's supposititious prosperity, and was the ideal log cabin of the Coeur d'Alêne. A thick-waisted chimney of country rock buttressed the long side-wall of peeled logs chinked with mud. The front room was twenty feet across, and had a stone hearth and a floor of dressed pine. Back of it were a small bedroom and a kitchen into which water was piped from a spring higher up on the mountain. The roof of cedar shakes projected over the gable, shading the low-browed entrance from the sun in summer, and protecting it in winter from the high-piled snows.

Like a swallow's nest it clung in the hollow of the peak, which slopes in vast, grand contours to the valley, as if it were the inside of a bowl, the rim half broken away. The valley is the bottom of the bowl, and the broken rim is the lower range of hills that completes its boundary. Great trees, growing beside its hidden streams far below, to the eye of a dweller in the cabin are dwarfed to the size of junipers, and the call of those unseen waters comes dreamily in a distant, inconstant murmur, except when the wind beats up the peak, which it seldom does, as may be seen by the warp of the pines and tamaracks, and the drifting of the snows in winter.

To secure level space for the passage of teams in front of the house, an embankment had been thrown up, faced with a heavy retaining-wall of stone. This bench, or terrace, was now all one with the mountain-side, heaped up and smoothed over with snow.

Jack, in his winter nest-building, had cleared a little space for air and light in front of each of the side windows, and with unceasing labor he shoveled out the snow which the wind as constantly sifted into these pits, and into the trench beneath the hooded roof that sheltered the gable entrance. The snow walls of this sunken gallery rose to the height of the door-frame, cutting out all view from without or within. A perpetual white twilight, warmed by the glow of their hearth-fire, was all that the fugitives ever saw of the day. Sun or stars were alike to them. One link they had with humanity, however, without which they might have suffered hardship, or even have been forced to succumb to their savage isolation.

The friendly Mule Deer across the mountain was in a state of winter siege, like the Dreadnaught, but had not severed its connections with the world. It was a working-mine, with a force of fifty or more men on its pay-roll, and regular communications on snow-shoes was had with the town. The mine was well stocked as well as garrisoned, and Jack was indebted to the friendship of the manager for many accustomed luxuries which Esmée would have missed in the new life that she had rashly welcomed for his sake. No woman could have been less fitted than she, by previous circumstances and training, to take her share of its hardships, or to contribute to its slender possibilities in the way of comfort. A servant was not to be thought of. No servant but a Chinaman would have been impersonal enough for the situation, and all heathen labor has been ostracized by Christian white labor from the Coeur d'Alêne.

So Jack waited upon his love, and was inside man and outside man, and, as he expressed it, "general dog around the place." He was a clever cook, which goes without saying in one who has known good living, and has lived eight years a bachelor on the frontier; but he cleaned his own kitchen, and washed his own skillets, which does not go without saying, sooner than see Esmée's delicate hands defiled with such grimy tasks. He even swept, as a man sweeps; but what man was ever known to dust? The house, for all his ardent, unremitting toil, did not look particularly tidy.

Its great, dark front room was a man's room, big, undraped and uncurtained, strongly framed, — the framework much exposed in places, — heavy in color, hard in texture, yet a stronghold, and a place of absolute reserve: a very safe place in which to lodge such a secret as Esmée. And there she was, in her exotic beauty, shivering close to a roaring fire, scorching her cheeks that her silk-clad shoulders might be warm. She had never before lived in a house where the fires went out at night, and water froze beside her bed, and the floors were carpetless, and as cold as the world's indifference to her fate. She was absolutely without clothing suited to such a change, nor would she listen to sensible, if somewhat unattractive, suggestions from Jack. Now, least of all times, could she afford to disguise her picturesque beauty for the sake of mere comfort and common sense, or even to spare Jack his worries about her health.

It was noon, and the breakfast-table still stood in front of the fire. Jack, who since eight o'clock had been chopping wood and "packing" it out of the tunneled snow-drift which was the wood-shed into the kitchen, and cooking breakfast, and shoveling snow out of the trenches, sat glowing on his side of the table, farthest from the fire, while Esmée, her chair drawn close to the hearth, was sipping her coffee, and holding a fan spread between her face and the flames.

"Jack, I wish you had a fire-screen—one that would stand of itself, and not have to be held."

"Bless you! I'd be your fire-screen, only I think I'm rather hotter than the fire itself. I insist that you take some exercise, Esmée. Come, walk the trench with me ten rounds before I start."

"Why do you start so early?"

"Do you call this early? Besides, it looks like snow."

"Then why do you go at all?"

"You know why I go, dearest. The boys went to town yesterday. I've had no mail for a week."

"And can't you exist without your mail?"

"Existence is just the hitch with us at present. It's for your sake I cannot afford to be overlooked. If I fall out of step in my work, it may take years to get into line again. I can't say, like those ballad fellows:

"Awake! arise! my love, and fearless be,
For o'er the southern moors I have a home for thee.

"I wish I had. We'll put some money in our purse, and then we'll make ourselves a home where we please. Money is the first thing with us now. You must see that yourself."

"I see it, of course; but it doesn't seem the nearest way to a fortune, going twice a week on snow-shoes to play solo at the Mule Deer mine. Confess, Jack dear, you do not come straight away as soon as you get your mail."

"I do not, of course. I must be civil, after a fashion, to Wilfrid Knight, considering all that he is doing for me."

"What is he doing for you?"

"He's working as hard as he can for me in certain directions. It's best not to say too much about these things till they've materialized; but he has as strong a backing as any man in the Coeur d'Alène. To tell you the truth, I can't afford not to be civil to him, if it meant solo everyday in the week."

Esmée smiled a little, but remained silent. Jack went around to the chimneypiece, and filled his pipe, and began to stalk about the room, talking in brief sentences as he smoked.

"And by the way, dearest, would you mind if he should drop in on us someday?" Jack laughed at his own phrase, so literally close to the only mode of gaining access to their cellarage in the snow.

Esmée looked up quickly. "What in the world does he want to come here for? Doesn't he see enough of you as it is?"

171

"He wants to see something of you, and it's howling lonesome at the Mule Deer. Won't you let him come, Esmée?"

"Why, do you want him, Jack?"

"I want him! What should I want him for? But we have to be decent to a man who's doing everything in the world for us. We couldn't have made it here, at all, without the aid and comfort of the Mule Deer."

"I'd rather have done without his aid and comfort, if it must be paid for at his own price."

"Everything has got to be paid for. Even that inordinate fire, which you won't be parted from, has to be paid for with a burning cheek."

"Not if you had a fire-screen, Jack," Esmée reminded him, sweetly.

"We will have one—an incandescent fire-screen on two legs. Will two be enough? A Mule Deer miner shall pack it in on his back from town. But we shall have to thank Wilfrid Knight for sending him. Well, if you won't have him here, he can't come, of course; but it's a mistake, I think. We can't afford, in my opinion, not to see the first hand that is held out to us in a social way—a hand that can help us if it will, but one that is quite as strong to injure us."

"Have him, then, if he's so dangerous. But is he nice, do you think?"

"He's nice enough, as men go. We're not any of us any too nice."

"Some of you are at least considerate, and I think it very inconsiderate of Mr. Wilfrid Knight to wish to intrude himself on me now."

"Dearest, he has been kindness itself, and delicacy, in a way. Twice he has sent a special man to town to hunt up little dainties and comforts for you when my prison fare—"

"Jack, what do you mean? Has Wilfrid Knight been putting his hand in his pocket for things for me to eat and drink?"

"His pocket's not much hurt. My own has suffered to the same extent quite frequently; but it is something to send a man fifteen miles down the mountain to pack the stuff. You might very properly recognize that, if you chose."

"I recognize nothing of it. Why did you not tell me how it was? I thought that you were sending for those things."

"How can I send Knight's men on my errands, if you please? I don't show up very largely at the mine in person. You don't seem to realize the situation. Did you suppose that the Mule Deer men, when they fetch these things from town, know whom they are for? They may, but they are not supposed to."

"Arrange it as you like, but I will not take presents from the manager of the Mule Deer."

"He has dined at your table, Esmée."

"Not at *my* table," said Esmee, haughtily averting her face.

"But you have been nice to him; he remembers you with distinct pleasure."

"Very likely. It is my rôle to be nice to people. I should be nice to him if he came here now; but I should hate him for coming. If *he* were nice, he would not dream of your asking him or allowing him to come."

"Darling, darling, we can't keep it up like this. We are not lords of fate to that extent. Fellows will pay you attention; they always have and they always will; but you must not, dearest, imply that I am not sensitive on the point of what you may or may not receive in that way. I should make myself a laughing stock before all men if I should begin by resenting things. I could not insult you so. I will resent nothing that a husband does not resent."

"Jack, don't you understand? I could have taken it lightly once; I always used to. I can't take it lightly now. I cannot have him come here—the first to see us in this *solitude à deux,* the most intimate, the most awful."

"Of course, of course," murmured Jack. "It is awful, I admit it, for you. But it always will be. Ours is a double solitude for life, with the world always eyeing us askance, scoring us, or secretly envying us, or merely wondering coarsely about us. It takes tremendous courage in a woman; but you will have the courage of your honesty, your surpassing generosity to me."

"Generosity!" Esmée repeated. "We shall see. I give myself just five years of this 'generosity.' After that, the beginning of the end. I shall have to eliminate myself from the problem, to be finally generous. But five years is a good while," she whispered, "to dare to love my love in, if my love loves me."

There could be no doubt of this as yet. Esmée could afford to toy sentimentally with the thought of future despair and final self-elimination.

"Come, come," said Waring; "this will never do; we ought to get some fresh air on this." He knocked the ashes out of his pipe, pocketed it, and marched into an inner room, whence he fetched a warm, loose cloak and a pair of carriage boots.

"Fresh air and exercise!"

Esmée, seeing there was to be no escape from Jack's favorite specific for every earthly ill, put out her foot, in its foolish little slipper, and Jack drew on the fur-lined boots, and laced them around the silken ankles.

He followed her out into the snow-walled foss, and fell into step beside her.

"May I smoke?"

"What affectation! As if you didn't always smoke."

"Well, hardly, when I have a lady with me, in such a public place."

"Oh me, oh me!" Esmée suddenly broke forth, "why did I not meet you when you were in New York the winter before! Well, it would have settled one or two things. And we might be walking like this now, before all the world, and every one would say we were exactly suited to each other. And so we are—fearfully and wonderfully. Why did that fact wait to force itself upon us when to admit it was a crime? And we were so helpless *not* to admit it. What resources had I against it?"

"God knows. Perhaps I ought to have made a better fight, for your sake. But the fight was over for me the moment I saw that you were unhappy. If you had seemed reasonably content with your life, or even resigned, I hope I should have been man enough to have taken myself off and had it out alone."

"I had no life that was not all a pretense and a lie. I began by thinking I could pretend to you. But you know how all that broke down. Oh, Jack, *you* know the man!"

"I wouldn't go on with that, Esmée."

"But I must. I must explain to you just once, if I can."

"You need not explain, I should hope, to me."

"But this is something that rankles fearfully. I must tell you that I never, never would have given in if I hadn't thought there was something in him, really. Even his peculiarities at first seemed rather picturesque; at least they were different from other men's. And we thought him a great original, a force, a man of such power and capacity. His very success was supposed to mean that. It was not his gross money that appealed to me. You could not think that I would have let myself be literally sold. But the money seemed to show what he had done. I thought that at least my husband would be a man among men, and especially in the West. But—"

"Darling, need we go into all this? Say it to yourself, if it must be said. You need not say it to me."

"*I* am saying it, not you. It is not you who have a monstrous, incredible marriage to explain. I must explain it as far as I can. Do you think I can afford to be without your respect and comprehension simply because you love me?"

"But love includes the rest."

"Not after awhile. Now let me speak. It was when he brought me out here that I saw him as he is. I measured him by the standards of the life that had made him. I saw that he was just a rough Western man, like hundreds of others; not half so picturesque as a good many who passed the window everyday. And all his great success, which I had taken as a proof of ability, meant nothing but a stroke of brutal luck that might happen to the commonest miner any day. I saw how you pretended to respect his judgment while privately you managed in spite of it. I could not help seeing that he was laughed at for his pretensions in the community that knew him best. It was tearing away the last rag of self-respect in which I had been trying to dress up my shameful bargain. I knew what you all thought of him, and I knew what you must think of me. I could not force myself to act my wretched part before you; it seemed a deeper degradation when you were there to see. How could I let you think that *that* was my idea of happiness! But from the first I never could be anything with you but just myself—for better or for worse. It was such a rest, such a perilous rest, to be with you, just because I knew it was no use to pretend. You always seemed to understand everything without a word."

"I understood *you* because I gave my whole mind to the business. You were in my thoughts night and day, from the moment I first saw you."

"Yes," said Esmée, passing over this confession as a thing of course in a young man's relations with his employer's wife. "It was as if we had been dear friends once, before memory began, before anything began; and all the rest came of the miserable accident of our being born—mis-born, since we could not meet until it was too late. Oh, it was cruel! I can never forgive life, fate, society—whatever it was that played us this trick. I had the strangest forebodings when they talked about you, before I saw you—a premonition of a crisis, a danger ahead. There was a fascination in the commonest reports about you. And then your perfectly reckless naturalness, of a man who has nothing to hide and nothing to fear. Who on earth could resist it?"

"I was the one who ought to have resisted it, perhaps. I don't deny that I was 'natural.' We're neither of us exactly humbugs—not now. If the law that we've broken is hunting for us, there will be plenty of good people to point us out. All that we shall have to face by and by. I wish I could take your share and mine too; but you will always have it the harder. That, too, is part of the law, I suppose."

"I must not be too proud," said Esmée. "I must remember what I am in the eyes of the world. But, Jack dear, if Wilfrid Knight does come, do not let him come without telling me first. Don't let him 'drop in on us,' as you said."

"He shall not come at all if it bothers you to think of it. I am not such a politic fellow. It's for your sake, dearest one, that I am cringing to luck in this way. I never pestered myself much about making friends and connections; but *I* must not be too proud, either. It's a handicap, there's no doubt about that; it's wiser to accept the fact, and go softly. My heavens! Haven't I got you?"

"I suppose Wilfrid Knight is a man of the world? He'll know how to spare the situation?"

"Quite so," said Jack, with a faint smile. "You needn't be uneasy about him." Then, more gravely, he added:

"He knows this is no light thing with either of us. He must respect your courage—the courage so rare in a woman—to face a cruel mistake that all the world says she must cover up, and right it at any cost."

"That is nonsense," said Esmée, with the violence of acute sensitiveness. "You need not try to doctor up the truth to me. You know that men do not admire that kind of courage in women—not in their own women. Let us be plain with each other. I don't pretend that I came here with you for the sake of courage, or even of honesty."

Esmée stopped, and turned herself about, with her shoulders against the wall of snow, crushing the back of her head deep into its soft, cold resistance. In this way she gained a glimpse of the sky.

"Jack, it does look like a storm. It's all over gray, is it not? And the air is so raw and chilly. I wish you would not go to-day."

"I'll get off at once, and be back before dark. There shall be no solo this afternoon. But leave those dishes for me. I despise to have you wash dishes."

"I hate it myself. If I do do it, it will be to preserve my self-respect, and partly because you are so slow, Jack dear, and there's no comfort in life till you get through. What a ridiculous, blissful, squalid time it is! Shall we ever do anything natural and restful again, I wonder?"

"Yes, when we get some money."

"I can't bear to hear you talk so much about money. Have I not had enough of money in my life?"

"Life is more of a problem with us than it is with most people."

"Let us go where nature solves the problem. There was an old song one of my nurses used to sing to me—

"Oh, islands there are, in the midst of the deep,
Where the leaves never fade, and the skies never weep.

"Can't we go, Jack dear? Let us be South Sea Islanders. Let's be anything where there will be no dishes to wash, or somebody to wash them for us."

"We will go when we get some money," Jack persisted hauntingly.

"Oh, hush about the money! It's so uncomplimentary of you. I shall begin to think—"

"You must not think. Thinking, after a thing is done, is no use. You must 'sleep, dear, sleep.' I shall be back before dark; but if I am not, don't think it strange. One never knows what may happen."

When he was gone Esmée was seized with a profound fit of dawdling. She sat for an hour in Jack's deep leather chair by the fire, her cloak thrown back, her feet, in the fur boots, extended to the blaze. For the first time that day she felt completely warm. She sat an hour dreaming, in perfect physical content.

Where did those words that Jack had quoted come from, she mused, and repeated them to herself, trying their sound by ear.

Then sleep, dear, sleep!

They gathered meaning from some fragmentary connection in her memory.

If thou wilt ease thine heart
Of love, and all its smart—
Then sleep, dear, sleep!
And not a sorrow—

She could recall no more. The lines had an echo of Keats. She looked across the room toward the low shelves where Jack's books were crammed in dusty banishment. It was not likely that Keats would be in that company; yet Jack, by fits and starts, had been a passionate reader of everybody, even of the poets.

She was too utterly comfortable to be willing to move merely to lay

the ghost of a vanished song. And now another verse awoke to
haunt her:

> But wilt thou cure thine heart
> Of love, and all its smart—
> Then die, dear, die!
>
> 'T is deeper, sweeter—

Than what? She could not remember. She had read the verses long
ago, as a girl of twenty measures time, when the sentiment had had
for her the palest meaning. Now she thought it not extravagant, but
simply true.

> Then die, dear, die!

She repeated, pillowing her head in the silken lining of her cloak. A
tear of self-forgiving pity stole down her cheek. Love of her own fair,
sensitive self; love of the one who could best express her to herself,
and magnify her day by day, on the highest key of modern poetic
sympathy and primal passion and medieval romance—this was the
whole of life to her. She desired no other revelation concerning the
mission of woman. In no other sense would she have held it worth
while to be a woman. Yet she, of Beauty's daughters, had been
chosen for that most fatal of all the stupid world's experiments in
what it calls success—a loveless marriage!

When at length the fire went down, and the air of the drafty room
began to change, Esmée languidly bestirred herself. The confusion
that Jack had left behind him in his belated departure began to afflict
her—the unwashed dishes on the table, the crumbs on the floor, the
half-emptied pipe and ashes on the mantel, the dust everywhere.
She pitied herself that she had no one at her command to set things
right. At length she rose, reluctantly dispensing with her cloak, but
keeping the fur boots on her feet, and began to pile up the breakfast
dishes, and carry them by separate journeys to the kitchen.

The fire had long been out in the cook-stove; the bare little place
was distressingly cold; neither was it particularly clean, and the
nature of its disorder was even more objectionable than that of the
sitting-room. Poor Jack! Esmée had profoundly admired and pitied
his struggles with the kitchen. What man of Jack's type and breeding
had ever stood such a test of devotion? Even young Sir Gareth, who
had done the same sort of thing, had done it for knighthood's sake,
and had taken pride in the ordeal. With Jack such service counted
for nothing except as a preposterous proof of his love for her.

Suppose she should surprise him in housewifely fashion, and treat him to a clean kitchen, a bright fire, and a hot supper on his return? The fancy was a pleasing one; but when she came to reckon up the unavoidable steps to its accomplishment, the details were too hopelessly repellent. She did not know, in fact, where or how to begin. She mused forlornly on their present situation, which, of course, could not last; but what would come next? Surely, without money, plucked of the world's respect and charity, they were a helpless pair. Jack was right: money they must have; and she must learn to keep her scruples out of his way; he was sufficiently handicapped already. She hovered about the scene of his labors for awhile, mourning over him, and over herself for being so helpless to help him. By this time the sitting-room fire had gone quite down, and she put on a pair of gloves before raking out the coals, and laying the wood to rebuild it. The room had still a comfortless air, now that she was alone to observe it. She could have wept as she went about moving chairs, lifting heavy bearskins, and finding dirt, ever more dirt, that had accumulated under Jack's superficial housekeeping.

Her timid attempt at sweeping raised a hideous dust. When she tried to open the windows everyone was frozen fast, and when she opened the door the cold air cut her like a knife.

She gave up trying to overhaul Jack's back accounts, and contented herself with smoothing things over on the surface. She possessed in perfection the decorative touch that lends an outward grace to the aspect of a room which may be inwardly unclean, and therefore unwholesome, for those who live in it.

It had never been required of her that she should be anything but beautiful and amiable, or do anything but contribute her beauty and amiability to the indulgent world around her. The hard work was for those who had nothing else to bestow. She laid Jack's slippers by the fire, and, with fond coquetry, placed a pair of her own little mouse-colored suèdes, sparkling with silver embroidery, close beside them. Her velvet wrap with its collar of ostrich plumes she disposed effectively over the back of the hard-wood settle, where the shimmering silk lining caught a red gleam from the fire. Then she locked the outer door, and prepared to take Jack's advice, and "sleep, dear, sleep."

At the door of her bedroom she turned for a last survey of the empty room—the room that was to live in her memory as the scene of the most fateful chapter of her life. That day, she suddenly remembered, was her younger sister's wedding-day. She would not permit the thoughts to come. All weddings, since her own, were hateful to her. "Hush!" she inwardly breathed, to quell her heart. "The thing is done. All that was left was dishonor, either way. This is my plea, O God! There was no escape from shame! And Jack loved me so!" About five o'clock of that dark winter day Esmée was awakened from her warm sleep by a loud knocking on the outside door. It could not be Jack, for he had carried with him the key of the kitchen door, by which way he always entered on his return. It was understood between them that in his absences no stranger could be admitted to the house. Guests they did not look for; as to friends, they knew not who their friends were, or if, indeed, they had any friends remaining since their flight.

The knocking continued, with pauses during which Esmée could fancy the knocker listening for sounds within the house. Her heart beat hard and fast. She had half risen in her bed; at intervals she drew a deep breath, and shifted her weight on its supporting arm.

Footsteps could be heard passing and repassing the length of the trench in front of the house. They ceased, and presently a man jumped down into the pit outside her bedroom window; the window was curtained, but she was aware that he was there, trying to look in. He laid his hand on the window-frame, and leaped upon the sill, and shook the sash, endeavoring to raise it; but the blessed frost held it fast. The man had a dog with him, which trotted after him, back and forth, and seconded his efforts to gain entrance by leaping against the door, and whining, and scratching at the lock.

The girl was unspeakably alarmed, there was something so imperative in the stranger's demand. It had for her startled ear an awful assurance, as who should say, "I have a right to enter here." Who was it, what was it, knocking at the door of that guilty house?

It seemed to Esmée that this unappeasable presence had haunted the place for an hour or more, trying windows, and going from door to door. At length came silence so prolonged and complete that she thought herself alone at last.

But Jack's brother had not gone. He was standing close to the window of the outer room, studying its interior in the strong light and shadow of a pitch-pine fire. The room was confiding its history to one who was no stranger to its earlier chapters, and was keen for knowledge of the rest.

This was Jack's house, beyond a doubt, and Jack was its tenant at this present time, its daily intimate inhabitant. In this sense the man and his house were one.

The Dreadnaught had been Jack's first important mining venture.

He had sunk in it his share of his father's estate, considerable time and reputation, and the best work he was capable of; and he still maintained, in accordance with his temperament, that the mine was a good mine, only present conditions would not admit of the fact being demonstrated. The impregnable nature of its isolation made it a convenient cache for personal properties that he had no room for in his quarters in town, the beloved impedimenta that every man of fads and enthusiasms accumulates even in a rolling-stone existence. He was all there; it was Jack so frankly depicted in his belongings that his young brother, who adored him, sighed restlessly, and a blush of mingled emotions rose in his snow-chilled cheek.

What is so characteristic a likeness of a man as the shoes he has lately put off his feet? And, by token, there were Jack's old pumps waiting for him by the fire.

But now suspicion laid its finger on that very unnamed dread which had been lurking in the young man's thoughts. Jack, the silent room confessed, was not living here alone. This could hardly be called "baching it," with a pair of frail little feminine slippers moored close beside his own. Where had Jack's feet been straying lately,—on what forbidden ground,—that his own brother must be kept in ignorance of such a step as this? If he had been mad enough to fetch a bride to such an inhuman solitude as this—if this were Jack's honeymoon, why should his bliss he hedged about with an awkward conspiracy of silence on the part of all his friends?

The silent room summoned its witnesses: one by one each mute, inanimate object told its story. The firelight questioned them in scornful flashes; the defensive shadows tried to confuse the evidence, and cover it up.

But there were the conscious slippers reddening by the hearth. The costly Paris wrap displayed itself over the back of Jack's honest hardwood settle. On the rough table, covered with a blanket wrought by the hands of an Indian squaw, glimpsed a gilded fan, half-open, showing court ladies, dressed as shepherdesses, blowing kisses to their ephemeral swains. Faded hot-house roses were hanging their heads—shriveled packets of sweetness—against the brown sides of a pot-bellied tobacco jar, the lid of which, turned upside down, was doing duty as an ash-receiver. A box of rich confectionery imported from the East had been emptied into a Dresden bowl of a delicate, frigid pattern, reminding one of such pure-bred gentlewomen as Jack's little mother, from whom he had coaxed this bit of the family china on his last home visit.

We do not dress up our brother's obliquity in euphemistic phrases. Jack might call it what he pleased; but not the commonest man that knew him had been willing to state in plain words the manner of his life at present, snowed in at the top of the Dreadnaught road. Behold how that life spoke for itself; how his books were covered with dust; how the fine, manly rigor of the room had been debased by contact with the habits of a luxurious dependent woman!

Here Jack was wasting life in idleness, in self-banishment, in inordinate affection, and in deceits of the flesh. The brother who loved him too well to be lenient to his weakness turned away with a sob of such indignant heartbreak as only the young can know. Only the young and the pure in heart can have such faith in anything human as Jack's brother had had in Jack.

Esmée, reassured by the long-continued silence, had ventured out, and now stepped cautiously forward into the broad, low light in the middle of the room. The fireshine touched her upraised chin, her parted lips, and a spark floated in each of her large, dark, startled eyes. Tip had been watching as breathless and as motionless as his companion, but now at sight of Esmée he bounded against the sash, and squealed his impatience to be let in. Esmée shrank back with a cry: her hands went up to her breast and clasped themselves. She had seen the face at the window. Her attitude was the instinctive expression of her convicted presence in that house. And the excluded pair who watched her were natural judges: Fidelity that she had outraged, and Family Affection that she had wronged.

Tip made further demonstrations at the window, but Esmée had dragged herself away out of sight into her own room.

The steps of the knocker were heard, a few minutes later, wandering irresolutely up and down the trench. For the last time they paused at the door.

"Shall we knock once more, Tip? Shall we give her one more chance? Any honest woman would ask a stranger's business, at least, on such a night, in such a place, as this. She has seen that I am no ruffian; she knows that you are a friend. For the last time, then!"

A terrific peal of knocking shocked the silence. Esmée could have screamed, there was an accent so scornfully accusative in this last ironical summons. No answer was possible. The footsteps turned away from the door, and did not come back.

II.

The snow that had begun to fall softly and quietly about the middle of the afternoon had steadily increased until now in the thickening dusk it spread a white blindness everywhere. From her bedroom window Esmée looked out, and though she could not see the sky, there were signs enough to tell her what the night must be. Fresh snow lay piled in the trench, and snow was whirling in. There was a blast outside that wailed in the chimney, and shook the house, and sifted snow in beneath the outer door.

Esmée was not surprised that Jack, when he came home, should be as dismal and quiet as she was herself; but it did surprise her that he should not at once perceive that something had happened in his absence.

At first there was supper to cook, and she could not talk to him then. Later, when they were seated together at the table, she tried to speak of that ghostly knocking; but Jack seemed preoccupied and not inclined to talk, and she was glad of an excuse to postpone a subject that had for her a peculiar terror in its suggestions.

It was nine o'clock before all the little house tasks were done, and they drew up to the fire and sought in each other's eyes the assurance that both were in need of, that nothing of their dear-bought treasure of companionship had altered since they had sat that way before. But it was not quite the same Esmée, not the same Jack. They were not thinking exclusively of each other.

"Why don't you read your letters, dear?"

"I can't read them," said Esmée. "They were not written to me—the woman I am now."

These were the home letters, telling of her sister's coming wedding festivities, that Esmée could not read, especially that one from Lilla—her last letter as a girl to the sister who had been a bride herself, and would know what a girl's feelings at such a time must be.

"I have tried to write to mama;" said Esmée, "but it's impossible. Anything I could say by way of defense sounds as if I were trying to lay the blame on someone else; and if I say nothing, but just state the facts, it is harsh, as if I were brazening it out. And she has never seen you, Jack. You are my only real defense. By what you are, by what you will be to me, I am willing to be judged."

"Dearest, you make me ashamed, but I can say the same of you. Still, to a mother, I'm afraid it will make little difference whether it's 'Launcelot or another.'"

"It certainly made little difference to her when she made her choice of a husband for me," said Esmée, bitterly. One by one she dropped the sheets of her letters in the fire, and watched them burn to ashes.

"When they know—if they ever write to me after that, I will read those letters. These have no meaning." They had too much meaning, was what Esmée should have said.

After a silence Jack spoke somewhat hoarsely. "It's a beastly long time since I have written to any of my people. It's a pity I didn't write and tell them something; it might have saved trouble. But how can a fellow write? I got a letter to-day from my brother Sid. Says he's thinking of coming out here."

"Heaven save us!" cried Esmée. "Do write at once—anything—say anything you like."

Jack smiled drearily. "I'm afraid it's too late. In fact, the letter was written the day before he was to start, and it's dated January 25. There's a rumor that someone is in town, now, looking for me. I shouldn't be surprised if it were Sid."

"What if it were?" asked Esmée. "What could you do?"

"I don't know, indeed," said Jack. "I'm awfully cut up about it. The worst of it is, I asked him to come."

"You asked him!"

"Sometime ago, dearest, when everything was different. I thought I must make the fight for both our sakes, and I sent for Sid, thinking it might help to have him here with me."

"Did you, indeed," said Esmée, coldly. "What a pity he did not come before it was too late; he might have saved us both. How long ago was it, please?"

"Esmée, don't speak to me like that."

"But do you realize what you are saying?"

"You should not mind what I say. Think—what shall we do if it should be Sid? It rests with you, Esmée. Could you bear to meet him?"

"What is he like?" said Esmée, trembling.

"Oh, he's a lovely fellow. There's nobody like Sid."

"What does he look like?"

"He's good-looking, of course, being my brother," said Jack, with a wretched attempt at pleasantry, which met with no response. Esmée was staring at him, a strange terror in her eyes. "But there is more to his looks, somehow, than to most pretty boys. People who are up in such things say he's like the Saint George, or Saint somebody, by Donatello. He's blond, you know; he's as fresh as a girl, but he has an uncommonly set look at times, when he's serious or a bit disgusted about something. He has a set in his temper, too. I should not care to have Sid hear our story—not till after he had seen you, Esmée. Perhaps even then he could not understand. He has never loved a woman, except his mother. He doesn't know what a man's full-grown passion means. At least, I don't think he knows. He was rather fiercely moral on some points when I talked to him last; a little bit inhuman—what is it, Esmée?"

"There is that dog again!"

Jack looked at her in surprise at her shocked expression. Every trace of color had left her face. Her eyes were fixed upon the door.

"What dog? Why, it's Tip."

A creature as white as the storm sprang into the room as he opened the door, threw himself upon Jack, and whimpered and groaned and shivered, and seemed to weep with joy. Jack hugged him, laughing, and then threw him off, and dusted the snow from his clothing.

Tip shook himself, and came back excitedly for more recognition from his master. He took no notice at all of Esmée.

"Speak to him, won't you, dear? It's only manners, even if you don't care for him," Jack prompted gently. But Tip refused to accept Esmée's sad, perfunctory greeting; his countenance changed, he held aloof, glancing at her with an unpleasant gleam in his bloodshot eyes.

He had satisfied the cravings of affection, and now made it plain that his visit was on business that demanded his master's attention outside of the house. Jack knew the creature's intelligent ways so well that speech was hardly needed between them. "What's the racket, Tip? What's wrong out there? No, sir; I don't go back to town with you to-night, sir. Not much. Lie down! Be quiet, idiot!"

But Tip stood at the door, and began to whine, fixing his eyes on his master's face. As nothing came of this, he went back and stood in front of him, wagging his tail heavily and slowly; troubled wrinkles stood out over his beseeching eyes.

"What under heaven's the matter with you, dog? You're a regular funeral procession." Jack shoved the creature from him, and again he took up his station at the door. Jack rose, and opened it, and playfully tried to push him out. Tip stood his ground, always with his eyes on his master's face, and whimpered under his breath with almost tearful meaning.

"He's on duty to-night," said Jack. "He's got something on his mind, and he wants me to help him out with it. I say, old chap, we don't keep a life-saving station up here. Get out with your nonsense."

"There was someone with him when he was here this afternoon," Esmée forced herself to say.

"Has Tip been here before?"

"Yes, Jack. But a man was with him—a young, strange man. It was about four o'clock, perhaps five; it was getting dusk. I had been asleep, and I was so frightened. He knocked and knocked. I thought he would never stop knocking. He came to my window, and tried to get in, but the sash was frozen fast." Esmée paused, and caught her breath. "And I heard a dog scratching and whining."

"Did you not see the man?"

"I did. I saw him," gasped Esmée. "It was all quiet after awhile. I thought he had gone. I came out into the room, and there he stood close by that window, staring in; and the dog was with him. It was Tip."

"And you did not open the door to Tip?"

"Jack dear, have you not told me that I was never to open the door when you were away?"

"But didn't you speak to the man? Didn't you ask him who he was or what he wanted?"

"How could I? He did not speak to me. He stared at me as if I were a ghost, and then he went away."

"I would have questioned any man that came here with Tip. Tip doesn't take up with toughs and hobos. What was he like?"

Esmée had retreated under this cross-questioning, and stood at some distance from Jack, pale, and trembling with an ague of the nerves.

"What was he like?" Jack repeated.

"He was most awfully beautiful. He had a face like—like a death-angel."

Jack resented this phrase with an impatient gesture. "Was he fair, with blue eyes, and a little shade of a blond mustache?"

"I don't know. The light was not good. He stood close to the window, or I could not have seen him. What have I done? Was it wrong not to open the door?"

"Never mind about that, Esmée. I want you to describe the man."

"I can't describe him. I don't need to. I know—I know it was your brother."

"It must have been; and we have been sitting here—how many

hours?"

"I did not know there could be anybody—who—had a right to come in."

"Such a night as this? Get away, Tip!"

Jack had risen, and thrown off his coat. Esmée saw him get down his snow-shoe rig. He pulled on a thick woolen jersey, and buttoned his reefer over that. His foot-gear was drying by the fire; he put on a pair of German stockings, and fastened them below the knee, and over these the India-rubber buskins which a snow-shoer wears.

"Tip had better have something to eat before we start," he suggested. He did not look at Esmée, but his manner to her was very gentle and forbearing; it cut her more than harsh words and unreasonable reproaches would have done.

"He seems to think that I have done it," she said to herself, with the instinct of self-defense which will always come first with timid natures.

Tip would not touch the food she brought him. She followed him about the room meekly, with the plate in her hand; but he shrunk away, lifting his lip, and showing the whites of his blood-rimmed eyes.

Except for this defect, the sequel of distemper or some other of the ills of puppyhood, Tip had been a good-looking dog. But this accident of his appearance had prejudiced Esmée against him at first sight. Later he had made her dislike and fear him by a habit he had of dogging his master to her door, and waiting there, outside, like Jack's discarded conscience. If chidden, or invited to come in, the unaccountable creature would skulk away, only to return and take up his post of dumb witness as before; so that no one who watched the movements of Jack's dog could fail of knowing how Jack bestowed his time. In this manner Esmée had come almost to hate the dog, and Tip returned her feeling in his heart, though he was restrained from showing it. But to-night there was a new accusation in his gruesome eye.

"He will not eat for me," said Esmée, humbly.

"He must eat," said Jack. "Here, down with it!" The dog clapped his jaws on the meat his master held out to him, and stood ready, without a change of countenance, at the door.

"Can't you say that you forgive me?" Esmée pleaded.

"Forgive you? Who am I, to be forgiving people?" Jack answered hoarsely.

"But say it—say it! It was your brother. If it had been mine, I could forgive you."

"Esmée, you don't see it as it is."

"I do see it; but, Jack, you said that I was not to open the door."

"Well, you didn't open it, did you? So it's all right. But there's a man out in the snow, somewhere, that I have got to find, if Tip can show me where he is. Come, Tip!"

"Oh, Jack! You will not go without—"Jack turned his back to the door, and held out his arms. Esmée cast herself into them, and he kissed her in bitter silence, and went out.

These two were seated together again by the fire in the same room. It was four o'clock in the morning, but as dark as midnight. The floor in spots was wet with melted snow. They spoke seldom, in low, tired voices; it was generally Esmée who spoke. They had not been weeping, but their faces were changed and grown old. Jack shivered, and kept feeding the fire. On the bed in the adjoining room, as cold as the snow in a deserted nest, lay their first guest, whom no house fire would ever warm.

"I cannot believe it. I cannot take it in. Are you sure there is nothing more we could do that a doctor would do if we had one?"

"We have done everything. It was too late when we found him."

"How is it possible? I have heard of persons lost for days—and this was only such a few hours."

"A few hours! Good God, Esmée! Come out with me, and stand five minutes in this storm, if you can. And he had been on snow-shoes all day; he had come all the way uphill from town. He had had no rest, and nothing to eat. And then to turn about, and take it worse than ever."

"It is an impossible thing," she reiterated. "I am crazy when I think of it."

Tip lifted his head uneasily, rose, and tapped about the room, his long-nailed toes rattling on the uncarpeted floor. He paused, and licked up one of the pools of melted snow. "Stop that!" Jack commanded. There was dead silence. Then Tip began again his restless march about the room, pausing at the bedroom door to whine his questioning distress.

"Can't you make him stay in the kitchen?" Esmée suggested timidly.

"It is cold in the kitchen. Tip has earned his place by my fire as long as I shall have one," said Jack, emphatically.

Down fell some crashing object, and was shivered on the floor. The dog sprang up, and howled; Esmée trembled like a leaf.

"It's only your little looking-glass," she whispered. There was no mystery in its having fallen in such a wind from the projecting log where Esmée, with more confidence than judgment, had propped it. In silence both recalled the light words that had passed when Jack had taken it down from its high nail, saying that the mirrors in his establishment had not been hung with reference to persons of her size; and Esmée could see the picture they had made, putting their heads together before it, Jack stooping, with his hands on her shoulders, to bring his face in line with hers. Those laughing faces! All smiles, all tremulous mirth, in that house had vanished as the reflections in a shattered mirror.

Jack got up, and fetched a broom, and swept the clinking fragments into the fire. The frame he broke in two, and tossed after them.

"Call me as soon as it is light enough to start," he said to Esmée.

"But not unless it has stopped snowing?"

"Call me as soon as it is light, please," Jack repeated. He stumbled as he walked, like an old man. Esmée followed him into the drear little kitchen, where a single candle on the table was guttering in the draft. The windows were blank with frost, the boards cracked with the cold. Esmée helped prepare him a bed on a rude bunk against the wall, and Jack threw himself down on his pallet, and closed his eyes, without speaking. Esmée stood watching him in silence a moment; then she fell on her knees beside him on the floor.

"Say that you can forgive me! How shall I bear it all alone!"

At first Jack made no answer; he could not speak; his breath came deep and hard. Then he rose on one elbow, and looked at her with great stern eyes.

"Have I accused you? You did not do it. I did not do it. It happened—to show us what we are. We are impossible. We have broken with all the ties of family. We can have no brother or sister—our brothers and sisters are the rebels like ourselves; the easy cynics, the reckless, the morbid, the insane; all who are tainted in reputation or maimed in character. Sooner or later we shall embrace them all. Anything healthy that comes near us must take harm from us. We are contamination to women and destruction to men. Poor Sid had better have come to a den of thieves and cut-throats than to the house of his own brother. He is dead through my sin. Now do you see what this means to me?"

"I see," said Esmée, rising from her knees. She went out of the room, closing the door gently between them.

Jack lay stretching his aching muscles in one position after another, and every way he turned his mind pursued him. The brutality of his speech to Esmée wrought its anguish equally upon him, now that it was too late to get back a single word. Still, she must understand—she would understand, when she came to think—how broken up he was in mind and body, how insane for want of rest after that horrible night's work. This feeling of irresponsibility to himself satisfied him that she could not hold him responsible for his words at such a time. The strain he was supporting, mentally and physically, must absolve him if she had any consideration for him left.

So at length he slept. Esmée was careful not to disturb him. She had no need of bodily rest, and the beating of her heart and the ceaseless thinking went on and on.

"I am to be left here along with *it*"—she glanced toward the room where the body lay—"while he goes for help to take it to town. He has not asked me if I can go through with this. If I should say to him, 'spare me this awful trial,' he would answer,—and of course he would be right—'There are only us two; one to go and one to stay. Is it so much to ask of you after what has happened?'

"He does not ask it; he expects it. He is not my tender, remorseful lover now, dreading for me, every day, what his happiness must cost me. He is counting what I have cost him in other possessions which he might have had if he had not paid too great a price for one."

So these two had come to judge each other in the common misery that drove them apart. Toward daylight the snow ceased and the wind went down. Jack had forgotten to provide wood for Esmée's fire; the room was growing cold, and the wood supply was in the kitchen, where he slept. She sat still, and suffered mutely, rather than waken him before the time. This was not altogether consideration for him. It was partly wounded pride, and partly that humility of the flesh which comes of a moral scourging either through one's own or another's conscience.

When the late morning slowly dawned, she went to waken him, obedient to orders. She made every effort to arouse him, but in vain. His sleep was like a trance. She had heard of cases of extreme mental and physical strain where a sleep like this, bordering on unconsciousness, had been nature's cure. She let him sleep.

Seeing that her movements did not disturb him, she went

cautiously about the room, trying, now in forlorn sincerity, to adapt herself to the necessities of the situation. She did her best to make ready something in the nature of a breakfast for Jack when he should at length awaken. It promised to be a poor substitute, but the effort did her good.

It was after noon before Jack came to himself. He had been awake some little time, and watching her, before she was aware of it. He could see for himself what she had been trying to accomplish, and he was greatly touched.

"Poor child!" he said, and held out his arms.

She remained at a distance, slightly smiling, her eyes on the floor.

He did not press the moment of reconciliation. He got upon his feet, and, in the soldierly fashion of men who live in camps and narrow quarters, began to fold his blankets, and straighten things in his corner of the room.

"If you will go into the sitting-room, I will bring in the breakfast, such as it is," said Esmée. Jack obeyed her meekly. The sitting-room fire had been relighted, and was burning brightly. It was strange to him to sit and see her wait upon him. Stranger still was her silence. Here was a new distress. He tried to pretend unconsciousness of the change in her.

"It is two o'clock," he said, looking at his watch. "I'm afraid I shall be late getting back; but you must not worry. The storm is over, and I know every foot of the way."

"Did I do wrong," Esmee questioned nervously, "not to call you? I tried very hard, but you could not wake up. You must have needed to sleep, I think."

"Do you expect me to scold you every time I speak, Esmée? I have said enough, I think. Come here, dear girl. *I* need to be forgiven now. It cuts me to the heart to see you so humble. May God humble me for those words I said!"

"You spoke the truth. Only we had not been telling each other the truth before."

"No. And we must stop it. We shall learn the truth fast enough. We need not make whips of it to lash each other with. Come here."

"I can't," said Esmée in a choking whisper.

"Yes, you can. You shall forgive me."

She shook her head. "That is not the question. You did not do it. I did not do it. God has done it—as you said."

"Did I say that? Did I presume to preach to you?"

"If I have done what you say—if I have cut you off from all human

191

relations, and made your house worse than a den of thieves and murderers, how can anything be too bad for me to hear? What does it matter from whom I hear it?"

"I was beside myself. I was drunk with sorrow and fatigue."

"That is when people speak the truth, they say. I don't blame you, Jack. How should I? But you know it can never be the same, after this, with you or with me."

"Esmée," said Jack, after a long and bitter silence, holding out his shaking hand, "will you come with me in there, and look at him? He knows the truth—the whole truth. If you can see in his face anything like anger or reproach, anything but peace,—peace beyond all conception,—then I will agree that we part this day, forever. Will you come?"

"Oh, Jack, you *are* beside yourself, now. Do you think that I would go in there, in the presence of *that* peace, and call on it for my justification, and begin this thing again? I should expect that peace would come to me—the peace of instant death—for such awful presumption."

"I didn't mean that—not to excuse ourselves; only to bring back the trust that was between us. Does this bitterness cure the past? Have we not hurt each other enough already?"

"I think so. It is sufficient for me. But men, they say, get over such things, and their lives go on, and they take their places as before. I want you to—"

"There is nothing for me—will you believe it?—more than there is for you. Will you not do me that much justice, not to treat this one passion of my life as—what shall I say? It is not possible that you can think such things. We must make up to each other for what we have each cost the other. Come. Let us go and stand beside him—you and I, before the others get here. It will do us good. Then we will follow him out, on his way home, as far as we can; and if there is anyone in town who has an account with me, he can settle it there and then. My mother may have both her sons shipped home to her on the same train."

Jack had not miscounted on the effect of these words. They broke down Esmée's purer resolution with their human appeal. Yet he was not altogether selfish.

He held out his hand to her. She took it, and they went together, shrinkingly, into the presence of the dead. When they came out, both were in tears.

Late as it was, it was inevitable that Jack must start. Esmée

192

watched him prepare once more for the journey. When he was ready to set out, she said to him, with an extreme effort:

"If anyone should come while you are gone, I am to let him in?"

"Do as you think best, dear; but I am afraid that no one will disturb you. It will be a lonely watch. I wish that I could help you through with it."

"It is my watch," said Esmée. "I must keep it."

She would have been thankful for the company even of Tip, to answer for something living, if not human, in the house; but the dog insisted so savagely on following his master that she was forced to set him free. She closed the door after him, and locked it mechanically, hardly aware of what she did.

There is a growth of the spirit which is gradual, progressive, healthful, and therefore permanent. There are other psychical births that are forced, convulsive, agonizing in their suddenness. They may be premature, brought on by the shock of a great sorrow, or a sin perhaps committed without full knowledge of its nature, or realization of its consequences. Such births are perilous and unsure. Of these was the spiritual crisis through which Esmée was now passing.

She had made her choice: human love was satisfied according to the natural law. Now, in the hours of her solitary watch, that irrevocable choice confronted her. It was as a cup of trembling held to her lips by the mystery of the Invisible, which says: Whoever will drink of this cup of his desire, be it soon, be it late, shall drain it to the dregs, and wring them out. Esmee had come very soon to the dregs of her cup of trembling.

In such anguish and abasement her new life of the spirit began. Will she have strength to sustain it, or must it pass like a shaken light into the keeping of a steadier hand?

She was but dimly aware of outward changes as the ordeal wore on. It had been pale day-light in the cabin, and now it was dusk. It had been as still as death outside after the night of storm, the cold relenting, the frost trickling like tears down the pane; but now there was a rising stir. The soft, wild gale, the chinook of the Northwest, came roaring up the peak—the breath of May, but the voice of March. The forest began to murmur and moan, and strip its white boughs of their burden, and all its fairy frost-work melted like a dream. At intervals in the deep timber a strange sound was heard, the rush and thump of some soft, heavy mass into the snow. Esmée had never heard the sound before; it filled her with a creeping dread. Every separate distinct pounce—they came at intervals, near or far, but with no regularity—was a shock to her overwrought nerves. These sounds had taken sole possession of her ear. It was hence a double shock, at the same hour of early twilight when her visitor had come the night before, to hear again a man's feet in the trench outside, and again a loud knock upon the door.

Her heart with its panting answered in her breast. There was a pause while the knocker seemed to listen, as he had done before. Then the new-born will of the woman fearfully took command of her cowering senses. Something that was beyond herself forced her to the door. Pale, and weak in every limb, she dragged herself to meet whatever it was that summoned her. This time she opened the door.

There stood a mild-faced man in the dress of a miner, smiling apologetically. Esmée simply stared at him, and held the door wide. The man stepped hesitatingly inside, taking off his hat to the pale girl who looked at him so strangely.

David Bruce modestly attempted to give an accidental character to his visit by inventing an errand in that neighborhood.

"Excuse me, ma'am," he said. "I was goin' along over to the Mule Deer, but I thought I'd just ask if Mr. Waring's brother got through all right yesterday evenin'. It was so ugly outside."

The girl parted her lips to speak, but no sound came. The light shone in her ashy face. Her eyes were losing their expression. Bruce saw that she was fainting, and caught her as she fell.

The interview begun in this unpromising manner proved of the utmost comfort to Esmée. There was nothing in Bruce's manner to herself, nothing in his references to Jack, that implied any curiosity on his part as to the relation between them, or the least surprise at their being together at the Dreadnaught. He had "spared the situation" with an instinct that does not come from knowledge of the world.

He listened to her story of the night's tragedy, which she told with helpless severity, almost with indifference, simply as if it had happened to himself.

He appeared to be greatly moved by it personally; its moral significance he did not seem to see. He sat and helplessly repeated himself, in his efforts to give words to his sorrow for the "kid." His vocabulary being limited, and half composed of words which he could not use before a lady, he was put to great inconvenience to do justice to his feelings.

He blamed himself and his brother for letting the young man go by their cabin on such a threatening day.

"Why, Jim and me we couldn't get to sleep for thinkin' about him, 't was blowin' such a blizzard. Seemed like we could hear him a-yellin' to us, 'Is this the way to the Dreadnaught mine?' Wished the Lord we'd 'a' said it wa'n't. Well, sir, we don't want no more such foolishness. And that's partly why I come. We never thought but what he *had* got through, for all we was pestered about it, or else me and Jim would 'a' turned out last night. But what we was a-sayin' this mornin' was this: Them folks up there ain't acquainted with this country as we be—not in the wintertime. This here is what we call snow-slide weather. Hain't you been hearing how things is lettin' go? The snow slumpin' off the trees—you must have heard that. It's lettin' go up above us, too. There's a million ton of snow up there a-settlin' and a-crawlin' in this chinook, just a-gettin' ready to start to slide. We fellers in the mountains know how 't is. This cabin has stood all right so far, but the woods above was cut last summer. Now, I want you to come along with me right now. I've got a hand-sleigh here. You can tuck yourself up on it, and we'll pull out for the Mule Deer, and likely meet with Mr. Waring on the way. And if there's a snow-slide here before morning, it'll bury the dead, and not the livin' and the dead."

At these words the blood rushed to Esmée's cheek, and then dropped back to her heart, leaving her as white as snow.

"I don't remember that I have ever seen you before," she said; "but I thank you more than I ever thanked anybody in all my life."

David Bruce thought of course that she was going with him. But that was not what she meant. God, in his great mercy, had given her one opportunity. Her face shone. The spirit burned clear.

"This is my watch, you know. I cannot leave this house. But I don't think there will be a snow-slide. Things don't happen so simply as that. You don't know what I mean? But think a moment. You know, do you not, who I am? Should you think really that death is a thing that any friend of mine would wish to save me from? Life is what I am afraid of—long life to the end. I don't think there will be a snow-slide, not in time for me. But I thank you so much. You have made me feel so human—so like other people. You don't understand that, either? Well, no matter. I am just as grateful. I shall remember your visit all my life; and even if I live long, I doubt if I shall ever have a kinder visitor—even though I did almost faint when you first came. That was because I had been alone so long, with some dreadful thoughts for company. They are all gone now. I am much better for your coming, though you may think you have come for nothing. Now you must go before it gets too dark. You will go to the Mule Deer, will you not, and carry this same message to—there."

"I'm goin' to stop right here till Jack Waring gets back."

"Oh, no, you're not. You are going this instant." She rose, and held out her hand. She had that power over him that one so much in earnest as she will always have over one who is amazed and in doubt.

"Won't you shake hands with me?" Her thrilling voice made a sort of music of the common words.

He took her hand, and wagged it clumsily in a dazed way, and she almost pushed him out of the house.

"Well, I'll be hanged if that ain't the meanest trick since I was born—to leave a little lone woman watchin' with a dead man in a cabin, with snow-slides startin' all over the mountains! What's the matter with me, anyhow? Seem to be knocked silly with her blamed queer talk. Heap of sense in it, too. Wouldn't think one of her kind would see it that way, though. Durned if I know which kind she is. B'lieve I'll go back now. Why, Lord! I must go back! What'll I say to Jim?"

David Bruce had gained the top of the road leading away from the mine before he came to himself in a burst of unconscious profanity. He could hear the howling of the wind around the horn of the peak. He looked up and down, and considered a second.

In another second it was too late—too late to add his life to hers, that instant buried beneath the avalanche.

A stroke out of a clear sky; a roar that filled the air; a burst of light snow mounting over the tree-tops like steam condensed above a rushing train; a concussion of wind that felled trees in the valley a hundred yards from the spot where the plunging mass descended—then the chinook eddied back, across the track of the snow-slide, and went storming up the peak.

Pilgrim Station

From the great plateau of the Snake River, at a point that is far from any main station, the stage-road sinks into a hollow which the winds might have scooped, so constantly do they pounce and delve and circle round the spot. Down in this pot-hole, where sand has drifted into the infrequent wheel-tracks, there is a dead stillness, while the perpetual land-gale is roaring and troubling above.

One noon, at the latter end of summer, a wagon carrying four persons, with camp-gear and provision for a self-subsisting trip, jolted down into this hollow, the horses sweating at a walk as they beat through the heavy sand. The teamster drew them up, and looked hard at the singular, lonely place.

"I don't see any signs of that old corral, do you?" objected the man beside him. He spoke low, as if to keep his doubts from their neighbors on the back seat. These, an old, delicate, reverend-looking gentleman and a veiled woman sitting very erect, were silent, awaiting some decision of their fellow-travelers.

"There wouldn't be much of anything left of it," the teamster urged on the point in question—"only a few rails and wattles, maybe. Campers would have made a clean-up of them."

"You think this is the place, do you not, Mr. Thane? This is Pilgrim Station?" The old gentleman spoke to the younger of the two men in front, who, turning, showed the three-quarter view of a tanned, immobile face and the keen side-glance of a pair of dense black eyes—eyes that saw everything, and told nothing.

"One of our landmarks seems to be missing. I was just asking Kinney about it," he said.

Mr. Kinney was not, it appeared, as familiar as a guide should be with the road, which had fallen from use before he came to that part of the country; but his knowledge of roads in general inclined him to take with allowance the testimony of any one man of merely local information.

"That fool Mormon at the ferry hain't been past here, he said himself, since the stage was pulled off. What was here then wouldn't be here now,—not if it could be eat up or burnt up."

"So you think this is the place?" the old gentleman repeated. His face was quite pale, and he looked about him shrinkingly, with a latent, apprehensive excitement, strangely out of keeping with the void stillness of the hollow,—a spot which seemed to claim as little on the score of human interest or association as any they had passed on their long road hither.

"Well, it's just this way, Mr. Withers: here's the holler, and here's the stomped place where the sheep have camped; and the cattle-trails getherin' from everywhere to the water; and the young rabbit-brush that's sprung up since the plains was burnt over. If this ain't Pilgrim Station, we're lost pilgrims ourselves, I guess. We hain't passed it, it's time we come to it, and there ain't no road but this: as I put it up, this here has got to be the place."

"I believe you, Mr. Kinney," the old gentleman solemnly confirmed him. "Something tells me that this is the spot. I might almost say," he added in a lower tone to his companion, while a slight shiver passed over him in the hot sunlight, "that a voice cries to us from the ground!"

Those in front had not heard him. After a pause, Mr. Thane looked round again, smiled tentatively, and said, "Well?"

"Well, Daphne, my dear, hadn't we better get out?" Mr. Withers conjoined.

She who answered to this pretty pagan name did so mutely by rising in her place. The wind had moulded her light-colored veil close to her half-defined features, to the outline of her cheeks and low-knotted hair; her form, which was youthful and slender, was swathed in a clinging raw-silk dust-cloak. As she stood, hesitating before summoning her cramped limbs to her service, she might have suggested some half-evolved conception of doubting young womanhood emerging from the sculptor's clay. Personality, as yet, she had none; but all that could be seen of her was pure feminine.

Thane reached the side of the wagon before the veiled young woman had attempted to jump. She freed her skirts, stepped on the brake-bar, and, stooping, with his support, made a successful spring to the ground. Mr. Withers climbed out more cautiously, keeping his hand on Thane's arm for a few steps through the heavy sand. Thane left his fellow-pilgrims to themselves apart, and returned to help the teamster take out the horses.

"It looks queer to me," Mr. Kinney remarked, "that folks should want to come so far on purpose to harrer up their feelin's all over again. It ain't as if the young man was buried here, nor as if they was goin' to mark the spot with one of them Catholic crosses like you see down in Mexico, where blood's been spilt by the roadside. But just to set here and think about it, and chaw on a mis'able thing that happened two years and more ago! Lord! I wouldn't want to, and I ain't his father nor yet his girl. Would you?"

"Hardly," said Thane. "Still, if you felt about it as Mr. Withers does, you'd put yourself in the place of the dead, not of the living; and he has a reason for coming, besides. I haven't spoken of it, because I doubt if the thing is feasible. He wants to see whether the water of the spring can be brought into the hollow here,—piped, to feed a permanent drinking-trough and fountain. Good for evil, you see,—the soft answer."

"Well, that's business! That gits down where a man lives. His cattle kin come in on that, too. There's more in that, to my mind, than in a bare wooden cross. Pity there won't be more teamin' on this road. Now the stage has hauled off, I don't expect as many as three outfits a year will water at that fountain, excusin' the sheep, and they'll walk over it and into it, and gorm up the whole place."

"Well, the idea has been a great comfort to Mr. Withers, but it's not likely anything more will ever come of it. From all we hear, the spring would have to run uphill to reach this hollow; but you won't speak of it, will you, till we know?"

"Gosh, no! But water might be struck higher up the gulch,—might sink a trench and cut off the spring."

"That would depend on the source," said Thane, "and on how much the old gentleman is willing to stand: the fountain alone, by the time you haul the stone here, will foot up pretty well into the thousands. But we'll see."

"Hadn't you better stay round here with them till I git back?" Kinney suggested, for Thane had taken the empty canteens from the wagon, and was preparing to go with him to the spring. "You kin do your prospectin' later."

"They would rather be by themselves, I think," said Thane. But seeing Mr. Withers coming towards him, as if to speak, he turned back to meet him.

"You are going now to look for the spring, are you not?" the old gentleman asked, in his courteous, dependent manner.

"Yes, Mr. Withers. Is there anything I can do for you first?"

"Nothing, I thank you." The old gentleman looked at him half expectantly, but Thane was not equal, in words, to the occasion. "This is the place, Mr. Thane," he cadenced, in his measured, clerical tones. "This is the spot that last saw my dear boy alive,—that witnessed his agony and death." He extended a white, thin, and now shaking hand, which Thane grasped, uncovering his head. Mr. Withers raised his left hand; his pale eyes blinked in the sunlight; they were dim with tears.

"In memory of John Withers," he pronounced, "foully robbed of life in this lonely spot, we three are gathered here,—his friend, his father, and his bride that was to have been." Thane's eyes were on the ground, but he silently renewed his grasp of the old man's hand. "May God be our Guide as we go hence to finish our separate journeys! May He help us to forgive as we hope to be forgiven! May He teach us submission! But, O Lord! Thou knowest it is hard."

"Mr. Withers is a parson, ain't he?" Kinney inquired, as he and Thane, each leading one of the team-horses, and with an empty canteen swinging by its strap from his shoulder, filed down the little stony gulch that puckers the first rising-ground to riverward of the hollow. "Thought he seemed to be makin' a prayer or askin' a blessin' or somethin', when he had holt of you there by the flipper; kind of embarrassin', wa'n't it?"

"That's as one looks at it," said Thane. "Mr. Withers is a clergyman: his manner may be partly professional, but he strikes one as always sincere. And he hasn't a particle of self-consciousness where his grief for his son is concerned; I don't know that he has about anything. He calls on his Maker just as naturally as you and I, perhaps, might take his name in vain."

"No, sir; I've quit doin' that," Mr. Kinney objected. "I drawed the line there some years ago, on account of my wife, the way she felt about it, and the children growin' up. I quit when I was workin' round home, and now I don't seem to miss it none. I git along jest as well. Course I have to cuss a little sometimes. But I liked the way you listened to the old man's warblin'. Because talkin' is a man's trade, it ain't to say he hasn't got his feelin's."

As the hill cut off sounds of retreating voices and horseshoes clinking on the stones, a stillness that was a distinct sensation brooded upon the hollow. Daphne sighed as if she were in pain. She had taken off her veil, and now she was peeling the gloves from her white wrists and warm, unsteady hands. Her face, exposed, hardly sustained the promise of the veiled suggestion; but no man was ever known to find fault with it so long as he had hopes; afterwards—but even then it was a matter of temperament. There were those who remembered it all the more keenly for its daring deviations and provoking shortcomings.

It could not have been said of Daphne that her grief was without self-consciousness. Still, much of her constraint and unevenness of manner might have been set down to the circumstances of her present position. Why she should have placed herself, or have allowed her friends to place her, in an attitude of such unhappy publicity Thane had asked himself many times, and the question angered him as often as it came up. He could only refer it to the singularly unprogressive ideas of the Far West peculiar to Far Eastern people. Apparently, they had thought that, barring a friend or two of Jack's, they would be as much alone with their tragic memories in the capital city of Idaho as at the abandoned stage-station in the desert where their pilgrimage had ended. They had not found it quite the same. Daphne could, and probably did, read of herself in the Silver Standard, Sunday edition, which treats of social events, heralded among the prominent arrivals as "Jack Withers's maiden widow." This was a poetical flight of the city reporter. Thane had smiled at the phrase, but that was before he had seen Daphne; since then, whenever he thought of it, he pined for a suitable occasion for punching the reporter's head. There had been more of his language; the paper had given liberally of its space to celebrate this interesting advent of the maiden widow with her uncle, "the Rev. Withers," as the reporter styled him, "father of the lamented young man whose shocking murder, two years ago, at Pilgrim Station, on the eve of his return to home and happiness, cast such a gloom over our community, in which the victim of the barbarous deed had none but devoted friends and admirers. It is to be hoped that the reverend gentleman and the bereaved young lady, his companion on this sad journey, will meet with every mark of attention and respect which it is in the power of our citizens to bestow during their stay among us."

Now, in the dead, hot stillness, they two alone at last, Daphne sat beside her uncle in the place of their solemn tryst; and more than ever her excitement and unrest were manifest, in contrast to his mild and chastened melancholy. She started violently as his voice broke the silence in a measured, musing monotone:

> " ' Drink, weary pilgrim, drink and pray
> For the poor soul of Sybil Grey,
> Who built this cross and well.' "

"These lines," he continued in his ordinary prose accent, "gave me my first suggestion of a cross and well at Pilgrim Station, aided, perhaps, by the name itself, so singularly appropriate; not at all consistent, Mr. Thane tells me, with the usual haphazard nomenclature of this region. However, this is the old Oregon emigrant trail, and in the early forties men of education and Christian sentiment were the pioneers on this road. But now that I see the place and the country round it, I find the Middle Ages are not old enough to borrow from. We must go back, away back of chivalry and monkish superstition, to the life-giving pools of that country where the story of man began; where water, in the language of its people, was justly made the symbol of their highest spiritual as well as physical needs and cravings. 'And David longed, and said, Oh, that one would give me drink of the water of the well of Bethlehem, that is at the gate!' It is a far cry here to any gate but the gate of sunset, which we have been traveling against from morning to evening since our journey began, yet never approaching any nearer. But this, nevertheless, is the country of David's well,—a dry, elevated plain, surrounded by mountains strangely gashed and riven and written all over in nature's characters, but, except for the speech of a wandering, unlettered people, dumb as to the deeds of man. Mr. Thane tells me that if the wells on this road were as many as the deaths by violence have been, we might be pasturing our horses in green fields at night, instead of increasing their load with the weight of their food as well as our own. Yes, it is a 'desolate land and lone'; and if we build our fountain, according to my first intention, in the form of a cross, blessing and shadowing the water, it must be a rude and massive one, such as humble shepherds or herdsmen might accidentally have fashioned in the dark days before its power and significance were know. It will be all the more enduring, and the text shall be"—

"Uncle," cried Daphne in a smothered voice, "never mind the text! *I* am your text! Listen to me! If your cross stood there now, here is the one who should be in the dust before it!" She pressed her open hand upon her breast.

The gesture, her emphasis, the extreme figure of speech she used, were repellent to Mr. Withers over and above his amazement at her words. As he had not been observing her, he was totally unprepared for such an outburst.

"Daphne, my dear! Do I understand you? I cannot conceive"—

But Daphne could not wait for her meaning to sink in. "Uncle John," she interrupted, taking a quick breath of resolution, "I read somewhere once that if a woman be dishonest, deep down, deliberately a hypocrite, she ought to be gently and mercifully killed; a woman not honest had better not be alive. Uncle, I have something to say to you about myself. Gently and mercifully listen to me, for it ought to kill me to say it!"

Mr. Withers turned apprehensively, and was startled by the expression of Daphne's face. She was undoubtedly in earnest. He grew quite pale. "Not here, my dear," he entreated; "not now. Let our thoughts be single for this one hour that we shall be alone together. Let it wait for a little, this woeful confession, which I think you probably exaggerate, as young souls are apt to have not learned to bear the pain of self-knowledge, or self-reproach without knowledge. Let us forget ourselves, and think of our beloved dead."

"Uncle, it must be here and now. I cannot go away from this place a liar, as I came. Let me leave it here, my cowardly, contemptible falsehood, in this place of your cross. I am longing, like David, for that water they have gone to find, but I will not drink at Pilgrim Station except with clean lips that have confessed and told you all."

Mr. Withers shrank from these unrestrained and, to him, indecorous statements of feeling; they shocked him almost as much as would the spectacle of Daphne mutilating her beautiful hair, casting dust upon her head, and rending her garments before him. He believed that her trouble of soul was genuine, but his Puritan reserve in matters of conscience, his scholarly taste, his jealousy for the occasion which had brought them to that spot, all combined to make this exaggerated expression of it offensive to him. However, he no longer tried to repress her.

"Uncle, you don't believe me," she said, "but you must. I am quite myself."

"Except for the prolonged nervous strain you have been suffering; and I am afraid I have not known how to spare you as I might, the fatigue, the altitude, perhaps, the long journey face to face with these cruel memories. But I will not press it, I will not press it," he concluded hastily, seeing that his words distressed her.

"Press it all you can," she said. "I wish you could press it hard enough for me to feel it; but I feel nothing,—I am a stone. At this moment," she reiterated, "I have no feeling of any kind but shame for myself that I should be here at all. Oh, if you only knew what I am!"

"It is not what you are, it is who you are, that brings you here, Daphne."

"Yes, who I am! Who am I? What right had I to come here? I never loved him. I never was engaged to him, but I let you think so. When you wrote me that sweet letter and called me your daughter, why didn't I tell you the truth? Because in that same letter you offered me his money—and—and I wanted the money. I lied to you then, when you were in the first of your grief—to get his money! I have been trying to live up to that lie ever since. It has almost killed me; it has killed every bit of truth and decent womanly pride in me. I want you to save me from it before I grow any worse. You must take back the money. It did one good thing: it paid those selfish debts of mine, and it made mother well. What has been spent I will work for and pay back as I can. But I love *you,* uncle John; there has been no falsehood there."

"This is the language of sheer insanity, Daphne, of mental excitement that passes reason." Mr. Withers spoke in a carefully controlled but quivering voice; as a man who has been struck an unexpected and staggering blow, but, considering the quarter it came from, is prepared to treat it as an accident. "The facts, John's own words in his last letter to me, cannot be gainsaid. 'I am coming home to you, dad, and to whom else I need not say. You know that I have never changed, but she has changed, God bless her! How well He made them to be our thorn, our spur, our punishment, our prevention, and sometimes our cure! I am coming home to be cured,' he said. You have not forgotten the words of that letter, dear? I sent it to you, but first—I thought you would not mind—I copied those his last words. They were words of such happiness; and they implied a thought, at least, of his Creator, if not that grounded faith"—

"They were hopes, only hopes!" the girl remorsefully disclaimed. "I allowed him to have them because I wanted time to make up my wretched, selfish mind. I had never made him a single promise, never said one word that could have given me the right to pose as I did afterwards, to let myself be grieved over as if I had lost my last hope on earth. I had his money all safe enough."

"Daphne, I forbid you to speak in that tone! There are bounds even to confession. If you think well to degrade yourself by such allusions, do not degrade me by forcing me to listen to you. This is a subject too sacred to be discussed in its mercenary bearings: settle that question with yourself as you will, but let me hear no more of it."

Daphne was silenced; for the first time in her remembrance of him she had seen her uncle driven to positive severity, to anger even, in opposition to the truth which his heart refused to accept. When he was calmer, he began to reason with her, to uphold her in the true faith, against her seeming self, in these profane and ruthless disclosures.

"You are morbid," he declared, "oversensitive, from dwelling too long on this painful chapter of your life. No one knows better than myself what disorders of the imagination may result from a mood of the soul, a passing mood,—the pains of growth, perhaps. You are a woman now; but let the woman not be too hard upon the girl that she was. After what you have been through quite lately, and for two years past, I pronounce you mentally unfit to cope with your own case. Say that you did not promise him in words: the promise was given no less in spirit. How else could he have been so exaltedly sure? He never was before. You had never before, I think, given him any grounds for hope?"

"No, I was always honest before," said Daphne humbly. "When I first refused him, when we were both such children, and he went away, I promised to answer his letters if he would let *that* subject rest. And so I did. But every now and then he would try me again, to see if I had changed, and that letter I would not answer; and presently he would write again, in his usual way. As often as he brought up the old question, just so often I stopped writing; silence was always my answer, till that last winter, when I made my final attempt to do something with my painting, and failed so miserably. You don't know, uncle, how hard I have worked, or what it cost me to fail,—to have to own that all had been wasted: my three expensive winters in Boston, my cutting loose from all the little home duties, in the hope of doing something great that would pay for all. And that last winter I did not make my expenses, even. After borrowing every cent that mother could spare (more than she ought to have spared; it was doing without a girl that broke her down) and denying myself, or denying her, my home visit at Christmas; and setting up in a studio of my own, and taking pains to have all the surroundings that are said to bring success,—and then, after all, to fail, and fail, and fail! And spring came, and mother looked so ill, and the doctor said she must have rest, total rest and change; and he looked at me as if he would like to say, 'You did it!' Well, the 'rest' I brought her was my debts and my failure and remorse; and I wasn't even in good health, I was so used up with my winter's struggle. It was then, in the midst of all that trouble and shame and horror at myself, his sweet letter came. No, not sweet, but manly and generous, —utterly generous as he always was. I ought to have loved him, uncle dear; I always knew it, and I did try very hard! He did not feel his way this time, but just poured out his whole heart once for all; I knew he would never ask me again. And then the fatal word: he said he had grown rich. He could give me the opportunities my nature demanded. You know how he would talk. He believed in me, if nobody else ever did; I could not have convinced him that I was a failure.

"It was very soothing to my wounds. I was absolutely shaken by the temptation. It meant so much: such a refuge from self-contempt and poverty and blame, and such rest and comfort it would bring to mother! I hope that had something to do with it. You see I am looking for a loop-hole to crawl out of; I haven't strength of mind to face it without some excuse. Well, I answered that letter; and I think the evil one himself must have helped me, for I wrote it, my first careful, deliberate piece of double-dealing, just as easily as if I had been practicing for it all my life. It was such a letter as any man would have thought meant everything; yet if I had wanted, I could have proved by the words themselves that it meant nothing that couldn't be taken back.

"I said to myself, if I can stand it, if I can hold out as I feel now, I will marry him; then let come what may. I knew that some things would come, some things that I wanted very much.

"Then came the strange delay, the silence, the wretched telegrams and letters back and forth. Ah, dear, do I make you cry? Don't cry for him: you have not lost him. Cry for me, the girl you thought was good and pure and true! You know what I did then, when your dear letter came, giving me all he had; calling me your daughter, all that was left you of John! I deceived you in your grief, hating myself and loving you all the time. And here I am, in this place! Do you wonder I had to speak?"

"Your words are literally as blows to me, Daphne," Mr. Withers groaned, covering his face. After awhile he said: "All I have in the world would have been yours and your mother's, had you come to me, or had I suspected the trouble you were in. I ought to have been more observant. My prepossessions must be very strong; doubtless some of the reader's faculties have been left out in my mental constitution. I hear you say these words, but even now they are losing their meaning for me. I see that your distress is genuine, and I must suppose that you have referred it to its proper cause; but I cannot master the fact itself. You must give me time to realize it. This takes much out of life for me."

"Not my love for *you*, Uncle John: there has been no falsehood there."

"You could not have spared yourself and me this confession?" the old man queried. "But no, God forgive me! You must have suffered grievous things in your young conscience, my dear; this was an ugly spot to hide. But now you have fought your fight and won it, at the foot of the cross. To say that I forgive you, that we both, the living and the dead, forgive you, is the very least that can be said. Come here! Come and be my daughter as before! My daughter!" he repeated. And Daphne, on her knees, put her arms about his neck and hid her face against him.

"Thank Heaven!" he murmured brokenly, "it cannot hurt him now. He has found his 'cure.' As a candle-flame would expire in this broad sunlight, so all those earthly longings"—the old gentleman could not finish his sentence, though a sentence was dear to him almost as the truth from which, even in his love of verbiage, his speech never deviated. "So we leave it here," he said at last. "It is between us and our blessed dead. No one else need know what you have had the courage to tell me. Your confession concerns no other living soul, unless it be your mother, and I see no reason why her heart should be perturbed. As for the money, what need have I for more than my present sufficiency, which is far beyond the measure of my efforts or deserts? I beg you never to recur to the subject, unless you would purposely wish to wound me. This is a question of conscience, purely, and you have made yours clean. Are you satisfied?"

"Yes," said Daphne faintly.

"What is the residue? Or is it only the troubled waters still heaving?"

"Yes, perhaps so."

"Well, the peace will come. Promise me, dear, that you will let it come. Do not give yourself the pain and humiliation of repeating to any other person this miserable story of your fault."

"It was more than a fault; you know that, Uncle. Your conscience could not have borne it for an hour."

"Your sin, then. A habit of confession is debilitating and dangerous. God has heard you; and I, who alone in this world could have the right to reproach you, have said to you, Go in peace. Peace let it be, and silence, which is the safest seal of a true confession."

"Do you mean that I am never to let myself be known as I am?" asked Daphne. Her face had changed; it wore a look of fright and resistance. "Why, that would mean that I am never to unmask; to go about all my life in my trappings of false widowhood. You read what that paper called me! I cannot play the part any longer."

"Are you speaking with reference to these strangers? But this will soon be over, dear; we shall soon be at home, where no one thinks of us except as they have known us all their lives. It will be painful for a little while, this conspicuousness, but these good people will soon pass out of our lives, and we out of theirs. Idle speculation will have little to do with us, after this."

"There will always be speculation," implored the girl. "It will follow me wherever I go, and all my life I shall be in bondage to this wretched lie. Take back the money, Uncle, and give me the price I paid for it,—my freedom, myself, as I was before I was tempted!"

"Ah, if that could be!" said the old gentleman. "Is it my poor boy's memory that burdens you so? Is it that you would be freed from?"

"From doing false homage to his memory," Daphne pleaded. "I could have grieved for him, if I could have been honest; as it is, I am in danger almost of hating him. Forgive me, Uncle, but I am! How do you suppose I feel when voices are lowered and eyes cast down, not to intrude upon my peculiar, privileged grief? 'Here I and Sorrow sit!' Isn't it awful, uncle? Isn't it ghastly, indecent? I am afraid some day I shall break out and do some dreadful thing, laugh or say something shocking, when they try to spare my feelings. Feelings! When my heart is as hard, this moment, to everything but myself, myself! I am so sick of myself! But how can I help thinking about myself when I can never for one moment be natural?"

"This is something that goes deeper," said Mr. Withers. "I confess it is difficult for me to follow you here; to understand how a love as meek as that of the dead, who asks nothing, could lay such deadly weights upon a young girl's life."

"Not his love: mine, mine! Is it truly in his grave? If it is not, why do I dare to profess daily that it is, to go on lying everyday? I want back my word, that I never gave to any man. Can't one repent and confess a falsehood? And do you call it confessing, when all but one person in the world are still deceived?"

"It is not easy for me to advise you, Daphne," said Mr. Withers wearily. "Your struggle has discovered to me a weakness of my own: verily, an old man's fond jealousy for the memory of his son. I could almost stoop to entreat you. I do entreat you! So long as we defraud no one else, so long as there is no living person who might justly claim to know your heart, why rob my poor boy's grave of the grace your love bestows, even the semblance that it was? Let it lie there like a mourning-wreath, a purchased tribute, we will say," the father added, with a smile of sad irony, "but only a rude hand would rob him of his funereal honors. There seems to be an unnecessary harshness in this effort to right yourself at the cost of the unresisting dead. Since you did not deny him living, must you repudiate him now? Fling away even his memory, that casts so thin a shade upon your life, a faint morning shadow that will shrink away as your sun climbs higher? By degrees you will be free. And speaking less selfishly, would there not be a certain indelicacy in reopening now the question of your past relations to one whose name is very seldom spoken? Others may not be thinking so much of your loss—your supposed loss," the old gentleman conscientiously supplied—"as your sensitiveness leads you to imagine. But you will give occasion for thinking and for talking if you tear open now your girlhood's secrets. Whom does it concern, my dear, to know where or how your heart is bestowed?"

Daphne's cheeks and brow were burning hot; even her little ears were scarlet. Her eyes filled and drooped. "It is only right," she owned. "It is my natural punishment."

"No, no; I would not punish nor judge you. I love you too well. But I know better than you can what a safeguard this will be,—this disguise which is no longer a deception, since the one it was meant to deceive knows all and forgives it. It will rebuke the bold and hasty pretenders to a treasure you cannot safely trust, even by your own gift, as yet. You are still very young in some ways, my dear."

"I am old enough," said Daphne, "to have learned one fearful lesson."

"Do I oppress you with my view? Do I insist too much?"

Perhaps nothing could have lowered the girl in her own eyes more than this humility of the gentle old man in the face of his own self-exposed weakness, his pathetic jealousy for that self above self,—the child one can do no more than grieve for this side of the grave. She had come to herself only to face the consciousness of a secret motive which robbed her confession of all moral value. Repentance, that would annul her base bargain, now that the costs began to outweigh the advantages, was gilt-edged, was a luxury; she was ashamed to buy back her freedom on such terms.

"Let it be as you say," she assented; "but only because you ask it.

It will not be wrong, will it, if I do it for you?"

"I hope not," returned Mr. Withers. "The motive, in a silence of this kind that can harm no one, must make a difference, I should say."

So it was settled; and Daphne felt the weight of her promise, which the irony of justice had fastened upon her, as a millstone round her neck for life; she was still young enough to think that whatever is must last forever. They sat in silence, but neither felt that the other was satisfied. Mr. Withers knew that Daphne was not lightened of her trouble, nor was he in his heart content with the point he had gained. The unwonted touch of self-assertion it had called for rested uneasily on him and he could not but own that he had made himself Daphne's apologist, which no confessor ought to be, in this disguise by which he named the deception he was now helping her to maintain.

After a time, when Daphne had called his attention to the fact, he agreed that it was indeed strange that their companions did not return: they had been gone an hour or more to find a spring said to be not half a mile away.

Daphne proposed to climb the grade and see if they were yet in sight, Mr. Withers consenting; indeed, under the stress of his thoughts, her absence was a sensible relief.

From the hilltop, looking down, she could see the way they had gone; the crooked gulch, a garment's crease in the great lap of the table-land, sinking to the river. She saw no one, heard no sound but the senseless hurry and bluster of the winds,—coming from no one knew where, going none cared whither; it blew a gale in the bright sunlight, mocking her efforts to listen. She waved her hand to her uncle's lone figure in the hollow, to signify that she was going down on the other side. He assented, supposing she had seen their fellow-travelers returning.

She had been out of sight some moments, long enough for Mr. Withers to have lapsed into his habit of absent musing, when Thane came rattling down the slope of the opposite hill, surprised to see the old gentleman alone. His long, black eyes went searching everywhere, while he reported a fruitless quest for the spring. Kinney and he had followed the gulch, which nowhere showed a vestige of water save in the path of the spring freshets, until they had come in sight of the river; and Kinney had taken the horses on down to drink, riding one and leading the other. It would be nearly three miles to the river from where Thane had left him, but that was where all the watched him prepare once more for the journey. When he was ready to set out, she said to him, with an extreme effort:

"If anyone should come while you are gone, I am to let him in?"

"Do as you think best, dear; but I am afraid that no one will disturb you. It will be a lonely watch. I wish that I could help you through with it."

"It is my watch," said Esmée. "I must keep it."

She would have been thankful for the company even of Tip, to answer for something living, if not human, in the house; but the dog insisted so savagely on following his master that she was forced to set him free. She closed the door after him, and locked it mechanically, hardly aware of what she did.

There is a growth of the spirit which is gradual, progressive, healthful, and therefore permanent. There are other psychical births that are forced, convulsive, agonizing in their suddenness. They may be premature, brought on by the shock of a great sorrow, or a sin perhaps committed without full knowledge of its nature, or realization of its consequences. Such births are perilous and unsure. Of these was the spiritual crisis through which Esmée was now passing.

She had made her choice: human love was satisfied according to the natural law. Now, in the hours of her solitary watch, that irrevocable choice confronted her. It was as a cup of trembling held to her lips by the mystery of the Invisible, which says: Whoever will drink of this cup of his desire, be it soon, be it late, shall drain it to the dregs, and wring them out. Esmée had come very soon to the dregs of her cup of trembling.

In such anguish and abasement her new life of the spirit began. Will she have strength to sustain it, or must it pass like a shaken light into the keeping of a steadier hand?

She was but dimly aware of outward changes as the ordeal wore on. It had been pale day-light in the cabin, and now it was dusk. It had been as death outside after the night of storm, the cold relenting, the frost trickling like tears down the pane; but now there was a rising stir. The soft, wild gale, the chinook of the Northwest, came roaring up the peak—the breath of May, but the voice of March. The forest began to murmur and moan, and strip its white boughs of their burden, and all its fairy frost-work melted like a dream. At intervals in the deep timber a strange sound was heard, the rush and thump of some soft, heavy mass into the snow. Esmée had never heard the sound before; it filled her with a creeping dread. Every separate distinct pounce—they came at intervals, near or far, but with no regularity—was a shock to her overwrought nerves. These sounds had taken sole possession of her ear. It was hence a double shock, at the same hour of early twilight when her visitor had come the night before, to hear again a man's feet in the trench outside, and again a loud knock upon the door.

Her heart with its panting answered in her breast. There was a pause while the knocker seemed to listen, as he had done before. Then the new-born will of the woman fearfully took command of her cowering senses. Something that was beyond herself forced her to the door. Pale, and weak in every limb, she dragged herself to meet whatever it was that summoned her. This time she opened the door. There stood a mild-faced man in the dress of a miner, smiling apologetically. Esmée simply stared at him, and held the door wide. The man stepped hesitatingly inside, taking off his hat to the pale girl who looked at him so strangely.

David Bruce modestly attempted to give an accidental character to his visit by inventing an errand in that neighborhood.

"Excuse me, ma'am," he said. "I was goin' along over to the Mule Deer, but I thought I'd just ask if Mr. Waring's brother got through all right yesterday evenin'. It was so ugly outside."

The girl parted her lips to speak, but no sound came. The light shone in her ashy face. Her eyes were losing their expression. Bruce saw that she was fainting, and caught her as she fell.

The interview begun in this unpromising manner proved of the utmost comfort to Esmée. There was nothing in Bruce's manner to herself, nothing in his references to Jack, that implied any curiosity on his part as to the relation between them, or the least surprise at their being together at the Dreadnaught. He had "spared the situation" with an instinct that does not come from knowledge of the world.

He listened to her story of the night's tragedy, which she told with helpless severity, almost with indifference, simply as if it had happened to himself.

He appeared to be greatly moved by it personally; its moral significance he did not seem to see. He sat and helplessly repeated himself, in his efforts to give words to his sorrow for the "kid." His vocabulary being limited, and half composed of words which he could not use before a lady, he was put to great inconvenience to do deceptive cattle-trails were tending. Thane, returning, had made a loop of his track around the hollow, but had failed to round up any spring. Hence, as he informed Mr. Withers, this could not be Pilgrim Station. He made no attempt to express his chagrin at this cruel and unseemly blunder. The old gentleman accepted it with his usual uncomplaining deference to circumstances; still, it was jarring to nerves overstrained and bruised by the home thrust of Daphne's defection. He fell silent, and drew within himself, not reproachfully, but sensitively. Thane rightly surmised that no second invocation would be offered, when they should come to the true Pilgrim Station; the old gentleman would keep his threnodies to himself, after this.

It would have been noticeable to any less celestial-minded observer than Mr. Withers, the diffidence with which Thane, in asking after Miss Daphne Lewis, pronounced her name. He did not wait for the old gentleman to finish his explanation of her absence, but, having learned the way she had gone, dropped himself at a great pace down the gulch, and came upon her unawares, where she had been sitting, overcome by nameless fears and creeping horror of the place. She started to her feet, for Thane's was no furtive tread that crashed through the thorny greaswood, and planted itself, a yard at a bound, amongst the stones. The horror vanished, and a flush of life, a light of joy, returned to her speaking face. He had never seen her so completely off her guard. He checked himself suddenly, and caught his hat from his head; and without thinking, before he replaced it, he drew the back of his soft leather glove across his dripping forehead. The unconventional action touched her keenly; she was sensitively subject to outward impressions, and "the plastic" had long been her delight, her ambition, and her despair.

"Oh, if I could only have done something simple like that!" the defeated, unsatisfied artist soul within her cried. "That free, arrested stride, how splendid! And the hat crumpled in his hand, and his bare head and strong brows in the sunlight, and the damp points of hair clinging to his temples! No, he is not bald,—that was only a tonsure of white light on the top of his head; still, he must be hard on forty. It is the end of summer with him, too; and here he comes for water, thirsting, to satisfy himself where water was plentiful in spring, and he finds a dry bed of stones. Call it The End of Summer; it is enough. Ah, if I could ever have thought out an action as simple and direct as that—and drawn it! But how can one draw what one has never seen!"

Not all this, but something else, something more, which Daphne could not have put into words, spoke in the look which Thane surprised. It was but a flash between long lashes that instantly fell and put it out; but no woman whose heart was in the grave ever looked at a living man in that way, and the living man could not help but know it. It took away his self-possession for a moment; he stood speechless, gazing into her face, with a question in his eyes which five minutes before he would have declared an insult to her.

Daphne struggled to regain her mask, but the secret had escaped her: shameless Nature had seized her opportunity.

"How did I miss you?" Daphne asked with forced coolness, as they turned up the gulch together. For the moment she had forgotten about the spring.

Thane briefly explained the mistake that had been made, adding, "You will have to put up with another day of us, now,—perhaps two."

"And where do you leave us, then?" asked Daphne stupidly.

"At the same place—Decker's Ferry, you know." He smiled, indulgent to her crass ignorance of roads and localities. "Only we shall be a day longer getting there. We are still on the south side of the river, you remember?"

"Oh, of course!" said Daphne, who remembered nothing of the kind.

"It was a brutal fake, our springing this place on you for Pilgrim Station," he murmured.

"It has all been a mistake,—our coming, I mean; at least I think so."

It was some comfort to Thane to hear her say it, he had been so forcibly of that opinion himself all along; but he allowed the admission to pass.

"It must have been a hard journey for you," he exerted himself to say, speaking in a surface voice, while his thoughts were sinking test-pits through layers of crusted consciousness into depths of fiery nature underneath.

She answered in the same perfunctory way: "You have been very kind; uncle has depended on you so much. Your advice and help have been everything to him."

He took her up with needless probity: "Whatever you do, don't thank me! It's bad enough to have Mr. Withers heaping coals of fire on my head. He gives me the place, always, in regard to his son, of

212

an intimate friend; which I never was, and God knows I never claimed to be! He took it for granted, somehow,—perhaps because of my letters at first, though any brute would have done as much at a time like that! Afterwards I would have set him right, but I was afraid of thrusting back the friendly imputation in his face. He credits me with having been this and that of a godsend to his son, when, as a fact, we parted, that last time, not even good friends. Perhaps you can forgive me for saying it? You see how I am placed!"

This iron apology, which some late scruple had ground out of Thane, seemed to command Daphne's deepest attention. She gave it a moment's silence, then she said, "There is nothing that hurts one, I think, like being unable to feel as people take for granted one must and ought to feel." But her home application of it gave a slight deflection to Thane's meaning which he firmly corrected.

"I felt all right, so did he, I dare say, but we never let each other know how we felt. Men don't have much use for sentiment, as a rule. Your uncle takes for granted that I knew a lot about him,—his thoughts and feelings; that we were immensely sympathetic. Perhaps we were, but we didn't know it. We knew nothing of each other intimately. He never spoke to me of his private affairs but once, the night before he started. It was at Wood River. Some of us gave him a little supper. Afterwards we had some business to settle, and I was alone with him in his room. It was then I made my break; and—well, it ended as I say: we quarreled. It has hurt me since, especially as I was wrong."

"What can men quarrel about, when they don't know each other well? Politics, perhaps?" Daphne endeavored to give her words a general application.

"It was not politics with us," Thane replied curtly. Changing the subject, he said, "I wish you could see the valley from that hogback over to the west." He pointed towards the spine of the main divide, which they would cross on their next day's journey. "Will you come up there this evening and take a look at the country? The wind will die down at sunset, I think."

There was a studied commonplaceness in his manner; his eyes avoided hers.

"Thanks; I should like to," she answered, in the same defensive tone.

"To go back to what we were saying," Daphne began, when they were seated, that evening, on the hilltop. All around them the view of the world rose to meet the sky, glowing in the west, purple in the east, while the pale planets shone, and below them the river glassed and gleamed in its crooked bed. "I ask you seriously," she said. "What was the trouble between you?" Doubtless she had a reason for asking, but it was not the one that she proceeded to give. "Had you—have you, perhaps—any claims in a business way against him? Because, if you had, it would be most unfair to his father"—The words gave her difficulty; but her meaning, as forced meanings are apt to be, was more than plain.

Thane was not deceived: a woman who yields to curiosity, under however pious an excuse, is, to say the least, normal. Her thoughts are neither in the heavens above nor in the grave beneath. His black eyes flashed with the provocation of the moment; it was instinct that bade him not to spare her.

"We quarreled," he said, "in the orthodox way, about a woman."

"Indeed!" said Daphne. "Then you must pardon me."

"And her name"—he continued calmly.

"I did not ask you her name."

"Still, since we have gone so far"—

"There is no need of our going any farther."

"We may as well,—a little farther. We quarreled, strangely enough, about you—the first time he ever spoke of you. He would not have spoken then, I think, but he was a little excited, as well he might have been. Excuse me?"

"Nothing!" said Daphne. She had made an involuntary protesting sound.

"He said he hoped to bring you back with him. I asked how long since he had seen you; and when he told me five years, I remarked that he had better not be too sure. 'But you don't know her,' he said; 'she is truth itself, and courage. By as many times as she has refused to listen to me, I am sure of her now.' I did not gather, somehow, that you were—engaged to him, else I hope I should not have gone so far. As it was, I kept on persisting, like a cynic who has got no one of his own to be sure of, that he had better not be too sure. He might have seen, I thought then, that it was half chaff and half envy with me; but it was a nervous time, and I was less than sympathetic, less than a friend to him. And now I am loaded with friendship's honors, and you have come yourself to prove me in the wrong. You punish me by converting me to the truth."

"What truth?" asked Daphne, so low that Thane had to guess her question.

"Have you not proved to me that some women do have memories?"

Daphne could not meet his eyes; but she suspected him of something like sarcasm. She could not be sure, for his tone was agitating in its tenderness.

"All things considered," she said slowly, "does it not strike you as rather a costly conversion?"

"I don't say I was worth it, nor do I see just how it benefits me, personally, to have learned my lesson."

He rose, and stood where he could look at her,—an unfair advantage, for his dark face, strong in it immobility, was in silhouette against the flush of twilight which illumined hers, so transparent in its sensitiveness.

"Is it not a good thing to believe, on any terms?" she tried to answer lightly.

"For some persons, perhaps. But my hopes, if I had any, would lie in the direction of disbelief."

"Disbelief?" she repeated confusedly. His keen eyes beat hers down.

"In woman's memory, constancy,—in youth, say? I am not talking of seasoned timber; I don't deserve to be happy, you see, and I look for no more than my deserts."

If he were mocking her now, only to test her? And if she should answer with a humble, blissful disclaimer? But she answered nothing, disclaimed nothing; suffered his suspicion,—his contempt, perhaps, for she felt that he read her through and through.

A widow is well, and a maid is well; but a maiden widow, who trembles and looks down,—in God's creation, what is she?

On the north side of the Snake, after climbing out of the cañon at Decker's Ferry, the cross-roads branch as per sign post: thirty miles to Shoshone Falls, one mile to Decker's Ferry,—"good road." This last assertion, as we have it on no less authority than that of Decker himself, must be true. Nothing is said of the road to Bliss—not even that there is such a Bliss,—only sixteen miles away. Being a station on the Oregon Short Line, Bliss can take care of itself.

At these cross-roads, on a bright, windy September morning, our travelers had halted for reasons, the chief of which was to say good-by. They had slept overnight at the ferry, parted their baggage in the morning, and now, in separate wagons, by divergent roads, were setting forth on the last stage of their journey.

Daphne had left some necessary of her toilet at the ferry, and the driver of Mr. Withers's team had gone back to ask the people at the ferry-house to find it. This was the cause of their waiting at the cross-roads. Mr. Withers and Daphe were on their devoted way, like conscientious tourists, though both were deadly weary, to prostrate themselves before the stupendous beauty of the great lone falls at Shoshone. Thane, with Kinney's team, was prosaically bound down the river to examine and report on a placer-mine. But before his business would be finished Mr. Withers and his niece would have returned by railroad via Bliss to Boise, and have left that city for the East; so this was likely to be a long good-by.

If anything could have come of Mr. Withers's project of a memorial fountain at Pilgrim Station, there might have been a future to the acquaintance, for Thane was to have had charge of the execution of the design; but nature had lightly frustrated that fond, beneficent dream.

Mr. Kinney had offered the practical suggestion that the road should go to the fountain, since the fountain could not come to the road. Its course was a mere accident of the way the first wagon-wheels had gone. The wheels were few now, and, with such an inducement, might well afford to cross the gulch in a new place lower down. But Mr. Withers would have none of this dislocation of the unities. There was but one place—the dismal hollow itself, the scene of his heart's tragedy—where his acknowledgment to God should stand, his mute "Thy will be done!"

Perhaps the whole conception had lost something of its hold on his mind by contact with such harsh realities as Daphne's disavowals and his own consequent struggle with a father's weakness. He had not, in his inmost conscience, quite done with that question yet.

Thane was touched by the meekness with which the old gentleman resigned his dream. The journey, he suspected, had been a disappointment to him in other ways,—had failed in impressiveness, in personal significance; had fallen at times below the level of the occasion, at others had overpowered it and swept it out of sight. Thane could have told him that it must be so. There was room for too many mourners in that primeval waste. Whose small special grief could make itself heard in that vast arid silence, the voice of which was God? God in nature, awful, inscrutable, alone, had gained a new meaning for Mr. Withers. Miles of desert, days of desert, like waves of brute oblivion, had swept over him. Never before had he felt the oppression of purely natural causes, the force of the physical in conflict with the spiritual law. And now he was to submit to a final illustration of it, perhaps the simplest and most natural one of all.

Daphne was seated at a little distance, on her camp-stool, making a drawing of the desert cross-roads with the twin sign-posts pointing separate ways, as an appropriate finish to her Snake River sketch-book. The sun was tremendous, the usual Snake River zephyr blowing forty miles an hour, and the flinty ground refused to take the brass-shod point of her umbrella-staff. Mr. Kinney, therefore, sat beside her, gallantly steadying her heavy sketching umbrella against the wind.

Mr. Withers, while awaiting the return of his own team from the ferry, had accepted a seat in Thane's wagon. (It was a bag, containing her curling-iron, lamp, and other implements appertaining to "wimples and crisping-pins," that Daphne had forgotten, but she had not described its contents. One bag is as innocent as another, on the outside; it might have held her Prayer Book.)

Thane was, metaphorically, "kicking himself" because time was passing, and he could not find words delicate enough in which to clothe an indelicate request,—one outrageous in its present connection, yet from some points of view, definitively his own, a most urgent and natural one.

"For one shall grasp, and one resign,
And God shall make the balance good."

To grasp is a simple act enough; but to do so delicately, reverently, with due regard for the prejudices and preferences of others, may not always be so simple. Thane was not a Goth nor a Vandal; by choice he would have sought to preserve the amenities of life; but a meek man he was not, and the thing he now desired was, he considered, well worth the sacrifice of such small pretensions as his in the direction of unselfishness.

The founding of a family in its earliest stages is essentially an egotistic and ungenerous proceeding. Even Mr. Withers must have been self-seeking once or twice in his life, else had he never had a son to mourn.

So, since life in this world is for the living, and his own life was likely to go on many years after Mr. Withers had been gathered to the reward of the righteous, Thane worked himself up to the grasping-point at last.

He never was able to reflect with any pride on the way he did it, and perhaps it is hardly fair to report him in a conversation that would have had its difficulties for almost any man, but his way of putting his case was something like the following: Mr. Withers guilelessly opening the way by asking, "You will be coming East, I hope, before long, Mr. Thane?"

"Possibly," said Thane, "I may run on to New York next winter."

"If you should, I trust you will find time to come a little further East and visit me? I could add my niece's invitation to my own, but she and her mother will probably have gone South for her mother's health. However, I will welcome you for us both,—I and my books, which are all my household now."

"Thanks, sir, I should be very glad to come; though your books, I'm afraid, are the sort that would not have much to say to me."

"Come and see, come and see," Mr. Withers pressed him warmly. "A ripe farewell should always hold the seeds of a future meeting."

"That is very kindly said," Thane responded quickly; "and if you don't mind, I will plant one of those seeds right now."

"So do, so do," the old gentleman urged unsuspiciously.

"Your niece"—Thane began, but could see his way no further in that direction without too much precipitancy. Then he backed down on a line of argument,—"I need not point out the fact," etc.,—and abandoned that as beset with too many pitfalls of logic, for one of his limited powers of analysis. Fewest words and simplest would serve him best. "It is hardly likely," then he said, "that your niece's present state of feeling will be respected as long as it lasts; there will be others with feelings of their own to think of. Her loss will hardly protect her all her life from—she will have suitors, in short! Nature is a brute, and most men, young men, are natural in that respect,—in regard to women, I mean. I don't want to be the first fool who rushes in, but there will be a first. When he arrives, sir, will you let me know? If any man is to be heard, I claim my right to speak to her, myself; the right, you understand, of one who loves her, who will make any sacrifice on earth to win her."

Mr. Withers remained silent. He had a sense of suffocation, as of waves of heat and darkness going over him. The wind sang in his ears, shouted and hooted at him. He was stunned. Presently he gasped, "Mr. Thane! You have not surely profaned this solemn journey with such thoughts as these?"

"A man cannot always help his thoughts, Mr. Withers. I have not

218

profaned any thoughts by putting them into words, till now; and I cannot do them justice, but I have made them plain. This is not a question of taste or propriety with me, or even of decency; it is my life, —all of it I shall ever place at the disposal of any woman. I am not a boy; I know what I want, and how much I want it. The secret of success is to be in the right place at the right time: here is where I ask your help."

"I do not question that you know what you want," said Mr. Withers mildly, —"it is quite a characteristic of the men of this region, I infer, —nor do I deny that you may know the way of success in getting it; but that I should open the door to you, —be your—I might say accomplice, in this design upon the affections of my niece—why, I don't know how it strikes you, but"—

"It strikes me precisely as it does you, —my part of it," said Thane impatiently. "But her part is different, as I see it. If she were sick, you would not put off the day of her recovery because neither you nor yours could cure her? Whoever can make her forget this shipwreck of her youth, heal her unhappiness, let him do so, would you not say? Give him the chance to try? A man's power in these things does not lie in his deserts. All I ask is, when other men come forward, I want the same privilege. But I shall not be on the ground. When that time comes, sir, will you remember me?"

For once Mr. Withers seized the occasion for a retort; he advanced upon the enemy's exposed position. "Yes, Mr. Thane, I will remember you, —better than you remember your friends when they are gone."

Thane accepted the reproach as meekly as if his friendship for John Withers had been of the indubitable stuff originally that Mr. Withers had credited him with. He rather welcomed than otherwise an unmerited rebuke from that long-suffering quarter.

But though Thane was silenced as well as answered, there was conscience yet to deal with. Mr. Withers sat and meditated sorely, while the wind buffeted his gray hairs. Conscience demanded that he give up the secret of Daphne's false mourning, which he would have defended with his life. "A silence that can harm no one." "So long as we defraud no living person who might claim a right to know your heart." The condition was plain; it provided for just such cases as the present. Then how could he hesitate? But he was human, and he did.

"I have gone too far, I see. Well, say no more about it," said Thane. "It was your generosity that tempted me. From those who

219

give easily much shall be asked. Forget it, sir, please. I will look out for myself, or lose her."

"Stop a bit!" exclaimed Mr. Withers. He turned to Thane, placing his hand above his faded eyes to shade them from the glare, and looked his companion earnestly in the face. Thane sought for an umbrella, and raised it over the old gentleman's head; it was not an easy thing to hold it steady in that wind.

"Thanks, thanks! Now I can look at you. Yes, I can look you in the eye, in more senses than one. Listen to me, Mr. Thane, and don't mind if I am not very lucid. In speaking of the affairs of another, and a young woman, I can only deal in outlines. You will be able to surmise and hope the rest. I feel in duty bound to tell you that, at the time of my son's death, there was a misunderstanding on my part which forced Miss Lewis into a false position in respect of her relations to my son. Too much was assumed by me on insufficient evidence,—a case where the wish, perhaps, was father to the thought. She hesitated at that sore time to rob me of an illusion which she saw was precious to me; she allowed me to retain my erroneous belief that my son, had he lived, would have enjoyed the blessing of her affection. As a fact, she had not given it to him,—could not have given it,—though she owns that her mind, not her heart, was wavering. Had she married him, other motives than love would have influenced her choice. So his death saved my dear boy from a cruel disappointment or a worse mistake, and her from a great danger. Had he lived, he must have had many hours of wretchedness, either with or without that dearest wish of his heart fulfilled.

"This she confessed to me not many days ago, after a long period of remorseful questioning; and I deem it my duty now, in view of what you have just told me, to acquaint you with the truth. I am the only one who knows that she was not engaged to my son, and never really loved him. The fact cut me so deeply, when I learned it first, that I persuaded her, most selfishly, to continue in the disguise she had permitted, sustained so long,—to rest in it, that my boy's memory might be honored through this sacrifice of the truth. Weak, fond old man that I was, and worse! But now you have my confession. As soon as I can speak with her alone I will release her from that promise. She was fain to be free before all the world,—our little part of it,—but I fastened it on her. I see now that I could not have invented a crueler punishment; but it was never my purpose to punish her. I will also tell her that I have opened the true state of the case to you."

"Would you not stop just short of that, Mr. Withers? To know that she is free to listen to him,—that is all any man could ask."

"Perhaps you are right; yes, she need not know that I have possessed you with her secret,—all of it that has any bearing on your hopes. I only thought it might save you, in her mind, from any possible imputation of—of want of respect for her supposed condition, akin to widowhood; but no doubt you will wait a suitable time."

"I will wait till we meet in Boise."

"In Boise!" the old gentleman cried, aghast.

"That will be three days from now," answered Thane innocently. Did Mr. Withers imagine that he would wait three years?

"But what becomes of the—the placer-mine?"

"The placer-mine be—I mean, the placer-mine will keep! She is shutting up her book; the sketch is finished. Will you hold the umbrella, or shall I put it down?"

Mr. Withers took hold of the umbrella-handle; the wind shook it and nearly carried it out of his grasp. "Put it down, if you please," he murmured resignedly. But by this time Thane was half across the road to where Daphne, with penknife and finger-tips, was trying to strip the top layer of blackened sand-paper from her pencil-scrubber; turning her face aside, because, woman-like, she would insist on casting her pencil-dust to windward.

Thane smiled, and took the scrubber out of her hands, threw away the soiled sheet, sealed up the pad in a clean stamped envelope, which bore across the end the legend, "If not delivered within ten days, return to"—"Robert Henry Thane," he wrote, with his address, and gave her back her property. It was all very childish, yet his hand trembled as he wrote; and Daphne looked on with the solemnity of a child learning a new game.

"May I see the sketch?" he asked.

They bent together over her book, while Daphne endeavored to find the place; the wind fluttered the leaves, and she was so long in finding it that Mr. Kinney had time to pack up her stool and umbrella, and cross the road to say good-by to Mr. Withers.

"Here it is," said Thane, catching sight of the drawing. He touched the book-holder lightly on the arm, to turn her away from the sun. Her shadow fell across the open page; their backs were to the wagon. So they stood a full half-minute, Thane seeing nothing, hearing his heart beat preposterously in the silence.

"Why don't you praise my sign-posts?" asked Daphne nervously. "See my beautiful distance,—one straight line!"

"I have changed my plans a little," said Thane. Daphne closed the book. "I shall see you again in Boise. This is good-by for three days. Take care of yourself." He held out his hand. "I shall meet your train at Bliss."

"Bliss! Where is Bliss?"

"You never could remember, could you?" he smiled. The tone of his voice was a flagrant caress. The color flew to Daphne's face. "Bliss," said he, "is where I shall meet you again: remember that, will you?"

Daphne drew down her veil. The man returning from the ferry was in sight at the top of the hill. Mr. Withers was alighting from Thane's wagon. She turned her gray mask towards him, through which he could discern the soft outline of her face, the color of her lips and cheeks, the darkness of her eyes; their expression he could not see.

"I shall meet you at Bliss," he repeated, his fingers closing upon hers.

Daphne did not reply; she did not speak to him nor look at him again, though it was some moments before the wagon started.

Kinney and Thane remained at the cross-roads, discussing with some heat the latter's unexpected change of plan. Mr. Kinney had a small interest in the placer-mine, himself, but it looked large to him just then. He put little faith in Thane's urgent business (that no one had heard of till that moment) calling him to Boise in three days. Of what use was it going down to the placers only to turn round and come back again? So Thane thought, and proposed they drive forward to Bliss.

"Bliss be hanged!"said Mr. Kinney; which shows how many ways there are of looking at the same thing.

Thane's way prevailed; they drove straight on to Bliss. And if the placer-mine was ever reported on by Thane, it must have been at a later time.

The Harshaw Bride

I wonder Charles Lamb did not include in his list of popular fallacies the saying, "It costs nothing to be polite." My dear, I am paying the price at this moment of one of my own imprudences in that line—a chance phrase with which I tried to round off a rather chilly leave-taking neatly, and cheaply, I flattered myself. But now, listen to the sequel!

I am to have a bride on my hands, or a bride-elect, for she isn't married yet. Her intended has been rustling for a home out here in the wilds of Idaho, while she has been waiting in the old country for success to crown his efforts. How much success in her case is demanded I don't know. She is a little English girl, upper middle-class, which Mrs. Percifer assures me is *the* class to belong to in England at the present day (it is her class, I infer), and the interesting reunion is to take place at our house. She sailed, poor thing, this day week, and will be forwarded to us by her confiding friends in New York as soon as she arrives. She has never seen either of us, but I suppose she will hear of us from the Percifers. That is something—enough for some persons, it seems.

The Percifers were really very nice to us in New York last winter, though one must not flatter one's self too much; it is all in the day's work for those commission men to be nice to a good shipper and his wife when they come out of the West. There was a rather impersonal note to *her* politeness, which made it difficult when we parted for me to speak of the possibility, to say nothing of the pleasure, of a visit from her. My natural "gush" was strangled in my throat. But one must say something, so I put it off on any friends or fellow-Britishers of theirs who might care to command us in the West; we should be so happy, and so forth. And, my dear, she writes me, quite as a matter of course (she's not impersonal now), that she is "so glad, for dear Kitty's sake," that we are here; and she is sure we will "be very good to her,—she is such a sweet girl no one could help

223

being,"—which doesn't leave much margin for our goodness. "The poor child" (I am quoting Mrs. Percifer) "knows absolutely nobody in the West but the man she is coming to marry" (it's a question if she knows him), "and cannot possibly have any conception of the journey she has undertaken"; she will be "so comforted" to find us at the end of it. And if anything unforeseen should detain Mr. Harshaw, the fiancé, that he could not meet her train, "Kitty's" friends will be "so relieved to know that the dear, brave little girl is in good hands"—ours, if you please, who never beheld her in our lives!

Mark the coolness with which she treats the possibility of the bridegroom's keeping the bride waiting—after she has traversed half the globe to compass her share of their meeting!

Well, it's not the American way; but perhaps it will be when bad times have humbled us a little more, and it's a question whether we can marry our daughters at all unless we can give them dowries, or professions to support their husbands on, and "feelings" are a luxury that only the rich can afford.

I hope "Kitty" won't have any; but still more I hope that her young man will arrive on schedule time, and that they can trot round the corner and be married, with Tom and me for witnesses, as speedily as possible.

I've had such a blow! Tom, with an effort, has succeeded in remembering this Mr. Harshaw who is poor Kitty's fate. He must have been years in this country, long enough to have citizenized himself and become a member of our first Idaho legislature (I don't believe you even know that we are a state!). Tom was on the supper committee of the ball the city gave them. They were a deplorable set of men; it was easy enough to remember the nice ones. Tom says he is a "chump," if you know what that means. I tell him that every man, married or single, is constitutionally horrid to any other man who has had the luck to be chosen of a charming girl. But I'm afraid Harshaw wasn't one of the nice ones, or I should have remembered him myself; we had them to dinner—all who were at all worth while.

Poor Kitty! There is so little here to come for but the man.

Well, my dear, here's a pretty kettle of fish! Kitty has arrived, and one Mr. Harshaw. Where the Mr. Harshaw is, quien sabe! It's awfully late. Poor Kitty has gone to bed, and has cried herself to sleep, I dare say, if sleep she can. I never have heard of a girl being treated so.

Tom and the other Mr. Harshaw are smoking in the dining room, and Tom is talking endlessly—what about I can't imagine, unless he is giving this young record-breaker his opinion of his extraordinary conduct. But I must begin at the beginning.

Mrs. Percifer wired us from New York the day the bride-elect started, and *she* was to wire us from Ogden, which she did. I went to the train to meet her, and I told Tom to be on the watch for the bridegroom, who would come in from his ranch on the Snake River, by wagon or on horseback, across country from Ten Mile. To come by rail he'd have had to go round a hundred miles or so, by Mountain Home. An American would have done it, of course, and have come in with her on the train; but the Percifers plainly expected no such wild burst of enthusiasm from him.

The train was late. I walked and walked the platform; some of the people who were waiting went away, but I dared not leave my post. I fell to watching a spurt of dust away off across the river toward the mesa. It rolled up fast, and presently I saw a man on horseback; then I didn't see him; then he had crossed the bridge and was pounding down the track-side toward the depot. He pulled up and spoke to a trainman, and after that he walked his horse as if he was satisfied.

That is Harshaw, I thought, and a very pretty fellow, but not in the least like an Idaho legislator. I don't seem to care for the sort of Englishman who is so prompt to swear allegiance to our flag, and take out his first papers and his second papers and all that; they never do unless they want to go in for government land, or politics, or something that has nothing to do with any flag. But this youngster looked ridiculously young. I simply knew he was coming for that girl, and that he had no ulterior motives whatever. He was ashy-white with dust—hair, eyebrows, eyelashes, and his fair little mustache all powdered with it; his corduroys, leggings, and hat all of a color. I saw no baggage, and I wondered what he expected to be married in. He leaned on his horse dizzily a moment when he first got out of the saddle, and the poor beast stretched his forelegs, and rocked with the gusts of his panting, his sides going in and out like a pair of bellows. The young fellow handed him over to a man to take to the stables, and I saw him give him a regular bridegroom's tip. He's all right, I said to myself, and Tom *was* horrid to call him a "chump." He beat himself off a bit, and went in and talked to the ticket-agent. They looked at their watches.

"I don't think you'll have time to go uptown," said the ticket-man.

Harshaw came out then, and *he* began to walk the platform, and to stare down the track toward Nampa; so I sat down. Presently he stopped, and raised his hat, and asked if I was Mrs. Daly, a friend of Mrs. Percifer of London and New York.

Not to be boastful, I said that I knew Mrs. Percifer.

"Then," said he, "we are here on the same errand, I think."

I was there to meet Miss Kitty Comyn, I told him, and he said so was he, and might he have a little talk with me? He seemed excited and serious, very.

"Are you *the* Mr. Harshaw?" I asked, though I hadn't an idea, of course, that he could be anybody else.

"Not exactly," he said. "I'm his cousin, Cecil Harshaw."

"Is Mr. Harshaw ill?" I asked.

He looked foolish, and dropped his eyes. "No," said he. "He was well last night when I left him at the ranch." Last night! He had come a hundred miles between dark of one day and noon of the next!

"Your cousin takes a royal way of bringing home his bride—by proxy," I said.

"Ah, but it's partly my fault, you know,"—he could not quell a sudden shamefaced laugh—"if you'd kindly allow me to explain. I shall have to be quite brutally frank; but Mrs. Percifer said"—here he lugged in a propitiatory compliment, which sounded no more like Mrs. Percifer than it fitted me; but mistaking my smile of irony for one of encouragement, he babbled on. I wish I could do justice to his "charmin' " accent and his perfectly unstudied manner of speech, a mixture of native and acquired colloquialisms, that is, British and American slang.

"It's like this, Mrs. Daly. A man oughtn't to be a dog-in-the-manger about a girl, even if he has got her promise, you know. If he can't get a move on and marry her before her hair is gray, he ought to step out and give the other fellows a show. I'm not speaking for myself, though I would have spoken three years ago if she hadn't been engaged to Micky—she's always been engaged to him, one may say. And I accepted the fact; and when I came over here and took a share in Micky's ranch I meant right by him, and God knows I meant more than right by her. Wasn't it right to suppose she must be tremendously fond of him, to let him keep her on the string the way he has? They've been engaged four years now. And was it any wonder I was mad with Micky, seeing how he was loafing along, fooling his money away, not looking ahead and denying himself as a man ought who's got a nice girl waiting for him? I'm quite frank, you see; but when you hear what an ass I've made of myself, you'll not begrudge me the few excuses I have to offer. All I tried to do was to give Micky a leg to help him over his natural difficulty—of laziness, you know. He's not a bad sort at all, only he's slow, and it's hard to get him to look things square in the face. It was for her sake, supposing her happiness was bound up in him, that I undertook to boom the marriage a bit. But Micky won't boom worth a—deuce. He's back on my hands now, and what in Heaven's name I'm to say to her—" His eloquence failed him here, and he came down to the level of ordinary conversation, with the remark, "It's a facer, by Jove!"

I managed not to smile. If he'd undertaken, I said, to "boom" his cousin's marriage to a girl he liked himself, he ought at least to get credit for disinterestedness; but so few really good acts were rewarded in this world! I seemed to have heard that it was not very comfortable, though it might be heroic, to put one's hand between the tree and the bark.

"Ah," he said feelingly, "it's unearthly! I never was so rattled in my life. But before you give me too much credit for disinterestedness, you know, I must tell you that I'm thinking of—that—in short, I've a mind to speak for myself now, if Micky doesn't come up to time."

I simply looked at him, and he blushed, but went on more explicitly. "He could have married her, Mrs. Daly, any time these three years if he'd had the pluck to think so. He's say, 'If we have a good season with the horses, I'll send for her in the fall.' We'd have our usual season, and then he'd say, 'It won't do, Cecy.' And in the spring we are always as poor as jack-rabbits, and so he'd wait till the next fall. I got so mad with his infernal coolness, and the contrast of how things were and how she must think they were! Still, I knew he'd be good to her if he had her here, and he'd save twice as much with her to provide for as he ever could alone. I used to hear all her little news, poor girl. She had lost her father, and there were tight times at home. The next word was that she was going for a governess. Then I said, 'You ought to go over and get her, or else send for her sharp. You are as ready to marry her now as ever you will be.'

" 'I'm too confounded strapped,' said he. I told him I would fix all that if he would go or write her to come. But the weeks went by, and he never made a move. And there were reasons, Mrs. Daly, why it was best that any one who cared for him should be on the ground. Then I made my kick. I don't believe in kicking, as a rule; but if you do kick, kick hard, I say. 'If you don't send for her, Micky, I'll send for her myself,' I said.

" 'What for?' said he.

" 'For you,' said I, 'if you'll have the manliness to step up and claim her, and treat her as you ought. If not, she can see how things are, and maybe she'll want a change. You may not think you are wronging her and deceiving her,' I said, 'but that's what you are; and if you won't make an end of this situation' (I haven't told you, and I can't tell you, the whole of it, Mrs. Daly), 'I will end it myself—for your sake and for her sake and for my own.' And I warned him that I should have a word to say to her if he didn't occupy the field of vision pretty promptly after she arrived. 'One of us will meet her at the train,' said I, 'and the one who loves her will get there first.'

"Well, I'm here, and he was cooking himself a big supper when I left him at the ranch. It was a simple test, Mrs. Daly. If he scorned to abide by it, he might at least have written and put her on her guard, for he knew I was not bluffing. He pawed up the ground a bit, but he never did a thing. Then I cabled her just the question, would she come? and she answered directly that she would. So I wired her the money. I signed myself Harshaw, and I told Micky what I'd done.

"And whether he is sulking over my interference, I can't say, but from that moment he has never opened his mouth to me on the subject. I haven't a blessed notion what he means to do; judging by what he has done, nothing, I should say. But it may be he's only waiting to give me the full strength of the situation, seeing it's one of my own contriving. There's a sort of rum justice in it; but think of his daring to insult her so, for the sake of punishing me!

"Now, what am I to say to her, Mrs. Daly? Am I to make a clean breast of it, and let her know the true and peculiar state of the case, including the fact that I'm in love with her myself? Or would you let that wait, and try to smooth things over for Micky, and get her to give him another chance? There was no sign of his moving last night; still, he may get here yet."

The young man's spirits seemed to be rising as he neared the end of his tale, perhaps because he could see that it looked pretty black for "Micky."

"If one could only know what he does mean to do, it would be simpler, wouldn't it?"

I agreed that it would. Then I made the only suggestion it occurred to me to offer in the case—that he should go to his hotel and get his luncheon or breakfast, for I doubted if he'd had any, and leave me to meet Miss Comyn, and say to her whatever a kind Providence might inspire me with. My husband would call for him and fetch him up to dinner, I said; and after dinner, if Mr. Michael Harshaw had not arrived, or sent some satisfactory message, he could cast himself into the breach.

"And I'm sorry for you," I said; "for I don't think you will have an easy time of it."

"She can't do worse than hate me, Mrs. Daly; and that's better than sending me friendly little messages in her letters to Micky."

I wish I could give you this story in his own words, or any idea of his extraordinary, joyous naturalness, and his air of preposterous good faith—as if he had done the only thing conceivable in the case. It was as convincing as a scene in comic opera.

"By the way," said he, "I didn't encumber myself with much luggage this trip. I have nothing but the clothes I stand in."

I made a reckless offer of my husband's evening things, which he as recklessly accepted, not knowing if he could get into them; but I thought he did not look so badly as he was, in his sun-faded corduroys, the whole of him from head to foot as pale as a plaster cast with dust, except his bright blue eyes, which had hard, dark circles around them.

"The train is coming," I warned him.

"*She* is coming! *À la bonne heure!*" he cried, and was off on a run, and whistled a car that was going up Main street to the natatorium; and I knew that in ten minutes he would be reveling in the plunge, while I should be making the best of this beautiful crisis of his inventing to Miss Comyn.

My dear, they are the prettiest pair! Providence, no doubt, designed them for each other, if he had not made this unpardonable break. She has a spirit of her own, has Miss Kitty, and if she cried upstairs alone with me,—tears of anger and mortification, it struck me, rather than of heart-grief,—I will venture she shed no tears before him.

As Mr. Michael Harshaw did not arrive, we gave Mr. Cecil his opportunity, as promised, of speech with his victim and judge. He talked to her in the little sitting-room after dinner—as long as she would listen to him, apparently. We heard her come flying out with a sort of passionate suddenness, as if she had literally run away from his words. But he had followed her, and for an instant I saw them together in the hall. His poor young face was literally burning;

229

perhaps it was only sunburn, but I fancied she had been giving him a metaphorical drubbing—"ragging," as Tom would call it—worse than Lady Anne gave Richard III.

She was still in a fine Shaksperian temper when I carried her off up-stairs. Reserves were impossible between us; her right to any privacy in her own affairs had been given away from the start; that was one of the pleasing features of the situation.

"*Marry* him! marry *him!*" she cried. "That impertinent, meddlesome boy, that I have known all my life, and never could have suspected of such work as this! That false, dishonorable—"

"Go slow, dear," I said. "I don't think he's quite so bad as that."

"And what do I want with *him!* And what do you think he tells me, Mrs. Daly? And whether there's any truth in him, how do I know? He declares it was not Michael Harshaw who sent for me at all! The message, all the messages, were from him. In that case I have been decoyed over here to marry a man who not only never asked me to come, but who stood by and let me be hoaxed in this shameful way, and now leaves me to be persecuted by this one's ridiculous offers of marriage, as if I belonged to all or any of the Harshaws, whichever one came first! Michael may not even know that I am here," she added in a lower key. "If Cecil Harshaw was capable of doing what he has done by his own confession, it would be little more to intercept my answers to his forgeries."

That was true, I said. It was quite possible the young man lied. She would, of course, give Mr. Michael Harshaw a chance to tell *his* story.

"I cannot believe," said the distracted girl, "that Michael would lend himself, even passively, to such an abominable trick. Could anyone believe it—of his worst enemy!"

Impossible, I agreed. She must believe nothing till she had heard from her lover.

"But if Michael did not know it," she mused, with a piteous blush, "then Cecil Harshaw must have sent me that money himself—the insolence! And after that to ask me to marry him!"

Men were fearfully primitive still, after all that we had done for them, I reminded her, especially in their notions of love-making. Their intentions were generally better than their methods. No great harm had been done, for that matter. A letter, if written that night, would reach Mr. Michael Harshaw at his ranch not later than the next night. All these troubles could wait till the real Mr. Harshaw had been heard from. My husband would see that her letter reached him promptly, and in the mean time Mr. Cecil need not be told that we were proving his little story.

I was forced to humor her own theory of her case; but I have no idea, myself, that Cecil Harshaw has not told the truth. He does not look like a liar, to begin with, and how silly to palm off an invention for to-day which to-morrow would expose!

Tom is still talking and talking. I really must interfere and give Mr. Cecil a chance to go. It is quite too late to look for the other one. If he comes at this hour, there is nothing he can do but go to bed.

. . . Well, the young man has gone, and Tom is shutting up the house, and I hope the bride is asleep, though I doubt it. Have I told you how charming she is? Not so discouragingly tall or so classic as the Du Maurier goddess who has posed for the English society girl so long; not so very much so either, but "comfy," much more "comfy," to my mind. Her nose is rudimentary, rather, which doesn't seem to prevent her having a mind of her own, though noses are said to have it all to say as to force of character. Her upper lip has the most fascinating little pout; her chin is full and emotional—but these are emotional times; and there is a beautiful finish about her throat and hands and wrists. She looks more dressed in a shirt-waist, in which she came down to dinner, her trunk not having come, than some of us do in the best we have. Her clothes are very fresh and recent, to a woman of Idaho; but she does not wear her pretty ears "cachées," I am glad to say. They are very pretty, and one—the left one—is burned pure crimson from sitting next the window of her section all the way from Omaha.

But why do I write all this nonsense at twelve o'clock at night, when all I need say by way of description is that we want her to stay with us, indefinitely if necessary, and let her countrymen and lovers go to—their ranch on the Snake River!

What do you suppose those wretches were arguing about in the dining-room last night, over their whisky and soda? Sentiment was "not in it," as they would say. They were talking up a scheme—a scheme that Tom has had in mind ever since he first saw the Thousand Springs six years ago, when he had the Snake River placer-mining fever. It was of no use then, because electrical transmission was in its infancy, its long distance capacities

231

undreamed of. But Harshaw was down there fishing last summer, and he was able to satisfy the only doubt Tom has had as to some natural feature of the scheme—I don't know what, but Harshaw has settled it, and is as wild as Tom himself about the thing. Also he wants to put into it all the money he can recover out of his cousin's ranch. (I shouldn't think the future of that partnership would be exactly happy!) And now they propose to take hold of it, together, and at once.

Harshaw, who, it seems, is enough of an engineer to be able to run a level, will go down with Tom and make the preliminary surveys. Tom will work up the plans and estimates, and prepare a report, which Harshaw will take to London, where his father has influence in the City, and the sanguine child sees himself placing it in the twinkling of an eye.

Tom made no secret with me of their scheme, and I fell upon him at once.

"You are not taking advantage of that innocent in your own house!" I said.

"Do you take him for an innocent? He has about as shrewd a business head—but he has no money, anyhow. I shall have to put up for the whole trip."

To be honest, that was just what I had feared; but it didn't sound well to say so. Tom is always putting up for things that never come to anything—for us.

He tried to propitiate me with the news that I was to go with them.

"And what do you propose to do with our guest?"

"Take her along. Why not? It's as hard a trip as any I know of, for the distance. Her troubles won't keep her awake, nor spoil her appetite, after the first day's ride."

"I don't know but you are right," I said; "but wild horses couldn't drag her if he goes. And how about the other Harshaw—the one she has promised to marry?"

"She isn't going to marry him, is she? I should think she had gone about far enough, to meet that fellow half-way."

Even if she wasn't going to marry him, I said, it might be civil to tell him so. She had listened to his accuser; she could hardly refuse to listen to him.

"I think, myself, the dear boy has skipped the country," said Tom, who is unblushingly on Cecil's side. "If he hasn't, the letter will fetch him. She will have time to settle his case before we start."

"Before we start! And when do you propose to start?" I shouldn't have been surprised if he had said "tomorrow"; but he considerately gives me until Thursday.

The truth is, Lou, it is years and years since I have been on one of these wild-goose chases with Tom. I have no more faith in this than in any of the other schemes, but who wants to be forever playing the part of Wisdom "that cries in the streets and no man regards her"? One might as well be merry over one's folly, to say nothing of the folly of other people. I confess I am dying to go; but of course nothing can be decided till the recreant bridegroom has been heard from.

This morning, when I went to Kitty's door for her letter, I found she hadn't written it. She made me come in while she "confessed," as she said.

"I couldn't submit to the facts last night," she faltered. "I had to pretend that I thought he didn't know; but of course he does; he must. I wrote him from home before I started, and again from New York. I can't suppose that Cecil would intercept my letters. He is not a stage villain. No; I must face the truth. But how can I ever tell it to mama!"

"We will arrange all that by and by," I assured her (but I don't see myself how she can tell the truth about this transaction to anybody, her mother least of all, who would be simply wild if she knew how the girl has been betrayed and insulted, among utter strangers); meantime I begged her to promise me that she would not waste—

She interrupted me quickly. "I have wasted enough, I think. No; don't be afraid for me, Mrs. Daly, and for heaven's sake don't pity me!"

I had just written the above when Tom came in and informed me that the "regular candidate had arrived," and requested to know if we were to have them both to dinner, or if the "dark horse" was to be told he needn't come.

"Of course he can't come," I screamed; "let him keep himself as dark as possible."

"Then you needn't expect me," said Tom. Cecy and I will dine at the Louvre." And I would give a good deal if I could dine there too, or anywhere but with these extraordinary lovers.

I went out to meet the real Harshaw, embarrassed with the guilty consciousness of having allowed my sympathies to go astray; for though in theory I totally disapprove of Cecil Harshaw, personally I defy anybody not to like him. I will except prejudiced persons, like his cousin and the lady he is so bent on making, by hook or by crook, a Mrs. Harshaw.

Mr. Harshaw the first (and last to arrive) has shaved off his mustache quite recently, I should say, and the nakedness of his upper lip is not becoming. I wonder if she ever saw him with his mouth bare? I wonder if she would have accepted him if she had? He was so funny about his cousin, the promoter; so absolutely unconscious of his own asinine position. He argued very sensibly that if, after waiting four years for him she couldn't wait one day longer, she must have changed in her feelings very decidedly, and that was a fact it behooved him to find out. Better now than later. I think he has found out.

All she said, upon his departure, was, "It's a long lane that has no turning."

One might infer that the engagement had been a long lane to her, and that she was glad to have come to the turn at last. Possibly he was nicer four years ago. Men get terribly down at heel, mentally, morally, and mannerly, poking off by themselves in these out-of-the-way places. But she has been seeing people, and steadily making growth, since she gave him her promise at eighteen. The promise itself has helped to develop her. It must have been a knot of perpetual doubt and self-questioning. No one need tell me that she really loves him; if she did, if she had, she could not take his treatment of her like this. Perhaps the family circumstances constrained her. They may have thought Harshaw had a fortune in the future of his ranch, with its river boundary of placer-mines. English girls are obedient, and English mamas are practical, we read.

She is practical, and she is beginning to look her situation in the face.

"I shall want you to help me find some way to return that money," she said to me later, with an angry blush—"that money which Cecil Harshaw kindly advanced me on my journey. I shall hate every moment of my life till that debt is paid. But for the insult I can never repay him, never!

"We are a large family at home—four girls besides me, and three boys; and boys are so expensive. I cannot ask mama to help me; indeed, I was hoping to help her. I should have gone for a governess if I had not been duped into coming over here. Would there be any one in this town, do you think, who might want a governess for her children? I have a few 'accomplishments,' and though I've not been trained for a teacher, I am used to children, and they like me, when I want them to."

I thought this a good idea for the future; it would take time to work it up. But for the present an inspiration came to me, on the strength of something Tom had said—that he wished I could draw or paint, because he could make an artist useful on this trip, he condescended to say, if he could lay his hand on one. All the photographs of the springs, it seems, have the disastrous effect of dwarfing their height and magnitude. There is a lagoon and a weedy island directly beneath them, and in the camera pictures taken from in front the reeds and willows look gigantic in the foreground, and the springs are insignificant out of all proportion. This would be fatal to our schemers' claims as to the volume of water they are supposed to furnish for an electrical power-plant to supply the Silver City mines, one hundred miles away. Hence the demand of Science for Art, with her point of view.

"Just the thing for her," I thought. "She can draw and water-color, of course; all English girls do." And I flew and proposed it to Tom. "Pay her well for her pictures, and she'll make your Thousand Springs look like Ten Thousand." (That was only my little joke, dear; I am always afraid of your conscience.) But the main thing is settled; we have found a way of inducing Kitty to go. Tom was charmed with my intelligence, and Kitty, poor child, would go anywhere, in any conceivable company, to get even with Cecil Harshaw on that hateful money transaction. When I told her she would have to submit to his presence on the trip, she shrugged her shoulders.

"It's one of 'life's little ironies,' " she said.

"And," I added, "we shall have to pass the ranch that was to have been—"

"Oh, well, that is another. I must get used to the humorous side of my situation. One suffers most, perhaps, through thinking how other people will think one suffers. If they would only give one credit for a little common sense, to say nothing of pride!"

You see, she will wear no willows for him. We shall get on beautifully, I've no doubt, even with the "irony" of the situation rubbed in, as it will inevitably be, in the course of this journey.

Tom solemnly assures me that the other Harshaw's name is not Micky, but "Denis;" and he explains his having got into the legislature (quite unnecessarily, so far as I am concerned) on the theory that he is too lazy even to make enemies.

I shall get the governess project started, so it can be working while we are away. If you know of anybody who would be likely to want her, and could pay her decently, and would know how to treat a nursery governess who is every bit a lady, but who is not above her business (I take for granted she is not, though of course I don't know), do, pray, speak a word for her. I'll answer for it that she is bright enough; better not mention that she is pretty. There must be a hundred chances for her there to one in Idaho. We are hardly up to the resident-governess idea as yet. It is thought to be wanting in public spirit for parents not to patronize the local schools. If they are not good enough for the rich families, the poor families feel injured, and want to know the reason why.

To return to these Harshaws. Does it not strike you that the English are more original, not to say queer, than we are; more indifferent to the opinions of others—certain others? They don't hesitate to do a thing because on the face of it it's perfectly insane. Witness the lengths they go, these young fellows out here, for anything on earth they happen to set their crazy hearts upon. The young fancy bloods, I mean, who have the love of sport developed through generations of tough old hard-riding, high-playing, deep-drinking ancestors; the "younger sons," who have inherited the sense of having the ball at their feet, without having inherited the ball. They are certainly great fun, but I should hate to be responsible for them.

I note what you say about my tendency to slang, and how it "seems to grow upon me." It "seems" to, alas! For the simple reason, doubtless, that it does. I can remember when I used carefully to corral all my slang words in apologetic quote-marks; as if they were range-cattle to be fenced out from the home herd—our mother-tongue which we brought with us from the East, and which you have preserved in all its conscientious purity. But I give it up. I hardly know any longer, in regard to my own speech, which are my native expressions and which are the wild and woolly ones I have adopted off the range. It will serve all human purposes of a woman irretrievably married into the West. If the worst come to the worst, I can make a virtue of necessity and become a member of the "American Dialect Society"—a member in good standing.

This is the morning of our glorious start. I am snatching a few words with you while the men are packing the wagon, which stands before the door. What a sensation it would make drawn up in front of—Mrs. Percifer's door, for instance, in Park Avenue! Here no one turns the head to look at it.

I told Tom he need make no concessions to the fact that he is to have two fairly well-dressed women along. We will go as they go, without any fuss, or they may leave us at home. I despise those condescending, make-believe-rough-it trips, with which men flatter women into thinking themselves genuine campaigners. Consequently our outfit is a big, bony ranch-team and a Shuttler wagon with the double-sides in; spring seats, of course, and the bottom well bedded down with tents and rolls of blankets. We don't go out of our way to be uncomfortable; that is the pet weakness of the tenderfoot. The "kitchen box" and the "grub box" sit shoulder to shoulder in the back of the wagon. The stovepipe, tied with rope, in sections, keeps up a lively clatter in concert with the jiggling of the tinware and the thumps and bumps of the camp-stove, which has swallowed its own feet, and, by the internal sounds, doesn't seem to have digested them.

I spent last evening covering the canteens with canvas. The maiden was quite cheerful, sorting her drawing-materials and packing her colors and sketch-blocks. She laughs at everything Tom says, whether she sees the point or not, and most when there is none to see. Tom will be cook, because he prefers his own messing to any of ours, and we can't spare room in the wagon for a regular camp chef. Mr. Harshaw is the "swamper," because he makes himself useful doing things my lord doesn't like to do. And Kitty is not Miss "Co-myn," as we called it, but Miss "Cummin," as they call it,—"the Comin' woman," Tom calls her. Mr. Billings, the teamster, completes our party.

Sept.—Never mind the date. This is tomorrow morning, and we are at Walter's Ferry. It seems a week since we left Bisuka. We started yesterday on the flank of a dust-storm, and soon were with the main column, the wind pursuing us, and hurling the sweepings of the road into the backs of our necks. The double-sides raised us out of the worst of the dust, else I think we should have been smothered. It was a test of our young lady's traveling manner. She kept her head down and her mouth shut; but when I shrieked at her to ask how she was standing it, she plucked her dusty veil from between her lips and smiled for answer.

We two sat on the back seat, Tom in front with Billings, and the "swamper" sat anywhere on the lumps and bumps which our baggage made, covered by the canvas wagon-sheet. He might have ridden his horse—everybody supposed he would; but that would have separated him from the object of his existence; the object sternly ignoring him, and riding for miles with her face turned away, her hand to her hat, which the wind persistently snatched at. It was her wide-brimmed sketching-hat—rather a daring creation, but monstrously becoming, and I had persuaded her to wear it, the morning being delusively clear, thinking we were to have one of our midsummer scorchers, that would have burned her fair English face to a blister.

Mr. Harshaw seemed to think she would be tired, wearing her hand continually in the air, and suggested various mechanical substitutes—a string attached to the hat-trimming, a scarf tied over her head; but a snubbing was all the reward he got for his sympathy.

"When this hand is tired I take the other one," she said airily.

We lunched at Ten Mile, by the railroad track. Do you remember that desolate place? The Oregon Short Line used to leave us there at a little station called Kuna. There is no Kuna now; the station-house is gone; the station-keeper's little children are buried between four stakes on the bare hill—diphtheria, I think it was. Miss Kitty asked what the stakes were there for. Tom didn't like to tell her, so he said some traveler had made a "cache" there of something he couldn't carry with him, and the stakes were to mark the spot till his return.

"And will nobody disturb the cache?" asked Miss Kitty. I couldn't bear to hear them. "They are graves," I whispered. "Two little children—the station keeper's—all they had." And she asked no more questions.

Mr. Harshaw had got possession of the canteen, and so was able to serve the maiden, both when she drank and when she held out her rosy fingers to be sprinkled, he tilting a little water on them slowly—with such provoking slowness that she chid him; then he let it come in gulps, and she chid him more, for spattering her shoes. She could play my Lady Disdain very prettily, only she is something too much in earnest at present for the game to be a pretty one to watch. I feel like calling her down from her pedestal of virgin wrath, if only for the sake of us peaceful old folks, who don't care to be made the stamping-ground for their little differences.

The horses were longer at their lunch than we, and Miss Kitty requested her traveling-bag. "And now," she said, "I will get rid of this fiend of a hat," whereas, she had steadily protested for miles that she didn't mind it in the least. She took out of her bag a steamer-cap, and when she had put it on I could see that poor Harshaw dared not trust himself to look at her, her fair face exposed, and so very fair, in its tender, soft coloring, against that grim, wind-beaten waste of dust and sage.

I shall skip the scenery on the road to Walter's Ferry, partly because we couldn't see it for the dust; and if we had seen it, I would not waste it upon you, an army woman. But Walter's Ferry was a hard-looking place when we crawled in last night out of the howling, dirt-throwing wind.

The little hand-raised poplars about the ferry-house were shivering and tugging and straining their thin necks in the gale, the windows so loaded with dust that we could barely see if there were lights inside. We hooted and we howled,—the men did,—and the ferry-keeper came out and stared at us in blank amazement that we should be wanting supper and beds. As if we could have wanted anything else at that place except to cross the river, which we don't do. We go up on this side. We came down the hill merely to sleep at the ferry-house, the night being too bad for a road camp.

The one guest-room at the Ferry that could be called private was given to Kitty and me; but we used it as a sitting-room till bedtime, there being nowhere else to go but into the common room where the teamsters congregate.

We stood and looked at each other, in our common disguise of dust, and tried to find our feet and other members that came awake gradually after the long stupor of the ride. There was a heap of sage-brush on the hearth laid ready for lighting. I touched a match to it, and Kitty dropped on her knees in front of its riotous warmth and glow. Suddenly she sprang up, and stared about her, sniffing and catching her breath. I had noticed it too; it fairly took one by the throat, the gruesome odor.

"What is this beastly smell?" She spoke right out, as our beloved English do. Tom came in at that moment, and she turned upon him as though he were the author of our misery.

"What *has* happened in this horrid room? We can't stay here, you know!" The proposition admitted of no argument. She refused to draw another breath except through her pocket-handkerchief.

By this time I had recognized the smell. "It's nothing but sagebrush," I cried; "the cleanest, sterilest thing that grows!"

"It may be clean," said Kitty, "but it smells like the bottomless pit. I must have a breath of fresh air." The only window in the room was a four-pane sash fixed solid in the top of the outside door. Tom said we should have the sweepings of the Snake River valley in there in one second if we opened that door. But we did, and the wind played havoc with our fire, and half the country blew in, as he said, and with it came Cecil, his head bent low, his arms full of rugs and dust-cloaks.

"You angel!" I cried, "have you been shaking those things?"

"He's given himself the hay-fever," said Tom, heartlessly watching him while he sneezed and sneezed, and wept dust into his handkerchief.

"Doesn't the man do those things?" Miss Kitty whispered.

"What, our next Populist governor? Not much!" Tom replied. Kitty of course did not understand; it was hopeless to begin upon that theme—of our labor aristocracy; so we sent the men away, and made ourselves as presentable as we could for supper.

I need not dwell upon it; it was the usual Walter's Ferry supper. The little woman who cooked it—the third she had cooked that evening—served it as well, plodding back and forth from the kitchen stove to the dining-room table, a little white-headed toddler clinging to her skirts, and whining to be put to bed. Out of regard for her look of general discouragement we ate what we could of the food without yielding to the temptation to joke about it, which was a cross to Tom at least.

"Do you know how the farmers sow their seed in the Snake River valley?" he asked Miss Kitty. She raised eyes of confiding inquiry to his face.

"They prepare the land in the usual way; then they go about five miles to windward of the plowed field and let fly their seed; the wind does the rest. It would be of no use, you see, to sow it on the spot where it's meant to lie; they would have to go into the next county to look for their crop, top-soil and all."

Now whenever Tom makes a statement Miss Kitty looks first at me to see how I am taking it.

It is a fair, pale morning, as still as a picture, after last night's orgy of wind and dust. The maiden is making her first sketch on American soil—of the rope-ferry, with the boat on this side. She is seated in perfect unconsciousness on an inverted pine box—empty, I trust—which bears the startling announcement, in legible lettering on its side, that it holds "500 smokeless nitro-powder cartridges." Now she looks up disgusted, to see the boat swing off and slowly warp over to the other side. The picturesque blocks and cables in the foreground have hopelessly changed position, and continue changing; but she consoles herself by making marginal notes of the passengers returning by the boat—a six-horse freight-team from Silver City, and a band of horses driven by two realistic cow-boys from anywhere. The driver of the freight-team has a young wildcat aboard, half-starved, haggard, and crazed with captivity. He stops, and pulls out his wretched pet. The cow-boys stop; everybody stops; they make a ring, while the dogs of the ferry-house are invited to step up and examine for themselves. The little cat spits and rages at the end of its blood-stained rope. It is not a pretty show, and I am provoked with our men for not turning their backs upon it.

Sunday, at Broadlands. From Walter's Ferry, day before yesterday, we climbed back upon the main road, which crosses the plateau of the Snake, cutting off a great bend of the river, to see it again far below in the bottom of the Grand Cañon.

The alkali growth is monotonous here; but there was a world of beauty and caprice in the forms of the seed-pods dried upon their stalks. Most of these pretty little purses were empty. Their treasure went, like the savings of a maiden aunt, when the idle wind got hold of it. There is an almost humorous ingenuity in the pains Nature has taken to secure the propagation of some of the meanest of her plant-children. The most worthless little vagabond seeds have wings or fans to fly with, or self-acting bomb-receptacles that burst and empty their contents (which nobody wants) upon the liberal air, or claws or prickers to catch on with to anything that goes. And once they have caught on, they are harder to get rid of than a Canadian quarter.

"And do you call this a desert?" cries Miss Kitty. "Why, millions of creatures live here! Look at the footprints of all the little beasties. They must eat and drink."

"That is the cheek of us humans," said Tom. "We call our forests solitudes because we have never shown up there before. Precious little we were missed. This desert subsisted its own population, and asked no favors of irrigation, till man came and overstocked it, and upset its domestic economies. When the sheep-men and the cattle-men came with their foreign mouths to fill, the natives had to scatter and forage for food, and trot back and forth to the river for drink. They have to travel miles now to one they went before. Hence all

241

these desert thoroughfares."

And he showed us in the dust the track of a lizard, a kangaroo-mouse, and a horned toad. We could see for ourselves Bre'r Jack-rabbit and Sis' Gopher skipping away in the greasewood. The horses and cattle had their own broad-beaten roads converging from far away toward an occasional break in the cañon wall, where the thirsty tracks went down.

We plodded along, and having with much deliberation taken the wrong road, we found ourselves about nightfall at the bottom of the cañon, in a perfect cul-de-sac. The bluffs ahead of us crowded close to the river, stretching their rocky knees straight down into deep water, and making no lap at all for our wagon to go over. And now, with this sweet prospect before us, it came on steadily to rain. The men made camp in the slippery darkness, while we sat in the wagon, warm and dry, and thanked our stars there were still a few things left that men could do without our aid or competition. Presently a lantern flashed out, and spots of light shifted over them as they slaved—pounding tent-pegs, and scraping stones away from places where our blankets were to be spread, hacking and hewing among the wet willows, and grappling with stovepipes and tent-poles; and the harder they worked the better their spirits seemed to be.

"I wish some of the people who used to know Cecil Harshaw in England could see him now," said Kitty.

"What did he do in England?" I asked.

"Well, he didn't hammer stovepipes and carry kitchen-boxes and cut fire-wood, you know."

"Don't you like to see men use their muscle?" I asked her. "Very few of them are reflective to any purpose at his age."

"Why, how old, or how young, do you take him to be?"

"I think you spoke of him as a boy, if I remember."

"If I called him a boy, it was out of charity for his behavior. He's within six months of my own age."

"And you don't call yourself a girl any longer?" I laughed.

"It's always 'girls' and 'men,' " she said. "If Cecil Harshaw is not a man now, he never will be."

I didn't know, I said, what the point at issue was between us. I thought Cecil Harshaw was very much a man, as men go, and I saw nothing, frankly, so very far amiss with his behavior.

"It's very kind of you, Mrs. Daly, to defend him, I am sure. I suppose he could do no less than propose to me, after he had brought me out to marry a man who didn't seem to be quite ready;

and if it had to be done, it was best to do it quickly."

So *that* was what she had been threshing out between whiles! I might have tried to answer her, but now the little tent among the willows began to glow with fire and candlelight, and a dark shape loomed against it. It was Cecil Harshaw, bareheaded, with an umbrella, coming to escort us in to supper.

I never saw such a pair of roses as Kitty wore in her cheeks that night, nor the girl herself in such a gale. Tom gave me a triumphant glance across the table, as if to say, See how the medicine works! It was either the beginning of the cure, or else it was a feverish reaction.

I shall have to hurry over our little incidents: how the wagon couldn't go on by way of the shore, and had to flounder back over the rocks, and crawl out of the cañon to the upper road; how Kitty and I set out vain-gloriously to walk to Broadlands by the river-trail, and Harshaw set out to walk with us; and how Kitty made it difficult for him to walk with both of us by staving on ahead, with the step of a young Atalanta. I was so provoked with her that I let her take her pace and I took mine. Fancy a woman of my age racing a girl of her build and constitution seven miles to Broadlands! Poor Harshaw was cruelly torn between us, but he manfully stuck to his duty. He would not abandon the old lady even for the pleasure of running after the young one, though I absolved him many times, and implored him to leave me to my fate. I take pride in recording his faithfulness, and I see now why I have always liked him. He wears well, particularly when things are most harassing.

It certainly was hard upon him when I gave out completely, toiling through the sand, and sat down to rest on the door-stone of a placer-miner's cabin (cabin closed and miner gone), and nowhere through the hot morning stillness could we catch a sound or a sight of the runaway. I could almost hear his heart beat, and his eyes and ears and all his keen young senses were on a stretch after that ridiculous girl. But he kept up a show of interest in my remarks, and paid every patient attention to my feeble wants, without an idea of how long it might be my pleasure to sit there. It was not long, however it may have seemed to him, before we heard the wagon wheels booming down a little side-canyon between the hills. The team had managed to drag it up through a scrubby gulch that looked like no thoroughfare, but which opened into a very fair way out of our difficulties.

When we had come within sight of Broadlands Ferry, all aboard except Kitty, and still not a sign or a sound of her, our hearts began to soften toward that wilful girl.

Tom requested Harshaw to jump out and see if he couldn't round up his country-woman. But Harshaw rather haughtily resigned—in favor of a better man, he said. Then Tom stood up in the wagon and gave the camp call, "Yee-ee-ip! yee-ip, ye-ip!" a brazen, barbarous hoot. Kitty clapped both hands to her ears when she was first introduced to it, but it did not fetch her now. Tom "yee-iped" again, and as we listened there she was, strolling toward us through the greasewood, with the face of a May morning! She wouldn't give us the satisfaction of seeing her run, but her flushed cheeks, damp temples, and quick, sighing breath betrayed her. She *had* been running fast enough.

"Kitty," I said severely, "there are rattlesnakes among those rocks."

"Are there?" she answered serenely. "But I wasn't looking for rattlesnakes, you know. See what lovely things I did find! I've got the 'prospecting' fever already."

She had filled her pockets with specimens of obsidian, jaspers, and chalcedonies, of colors most beautiful, with a deep-dyed opaqueness, a shell-fracture, and a silken polish like jade. And she consulted us about them very prettily—the little fraud! Of course she was instantly forgiven.

But I notice that since our arrival at Broadlands Harshaw has not troubled her with his attentions. They might be the most indifferent strangers, for all that his manner implies. And if she is not pleased with the change, she ought to be, for she has made her wishes plain.

II.

Camp at the Thousand Springs—A little grass peninsula running out between the river and a narrow lagoon, a part of Decker's ranch, two miles by water below the Springs, and half a mile from Decker's Ferry, set all about with a hedge of rose, willow, and wild-currant bushes, sword-grass, and tall reeds,—the grasses enormous, like Japanese decorations,—crossing the darks of the opposite shore and the lights of the river and sky. Our tents are pitched, our blankets spread in the sun, our wagon is soaking its tired feet in the river. Tom and Harshaw are up-stream somewhere, fishing for supper. Billings is bargaining with Old Man Decker for the "keep" of his team. Kitty and I are enjoying ourselves. There is a rip in one of the back seams of my jacket, Kitty tells me, but even that cannot move me.

I say we are enjoying ourselves; but my young guest has developed a new mood of late, which gives poignancy to my growing tenderness for the girl. She has kept up wonderfully, with the aid of her bit of temper, for which I like her none the less. How she will stand this idleness, monotony, and intimacy, with the accent of beauty pressing home, I cannot say. I rather fear for her.

The screws have been tightened on her lately by something that befell at the Harshaw ranch. Our road lay past the place, and Harshaw had to stop for his surveying instruments, also to pack a bag, he said, with apologies for keeping us waiting.

I think we were all a little nervous as we neared the house. Very few women could have spelled the word "home" out of those rough masculine premises. I wondered if Kitty was not offering up a prayer of thanksgiving for the life she had been delivered from.

Harshaw jumped down, and, stooping under the wire fence, ran across the alfalfa stubble to the house as fast as he could for the welcome of a beautiful young setter dog—Maisie he called her—that came wildly out to meet him. A woman—not a nice-looking woman—stood at the door and watched him, and even at our distance from them there was something strange about their recognition.

Kitty began to talk and laugh with forced coolness. Tom turned the horses sharply, so that the wagon's shadow lay on the roadside, away from the house. "Get out, hadn't you better?" he suggested, in the tone of a command. We got out, and Kitty asked for her sketching-bag.

"Kitty," I whispered, pointing to the house, "draw *that,* and send it to your mother. She will never ask again why you didn't care to live there."

"That has nothing to do with it," she retorted coldly. "I would have lived there, or anywhere else, with the right person."

There was no such person. I couldn't help saying it.

She is very handsome when she looks down, proud and a trifle sullen when you "touch her on the raw," as the men say.

"But there *is* such a person, Kitty," I ventured. I had ventured, it seemed, too far.

"You are my hostess. Your house is my only home. Don't be his accomplice!" I thought it rather well said.

Now that woman's clothes were hanging on the line (and very common-looking clothes they were), so she could not have been a casual guest. Moreover, she was pacing the hard ground in front of the house, and staring at us with a truculent yet uneasy air. Curiosity was strong, and a sort of anger possessed me against the place and everybody connected with it.

When Cecil came out, looking very hot and confused for him, who is always so fresh and gay, I inquired, rather shortly perhaps, "Who is your visitor?"

"I have no visitor," he answered me, as cool as you please. But there was a sort of protest in his eye. I was determined not to spare him or any of the Harshaws.

"Your housekeeper, then?"

"I have no housekeeper."

"Who is the lady stopping at your house?"

"I have no house."

"Your cousin's house, then?"

"She is my cousin's housekeeper, I suppose."

Tom gave me a look, and I thought it time to let the subject drop. This was in Kitty's presence, though apparently she neither saw nor heard. I walked on ahead of the wagon, so angry that I was almost sick. Instantly Harshaw joined me, with a much nicer, brighter look upon his face.

"Mrs. Daly," he said, "I want to beg your pardon. I could not answer your question before Miss Comyn. The lady, as you were pleased to call her, is Mrs. Harshaw, *my cousin*—Micky's wife, you understand."

"Since when?"

"Day before yesterday, she tells me. They were married at Bliss."

"Well, I should say it was 'Bliss' for Kitty Comyn that *she* is not Mrs. Harshaw too." I was about to add, but that would be going rather far. "And what did you want to bring that girl over here for?"

"Mrs. Daly, I have told you, I thought she loved him."

"And what of his love for her?"

"Good heavens! You don't suppose Micky cares for that old thing he has married! *That* was what I was trying to save him from. He'd have had to be the deuce of a lot worse than he is to deserve that."

Had it occurred to him, I put it to Cecil Harshaw, to ask himself what the saving of his precious cousin might have cost the girl who was to have been offered up to that end?

"You leave out one small feature of the case," said Harshaw, with a sick and burning look that made me drop my eyes, old woman as I am. "I love her myself so well that, by Heaven! if she had wanted Micky or any other man, she should have had him, if that was what

246

her heart was set upon. But I didn't believe it was. I wanted her to know the truth, and, hang it! I couldn't write it to her. I couldn't peach on Micky; but I wanted to smash things. I wanted something to happen. Maybe I didn't do the right thing, but I had to do something."

I couldn't tell him just what I thought of him at that moment, but I did say to him that he had some very simple ideas for an end-of-the-century young Englishman. At which he smiled sweetly, and said it was one of his simple ideas that Kitty need not be informed who or what her successor was, or how promptly she had been succeeded.

"But just now you said you wanted her to know the truth."

"Not the whole truth. Heavens! she knows enough. No need to rub it in."

"She knows just enough about this to misunderstand, perhaps. In justice to yourself,—she heard you beating about the bush,—do you want her to misunderstand you?"

"Oh, hang me! I don't expect her to understand me, or even tolerate me, yet. Mine is a waiting race, Mrs. Daly."

"Very well; you can wait," I said. "But news like this will not wait. She will be obliged to hear it; you don't know how or where she may hear it. Better let her hear it first in as decent a way as possible."

"But there is no decent way. How can I explain to you, or you to her, such a measly affair as this? It began with a question of money he owed that woman on the ranch. He bought it of her,—and a cruel, bad bargain it was,—and he never could make his last payment. She has threatened him, and played the fool with him when he'd let her, and bored him no end. His governor would have helped him out; but, you see, Micky has been a pretty expensive boy, and he has given the old gentleman to understand that the place is paid for,—to account for money sent him at various times for that ostensible purpose,—and on the basis the bargain was struck, between our governors, for my interest in the ranch. My father bought me in, on a clear title, as Uncle George represented it, in perfect good faith. I've never said a word, on the old gentleman's account; and Micky has never dared undeceive his father, who is the soul of honor in business, as in everything else. I am sorry to bore you with family affairs; but it's rather rum the way Micky's fate has caught up with him, through his one weakness of laziness, and perhaps lying a little, when he was obliged to. How this affair came about so suddenly I can't say. Didn't like to ask her too many questions, and Micky, poor devil, faded from view directly he saw us coming. But at a venture: she had heard he was going to be married, and came down here to make trouble when he should arrive with his bride; but he came back alone, disgusted with life, and found her here, and it was easier to marry her than—pay her, we'll say. She has been something over-generous, perhaps. She would rather have had him, anytime, than her money, and now was the time. She took advantage of a weak moment."

"A weak and a spiteful moment," I kindly added. "Now if he hastens the news to England, and the Percifers hear of it in New York, how pleasant for Kitty to have all her friends hear that *he* is married and *she* is not!"

"Great Heavens!" said the young fellow, "if she would let me hasten the news—that she is married to me!"

"Why don't you appeal to her pride and her spirit now while they are in the dust? Why do you bother with sentiment now?"

I liked him so much at that moment that I would have had him have Kitty, no matter what way he got her.

"Yes," he said; "why not take advantage of her, as everybody else has done?"

"Some people's scrupulousness comes rather late," I said.

"To those who don't understand," he had the brazenness to say. "What is done is done. It's a rough beginning—awfully rough on her. The end must atone somehow. If I don't win her I shall be punished enough; but if I do, it will be because she loves me. And pray God—" He stopped, with that look. It is a good many years since a young man has looked at me in that way, but a woman does not forget.

It was rather difficult telling to Kitty the story of her old lover's marriage, as I took it on myself to do. Not that she winced perceptibly; but I fear she has taken the thing home, and is dwelling on it—certain features of it—in a way that can do no good. From a word she lets slip now and then I gather that she is brooding over that fancy of hers that Cecil Harshaw offered himself by way of reparation, as she was falling between two stools,—her own home and her lover's,—to save her from the ground. As since that rainy night in the wagon she has never distinctly referred to this theory of his conduct, I have no excuse for bringing it up, even to attack it. In fact, I dare not; she is in too complicated a mood. And, after all, why should I want her to marry either of them? Why should the "hungry generations" tread her down? She is nice enough to stay as she is.

Another thing happened on our way here which may perversely

have helped to confirm her in this pretty notion of Harshaw's disinterestedness.

At a place by the river where the current is bad (there are many such places, and, in fact, the whole of the Snake River is a perfect hoodoo) Harshaw stopped one day to drink. The wagon had struck a streak of heavy sand, and we were all walking. We stood and watched him, because he drank with such deep enjoyment, stooping bareheaded on his hands and knees, and putting his hot face to the water. Suddenly he made a clutch at his breast pocket: his Norfolk jacket was unbuttoned. He had lost something, and the river had got it. He ran along the bank, trying to recover it with a stick, and, not succeeding, he plopped in just as he was, with his boots on. We saw him drop into deep water and swim for it, a little black object, which he caught, and held in his teeth. Then he turned his face to the shore; and precious near he came to never reaching it! We women had been looking on, smiling, like idiot dolls, till we saw Tom racing down the bank, throwing off his coat as he ran. Then we took a sort of dumb fright, and tried to follow; but it was all over in a second, before we saw it, still less realized it—his struggle, swimming for dear life, and not gaining an inch; the stick held out to him in the nick of time, just as he passed a spot where the beast of a current that had him swooped inshore.

I am sorry to say that my husband's first words to the man he may be said to have saved from death were, "You young fool, what did you do that for?"

"For this," Harshaw panted, slapping his wet breast.

"For a pocket-book! Great Sign! What had you in it? I wouldn't have done that for the whole of the Snake River valley."

"Nor I," laughed Harshaw.

"Nor the Bruneau to boot."

"Nor I."

"What did you do it for, then?"

"For this," Harshaw repeated.

"For a piece of pasteboard with a girl's face on it, or some such toy, I'll be sworn!"

Harshaw did not deny the soft impeachment.

"I didn't know you had a girl, Harshaw," Tom began argumentatively.

"Well, I haven't, you know," said Harshaw. "There was one I wanted badly, a few years ago," he added, with engaging frankness.

"When was it you first began to pine for her? About the period of second dentition?"

"Oh, betimes; and betimes I was disappointed."

"Well, unless it was for the girl herself, I'd keep out of that Snake River," my husband advised.

Kitty's face wore a slightly strained expression of perfect vacancy.

"Do *you* know who Harshaw's girl was?" I asked her the other night, as we were undressing, without an idea that she wouldn't see where the joke came in. She was standing, with her hair down, between the canvas curtains of our tent. It looks straight out toward the Sand Springs Fall, and Kitty worships there awhile every night before she goes to bed.

"No," she said. "I was never much with Cecil Harshaw. It is the families that have always known each other." The simple child! She hadn't understood him, or would she not understand? Which was it? I can't make out whether she is really simple or not. She is too clever to be so very simple; yet the cleverness of a young girl's mind, centered on a few ideas, is mainly in spots. But now I think she has brought this incident to bear upon that precious theory of hers, that Harshaw offered himself from a sense of duty. Great good may it do her!

The Sand Springs Fall, a perfect gem, is directly opposite our camp, facing west across the lagoon. We can feast our eyes upon it at all hours of the day and night. Tom has told Kitty, in the way of business, that he has no use for that fall. She may draw it or not, as she likes. She does draw it; she draws it, and water-colors it, and chalks it in colored crayons, and India-inks it, loading on the Chinese white; and she charcoals it, in moonlight effects, on a gray-blue paper. But do it whatever way she will, she never can do it.

"Oh, you exquisite, hopeless thing! Why can't I let you alone!" she cries; "and why can't *you* let *me* alone!"

"It is rather hard, the way the thing doubles up on you," says Tom. "The real fall, right side up, is bad enough; but when it comes to the reflection of it, standing on its head in the lagoon, I should lie right down myself. I wouldn't pull another pound."

(*"Lay* down," he said; but I thought you wouldn't stand it. Tom never would spoil a cherished bit of dialect on account of shocking anybody with his grammar.)

Kitty throws herself back in the dry salt-grass with which the whole of our little peninsula is bedded, the willows and brakes being our curtains, through which the rising moon looks in at us, and the setting sun; the sun rises long before we see him, above the dark-blue mountains beyond the shore.

"Won't somebody repeat

> There is sweet music here that softlier lies?"

Kitty asks, letting her eyelashes fall on her sun-flushed cheeks. Her face, as I saw it, sitting behind her in the grass, was so pretty—upside down like the reflection of the waterfall, its colors all the more wonderfully blended.

We did not all speak at once. Then Harshaw said, to break the silence, "I will read it to you, if you don't mind."

"Oh, have you the book?" Kitty asked, in surprise.

He went to his tent and returned with a book, and sitting on the grass where she could hear but could not see him, he began. I trembled for him; but before he had got to the second stanza I was relieved: he could read aloud.

"Now *there* is a man one could live on a Snake River ranch with," I felt like saying to Kitty. Not that I am sure that I want her to go.

When he had finished,

> O rest ye, brother mariners; we will not wander more!

Tom remarked, after a suitable silence, that it was all well enough for Harshaw, who would be in London in six weeks, to say, "We will not wander more!" But how about the rest of us?

Kitty sat straight up at that.

"Will Mr. Harshaw be in London six weeks from now?" The question was almost a cry. "Will you?" she demanded, turning upon him as if this was the last injury he could do her.

"I suppose so," he said.

"And you will see my mother, and all of them"

"I think so—if you wish."

She rose up, as if she could bear no more. Harshaw waited an instant, and then followed her; but she motioned him back, and went away to have it out with herself alone.

I took up the book Harshaw had left on the grass. It was "Copp's Manual"—"For the use of prospectors," etc.

After all, it is not so sure that Harshaw will go to London. There has been an engineer on the ground since last summer, when all the water was free. He has located a vast deal of it, perhaps the whole. Tom says he can hold only just as much as he can use; I hope there will be no difference of opinion on this point. There generally is a difference of opinion on points of location when the thing located is proved to have any value. The prior locator has gone East, they tell us at the ranch, on a business visit, presumably to raise capital for his scheme, which, as I understand it, is to force the water of the springs up on the dry plains above for irrigation (the fetish of the country), by means of a pneumatic pumping arrangement. His ladders and pipes, and all his hopeful apparatus, are clinging now like cobwebs to the face of the bluff, against that flashing, creaming broadside of the springs, at their greatest height and fall. I was pitying the poor man and his folly, but Tom says the plan is perfectly feasible.

The wall of the river canyon is built up in stories of basalt rock, each story defined by a horizontal fissure, out of which these mysterious waters gush, white and cold, taking glorious colors in the sunlight from the rich underpainting of the rock. There is an awfulness about it too, as if the sheer front of rock were the retaining-wall of a reservoir as deep as the bluffs are high, which had sprung a leak in a thousand places, and might the next instant burst and ingulf the lagoon, and wipe out the pretty island between itself and the river. Winter and summer the volume of water never varies, and the rate of discharge is always the same, and the water is never cold, though I have just said it is. It looks cold until the rocks warm it with their gem-like tints, like a bride's jewels gleaming through her veil. Back of the bluffs where it might be supposed to come from, there is nothing for a hundred miles but drought and desert plains. I don't care for any of their theories concerning its source. It is better as it is—the miracle of the smitten rock.

You can fancy what wild presumption it must seem that a man should think to reverse those torrents and make them climb the bluff, or cram them into an iron pipe and send them like paid laborers to hoist and pump and grind, and light the streets at Silver City, a hundred miles away. And how the cataracts will shout while these two boys compare their rival claims to ownership in a force that with one stroke could lay them as flat as last year's leaves in the bottom of a mill-race!

The particular fall my schemer has located for his own—other claims to be discussed hereafter—is called the "Snow Bank." He says he doesn't want the earth: this one cataract is enough for him. To look at the whole frontage of the springs and listen to their roar, one would think there might be water enough for them both, poor children! Hardly what you'd call two bites of a cherry!

If the springs were the half of a broken diamond bracelet, the

252

Snow Bank would be its brightest gem, lying separate in the case—perhaps the one that was the clasp. It is half hidden by the shoulder of a great barren bluff that, at a certain angle of the sun, throws a blue shadow over it. At other times the fall is almost too bright in its foaming whiteness for the eye to endure.

Kitty is painting it with this shadow half across it; but the light shines upon it at its source. Tom is doubtful if she is showing the fall to the best advantage for his purpose, but he is obliging enough to let the artist try it in her own way first.

"Go up there," she says, "and stand at the head of the spring, if you want to show by comparison how big it is, or how small you are."

He goes, and gets in position, and Kitty makes some pencil-marks on the margin of her sketch. Then she waves her hands to tell him, across the shouting torrent, that she is done with him. She has been so quick that he thinks he must have mistaken her gesture. Then Harshaw makes the train-conductor's signal for the train to move on.

"You see," she says to Harshaw and me, who are looking over her shoulder, "that would be the size of him in my sketch." She points to the marginal pencil-mark, which is not longer than the nib of a stub-pen. "I can't make a little black dot like that look like a man."

"In this particular sketch for his purpose, he'd rather look like a dot than a man, I dare say," said Harshaw.

"Well, shall I put him in? I can make a note of it on the margin: 'This black dot is Mr. Daly, standing at the spring-head. He is six feet—'"

"But he isn't, you know," Harshaw says. "He's five feet ten—if he's that."

"Ten and a half," Tom's wife corrects.

Our lunch that day had been left in the boat. We went down and ate it under the mountain birches at a spot where the Snow Bank empties into the lagoon—not *our* lagoon, as we called it, between our camp and the lovely Sand Springs Fall, but the upper one, made by the springs themselves, before their waters reach the river. In front of us, half embraced by the lagoon and half by the river, lay a little island-ranch of about ten acres, not cut up in crops, but all over green in pasture. A small cabin, propping up a large hop-vine, showed against a mass of birch and cottonwood on the river side of the island.

"What a place for a honeymoon!" said I.

"There is material there for half of a honeymoon," said Tom—"the feminine half; not bad material, either."

"Oh, yes," I said; "we have seen her—that is, we have seen her sunbonnet."

"Kitty, you've got a rival," I exclaimed; for there in the sunny center of the island, planted with obvious design right in front of the Snow Bank, *our* Snow Bank, was an artist's big white umbrella.

"Why should I not have in a place like this?" she said. "If the schemers arrive by twos, why not two of my modest craft? We shall leave it as we find it; we don't intend to carry it away in our pockets." She stopped, and blushed disdainfully. "I forgot," she murmured, "my own mercenary designs."

"I have not heard of these mercenary designs of yours. What are they, may I ask?" Harshaw had turned on his side on the grass, and half rose on one elbow as he looked at her.

"That is strange," mocked Kitty, with supreme coldness. "You have always been so interested in my affairs!"

"I always shall be," he replied seriously, with supreme gentleness.

"I ought to be so grateful."

"But unfortunately you are not."

"I should be grateful if you would move a little farther to the right, if you please. That young person in the pink sunbonnet is coming down to water her horses again."

Harshaw calmly took himself out of her way altogether, lighted his pipe, and went down close to the water, and sat there on a stone, and presently, as we could hear, entered into easy conversation with the pink sunbonnet, the face of which leaned toward him over the pony's neck as it stooped to drink. The splashed waters became still, and softly the whole picture—pink sunbonnet, clay-bank pony, pale, shivery willows, and deep blue sky—developed on the negative of the clear lagoon.

There was no use in saying how pretty it was, so we resorted to the other note, of disparagement. I remarked that I should not think a pink sunbonnet would be ravishingly becoming to the average Snake River complexion, as I had seen it.

"*That* sunbonnet is becoming, you bet!" Tom remarked. "Wait till you see the face inside it."

"Have you seen it?"

"Quite frequently. Do you think Harshaw would sit there talking with her, as he does by the hour, if that sunbonnet was not becoming?"

"As he does by the hour! And why have we not heard of her

before?" I requested to be told.

"Business, my dear. She is a feature of the scheme—quite an important one. She represents the hitch which is sure to develop early in the history of every live enterprise."

"Indeed?" I said. And if Harshaw talked with her on business, I didn't see what his talking had to do with the face inside her bonnet.

"I don't say that it's always on business," Tom threw in significantly.

"Who is the lady in the pink sunbonnet, and what is your business with her?" I demanded.

"I question the propriety of speaking of her in just that tone," said Tom, "inasmuch as she happens to be a lady—somewhat off the conventional lines. She waters her own stock and milks her own cow, but that is because the old Indian girl who lives with her is laid up at present with a fever. Her father was an artist—one of the great unappreciated—"

"So that was her father painting the Snow Bank?" I interrupted.

"Her father is dead, my dear, as you would have learned if you had listened to my story. But he lived here a good many years before he died. He had made a queer marriage, old man Decker tells me, and quarreled with the world on account of it. He came here with his disputed bride. She was somebody else's wife first, I believe, and there was a trifling informality about the matrimonial exchange; but it came out all right. They both died, and a sweeter, fresher little thing than the daughter! Adamant, though—bedrock, so far as we are concerned."

"What do you want that belongs to her?" I asked. "Her island, perhaps?"

"Only right of way across it. But 'that's a detail.' She is the owner of something else we do want—this piece of ground,"—he looked about him and waved his hand,—"and all this above us, where our power-plant must stand. And our business is to persuade her to sign the lease, or, if she won't lease, to sell it when we are ready to buy. We have to make sure of that piece of ground. This place is so confoundedly cut up with scenery and nonsense that there's not a spot available for our plant but this. We'll bridge the lagoon and make a landing on that point of birches over there."

"You will! And do you suppose she will sign a lease to empower you to wipe her off the face of the earth—abolish her and her pretty island at one fell swoop?"

"She knows nothing yet about our designs upon her toy island.

We haven't approached her on that. We could manage without it at a pinch."

"So good of you!" I murmured.

"But we can't manage without a place to put our power-house."

"She'll have to sign her own death-warrant, of course. If you get a footing for your power-house you'll want the island next. I never heard of such grasping profanation."

"Well, if Cecy could see his way to fall in love with her,—I wouldn't ask him to woo her in cold blood,—it would be a monstrous convenient way to settle it."

"Why do you say such things before her?" I asked Tom when we were alone. "They are not pretty things to say, in the first place."

"Have you noticed how she is always snubbing him? I thought it time somebody should try the counter-snub. He's not solely dependent for the joys of life on the crumbs of her society."

"Do you suppose she cares whom he talks to, or whom he spends his time with?"

"Perhaps she doesn't care. I should like to give her a chance to see if she cares, that's all."

Tom's location notice being plain for all eyes to read, the mistress of the island naturally inquired what he wanted with the Snow Bank; and he, thinking she would see at once the value to her ranch of such a neighboring enterprise, frankly told her of his scheme. Nothing of its scientific interest, its difficulties, its commercial value, even its benefit to herself, appealed to the little islander. To her it was simply an attempt to alter and ruin the spot she loved best on earth; to steal her beautiful waterfall and carry it away in an ugly iron pipe. Whether the thing could be done, she did not ask herself; the design was enough. Never would she lend herself, or anything that was hers, to such an impious desecration! This was her position, which any child might have taken in defense of a beloved toy; but she was holding it with all a woman's force and constancy.

I was glad of it, I said to Tom, and I hoped she would stand them off for all she was worth. But I am not really glad. What woman could love a waterfall better than her husband's success? There are hundreds of waterfalls in the world, but only this one scheme for Tom.

But anent this hitch, it teases me a little, I confess, on Kitty's account, when Cecil meanders over to the island at all hours of the day. To be sure, it relieves Kitty of his company; but is she so glad, after all, to be relieved?

It was last Friday, after one of Harshaw's entirely frank but perfectly unexplained absences, that he came into camp and inquired if there was any clam-broth left in the kitchen. I referred him to the cook. Finding there was, he returned to me and asked if he might take a tin of it to Miss Malcolm for her patient.

"Who is Miss Malcolm?" I asked. But of course who could she be but the lady of the island, where he spends the greater part of his time? He was welcome to the clam-broth, or anything else he thought would be acceptable in that quarter, I said. And how was the patient?

"Oh, she's quite bad all the time. She doesn't get about. I wonder if you'd mind, Mrs. Daly, if I asked you to look in on her some day? The old creature's in a sad way, it seems to me."

Of course I didn't mind, if Miss Malcolm did not. Harshaw seemed to feel authorized to assure me of that fact. So I went first with Tom, and then I went again alone, leaving Harshaw in the boat with Kitty.

Miss Malcolm's maid-or man-servant, or both—for she does the work of both,—and looks in her bed (dressed in a flannel bed-sack, her head tied up in an old blue knitted "fascinator") less like a woman than anything I ever beheld,—appears to have had a mild form of grippe fever, and having never been sick in her life before, she thought she was nearing her end. My simple treatment, the basis of which was quinine and whisky, seemed to strike old Tamar favorably; and after the second visit there was no need to come again to see her. But by this time I was deep in the good books of her mistress, who knows too little of illness herself to appreciate how little has been done, by me at least, or how very little needed to be done after restoring the old woman's confidence in her power to live. (The last time I saw her she still wore the blue fascinator, but with a man's hat on top of it; she was waddling toward the cow-corral with half a haystack, it looked like, poised on a hay-fork above her head. She was certainly a credit to her doctor, if not to her corsétière, she and the haystack being much of a figure.)

Miss Malcolm's innocent gratitude is most embarrassing, really painful, under the circumstances, and the poor child cannot let the circumstances alone. She imagines I am always thinking about Tom's scheme. It is evident that she is; and not being exactly a woman of the world, out of the fullness of her heart her mouth speaketh. That would be all right if she would speak to somebody else. I don't want to take advantage of her gratitude, as she seems determined I shall do.

"You must think me a very strained, sentimental creature," she said to me the last time, "to care so much for a few old rocks and a little piece of foamy water."

I didn't think so at all, I told her. If I had lived there all my life, I should feel about the place just as she did.

Here she began to blush and distress herself. "But think how kind you have all been to me! Mr. Harshaw was here every day, after he found how ill poor Tamar was. He did so many things: he lifted her, for one thing, and that I couldn't have done to save her life. And your two visits have simply cured her! And here I am making myself a stumbling-block and ruining your husband's plans!"

I said he was quite capable of taking care of himself.

"Does your husband want *all* the water?" she persisted. "Do I understand that he must have it all?"

I supposed she was talking of the Snow Bank, and since she was determined we should discuss the affair in this social way, I said he would have to have a great deal; and I told her about the distance the power would have to be sent, and about the mines and the smelters, and all the rest of it, for it was no use to belittle the scheme. I had got started unintentionally, and I saw by her face that I had made an impression. It is a small-featured, rather set, colorless face, not so pretty as Tom pretended, but very delicate and pure; but now it became suddenly the face of a fierce little bigot, and enthusiast to boot.

"It shall never go through—not *that* scheme—not if—" Then she remembered to whom she was talking, and set her lips together, and two great shiny drops stood in her eyes.

"Don't, don't, you child!" I said. "Don't worry about their old scheme! If it must come it will come; but as a rule, a scheme, my dear, is the last thing that ever does go through. There's plenty of time."

"But I can't give in," she said. "No; I *must* try to hinder it all I can. I will be honest with you. I like you all; of all the strangers who have come here I never liked any people better. But your husband—must not—set his heart on *all* that water! It doesn't belong to him."

"Does it belong to you, dear?"

"The *sight* of it belongs to me," she said. "I will not have the place all littered up with their pipes and power-plants. Look out there! Look at that! Has anyone the right to come here and spoil such a lovely thing as that?" This is what it is to be the daughter of an artist.

"And how about the other despoiler," I asked—"the young man

with the pneumatic pipe?"

"The 'pneumatic pipe'!" she repeated.

" 'Pump,' I mean. Is he to be allowed all over the place to do as *he* pleases? His scaling-ladders are littering up the bluffs—not that they incommode the bluffs any; but if I lived here, I should want to brush them away as I would sweep the cobwebs from my walls."

"I do not own the bluffs," she said in a distant, tremulous voice.

But the true answer to my question, as I surmise, was the sudden, helpless flush which rose, wave upon wave, covering her poor little face, blotting out all expression but that of painful girlish shame. Here, if I'm not mistaken, will be found the heart of the difficulty. Miss Malcolm's sympathies are evidently with compressed air rather than with electrical transmission. I shall tell Tom he need waste no more arguments on her. Let him first compound with his rival of the pump.

I suppose there is just such a low, big moon as this looking in upon you where you sit, you little dot of a woman, lost in the piazza perspectives of the Coronado; and you might think small things of our present habitation—a little tent among the bushes, with wind-blown weeds against the moon, shifting their shadow-patterns over our canvas walls. But you'd not think small things of our Sand Springs Fall by night, that glimmers on the dark cliff opposite—cliff, and noiseless, mist-like cataract, and the low moon throwing the shadow of the bluff across it, all repeated in the stiller, darker picture of the lagoon. I shall not inflict much of this sort of thing upon you; but the senseless beauty of it all gives one a heartache. Why should it be here, where you and I shall never see it together—where I shall leave it soon, never to see it again? Tom says we are coming back—when the great scheme is under way. Ah, the scheme, the scheme! It looks very far away to-night, and so do some other schemes that I seem to have set my heart on unaware, foolish old woman that I am. As if there was only one way in this world for young men and women to be happy!

Harshaw brought me your sweet letter yesterday. It was stage-day, and he went up over the bluffs to the ferry mail-box at the cross-roads, where the road to Shoshone Falls branches from the road to Bliss.

I read to Kitty what you wrote me about the Garretts and their children, and the going to New York and then to Paris. (Thank you so much, dear, for your prompt interest in my little bride that isn't to be!) She had two letters of her own which she had read by herself, and afterward I thought she had been crying; but with her it is best not to press the note of sympathy. Neither does she like me to handle her affairs with gloves on, so to speak. So I plunged into the business in a matter-of-fact tone, and she replied in the same. Her objection is to going east to New York, and then to the other side. "I had rather stay in California," she said, "or anywhere in the West." Naturally; westward lies the way of escape from social complications.

She is afraid of the Percifers, and of meeting people she knows in Paris. But an offer like this was exceptional in this part of the world, I reminded her. A nurse for the boy, a maid, and only two little girls of eight and ten on her hands; and such nice people as the Garretts, who have been all over the world!

"Well," she said, "I should certainly like to get away from here as soon as possible. From *here*, not from *you!*" she added, looking me in the face. Her eyes were full of tears. We clasped hands on that.

"What is it? Has anything else happened?" I asked; for I knew by her looks that something had.

"Oh, dear!" she sighed, "I should so like to take myself and my troubles seriously once in a while. No sooner do I try, but something perfectly farcical is sure to happen. If I tell you this, promise me you won't laugh. It's indecent for me to laugh; mama would never forgive me. The old dear! I'm so fond of him!"

The "old dear," it seems, is Micky's father—a very superior sort of father for such a son to have, but accidents will happen in the best-regulated families. He is a gallant widower of fair estate, one of those splendid old club-men of London; a very expensive article of old gentleman, with fine old-fashioned manners and morals, and a few stray impulses left, it would seem by what follows. According to the father's code, the son has not conducted himself in his engagement to Kitty Comyn as a gentleman should. Thereupon the head of the house goes to Miss Kitty's mother and makes the *amende honorable* by offering his hand and heart and fortune to his son's insulted bride! The mother is touched and pleased not a little by this prompt espousal of her daughter's cause; and having wiped away all tears from *her* eyes, this gallant old gentleman is coming over to America, for the first time in his life, to make his proposal to the bride herself! He is not so old, to get down to particulars; sixty-three doesn't seem so old to some of us as it does to Miss Kitty. He is in fine health, I doubt not, and magnificently preserved. Kitty's mother is not at all averse, as I gather, to this way of settling her child's difficulties. She rather pleadingly assures Kitty that Mr. Harshaw senior has solemnly sworn that this is no unpleasant duty he feels called on to perform; not only his honor, but his affections are profoundly enlisted in this proposal. Kitty has had for years a sacred place in his regard; and from thinking of her as a daughter absolutely after his own heart, it is but a step to think of her in a still nearer—the nearest—relation. He begs her mother to prepare her for no perfunctory offer of marriage, but one that warms with every day's delay till he can take the dear child under his lifelong protection. Not to punish or to redress does he come, but to secure for himself and and posterity a treasure which his son had trampled under foot. Somehow we did not feel like laughing, after all. Kitty, I think, is a little frightened. She cannot reach her mother, even with a cable despatch, before this second champion will arrive.

"He's an awfully grand old fellow, you know. I could never talk to him as I do to the boys. If he thinks it his duty to marry me, I don't know if I can help myself. Poor Uncle George! I've always called him 'uncle' like his own nieces, who are all my friends. I never thought that I should be 'poor-ing' Uncle George! But he can't have heard yet of Micky's marriage. Fancy his going down to the ranch to stay with Micky and that woman! And then for a girl like me to toss him aside, after such a journey and such kindness! I don't know how I shall ever have courage to do it. There are fine women in London who would jump at the chance of being Mrs. Harshaw—not Mrs. Micky, nor Mrs. Stephen, nor Mrs. Sidney, but *Mrs. Harshaw,* you understand?" I understood.

"And now," she said, producing the second letter, "you *will* laugh! And you may!"

The envelop contained a notification, in due form, of the arrival from New York, charges not paid, of some five hundred pounds of second-class freight consigned to Mrs. Harshaw, Harshaw's ranch, Glenn's Ferry (via Bisuka).

"These things belong to me," said Kitty. "I paid for them, at least. They cost me the last bit of money I had that was my own. Mrs. Percifer, who is so clever at managing, persuaded me I should need them directly on the ranch—curtains and rugs and china, and heaven knows what! She nearly killed me, dragging me about those enormous New York shops. She said it would be far and away cheaper and better to buy them there. I didn't mind about anything, I was so scared and homesick; I did whatever she said. She saw to getting them off, I suppose. That must have been her idea, directing them to Mrs. Harshaw. She thought there would be no Kitty Comyn, no *me,* when these got here. And there isn't; *this* is not the Kitty Comyn who left England—six weeks, is it?—or six years ago!

"How did the letter reach you?" I asked. We examined the envelop. It bore the postmark, not of Bisuka, but of Glenn's Ferry, which is the nearest post-office to the Harshaw ranch. Micky's wife had doubtless opened the letter, and Micky, perceiving where the error lay, had reinclosed, but someone else had directed it—the post-master, probably, at his request—to Kitty, at our camp. That was rather a nice little touch in Micky, that last about the direction.

"Come, he is honest, at the least," I said, "whether Mrs. Micky would have scrupled or not. She could claim the things if she chose."

"She is quite welcome," said Kitty. "I don't know what in the world I shall do with them. There'll be boxes and bales and barrels—enough to bury me and all my troubles. I might build me a funeral pyre!"

We fell into each other's arms and screamed with laughter.

"Kitty, we'll have an auction," I cried. "There's nothing succeeds like an auction out here. We'll sell the things at boom prices—we'll sell everything."

"But the bride," said Kitty; "you will have to keep the bride." And without a moment's warning, from laughing till she wept, she began to weep in earnest. I haven't seen her cry so since she came to us, not even that miserable first night. She struggled with herself, and seemed dreadfully ashamed, and angry with me that I should have seen her cry. Did she suppose I thought she was crying because she wasn't going to be a bride, after all?

"Oh, Mrs. Daly, I feel so ill!" were Kitty's first words to me when I woke this morning. I looked her over and questioned her, and concluded that a sleepless night, with not very pleasant thoughts for company, might be held responsible for a good share of her wretchedness.

"What were you lying awake about? Your new champion, Uncle George?" I asked her.

She owned that it was. "Don't you see, Mrs. Daly, mama doesn't leave room for the possibility of my refusing him. And if I do refuse him, he'll simply take me back to England, and then, between him and mama, and all of them, I don't know what will happen."

"Kitty," I said, "no girl who has just escaped from one unhappy engagement is going to walk straight into another with her eyes wide open. I won't believe you could be so foolish as that."

"You don't understand," she said, "what the pressure will be at home—in all love and kindness, of course. And you don't know Uncle George. He is so sure that I need him, he'll force me to take him. He'll take me back to England in any case."

"And would you not like to go, Kitty?"

"Ah, wouldn't I! But not in that way."

She sat up in her flannel camp-gown, and began to braid up her loosened hair.

"Kitty," I commanded, "lie down. You are not to get up till luncheon."

"I have a plan," she said, "and I must see Mr. Harshaw; he must help me carry it out. There is no one else who can."

"You have all day to see him in."

"Not all day, Mrs. Daly. He must be ready to start to-morrow. Uncle George will reach Bisuka on the fifteenth, not later. Cecil must meet him there, first, to prepare him for Micky's new arrangement, and second, to persuade him that he does not owe me an offer of marriage in consequence. Cecil will know how to manage it; he must know! I will not have anymore of the Harshaws offering themselves as substitutes. It's passing strange if I cannot exist without them somehow."

It struck me that the poor child's boast was a little premature, as she seemed to be making rather free use of one of the substitutes still, as a shield against the others; but it was a piece with the rest of the comedy. I kept her in bed till she had had a cup of tea; afterward she slept a little, and about noon she dressed herself and gave Cecil his audience. But first, at her request, I had possessed him with the main facts and give him an inkling of what was expected of him. His face changed; he looked as he did after his steeplechase the day I saw him first,—except that he was cleaner,—grave, excited, and resolved. He had taken the bit in his teeth. When substitute meets substitute in a cause like this! I would have left them to have their little talk by themselves, but Kitty signified peremptorily that she wished me to stay, with a flushed, appealing look that softened the nervous tension of her manner.

"I would do anything on earth for you, Kitty," Cecil said most gently and fervently; "but don't ask me to give advice—to Uncle George of all men—on a question of this kind—unless you will allow me to be perfectly frank."

"It's a family question," said Kitty, ignoring his proviso.

"I think it would get to be a personal question very soon between Uncle George and me. No; I meddled in one family question not very long ago."

"It's very strange," said Kitty, restlessly, "if you can't help me out of this in some way. I cannot be so disrespectful to him, the dear old gentleman! I ought not to be put in such a position, or he either. How would you like it if it were your father?"

Cecil reddened handsomely at this home question. "I'd have a deuce of a time to stop him if he took the notion, you know; it's not exactly a son's or a nephew's business. There is only one way in which I can help you, Kitty. You must know that."

He had struck a different key, and his face was all one blush to correspond with the new note in his voice. I think I never saw a manlier, more generous warmth of ardor and humility, or listened to words so simple uttered in such telling tones.

"What way is that?" asked Kitty, coldly.

"Forgive me! I could tell him that you are engaged to me."

"That would be a nice way—to tell him a falsehood! I should hope I had been humiliated enough—"

She snatched her handkerchief from her belt and pressed it to her burning face. I rose again to go. "Sit still, pray!" she murmured.

"It need not be a falsehood, Kitty. Let it be anything you like. You may trust me not to take advantage. A nominal engagement, if you choose, just to meet this exigency; or—"

"That would be cheating," cried Kitty.

"The cheat would bear a little harder on me than on any one else, I think."

"You are too good!" Kitty smiled disdainfully. "First you offer yourself to me as a cure, and now as a preventive."

"Kitty, I think you ought at least to take him seriously," I remonstrated.

"By all that's sacred, you'll find it's serious with me!" Cecil ejaculated.

"Since when?" retorted Kitty. "How many weeks ago is it that I came out here by your contrivance to marry your cousin? Is that the way a man shows his seriousness? You sacrificed more to marry me to Micky than some men would to win a girl themselves."

"I did, and for that very reason," said Cecil.

"I should like to see you prove it!"

"Kitty, excuse me," I interrupted. "I should like to ask Mr. Harshaw one question, if he does not mind. Do you happen to have that picture about you, Mr. Harshaw?"

I thought I was looking at him very kindly, not at all like an inquisitor, but his face was set and stern. I doubt if he perceived or looked for my intention.

" 'That picture,' Mrs. Daly?" he repeated.

"The photograph of a young lady that you jumped into the river to save—don't you remember?"

Cecil smiled slightly, and glanced at Kitty. "Did I say it was a photograph of a lady?"

"No; you did not. But do you deny that it was?"

"Certainly not, Mrs. Daly. I have the picture with me; I always have it."

"And do you think *that* looks like seriousness? To be making such protestations to one girl with the portrait of another in your coat pocket? We have none of us forgotten, I think, that little conversation by the river."

He saw my intention now, and thanked me with a radiant look. "Here is the pictu e, Mrs. Daly. Whose portrait did you think it was? Surely *you* might have known, Kitty! This is the girl I wanted years ago, and have wanted ever since; but she belonged to another man, and the man was my friend. I tried to save that man from insulting her and dishonoring himself, because I thought she loved him. Or, if he couldn't be saved, I wanted to expose him and save her. And I risked my own honor to do it, and a great fool I was for my pains. But this is the last time I shall make a fool of myself for your sake, Kitty."

I rose now in earnest, and I would not be stayed. In point of fact, nobody tried to stay me. Kitty was looking at her own face with eyes as dim as the little water-stained photograph she held. And Cecil was on his knees beside her, whispering: "I stole it from Micky's room at the ranch. That was no place for it, anyhow. May I not have one of my own, Kitty?"

I think he will get one—of his own Kitty.

Our rival schemer, Mr. Norman Fleet, has arrived, and electrical transmission has shaken hands with compressed air. The millennium must be on the way, for never did two men want so nearly the same thing, and yet agree to take each what the other does not need.

Mr. Fleet does not "want the earth," either, nor all the waters thereof; but the most astonishing thing is, he doesn't want the Snow Bank! He not only doesn't want it himself, but is perfectly willing that Tom should have it. In fact, do what we will, it seems to be impossible for us to tread on the tail of that young man's coat. But having heard a little bird whisper that he is in love, and successfully so, I am not surprised at his amiability. Neither am I altogether unprepared, if the little bird's whisper be true, for the fact that Miss Malcolm is becoming reconciled to Tom's designs upon her beloved scenery. For the sake of consistency, and that pure devotion to the Beautiful, so rare in this sordid age, I could have wished that she had not weakened so suddenly; but for Tom's sake I am very glad. She is clay in the hands of the potter, now that she knows my husband does not want "all the water," and that his success does not mean the failure of Mr. Norman Fleet.

Harshaw will take the Snow Bank scheme when he takes Kitty back to London. If he promotes it, I tell Tom, after the fashion in which he "boomed" Kitty's marriage to his cousin, we're not likely to see either him or the Snow Bank again. But "Harshaw is all right," Tom says; and I believe that the luck is with him.

The Far West Illustrations

Looking For Camp

In that portion of the arid belt which lies within the borders of Idaho between the rich irrigated valleys and the mining-camps of the mountains there is a region whereon those who occupy it have never labored—the beautiful "hill country," the lap of the mountain ranges, the free pastures of the plains. Here, without help of hands, are sown and harvested the standing crops of wild grass which constitute the wealth of the cattle-men in the valleys.

Of all the monotonous phases of the Western landscape these high, solitary pastures are the most poetic. Nothing human is suggested by the plains except processions of tired people passing over, tribal movements, war-parties, discoverers, and fortune-seekers. But the sentiment of the hills is restful. Their stillness is not lifeless; it is as if these warm-bosomed slopes were listening, like a mother to her child's breathing, for sounds from all the shy, wild communities which they feed and shelter—the slow tread of grazing herds, the call of a bird, the rustle of the stiff grass on the hill-slopes, the lapsing trickle of water in gulches hidden by willows, and traced by their winding green from far off across the dry slopes.

All the life of the hills tends downwards at night; the cattle, which always graze upwards, go down to the gulches to drink; the hunter makes his camp there when darkness overtakes him. He may travel late over the hills in the twilight, prolonged and colored by the sunset. There is seldom a cloud to vary the slow, deep gradation where the sun has gone down and the dusty valley still smolders in orange and crimson, with a cold substratum of pale blue mist above the river channel. Through a break in the line of the hills, or from a steep rise, one can track the sun from setting to setting till he is gone at last, and the flaming sky colors the opposite hilltops so that they glow even after the rising moon casts shadows. At this hour the stillness is so intense that the faintest breeze can be heard, creeping along the hillslopes and stirring the dry, reed-like grasses with a sound like that of a muted string.

The Coming of Winter

One year's occupation of a quarter-section of wild land means but a slight foothold in a new country—a cabin, rude as a magpie's nest; a crop of wild hay, if the settler is near a river-bottom; the tools and stock he brought with him; a few chickens not yet acclimated; a few seeds and slips from the last home; probably a new baby.

Now that the wild-geese are beginning to fly, a chance shot may furnish a meal, where every meal counts. The young wife holds the baby's blanket close to its exposed ear to deaden the report of the gun. She is not so sure of the marksman's aim as she would have been a year before she married him. He is one of an uncertain crop of husbandmen that springs up quickly on new soil, but nowhere strikes deep roots.

The prettiest girl of his native village, somewhere in the Southwest, will have fancied him, and have consented to take her place beside him on the front seat of his canvas-topped wagon when the inevitable vague westward impulse seized him. As the miles lengthen behind them and "their garments and their shoes become old by reason of the long journey," she will lose her interest in the forward outlook and spend more and more of her time among the bedquilts and hen-coops in the rear of the wagon, half asleep, or watching listlessly the plains they crawl across and the slow rise and fall of the strange hills they climb.

When the settlers stop, it is not because they have reached the place to which they meant to go, but because they have found a sheltered valley with water and wild grass. The wagon needs mending, they and their cattle are tired. While they rest, they build a rude cabin, the baby is born, summer has passed. It is too late to move that winter.

The home-seeker, with all the West before him, will be wary of the final choice which costs him the freedom of the road. He is like a child in a great toy-shop full of high-priced, remotely imaginable joys, and with but a single penny in his pocket. So long as he nurses

269

the penny unspent he is the potential possessor; a man of much wider scope, much larger resources, than the actual possessor. Birds in the bush that beckon and call are not of the same species as the bird that lies tamely in hand.

Teamsters, toiling across the great lava beds, on their way to the mountain mining-towns, make camp near the cabin in the willow-brake, sit by the settler's fire, and their talk is the large talk of the men of the road—of placer claims on the rivers far to the north, where water is plentiful all the year; of the grass, how rich and tall it grows in Long Valley, and how few stock-men with their herds have got into that region as yet.

The settler's eye is brilliant as he listens. He is losing time; he yearns for the spring, and the dawn of new chances. But he is a restless, not a resolved man, and with spring come back the birds of promise, the valley rings with their music, the seeds are up in the garden, and the baby is learning to walk.

Out of the poorest thousand in Manasseh was Gideon chosen. It may be that the child, so soon escaping out of the languid mother's arms, may be one of the mighty men in the new country where his parents waited to rest awhile before moving farther on.

The Sheriff's Posse

This picture is not so sincere as it might be. The artist, in the course of many rides over these mountain pastures, by daylight or twilight or moonrise, has never yet encountered anything so sensational as a troop of armed men on the track of a criminal. Yet rumors are passing, from turbulent camps above us in the mountains or from the seductive valley towns, that easily suggest some such night journey as this. The riders make haste slowly, breasting slope after slope of the interminable cattle-ranges, on the alert, as they climb out of gulch after gulch of shadow, for the next long outlook ahead.

It may be mentioned that by far the greater number of criminals confined in the jails of the far West are there for a class of offenses peculiar to the country. They are men dangerous in one direction, perhaps, but generally not depraved. The "trusties" are often domesticated upon ranches near the town, and apparently are unwatched, and on the best of terms with the ranchman's family. They have a simple faith in the necessity for a certain sort of action, under given circumstances, which supports them under sentence of the law, and serves instead of a clear conscience. They have done nothing of which they are ashamed.

For example, a cattle-man meets a sheep-man on the hills. The sheep-man represents to the cattle-man that his only possible course is to take his band across the cattle-man's range—to "sheep" him, in the local phrase. A sheep-man makes no treaty with the owners of the land he crosses that he will not "turn into the fields, or into the vineyards;" that he will not "drink of the water of the well"; but go by the highway until he has passed on. The land belongs to him as much as to the cattle-man who has pitched in its borders. But it is a perfectly clear case to the cattle-man that the sheep-man's multitude will lick up all before them, and that his own multitude must starve on what is left. He does not waste time praying, "Curse me this sheep-man!" He goes out against the sheep-man, without prayerful

272

preliminaries. He "lays for him" at night, when he has lighted his solitary fire in the sage-brush. The next day a disorganized band of sheep, minus a grimy shepherd, goes wandering back to the river, to the despair of a masterless dog.

The case is tried in the valley town and the murderer is acquitted, the sentiment of the community being with him to a much greater extent than would be generally admitted. No judge nor jury nor term of punishment could have altered his personal conviction and that of his friends that his deed was only an effort in self-defense and an act of public justice.

If such a fugitive as this is overhauled in a night-chase by the sheriff and his men, he is treated as a comrade "in trouble." To quote a description, given in Hibernian good faith, of a young man at large with the murder of his father—in defense of his mother, it is claimed—on his head, "He is a perfect gentleman if he isn't crossed."

The Orchard Windbreak

It was late in May; the apple blossoms, which are in full beauty in the valley of the Boise about the first of the month, had fallen when we discovered this pioneer orchard and first walked its length between the young trees, leafing out, and the dark wall of poplars which shelters it from the north-east winds. The "wind-break" bounds the orchard along the brink where the land drops to the level of the meadow below. A path follows the wind-break on the orchard side: walking this path, one may look out, as from high Gothic windows, upon the broad, bright meadows beneath.

An irrigating ditch traverses the meadows, skirting the edge of the higher land. Each farmer on the ditch has his wheel,—called a Chinese wheel, though it is like the Persian *noria,* lifting water to the upper fields. These upper and lower fields, with the sky-pierced screen of poplars between them, divide the water of the ditch as it passes. The lower fields, which get it first, hand it up to the fields above, and these return it again in drainage or in drippage from the creaking buckets that ladle it into the flumes and boxes that distribute it to the higher plantations. The system is supposed to be an improvement upon the "useful trouble of the rain."

In all these new holdings of the old West it would be difficult to find a prettier walk than this,—along the brink of these upper fields, in the shade of the poplars, with all the sunny land below,—on a May morning when the air is as cool as the sun is hot, when the clustering spires of young leaves glisten in the light like strung jewels, when shadows lose themselves in the short tufted grass, when the mosquitoes are as yet in abeyance.

To reach the orchard we cross the garden of the penitentiary: there is no other way, unless we pass through the home lot of the proprietor of the orchard. The first way, the way of the discovery, is much the better, for when we came upon it first by way of the penitentiary garden, the orchard was a surprise in its effect of overlooking the lower fields.

It was Sunday; the penitential gardeners were not at work—we saw not a single fallen Adam of them all. A stout wire fence separates the field of the just from the field of the unjust. For the woman of the party to go between the barbed wires and not to leave a large part of her drapery attached to the fence was a problem. It was solved by the man of the party, who muffled the lower wire of the fence in the folds of the cloak he carried, as the matador casts his cloak over the horns of the bull, and lifted the wire next above, to widen the way between.

Beyond the barricade lay the lovely spaces of light and shadow—the familiar little trees, the trees of home, with their stiff, up-springing shoots and queer knots and angles, showing how Nature had been assisted or thwarted in her work by the hand of man. Down the middle of the picture, ranging upward in perspective to the towering deep blue sky, strode the dark monkish procession of poplars. We saw before us the cloister and the home, and behind us was the garden of the penitentiary.

We did not see the lady and the fawn that day, nor indeed on any other day, it must be confessed, in that particular spot. But she was needed there. Something was lacking in the pretty scene in its Sunday morning silence and quiet sunshine—a step upon the grass, a white shape against the poplars, a head, in light, in the midst of the tender May greens.

By her permission the lady is there, with the fawn that long ago escaped to the hills—or was it sold, or given away, or quietly put out of its warped existence? For these wild nurslings that are brought down to the valley town for playthings lose, it is said, after a few months of petted bondage, their fitness for freedom. They are rejected forever by their kind as a thing which has been tainted by the touch of man—a creature that might betray, or renounce in favor of the slavish past.

The planting of an orchard by a new settler is accepted as his final expression of content with his choice, a guaranty that he means to stay. He may build a cabin, or plow a field, or dig a well or a ditch to water his garden, for seed springs up and is gathered in a summer; but the planting of a tree, the life of which is more than the age of man, is the seal of civilization set upon virgin soil. An orchard is a creation, with potential values not to be hastily measured; it is money in the bank of nature, which rarely acknowledges a draft at sight, nor dishonors a final payment. He who plants apple trees plants for himself, but "he who plants pears plants for his heirs." They are planting pear orchards in the valley of the Boise.

277

The Choice of Reuben and Gad

As the stage-road climbs eastward out of a certain river-valley there is a bit of wild, broken country at the meeting of two roads which gives the keynote to that biblical suggestion in the scenery of the far West that often impresses the traveler with an historic familiarity. The lower road follows the river, leading to neighboring ranches on its shore; the upper, and less traveled, skirts the base of the hills and leads—anywhere one chooses to fancy: to the fastnesses, it might be, of the five kings of the Amorites.

It is a sad, strange, yet inviting region, suggestive of primitive occupation; and indeed, for many years, it may be said to have been the inheritance of the children of Reuben and Gad. It is "a place for cattle." Whether it was their weary choice to remain here, like their prototypes of Israel, content and unambitious for the fulfillment of the promise, and whether there were subsequent wars with the heathen, we were not curious to discover; it is a place one passes by but remembers afterwards. No doubt the first occupants had their struggles, of one sort or another, before they came in possession, with their wives and little ones and their "very great multitude of cattle," and built them sheepfolds and fenced cities.

We had been reading to the children one evening the story of the conquest of Canaan and had got as far as the battle of Beth-horon, when, in one of those sudden flashes of association by which memory aids the mental vision, we saw that bit of broken country, that lonely road pursuing its way into the hills: the place and the story were one. So looked the pass that goeth up to Beth-horon; so, between sunset and moonrise, looked the valley of Ajalon. Those dark hills to the eastward were the outgoings of the mountain of Ephraim, where Joshua was buried, and Eleazar, in the hill that pertained to Phineas his son.

The presence and company of an unknown landscape wherein one has set up no landmarks, a landscape that has no history set forth in guide-books, that has no haunting place in one's reading, restores us to the attitude of a child towards its first surroundings. Children are too wise to ask questions and so disturb the dream with which they people the places it suits the convenience of their elders they should dwell in. Much is lost by insisting upon contemporary evidence, especially in a land poor in tradition but rich in suggestion, of a vague, large, melancholy sort.

If we ask who is this dark-faced rider hurrying bands of shock-haired ponies down from the hills, we are told it is Packer Nelson, or his brother John, from the horse-ranch up the river. When we go deeper than the fact and enter into the hopes and hardships and scant rewards of a patient, much-enduring people, we are scarcely the happier, but we may be better satisfied with ourselves; for it is a cheap sort of indulgence, dressing real people up in rags of fancy and trite symbolism.

We know that the cowboy is as genuine, and probably as historic, an outgrowth of the western border of the Platte as was the wily Gibeonite of the eastern borders of the Jordon. We accept him; we know he is as interesting in reality as an Amorite or a Hivite chieftain. But we would like to keep our play-names for this solemn, Old World landscape. This hither shore of the river, rich in grass, broken by hills into shelter from the winds, is our land of Gilead; those hills to the eastward, with their strange copper-colored lights at sunset, are the lonely hills of sepulture; the Promised Land lies just beyond the river's twilight gleam, where the mesa steps down by treads ten miles long to the dim, color-washed line of the plain.

Cinching Up

It is difficult to define the charm of a day's riding in the West where the sun is hot, the country barren, the horses generally bad. It must be the simplicity, the touch of reality so prized by children in their play, the truth to circumstances, that distinguish it, as a pursuit, from showy meets of town and country clubs, anise-seed hunts, and masquerading of one sort or another in the saddle.

One must go far to find the indispensable conditions: they are usually the reward of a rather bad time in other ways. The play must be played in earnest, not with an eye to spectators. If possible, it should be part of the business of one's life, yet only lately so, for novelty is one of the conditions; good company, and not too much of it, is another.

One should start early in the morning, with serious intentions. The horses should know their business as well as the men, and for this reason the horses of the country are the best. If there is a woman in the party, she should return in spirit to her primitive condition of dependence upon direct masculine protection and leadership: by the abandonment of her rights she will receive a corresponding measure of her privileges. There should be food in the saddle-bags; for women cannot travel as men can, hour after hour without eating, however sure of their powers in this respect they may be at the start. Without food a woman's courage in the saddle, and frequently her temper, give out; and it is not wisdom on a journey to strain either the one or the other more than is necessary. An inevitable strain a woman will endure with dignity, while a trifling but needless one irritates her.

There should be no definite picture of the country in the minds of the adventurers beyond such suggestions as the local names afford—Robie's Gulch, Sour-dough Dick's, the Idaho City road, the road to Silver Mountain. There should be some discomfort to remember with complacency when the ride is over, and the stages

Cinching U[...]

should be long enough to give the women of the party the simple pride of showing that they can keep the pace beside the men, with the odds against them of a side-saddle instead of a pair of stirrups. There should be important changes of scenery by the way, such as every few hundred feet of elevation will give in the West, from plain or treeless park to lightly wooded foothills; from these to the deep old timber upon the flanks of the range; and from this again to the crooked trees and dwarfish vegetation on the borders of the snow.

But a journey from valley to valley across the divides between, if not so sensational, is more beautiful and less severe than a steady climb; for in every valley there will be a cabin or a ranch, if not a settlement, and the sight of new faces and strange interiors is part of the rest.

Montaigne, who seems to have been one of the most sensible as well as (by his own account) hardiest of horsemen, says: "I have learnt to frame my journeyes after the Spanish fashion, all at once and outright, great or reasonable. And in extreme heats I travell at night, from sunne-set to sunne rising."

It is impossible to read the mere statement and think of the countries he traversed in this manner without a vivid conception of his wisdom. No woman who has ridden in the blazing West but can sympathize with him when he says, "No weather is to me so contrary as the scorching heat of the parching sunne; for those umbrels or riding canopies which, since the ancient Romans the Italians use, doe more weary the armes than ease the head."

Have we not dreamed—all of us who are amateurs, and not proud, like the cowboy, of wearing upon our cheeks "the shadowed livery of the burnished sun"—of cool night marches during the season of unvarying weather, when Perseus is striding up the east, and Lyra the beautiful hangs like a lamp in the heavens? That lack of atmosphere which leaves the traveler at the sun's mercy by day gives wonderful brilliancy to the spectacle of the night sky. Soon after sunset the dry summer gale begins to blow; the stars "rush out"; the cloudlesss sky is dark as on frosty winter nights. Or if there be a moon, the breadth and tenderness of her light in a wide and treeless landscape will be a revelation to those who only know moonlight beset by shadows.

All the night journeys in the fiction of one's early reading come back to revive the restlessness such nights will bring: Sir Kenneth, exiled from honor and slave of the Arab physician, looking back at the Crusaders' camp, at the tents and banners glimmering in the moonlight, as he rides away into the desert; Quentin Durward mustering his little troop of lances at the hour of midnight beneath the Dauphin's tower. The days of errant heiresses, of Lady Ediths in Palestine, are no more: the Kenneths and the Quentins are engaged in earning their individual livings, instead of guarding banners or convoying disguised ladies across unscientific frontiers. Yet there are nights of the dry season as haunting in their lonely beauty as the nights of Palestine or that hour of the rendezvous at the Dauphin's tower; there are stretches of uncelebrated country as lovely by moonlight as the Syrian desert or the majestic plain of the Loire. And there may be a man, now and then, in the West, though he rides a shock-haired cayuse instead of a stately war-horse, as brave in his way and as simply true as the young gentlemen to whom those important undertakings were intrusted so long ago. And it is to be hoped that such confidence as that of the noble ladies of Croye, who asked but the name of their knight, his degree, and one look at his face, may be ready when called for in the women of the West.

The Irrigating Ditch

The word "desert" is used, in the West, to describe alike lands in which the principle of life, if it ever existed, is totally extinct, and those other lands which are merely "thirsty."

West of the Missouri there are immense, sad provinces devoted to drought. They lie beneath skies that are pitilessly clear. The great snow-fields, the treasury of waters, are far away, and the streams which should convey the treasure are often many days' journeys apart. These wild water-courses are Nature's commissaries sent from the mountains to the relief of the plains; but they scamper like pickpockets. They make away with the stores they were charged to distribute. They hurry along, making the only sound to be heard for miles in those vacant lands which they have defrauded. Year by year, or century by century, they plow out their barren channels: gradually they sink, beyond any possibility of fulfilling their mission. Now and then one will dig for itself a grave in the desert, bury its mouth in the sand, and be known as a "lost" river.

Meantime the long-repressed soil vents itself in extravagant, contorted growths of sage-brush. Where the sage grows rank and covers the ground like a dwarfed forest the settler chooses his location. But the prospector usually comes before the settler; he takes the greater risks which go with the higher chances. He has found, or fought, his way into the mountains, whence rumors of rich strikes quickly breed the mining fever. Hard upon the news of the first "boom" comes the settler, sure of his market. He ventures into the nearest valley, taps the runaway river, makes a hole in its pocket, and a little of the wrested treasure leaks out and fertilizes his wild acres. The new crops are miracles of abundance: mining-camp markets, while they last, are the romance of farming; very soon the primitive irrigator can afford to enlarge his ditches and improve his "system." New locators crowd into the narrow valley; the ranches lock fences side by side. Small ventures in stock are cast, like bread

The Irrigating Ditch

upon the waters, far forth into the hills, which are the granaries of the arid belt.

The river and its green dependencies strike a new and shriller color-note, which quavers through the dun landscape like the note of a willow-whistle on warm spring days—clear, sweet, but languid with the oppression of the bare, unshaded fields around. It is the human note, familiar in its crudeness, but dearly welcome to the traveler after days of nothing but sky and sage-brush, sun and silence.

The new settlement is but an outpost of the frontier: if the mines hold out, if the railroads presently remember that it is there, its young fields need not wither nor its ditches be choked with dust. Twenty years, if it should survive, will have brought it beauty as well as comfort and security. The older ranches will show signs of prosperous tenantage in their tree-defended barns and long lines of ditches, dividing, with a still sheen, the varied greens of the springing crops. Each freshly plowed field that encroaches upon the aboriginal sage-brush is a new stitch taken in the pattern of civilization which runs, a slender, bright border, along the skirt of the desert's dusty garment.

Faces, too, will soften, and forms grow more lovely as the conditions of life improve. The men and women who took the brunt of the siege and capture of those first square miles of desert will carry in their countenances something of the record of that achievement. The second generation may seek to forget that its fathers and mothers "walked in" behind a plains' wagon; but in the third, the story will be proudly revived, with all the honors of tradition; and in the fourth generation from the sage-brush the ancestral irrigator will be no less a personage, in the eyes of his descendants, than the Pilgrim Father, the Dutch Patroon, or the Virginia Cavalier.

The Last Trip In

The teamster, as one of the types of the frontier, is seldom introduced in print without allusions to his ingenious and picturesque profanity; whereas it is his silence, rather than his utterances, that gives him among his brethren of the way almost the distinction of a species.

The sailor has his "chanty," the negro boat-man his rude refrain; we read of the Cossack's wild marching chorus, of the "begging-song" of the Russian exiles on the great Siberian road, of the Persian minstrel in the midst of the caravan, reciting, in a high, singing voice, tales of battle and love and magic to beguile the way. For years the parlor vocalist has rung the changes upon barcarolles and Canadian boat-songs, but not the most fanciful of popular composers has ventured to dedicate a note to the dusty-throated voyageur of the overland trail.

He is not unpicturesque; he has every claim that hardship can give to popular sympathy; yet, even to the most inexperienced imagination, he pursues his way in silence along those fateful roads, the names of which will soon be legendary. As a type he was evolved by these roads to meet their exigencies. He was known on the great Santa Fe trail, on the old Oregon trail, on all the historic pathways that have carried westward the story of a restless and a determined people. The railroads have driven him from the main lines of travel; he is now merely the link between them and scattered settlements difficult of access. When the systems of "feeders" to the main track are completed, his work will be done. He will have left no record among songs of the people or lyrics of the way, and in fiction, oddly enough, this most enduring and silent of beings will survive—through the immortal rhetoric of his biographers—as one whose breath is heavy with curses.

The teamster is usually a man of varied experience, acquainted with life through its misfortunes. His philosophy easily condenses itself into the phrase, "It's dogged that does it." He is a fatalist, but he has not ceased to plan. In this, whatever his nationality, he is always American. It is a big country, and though he gets over it but slowly, he has all the more time to collect his faculties, and his chance is as good as another's, should luck take a turn.

As he plods along he nurses a passive discontent. The future does not press him. It is the season of summer travel; the sun is hot upon the road; from two to three miles an hour is his average rate of progress. The monotonous shuffle of feet, the clanking of bits and chain-traces, the creak and roll of the heavy wagons as they trundle along, the wind that bellies the wagon-sheet and carries the dust before him, are opiates that might dull a livelier fancy than his. But the cadence in his brain does not make itself audible in musical phrases; his is the silence of solitude and latent resistance.

The teamster either has or affects a great contempt for his calling—unlike the stage-driver, who is always, figuratively speaking, on the box. He calls himself, and submits to be called, by derogatory epithets allusive to the animals he is driving. He will tell you that he is a "bull-puncher" or a "mule-skinner," but he says it with more of ostentation than humility. It is part of that ironical acceptance of fortune's latest freak so characteristic of the Western man, who never apologizes for his circumstances but by making sport of them.

The teamster is a man of simple habits. In a life of rough passages he has "lightened ship" by dispensing with all useless wants and conventions that tend to complicate existence. He has forgotten the use of a bed. When he arrives he sleeps in his blankets in the corral, which is his hotel. On the journey he spreads his bedding in the dust or the mud or the snow, at the hind wheels of his wagon. When he makes camp for the night he barely "hauls out" of the road, his inertia being equal to that of "Brer Tarrypin" when the man set the field on fire, and his philosophy much the same. The harness belonging to each mule of the string, 14, 16, or 20, as the case may be, is dropped in the animal's tracks on the spot where he came to a halt. When that proud society man and aristocrat of the road, the stage-driver, comes spanking along about nightfall, six-in-hand, and the pick of his passengers on the box beside him, he encounters the freighter's outfit distributed in heaps along the road. If he be a placable man he will submit to swing his team out, contenting himself with cursing the slumbering teamster in his blankets; but should he have wrongs in the past to avenge, or happen to be in a grim, joking humor, he will, as likely as not, drive straight on, smashing hames

THE LAST TRIP IN.

and grinding collars into the dust. On his return trip next day he meets the freighter where he has crawled, scarcely a mile from his last camp, his crippled harness tied up with "balin' rope," and the two men will pass each other without a word; but a counter-grudge is saving up in the heart of the teamster, to be worked out by degrees on the road.

Relatively the teamster is but a small figure in that imposing procession of the forces of civilization on its march westward. But upon his humble chances of one sort or another, his luck as regards the weather, his personal influence with his team,—perhaps upon some incantation of sounds with which he conjures those mysterious brute natures in their spellbound moments,—as well as upon his endurance and dogged resolution, the fate of many of the bravest experiments has rested. And as the season advances and the question presses, in some doubtful foothold of men in the wilderness, "Can we hold out till spring?" the arrival of the last freighter "in " is looked for as, on the verge of winter, on the Atlantic coast the colonists watched for the promised shipload of supplies from the mother country.

Afternoon At A Ranch

Houses in the West, in accordance with their owners' tendencies, are showy, imaginative, practical, reminiscent, or shiftless; though there is a sort of building, *in transitu,* which may indicate economy and good judgment.

Such a dwelling stood in the midst of the sage-brush common, on the outskirts of a frontier town where we once lived, facing the foothills which were the seat of a military post. It was first a wall tent, set up a few feet from the ground on a foundation of boards. Here, in the course of the summer, a child was born. It occurred to us that some of the comforts needed at such a time might be wanting in this Ishmaelitish household, as we supposed it to be. But we were told by the daughter of a neighbor, who knew, through her mother's good offices, more of the family than we, that they were people of means—stock-raisers looking about them, like the tribe of Reuben in the land of Jazer and of Gilead, in search of good grazing valleys where the winters were not severe.

A few months later we saw the mother, bearing her babe in her arms, walking, after sunset, bareheaded, along the paths of the common. She looked a woman to be the mother of pioneers—the gipsy-like tan of her long journeys showing on her cheeks through the paleness of recent maternity. To have thought of her as an object of charity seemed ridiculous.

They continued to look about them all the rest of the summer, driving their stock up into the hills in the morning, and down to the ditches to water at evening. In the autumn a cabin was added to the tent, the rear of the one opening into the door of the other; wagon-sheets drawn over the wagon-body, close by, enlarged their winter accommodations. All these arrangements had a thoroughly competent and experienced look. In the spring we went away ourselves and saw no more of our nomadic neighbors on the common.

In every Western town which has known a period of prosperity there will be a few houses built by persons who have had the means to proclaim their taste. "Oh that mine enemy would build him a house!" one might reflect looking upon some of these monuments. But with regard to our neighbor's house, as well as his management in most other respects, the point of view is personal, and where one lightly scoffs in passing another may pause and respectfully admire.

"He jests at scars that never felt a wound." He that has never disappointed himself with results of his own planning may laugh at his neighbor's follies in bricks, or boards, or stone. If there lives a man that, having had the license money gives to clothe his caprice, finds himself entirely satisfied, let him not obtrude the fact. There is something offensive in our neighbor's complacency with the fine shell of his own making. We will grant him whatever God gave him as his portion in other particulars, but he must be modest about his house. We forgive him if his chimney smokes—we love him as a brother if he is generous enough to confess to one fundamental regret concerning the whole!

Besides the houses that celebrated their owners' success, there are the modest homes built in this far land in fond remembrance of the cherished ideals of home, wherever home may be. The white paint; the neat door-yard fence; the little fruit trees close to the house; the old-fashioned flowers, tended in beds and borders and fed by foreign irrigation instead of the pleasant showers of home—all have a wistful look. Yet this may be the fancy of some homesick passer-by; another may see only the look of contented achievement. No more than this was expected or desired. Here ambition ceases, and the householder would not exchange the new home of his own making for the soundest inheritance, of equal value, at home.

The imaginative builder in the West, as in the East, frequently "slips up" in practice; but it will be he that first catches the spirit of the landscape and makes its poetry of suggestion his own. The people of certain races build with an unconscious truth to the nature around them which is like an instinct; or perhaps it is part of that providence which is said to attend upon the lame and the lazy. They are crippled by their poverty; they have the temperament that can wait. They cannot afford to "haul" expensive lumber or pay for carpenters to aid them in their experiment; so they scrape up the mud around them, make it into adobes and wait for them to dry, and pile them up in the simplest way, which proves to be the best. They build long and low because it is less trouble than to build high; for the same reason,

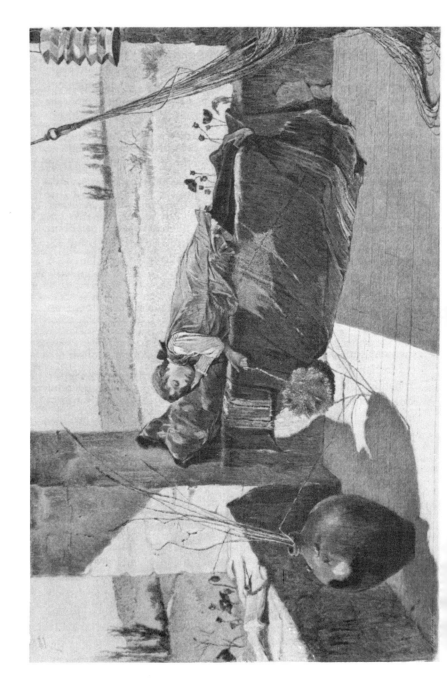

perhaps, they do not cut up their wall space into windows. The result is the architecture of simplicity and rest; and it goes very well with a country that pauses, for miles, in a trance of sky and mountain and plain, and forgets to put in the details.

The practical builders are as successful as the lazy builders, for they build with the same directness. The ranch buildings of the West, like the old Eastern farm-houses, are good in this way. There is no nonsense about them. If the buildings belong to a show ranch there will be ample opportunity for the exercise of a trained intelligence in the adaptation of historic styles that were inspired by similar sites and conditions.

The houses of these great desert landscapes should convey the idea of monotonous and concentrated living. Sun and wind beleaguered fortresses, they should never look as if they cared in the least what an outsider thought of their appearance. They should wrap themselves in silence and blind-walled indifference, as a bathless, breakfastless Mexican smokes his cigarette against a sunny wall of a morning, wrapped to the ears in his dingy serape. It is not presumed to offer this somewhat squalid suggestion to the ranch gentry, but to their humble neighbors of the railroad outpost, the cattle-feeding station, and the engineers' camp, who have winters as well as summers to provide for.

It may be added that the best houses in the West, those best worth describing, like the best people, are not the ones that are typical.

The Pretty Girls in the West

The wish so often expressed by mothers in the West that their daughters should have a "good time," suggests an inquiry as to what precisely is meant by this fond aspiration.

A mother's idea of a "good time" for her daughter usually signifies the sort of time she has failed to have herself. If she has been a hard-working woman, with many children to care for, she will desire that her daughter shall live easy and be blessed, in the way of offspring, with something less than a quiver-full. Where in the past labor has urged her, often beyond her strength, pleasure in the future shall invite her child.

So the mothers of the West, women of the heroic days of pioneering, unconsciously tell the story of their own struggles and deprivations in the ambitions which they indulge for their children.

Along the roads over which her parents journeyed in their white-topped wagon, their tent by night, their tabernacle, their fortress in time of danger, the settler's daughter shall ride in a tailor-made habit, or fare luxuriously in a drawing-room car. Where the mother's steadfast face grew brown with the glare of the alkali plain, the daughter shall glance out carelessly from behind the tapestry blind of her Pullman "section." Where the mother's hands washed and cooked and mended, and dressed wounds, and fanned the coals of the camp-fire, the daughter's shall trifle with books and music, shall be soft and "manicured" and daintily gloved.

It is one of the curious sights in the shops of a little town of frame houses—chiefly of one story, where the work of the house is not unfrequently done by the house-mother, not from poverty, but from the want in a new community of a servant class—to behold about Christmas time the display of sumptuous toilet articles implying hours spent upon the care of the feminine person, especially the feminine hands. This may be one of the indications of the sort of good time that is preparing for the daughters of the town. There are other and more hopeful suggestions, but none that seriously counteract the plainly projected revolt, on the part of the mothers, against a future of physical effort for their girls.

There are girls and girls in the West, of all degrees and styles of prettiness; but here, as elsewhere, and in all her glory, is seen the preeminently pretty girl—who by that patent exists, to herself, to her world, and in the imagination of her parents. The career of this young lady in her native environment is something amazing to persons of a sober imagination as to what should constitute a girl's "good time." The risks that she takes, no less than her extraordinary escapes from the usual consequences, are enough to make one's time-honored principles reel on the judgment seat of propriety.

It is true she does not always escape; but she escapes so often that it is quite impossible to draw any wholesome deductions from her. The only thing that can be done with her is to disapprove of her (with the consciousness that she will not mind in the least) and forgive her, because she knows not what she does. Why should she not take the good time for which, and for little else, she has been trained—the life of pleasure for which some one else pays!

In the novels she goes abroad and marries an English duke; in real life not quite so often; but she is an element of confusion, morally, in all one's prophecies with regard to her. She may have talent and make an actress or a singer, if she has any capacity for work; or she may marry the man she loves and become an exemplary wife. That which in her history appeals most deeply to one's imagination is the contrast between her fortunes and those of her mother.

If Creusa had survived the fall of Troy to accompany Aeneas on his wanderings, with a brood of fast-growing boys and girls, whose travel-worn garments she would have been mending while her hero entertained Dido with the tale of his misfortunes, it is not unlikely that that much-tried woman would have had her ideas as to those qualities in her sex that make for a "good time," and those which mostly go to supply a good time for others. And we may be sure that in planning the futures of the Misses Aeneas she would not have chosen for them the virtues that go unrewarded; rather shall they sit, white-handed and royally clad, and turn a smiling face upon some eloquent adventurer—who shall not be, in all respects, a copy of father Aeneas.

Whoever has lived in the West must have observed that here it is the unexpected that always happens; therefore it will be a mistake to take the pretty girl too seriously, or to regard her as a fatal sign of the

tendency of the life she is so fitted to enjoy. She is merely a phase,—an entertaining if not an instructive one,—for which her parents' hard lives and changes of fortune are mainly responsible. Her children will reverse the tendency, or carry it to the point of fracture, where nature steps in, in her significant way, and rubs out the false sum.

But as often as not nature permits the whole illogical proceeding to go on, and nothing happens of all that we have prophesied. We see that the fountain *does* rise higher than its source, that grapes *do* grow upon thorns and figs upon thistles, on some theory of cause and effect unknown to social dynamics.

The pretty girl from the East is hardly enough of a "rusher" to please the young Western masculine taste; but there will not be wanting pilgrims to her shrine. Her Eastern hostess will be proud of the chance to demonstrate that she isn't at all the same sort of pretty girl as her sister of the West,—it is the shades of difference that are vital,—and she will receive an almost pathetic welcome at the hands of her young countrymen, stranded upon cattle-ranches, or in railroad or mining camps, or engaged in hardy attempts of one sort or another wherein there is room for feminine sympathy.

Whether she takes her pleasure actively, in the saddle or in the canoe, or sits out the red summer twilights on the ranch piazza, or tunes her guitar to the ear of a single listener who has ridden over miles of desert plain for the privilege, she will be conscious that she supplies a motive, a new meaning to the life around her.

All this is very dangerous. She is in a world of illusions capable of turning into ordeals for those who put them to the proof—ordeals for which there has been no preparation in the life of the pretty girl. Even the ordeal of taste is not to be despised—taste, which environs and consoles and unites and stimulates women in the East, and which disunites and tortures and sets them at defiance, one with another, in the West.

The life of the men may be large and dramatic, even in failure; but the life of women, here, as everywhere, is made up of very small matters—a badly cooked dinner, a horrible wall-paper, a wind that tears the nerves, a child with something the matter with it which the doctor "doesn't understand," an acquaintance that is just near enough *not* to be a friend: it is the little shocks for which one is never prepared, the little disappointments and insecurities and failures and postponements, the want of completeness and perfection in anything, that harrows a woman's soul and makes her forget, too often, that she has a soul.

So let our pretty Eastern girl remember, before she pledges herself irrevocably to follow the fortunes of some charming young man she has had a "good time" with on the frontier, that—all good times and masculine assurances to the contrary notwithstanding—the frontier is not yet ready for her kind of pretty girl. There is more than one generation between her and the mother of a new community—unless she be minded to offer herself up on the altar of social enlightenment, or for the particular benefit of her particular young man. This is a fate which will always have a baleful fascination for the young woman who is capable of arguing that, if the frontier be not ready for her, the young man is.

The pity of it is that these young gentlemen always will pick out the pretty girl, when a less expensive choice would be so much more serviceable and fit the conditions of their lives so much better. But they are all potential millionaires, these energetic dreamers. They do not pinch themselves in their prospective arrangements, including the prospective wife. Between them both, the girl who expects to have a good time, and the young man who is confident that he can give it to her, there will probably be a good deal to learn.

The Winter Camp—A Day's Ride From the Mail

Since the West began to call for specialists the life of the frontier has offered peculiar inducements to young men of technical training. It combines the inspiration that comes of action with opportunities for practical experience and early responsibility. It would be surprising to note the ages of some of the men in positions of tried sagacity in the West, not to mention the phenomenal successes of those who have gone up on a wave of chance. It is also the life of conspicuous tests, moral and physical. A few months will effectually place a new-comer with one or the other of the primitive forces that divide the suffrages of every new community, or leave him on that modern pillory, the unhappy middle-ground of postponed issues and divided judgments.

Of these tests there is one which might be given greater prominence in pictures of Western life. It is a very commonplace ordeal, to be met with anywhere by the least interesting of us; but it is a peculiarly searching experience under the conditions of life on the frontier. It is assumed that every person in these new communities has some practical reason for being there and doesn't mean to "get left." But occasionally it happens that a man's life pauses in the West, even if he be not altogether "left." The pause may last for months or for years; in the course of it hope and faith in the purpose which brought him there alternate with a sense of absurdity and defeat. His situation is not unlike that of a man in the trenches on a field of battle. The balls are flying over his head; his part is to lie low and wait for orders. He jokes with the man next him; he shifts from one attitude of constraint to another; he wonders how long this sort of thing is going to last.

We enforce upon children the saying that one can always "find something to do"; but the capable man with his hands tied, in a community where life means nothing if not action, finds there is a bitter difference between the "something" that takes the place of

301

work—that is invented, nursed, stooped to, as a sick man carves jack-straws or pastes scrap-books—and the divine gift of a man's own work that comes to him like the angel to Peter in prison, with the keys of deliverance.

We read in an engineering journal, a year or two ago, an account of the ceremonies at the opening of a canal for irrigation, unlocking to settlement an immense valley of rich but arid land. It was made a great occasion, with bands of music, and "tributes" to the persons chiefly concerned in the achievement. We learned that this great success had been fifteen years in coming, and that it had not come to all of those who were joined to its fate in the beginning. The originators had held it up for ten years, and when they could no longer support the burden a new combination carried it on to its completion. It did not appear what share the originators had in the triumph; but during those ten years of bondage to a scheme they must at least have got some experience, of the sort that all triumphs do not supply.

It would be too much to imply that always in the West success is the child of failure, and that back of every five years of fortunate activity one may look for ten years of unrewarded waiting. The best things are not always those that come hardest; but it may be accepted that a certain proportion of all the young men who rush into the fields of action west of the Missouri will have to wait for their success, without the privilege of laboring while they wait. In stories and pictures of the West we see these young men on horseback, on forced marches or exploring expeditions, engaged in exploits of love or war or money-making. A survey of the actual field of observation as regards the college graduate would find a good many of him much less picturesquely employed. He is quite as likely to be found "holding down a claim" in some sun-baked valley a day's ride from the mail, or in charge of a suspended mine or comatose smelter, or wearing out the winter in an engineer's camp waiting for orders—becalmed in heart-sick idleness. There is no prayer for him in the church service; he is not a sick person or a malefactor or in peril of his life. But mothers and wives know the peculiar nature of his trial, and pray that he may be remembered in the hour of the march forward, or that he may be loosed from the vow, the enchantment, the delusion—whatever the spell may be that keeps him, dreaming of activity, fast bound in the toils of suspense and enforced idleness.

NOTES ON THE TEXT

The stories and essays are printed from the texts of the magazines in which they were first published. The nineteenth century publishers' use of hyphenated words is maintained. Modernized forms for printing quotation marks and for printing contractions are incorporated in the text.

"A Cloud on the Mountain"
First published in *Century Magazine* 31 (Nov. 1885): 28-38. Collected in *In Exile, and Other Stories*. Boston: Houghton, 1884.

"The Fate of a Voice"
First published in *Century Magazine* 33 (Nov. 1886): 61-73. Collected in *The Last Assembly Ball: A Pseudo Romance of the Far West*. Boston: Houghton, 1889.
In the third paragraph, Foote first used the phrase "angle of repose," which in her reminiscences became a phrase symbolic of the Footes' lives in Idaho. The phrase was appropriated by Wallace Stegner for the title of his novel based on Foote's life.
Foote was particularly perturbed by the number of errors she found in the story as it was printed. She wrote to the "Editors of the Century," chastising them for not sending her the proofs to correct and listing the errors which most distressed her, particularly the error in the name of the heroine: "The name of my girl was meant to be HENDRIE and it comes out in print Hendric; a name which in no name at all, or rather one misspelled" (7 Nov. 1886. MHF Collection. The Huntington, San Marino).

"The Rapture of Hetty"
First published in *Century Magazine* 43 (Dec. 1891): 198-201. Collected in *In Exile, and Other Stories*. Boston: Houghton, 1894.

"The Watchman"
First published in *Century Magazine* 47 (Nov. 1893): 30-41. Collected in *In Exile, and Other Stories*. Boston: Houghton, 1894.

"Maverick"
First published in *Century Magazine* 48 (Aug. 1894): 544-50. Collected in *The Cup of Trembling, and Other Stories*. Boston: Houghton, 1895.

"The Trumpeter"
First serialized in *Atlantic Monthly* 74 (Nov. 1894): 577-97 and 74 (Dec. 1894): 721-29. Collected in *The Cup of Trembling, and Other Stories*. Boston: Houghton, 1895.

"On a Side-Track"
First published in *Century Magazine* 50 (June 1895): 271-83. Collected in *The Cup of Trembling, and Other Stories*. Boston: Houghton, 1895.
Foote wrote to the "Editors Century Magazine" to inform them that she had sent "On a Side-Track" and to give the editors her family's opinion about the story: "My 'general public' here say it is my strongest story yet: so if I am crowding the market of the magazine, perhaps you would rather have this story and let 'The Watchman' go elsewhere" (18 Feb. 1892. MHF Collection. The Huntington, San Marino).

On Nov. 23, 1893, Foote wrote Richard Gilder about illustrations for the story: "Yes I remember I declined to illustrate this story, but I have made a rather 'happy' sketch of 'Phebe' sitting between her father's berth curtains, and I am just finishing a snow-plow engine bit of landscape which will 'place' the story. . ." She concludes with some observations about the plot: "They say, the men, that Ludovic must not go so far as Omaha before he turns back: and I tried to change that, but it involves too many other changes, and does not give him enough time on the sleeper with the girl: and nobody knows where Pocatello is" (MHF Collection. The Huntington, San Marino).

"The Cup of Trembling"

First published in *Century Magazine* 50 (Sept. 1895): 673-90. Collected in *The Cup of Trembling, and Other Stories*. Boston: Houghton, 1895.

In a letter to Richard Gilder, Foote revealed her understanding of the story's theme and also how it might be perceived by others: ". . .I'm afraid you will say won't do; but please don't say it till you've read it through. I know it's an ugly theme, but it would have to come in once, at least in any true series of western tales. . . .I think it a moral tale, myself—and I'm not afraid but you will,—but of course you know your 'general reader' " (15 Jan. 1894. MHF Collection. The Huntington, San Marino). Her concern about the theme was also apparent in her reply to C.C. Buel at the *Century*: "It was very kind of you to send me those pleasant words about the story. I hope indeed that it will appeal to my readers, or the Century's readers,—because it is a theme one would not like to touch on only to blunder and strike false notes" (18 Oct. 1895. MHF Collection. The Huntington, San Marino).

"Pilgrim Station"

First published in *Atlantic Monthly* 77 (May 1896): 596-613. Retitled "The Maid's Progress" and collected in *A Touch of Sun, and Other Stories*. Boston: Houghton, 1903.